Slaughter

ELMER KELTON

Slaughter

DOUBLEDAY
New York London Toronto Sydney Auckland

PUBLISHED BY DOUBLEDAY
a division of Bantam Doubleday Dell Publishing Group, Inc.
666 Fifth Avenue, New York, New York 10103

DOUBLEDAY and the portrayal of an anchor with a dolphin
are trademarks of Doubleday, a division of
Bantam Doubleday Dell Publishing Group, Inc.

Library of Congress Cataloging-in-Publication Data

Kelton, Elmer.
Slaughter/Elmer Kelton.—1st ed.
    p.   cm.
1. Comanche Indians—Wars—Fiction.   2. Texas—History—1846–1950
Fiction. I. Title.
PS3563.A2932S5   1992
813'.54—dc20   92-10317
CIP

ISBN 0-385-24894-6

Printed in the United States of America
November 1992
First Edition

10 9 8 7 6 5 4 3 2 1

This book is dedicated to Stanley and Robert Frank, Fred Ball, Edgar Talley, Jerry Lackey and Forrest Salter, who have been good partners, all.

Slaughter

One

THE COMANCHE meat-hunting party had come across the horned toad a while after dawn and interrupted its feasting at the edge of an ant bed. Crow Feather, naked except for a breechclout and the broad tailfeather of an eagle tied in his heavily greased black hair, had stepped down from his bay horse to kneel and ask the scaly-hided lizard where the buffalo were to be found. The creature had paused a moment, as if in reflection, then had scurried westward the length of Crow Feather's shadow into the protection of a low bush.

That was answer enough, for the formidable-looking lizard was known among the People as Asking About the Buffalo. Many regarded it as more reliable than the raven, which might circle overhead and then fly off in the direction of the buffalo but might as often decline any answer, no matter how earnest the pleading or how severe the need for fresh meat.

The sign had been good, for a while later the riders put their horses to the top of a rise in the plains and saw their quarry. But Asking About the Buffalo had not warned them that interlopers were already there, already surrounding the small herd, bringing the shaggy beasts down with arrows and lances. It was a moment of high indignation, for Crow Feather's band had long claimed the right to this hunting ground. Others came only with the band's permission, or at their peril.

Man Who Stole the Mules loudly advocated a swift and merciless attack upon these challengers who poached where they had no right. Mules was always quick to fight, for he sought to improve his stature as a warrior. He was also eager to earn approval of his two wives' father, for he wanted to marry a third daughter, the youngest and choicest of them all. Crow Feather agreed with the others, however, that it would be wise first to establish the identity of these hunters. If they were not an implacable enemy such as the Apache or the Ute, perhaps it would be well to treat with them. They appeared to be fewer than the five times four who rode with Crow Feather. There would be time enough to kill them if council failed to produce a satisfactory agreement and division of the meat.

As Crow Feather's party rode down the hill toward the buffalo herd, the other hunters disengaged from the chase and hurried together into a defensive line. It was quickly evident that these were not enemy Apaches, or even the Kiowas with whom the Comanches often allied. These were of the People, though not of a band Crow Feather recognized. He guessed they might be of a northern group who had dropped out along the way as the People generations ago made their gradual southward migration from the eastern slope of the great white mountains. Seldom did such bands venture this far south except in occasional raiding parties bound for the Tejano settlements or to cross the river known as Quannah Coth-cho Pah to seek blood and booty in Mexico.

As the hunt leader, Crow Feather pushed his horse a length ahead of the others and raised his hand in sign that he and his party meant the strangers no hostility. He was met by a gaunt warrior a few years his elder, a man in whose face the hardships of many cold winters and blazing summers had etched deep lines, and across whose head a large scar bore mute evidence of some long-ago battle. They exchanged polite but suspicious greetings. Crow Feather was gratified that though they were strangers to one another, their language was the same. It was not like having to treat with the Kiowas, whose words had no meaning to him and with whom he could make himself understood only by *maw-taquoip*, the language of the hands.

"You are far from your hunting grounds," he said, a cautious way of presenting a challenge without overt belligerence.

"If we have taken meat that belongs to you, we are willing to share," the older warrior said in an even tone, friendly but careful not to be submissive. "We have come far, and these are the first of the *coth-cho* we have found. Our families are without meat." He pointed. Crow Feather saw others in the distance, women and children and the old ones, waiting for the killing to finish so the skinning and the butchering could begin. Crow Feather's band had its own families following hopefully at a short distance, eager to be about the same work.

There was more than enough to feed everybody. He said in a conciliatory manner, "It is not good for the children and the old ones to be hungry. Keep what you have killed." The surviving buffalo were running in a northwesterly direction, their awkward rocking gait carrying them into the wind. "Our camp is that way," he added, pointing eastward. "There is wood and water enough for all." He dismounted and removed the rawhide-covered saddle, coiling a horsehair rope in its place around the horse's body. He would tuck his knees under it for security and ride light, unhampered by the saddle's bulk. The other men followed his example. He signaled, and they set out in pursuit of the herd.

The hunt had a purpose beyond simply the necessity of providing meat. It was sport, and it carried an element of danger that aroused a high exhilaration in Crow Feather's hunters. They pushed their horses hard as they closed on the fleeing buffalo. Crow Feather saw a horse strike a soft spot, an animal burrow of some kind, and go down. Its rider was a lean lad on only his second hunt, a good horseman despite his youth. He hit the ground on hands and knees, scrambling out of the way as the horse rolled over, then grabbing the rawhide rein that had been wrested from his hand and jumping once more upon the horse's back as the animal struggled to its feet. Instantly he was beating his heels against the animal's ribs, trying to catch up.

The fact that the buffalo were running made it difficult to start a surround, the easiest method for acquiring meat. This way the carcasses would be spread across a considerable distance rather than grouped close together. It meant extra work for the women, but the primary consideration was meat, not the labor required in its taking. Crow Feather decided upon a mature cow and asked her pardon for killing her. He pressed the bay up close on her right-hand side and drove an arrow between the last rib and her hipbone. The shaft disappeared most of the way to the feathers. The horse pulled to the right to be out of range of the sharp black horns should the cow turn to hook at him. She slowed but did not show fight. Crow Feather leaned down, grasped what he could of the arrow's shaft and gave it a sharp tug. It came out, dripping blood. He would not need the arrow to identify the cow; he would know she was his. He might need the arrow if his luck ran good and he killed many buffalo. He saw the cow go to her knees, blood running from her nose, and knew he had mortally wounded her. He pressed on after another, and another and another, hooves pounding all around him. He was aware that the other hunters were taking their share, but he did not let them be a distraction. He wanted to kill as many as he could before the opportunity slipped away.

His quiver was nearly emptied of arrows by the time he felt the bay horse faltering and knew it was time to stop. Buffalo were plentiful, but good hunting horses were not. He had no wish to run this one into the ground. Stopping to catch his breath and look around him, he saw that most of the hunters had already pulled back. Two young boys still pursued the remnant of the herd across the flat prairie. This was their first hunt, and they had not done as well as the veterans. They would not want to be shamed in camp tonight for coming up short. Crow Feather smiled, remembering his own first hunt. He had lived through more than thirty winters, and he no longer had anything to prove.

Through the settling dust he saw dead and dying buffalo scattered over a long stretch of open grassland. The women were coming, dragging the dual-pole travois upon which they would haul the meat and hides back to camp when the butchering was done. Among them would be his two wives, both daughters of Stands His Ground. It was generally agreed among the People that it was wise to marry sisters, for sisters as a rule got along better together than strangers, given that they must share a husband. And marrying sisters meant only one set of in-laws would expect to be enriched by whatever the hunter brought to camp. Old Stands His Ground, a good hunter in his own time, would be pleased at the feast tonight and boast about his son-in-law.

Crow Feather met the two women and pointed out the first of the cows he had killed. He would attend to the heaviest task, the skinning and quartering. Cutting the meat into more manageable portions was essentially woman's work. Among his kill were two bulls on which he must do more of the butchering because they were larger and heavier than the cows. They would be a strain on even a strong woman.

White Deer was the older of the pair by three winters and by nature the hardest worker. He had married her first, though he had always had an eye on Rabbit, prettiest of the sisters. Rabbit did not labor as hard or quite so skillfully as White Deer, but she had compensating talents. White Deer would be tired tonight, and once the feasting was done she would prefer only to sleep. Rabbit always held some energy in reserve.

He rode back to the first cow and began the skinning while his women brought up the horses. His two children rode on a travois together atop an old buffalo robe, behind White Deer's mare. The oldest was a son from White Deer, his skin toughened by the suns of five summers. Little Squirrel was old enough that Crow Feather must soon find a pony for him and begin teaching him to use a boy-size bow. The girl, Rabbit's daughter, was just beginning to say a few understandable words. She did a lot of chattering that made no sense to anyone except herself, but it was like the music of a flute to Crow Feather's ears.

He smiled indulgently, listening to the two wives of Man Who Stole the Mules quarreling with the wife of Goes His Own Way over the rightful ownership of a cow brought down by arrows bearing the markings of both men. The two hunters rode up and squelched the quarrel by agreeing to divide the meat half and half. As the men moved on to examine their other kills, the wives of Mules continued to grumble that because there were two of them and Goes His Own Way had but one wife, they should receive twice as much.

Crow Feather was tempted to point out that the kill had been abundant and that there was more than enough meat for everyone, including the widows and the old in camp. But long ago he had decided it was not well to intrude into the quarreling of women, especially other men's women, for likely as not they would stand together and turn on him.

As families pitched into the butchering, children clustered noisily around, clamoring for a chance at fresh warm liver with all the juice still in it. Crow Feather had to warn his two to remain on the travois and out of their mothers' way. Remembering the pleasures of his own boyhood, he sliced off two pieces of liver and carried it to the pair. Grinning in anticipation, the boy eagerly began to chew. The girl was put off a bit at first, passing the meat from one hand to the other, dismayed over the sticky blood it left on her fingers.

"Taste it," Crow Feather told her. "It is good." He demonstrated by taking a generous bite.

Hesitantly she brought the liver to her mouth. Her big black eyes widened with delight as she bit down with her few baby teeth and found the rich, full flavor of the raw meat. Crow Feather lovingly placed his hand on top of her head, then that of the boy. "I must go now. You do what your mothers tell you."

A stranger in camp would have difficulty determining which child belonged to which woman. The two wives treated both as if each were her own. It was the way of the People that all children were treasured, for birth rates were low and death rates relatively high, both from natural causes and from the violence that attended a hunter-warrior tribe.

White Deer was quick and competent with the knife, cutting the meat so it would be easier to transport back to camp on the travois. Rabbit let her take the lead, content to be a follower and let the older sister do the heavier work. Nearby, the wives of Mules had quit grumbling about the wife of Goes His Own Way and quarreled with each other over the fact that the eldest had a good steel knife while the younger had to make do with a sharp-edged piece of flint. Crow Feather's wives each had a good steel knife that he had acquired from Mexican Comanchero traders who came periodically to the plains encampments to buy buffalo robes and dried meat. Crow Feather was wealthy by Comanche standards. He owned many horses. Life was good.

He rode to where his first bull had fallen. He had not chosen an old one, for the old ones were stringy and tough, but it was heavy enough that he had to struggle to turn it onto its belly. He spread its legs and slit the hide down the spine without cutting the sinews, needed for sewing and patching and securing the heads to arrows. He peeled the hide down either side and began disjointing the hindquarters. The labor brought sweat, for the morning sun was beginning to warm him. Far in the rear, he could see the other band at work, butchering their own kill. He could not begrudge them, for in a broad sense they were kin, no matter their band. Comanches, like most plains Indians, regarded their own as *the* People, the chosen ones. Other tribes were higher than the animals, perhaps, but something less than the True Human Beings.

In a while his women had all the meat they could pack onto both travois, wrapped in the soft and bloody hides to protect it from dust as it was dragged back to camp. White Deer took the girl in front of her on one mare. The boy climbed on top of the load behind her. The second mare was trained to follow without a rider, though as a precaution White Deer held onto a long lead rope of pleated rawhide in case the animal took it in her head to go her own direction. Rabbit remained to continue with the cutting-up of the meat. Convention did not require that Crow Feather help her, but he enjoyed being close to Rabbit, finding excuses to touch her as they worked together. Rabbit needed no excuses. She was always willing.

They took virtually all of the carcass but left the heart as tribute and to insure that there would always be more buffalo. By the time the last of the meat had been packed, several gray wolves skulked in the grass, moving as near as they dared, waiting impatiently for the skinners to be gone so they could scavenge from whatever offal was left on the killing ground. In reality they had nothing to fear, for among the People harm to a wolf or a coyote was taboo. They were all of a brotherhood, the wolves and the prairie-born People. Unlike most other plains tribes, a Comanche would not even eat dog. The dog, though of a much lower order, was distant cousin to the wolf and the coyote.

In camp, White Deer and Rabbit began cutting long strips of meat to be hung and dried upon racks built of thin limbs. Crow Feather cautioned the children to play elsewhere and not raise dust where their mothers and other women were working with the meat.

He decided it was time to visit the encampment of the band from the north. He would invite them to share in the feast tonight, for meat was plentiful. The newcomers had camped downstream. They would have been poor guests to have gone upstream, where any refuse they threw into the creek would drift by their hosts. He had turned his hunting horse loose for a well-earned rest but caught a sorrel out of the herd for the ride to the other camp. That took him twice as long as if he had walked, but a warrior did not walk where he could ride.

He found the band's hunt leader, Three Bears, supervising his wife and young daughters while the women set up their tepee, though they knew the routine as well or better than he did. They spread a number of poles, each nearly four times the length of a man's body. They tied the poles together where they met near the top, then laced tanned buffalo skins together around them. By custom, the front flap faced east so the first light of the morning sun would fall upon those inside and offer its blessing. Though the man gave instructions, he did not lend a hand to the actual work. Tradition dating back to the grandfathers of old had clearly defined the division of labor between men and women. A married man risked loss of stature if he did work that properly belonged to his wife or wives.

Crow Feather waited, watching small children playing at the edge of camp. At their age he had loved the excitement of moving, for it broke the monotony that came after spending a time in one camp. The grazing needs of the large horse herd had always been as much a factor in the frequency of these moves as the necessity of following the buffalo.

Three Bears joined Crow Feather after a bit, bringing a ceremonial pipe, its long antelope-bone stem wrapped with buffalo ligament, its bowl carved from soft soapstone. They walked down to the edge of the creek, away from the women's work. The elder of the men lighted the pipe and offered smoke to each of the four directions, then to the spirits of the sky and the earth. He passed the pipe to Crow Feather, who did the same.

"You have come far," Crow Feather said.

"We came in search of meat," replied the man with the deeply lined face.

"I have ridden far north more than once. I have seen many buffalo there. Have they all gone back into the earth?"

The People accepted a legend that in the first days the buffalo had escaped from a hole in the ground and had spread out across the land in abundance to guarantee that the chosen ones were never in need.

"Many from the north have moved down onto our hunting grounds because they find nothing on their own. Kiowas, Cheyennes, some of the others. They say it is the white man. They say his thundersticks have killed all the buffalo in the north. They say he kills only to take the skin and leaves the meat to rot."

Crow Feather frowned in disbelief. Such a notion was unthinkable. The People did not believe in waste, for that could lead to want. In the good feast days one put up meat for the lean days certain to come. One found uses for every part of the animal. Even the wolf did not waste; he killed to eat, and what he did not eat, the buzzards and the other scavengers found to their liking. Mother Earth provided for all.

Tejanos from the south occasionally ventured up onto the buffalo ranges in search of meat, but they usually took no more than they could pack away. The People stopped them when they found them and killed them if they could, but it was for principle only. The Tejanos had been enemies since Crow Feather's father had been a boy. There had been no fear that the white man could ever kill off all the buffalo. They did not take as many, even, as the wolves that stalked the fringes of the herds, searching for the young, the lame or the unlucky.

Crow Feather had raided the Tejano settlements many times, taking horses and mules, accepting fight where fight was offered, turning back with the ferocity of a badger upon those bold but foolish Tejanos who attempted pursuit. "Why do they not simply kill the white man? I have never found it difficult." Several of their scalps had adorned his lodge.

"I have seen little of the *teibo* myself, but the Cheyennes say killing him is like killing the flies. When one dies, two more appear in his place. They say the iron road keeps bringing more and more, like wasps coming out of a nest."

Crow Feather had heard stories of an iron road far to the north and of a great iron horse which traveled upon it, smoking some foul type of tobacco. Some said it ran over the buffalo and cut them to pieces like a butchering knife, that it gave out great piercing screams and sent horses stampeding in fright. He did not believe. These tales reminded him of those the old men used to tell when he was a boy, of the malevolent *nenuhpee*, the tiny men, and of monsters like the Great Cannibal Owl, that lived in the earth. He had never known anyone who actually had seen one of these creatures; always it had been someone else.

Skeptically he asked, "Have you seen this iron road and this iron horse?"

"No, but I have talked to those who say they have."

Like the rest of the monsters, Crow Feather thought, seen by others than those who told the stories. What he had not seen for himself, he could not accept without reservation.

"The buffalo are as many as the stars in the skies," he declared. "They are more than all the white men, and they become more with every calf."

"If the white man kills the cow, she will produce no calf."

The grave face of his distant kinsman said he believed, even if Crow Feather did not. Crow Feather said, "The buffalo has been here since the first days. He will be here when our children are old. What the spirits have given to us, they will not allow the white man to take away."

The older man gave him a look of sadness and pity. "I did not want to believe either, at first, but a dark wind is blowing, my cousin. I can already feel its chill. You will feel it too, for it is moving in your direction."

Crow Feather left, after a time, still not believing. But something in Three Bears's eyes left him uneasy.

Two

JEFFERSON LAYNE had hunted these Kansas prairies for three days without seeing so much as a fresh buffalo chip. The Sharps Big Fifty rifle balanced across his lap had not seemed so heavy when game was plentiful, but now it felt as if it weighed two hundred pounds. It was difficult to accept that these long rolling hills with their abundant blanket of fall-curing bluestem grasses could be barren of buffalo. Only a little while ago the shaggy beasts had been so plentiful that they appeared like a solid but dusty black robe blanketing the open ground to the farthest horizon as they migrated in a shuffling, chuffing mass, following some primeval instinct to water and fresh grazing grounds. No man could have counted them.

He had seen the earth churned like plowed ground in their wake, the rivers a muddy, putrid ruin where the migration had crossed—drowned, bloated bodies scattered along the banks, stinking so badly that he held his breath and lingered no longer than it took him to put a reluctant horse across and be gone. He would have thought the land and the water would never recover, but given time and healing rain the grass would rise green and tall, bending in obedience to the clean prairie wind. The water again would flow clear and sweet. Nature had rejuvenating processes that he accepted on faith because he would never understand how they worked.

Even here, far from the river, the remembered smell came back to him often as he rode upon old killing grounds where the return of bodies to the earth was not yet complete, where wolves still prowled to salvage carrion, where the buzzards still came to clean the whitening bones of the once-great herds. It was a reminder, if he needed one, of the devastation man could cause when he unleashed his full destructive powers. But business was business, they said in Dodge City. It had been a lucrative one when hides brought better than two dollars apiece and the buffalo were so many that the only limitation to the kill was the number a skinning crew could handle before spoilage set in.

Even as the great ricks of stinking hides stretched farther and farther along the Atchison, Topeka & Santa Fe tracks, high as men could throw them from the bed of a wagon, he would not have believed the hunters could ever cut significantly into the number of buffalo. Only yesterday, it seemed, they had been estimated in the millions. Today they were nearly gone from these Kansas hills between the Arkansas River and the Pawnee.

"Maybe yonder," he said to the tall black horse he rode. "Maybe over that little hill yonder."

But the words were hollow, spoken only to break the long silence of the plains, for he knew that when he rode upon the next hill he would see no more than he had seen from the last.

It was not that he enjoyed the business of killing buffalo; he tolerated it for lack of something better. He had had enough of guns in the war, fighting futilely for the Southern cause. He had returned to his native Texas tired and sick in soul, intending never to fire a rifle again except for meat. Sadly, he had found that in weary, impoverished Texas the war was not really over. Guns remained a bleak fact of life—and death.

In time, to escape, he had come north up the trail to Kansas, a hired man in a crew of hired men, driving a herd of Longhorn cattle to be shipped east from Abilene on the newly built railroad. He had not gone south again; he *could* not. He had blistered his hands on pick, shovel and sledge, one of the anonymous army of workmen helping to lay the steel rails as they slowly stretched southwestward from Abilene across the open plains. He had put all he could of Yankee dollars into his pockets, spending only for the occasional warming company of a woman, for whiskey to help him burn away the pain of old memories, of youthful dreams gone sour in the wake of a war he had neither wanted nor seen a reason for.

When Indians killed a railroad hunter who had furnished buffalo meat and venison to the construction camp, Jeff Layne had volunteered for the job. The rifle in his hands reminded him of much he had rather forget, but it paid better than carrying rails and driving spikes, and put less strain on his back. He was long past thirty now; forty was standing at the door. Time had taught him that comfort was a seldom thing. One took it gratefully where he found it, in whatever measure it might be afforded. Kansas had been passable enough, but his gaze often turned wishfully south . . . wishfully and in vain.

For decades, buffalo robes had been a prime commodity, traded from the Indians, but no market existed for raw hides. Then a new tanning technique emerged, and with it a sudden, broad demand. Jeff had found his keen marksmanship more profitable in killing for skins than for meat. Lacking capital to acquire his own outfit, he killed on shares for a former Union officer who might have shot at him in the war, who for all he knew might have been responsible for a lead ball he had taken in his hip.

Damon Cregar, one of the largest men he had ever known, owned the wagons and teams. He had the financial strength to put a good outfit together and the physical strength to keep driving it forward. Jeff had added to Cregar's wealth and had managed to salt away some healthy savings for himself. Someday, if he could ever go back to Texas, he would put that money to good use. Someday, if . . . It was a haunting thought, and a futile one. They had long memories down there, the carpetbag regime that ruled the state. They had not forgotten the Layne name.

That damnyankee'll bust a gut when he sees how near empty the wagons are coming in, he thought. The skinners already dreaded him, for Cregar could rear up and roar like an angry bear. He held no terror for Jefferson Layne. Since the war, very little did. *The hell with him. Let him come and look for himself if he's not satisfied the buffalo are gone.*

He started the black horse up the hill, the wind in his face, and stopped abruptly just before he reached the top. "Whoa, Tar Baby. Damned if I didn't see a buffalo after all."

He took the horse partway back down the hill and swung carefully from the saddle, favoring the hip that never let him forget the war. He untied the tripod that allowed him to steady the rifle's long, heavy barrel, and the pouch that contained the fifty-caliber ammunition. The black horse was trained to stand without being tied. Jeff carried the load up the hill, crouching as he reached the top. The wind was in his favor, and buffalo had notoriously poor eyesight, but he had been at this work too long to take unnecessary chances.

He had hoped, from his one quick glimpse, to find a sizeable herd. Disappointment touched him as he saw just a bull and two cows, one trailed by a reddish calf. The bull carried one leg stiffly. Layne guessed that some other hunter had recently wounded him but let him get away. *Well, I've got no such intention.* He sat down cross-legged at the top of the hill, spread the tripod and rested the barrel upon it. He estimated the range at a hundred yards and set the sights accordingly. He brought the rifle around until the bull was squarely in the sights. His finger tightened on the trigger, then eased. A bead of sweat trickled down into his right eye, setting it to burning, and he had to pause to wipe a sleeve over his face. He blinked until the burning subsided, then sighted again. The buffalo had turned its rump toward him. He could not shoot it that way. He shifted his sights to one of the cows. The calf chose that moment to push itself against her belly and punch at her udder, seeking warm milk.

He eased the rifle stock down, the barrel rising up. Just three hides, that and a kip if he chose to take the calf. He guessed that the wagons were waiting three, maybe four miles behind him. He would have to ride that far, then fetch them all this way, and for so little. He looked at the calf, eagerly taking all the nourishment its mother could give it, oblivious to the threat of the great rifle. He looked at the bull, which had already been down the long, dark valley and somehow had come out alive.

Don't seem fair after all he's been through to take him now. And for what? The whole bunch won't fetch but six, maybe seven dollars in Dodge.

With so many hunters roaming these hills, it was probable that someone would soon find and take these miserable few. *But it won't be me. Damned if it's going to be me.* He lifted the rifle, folded the tripod and remained low until he had moved far enough down the hill that the animals would not see him and take fright.

Damon Cregar would raise hell if he knew, but Damon Cregar was not here.

Expecting to be on the move again, the horse cropped at the grass with a special urgency as Jeff tied the tripod and the bag of ammunition upon his trail-worn Texas saddle. Jeff gave him time to graze. *Somebody ought to get something out of all this effort,* he thought.

The black was not necessarily the smartest horse Jeff had ever owned, but patience and dependability counted for much, and his eyes were sharp. He saw everything that moved and some things that did not. Tar Baby jerked his head up, ears pointing. Four or five hundred yards away, a man sat on a horse, watching. Another hunter, Jeff thought for a moment, then changed his mind. *A hunter, maybe, but not one like me.* Though he could make out no detail, a wary stirring deep in his gut told him this was an Indian. He looked around for sign of more, his hand tight on the rifle. He saw only the one.

He could not tell whether the Indian was armed with a bow or with a rifle. Many these days had rifles, though none of their weapons had the range and accuracy of the big Sharps. Jeff was not overly concerned about a single Indian, or even two or three, for the buffalo rifle gave him a strong advantage. But a bunch of them coming over the hill could complicate his situation in a hurry.

The black seemed to have lost interest in grass, giving his attention to the other horse. Jeff said, "Too bad, but you've had all the grazin' you're goin' to get for a while." He mounted, swinging the barrel around and resting the rifle across his lap, his right hand firmly grasping the trigger guard. It was not an ideal weapon for firing from horseback. It was too long and heavy to hold steady, and its recoil could knock a man out of the saddle. But in a pinch he could dismount, rest the barrel across the saddle and fire a round with high accuracy before an adversary could bring a smaller rifle into favorable range. He wore a pistol, but he did not intend to allow any hostile Indian to get close enough that it would be effective.

He put the horse into an easy walk. He did not want to appear to be running away, for this would only embolden the Indian if his intentions were warlike. Jeff thought it likely that those *were* his intentions. Several hunters caught alone had been killed on these prairies in recent weeks. Often now they traveled in pairs, one to watch for danger while the other concentrated on shooting buffalo, if they managed to find any. Jeff had not chosen to work in this manner. War had taught him that other men could be fallible, that he should trust his own instincts and the movement of his horse's ears. It had taught him that the man who looks out for himself is likely to live longer.

He kept watching over his shoulder as he sought his way back to the wagons, but if the Indian followed he was careful not to show himself. Jeff thought he might have been a lone hunter, like himself, trying to find meat for his people. He did not engage in long introspection about his part in curtailing the food supply for these nomads of the plains, nor did he indulge himself in more than an occasional brief sense of guilt. That the Indians were being displaced from their homeland was obvious to him, but he had been displaced from his own as well. He had been forced to change his life in ways he had not foreseen and had not wanted. He rationalized that the Indians had been fighting over this land for ages, one tribe driving out another and in turn eventually being driven out by some stronger force. What the white man was doing was nothing new except that his weapons were more effective, his numbers of a magnitude that assured his eventual victory.

Once the Indian was gone, the same old struggle would continue. It would be white man against white man, but the prize would remain essentially the same: the land.

He had made a wide circle during the day in his search for buffalo, but always he had kept track of directions and distances so he would know where he was in relation to the wagons, camped on the forks of a creek. An elderly man with bent shoulders walked out a few yards from the cottonwoods to meet him. He was thin, his old clothes too large for him, though they had not always been. He seemed to have shrunk in recent years.

"Didn't hear no shootin', Son."

"No, Dad, you didn't." It would be a waste of words to tell his father there had been nothing to shoot at. That was obvious.

Elijah Layne squinted against the glare of late-afternoon sun as he took a sweeping look across the expanse of treeless prairie beyond the creek. His eyes, once a bright, deep blue, looked clouded now, but Jeff could still see something of his own face in his father's. Elijah's voice was slow and Southern, cracking a little. "Indians say the buffalo've all gone back into the ground to wait till us white folks leave the country."

"I'm afraid they've gone to ground, all right. There's damned little left but a scatterin' of bones and the hide yards over in Dodge." He would have turned the wagons back days ago, but that would have been too early for the scheduled rendezvous with Damon Cregar. He wished he had a stiff shot of whiskey now to wash down the day's disappointment.

Elijah said, "We could go back home. A man can always find some way to make a livin' in Texas."

Jeff dismounted stiffly, his hip hurting him. He extracted the cartridge he had kept in the Big Fifty's breech in case the Indian had turned up. He disliked loaded guns in camp; he had seen a couple of soldiers killed that way. It was bad enough losing them to the Yankee enemy; it was worse having them lost to their own friends' foolishness. "You know we can't go back."

"Maybe they've forgotten by now. It's been a long time."

"People don't forget a killin'." He turned away from his father, toward the campfire. "You-all got any coffee made?" He had carried along some camp bread and buffalo hump to ward off hunger during the day, and had drunk water from his canteen.

The last couple of hundred yards he had been watching a skinner sitting on the ground, leaned back against a wagon wheel. The skinner was too lethargic to arise as Jeff led the black horse in and removed the saddle. In the weeks they had been out on this round, Jeff had never seen Gantry Folsom take a bath though they had camped more often than not at some spring or creek where it would have been easy to do. Folsom's black whiskers had felt neither razor, scissors nor comb. His bloodstained old Union army britches could have stood by themselves if he ever took them off, and he smelled like something two weeks dead. Jeff contrived to stay upwind of him as much as he could.

Folsom pointed his thumb back over his shoulder toward the small stack of hides lashed upon the wagon against which he had made himself comfortable. "Goddamned little to show for all the time we been out. Ol' Cregar'll raise hell and shove a chunk under it."

Grittily, for he sensed a tone of reproach, Jeff said, "You afraid of him, Gant?"

"Hell no! Just because he was a colonel in the Goddamned army don't make him no better than them of us that was just foot soldiers. Anyway, all I can do is peel them after you shoot them. If you can't find them, it ain't no Goddamned skin off of my nose."

Jeff could not remember hearing Gant speak two sentences without throwing in a *Goddamn*. Take the profanity away from him and he could not communicate. Truth be known, Jeff thought, Gant was probably happy the way things were. He was paid by the day whether he did any skinning or not. Jeff had had a few such soldiers under his sergeancy in the war. Usually he had sought the meanest, dirtiest work he could find for them. Here, skinning was the meanest, dirtiest work there was.

Jeff turned back to his father. "Come mornin' we'll break camp and head for the rendezvous point. We won't find anything more that's worth the time and expense of stayin' out."

Elijah Layne shrugged, accepting with an old man's stoic fatalism. He never fought back anymore. There had been a time when he accepted nothing without a fight if it did not come on his own terms. Age and illness had drained that old wildcat strength from him; they had left him diminished in body and mind. He talked a lot about the good old times in Texas, but he would not have the stamina now to relive them even if opportunity allowed. Jeff laid his blanket and bridle atop his saddle on the ground and watched in regret as his father crippled off to fetch him a cup of coffee. It should have been the son who fetched coffee for the father, but that had ended years ago. Somehow it was as if father had become child and the son the father. Jeff wondered if someday it might be the same for him, except that he had no son, and no prospects for one.

He accepted the black coffee with gratitude. "I could've gone for myself."

"You've had a long ride. You look tired."

They had had their quarrels in times past, as fathers and sons did, but those seemed a small thing now. *I wish I had him back the way he was.* He looked into the clouded eyes of the older man and saw himself in twenty or thirty years. *Better I let the Indians get me.*

Elijah began retelling an old story about when he had moved his family from Alabama to Texas in the days of the republic. "We didn't have no coffee then," he reminisced. "We was poor as church mice. I reckon you was too young to remember."

Jeff remembered a little of it. He didn't remember the hardship. He had been too small to realize that hardship was not necessarily a normal way of life. He slumped in fatigue, only half listening to his father. Memories were about all the old man had left to show for a long life. He lived in them most of his waking hours and, Jeff suspected, in his dreams as well.

The cook was a young wagon driver out of New York who had come west seeking adventure and fortune and had found little of either. Jeff suspected that Kid, no more than eighteen or nineteen, would disappear like a ship-jumping sailor as soon as they reached Dodge, escaping back to the more-ordered life he had come here to put behind him. The pay for a driver or skinner was poor. There hadn't been much adventure, looking at the rear end of a mule team when they moved camp, staking out hides as the skinners brought them in, cooking three times a day for a crew that showed little respect for his efforts, for good reason. He had probably never cooked so much as a pot of beans before he had signed on with Damon Cregar, though he had claimed to be an expert so he could get the job. Gantry Folsom had teased Kid about the likelihood that the Indians would catch him and stake him out on an anthill, to a point that he saw savages in every shadow.

Jeff was not surprised, then, when Kid hollered, "Indians!" He had done it before. Jeff nursed the coffee cup in both hands and did not even look up until he heard Gant's strained voice. "He's right, Jeff. Goddamn, must be twenty of the bastards."

Jeff turned, squinting into the sinking sun. Gant was exaggerating, but Jeff counted ten Indians on horseback, skirting the west side of the hunting camp. The range was about three hundred yards. It was no great challenge for the fifty-caliber rifle but long for anything else in the hands of someone less than a marksman. The horsemen halted, stretching out in a line and facing the camp. Jeff's pulse quickened as he retrieved the rifle and poked a big buffalo-killing cartridge into the chamber.

Elijah Layne squinted, trying to see with his failing eyes. Jeff doubted that his father could make them out well enough even to count them. "They fixin' to charge us, Son?"

"Who knows? There's enough to give us a right smart of a fight if they took the notion."

Gant and another skinner, a rangy farmer from Minnesota who always wore an old plug hat, fetched rifles and sighted them over the beds of two wagons. Gant had demonstrated that he was not much of a marksman. Jeff had never seen the farmer even try. He said, "Don't anybody fire unless they act like they're comin' in. We don't need trouble, and maybe they're not lookin' for any."

Gant grumbled, "Goddamned Indians have got trouble in their nature."

"You might too if somebody was killin' off your buffalo and you couldn't find enough meat to feed your young'uns."

"You siding with the sons of bitches?"

"This is a damned poor time and place to do that."

The young cook crouched beneath a wagon, trembling, his lips moving in silent prayer. He made no effort to get a weapon. Jeff doubted that he knew how to use one. Elijah stood beside Jeff, a rifle in his hand. He wouldn't be able to see well enough to aim it until the Indians were almost in his lap. Jeff moved up beside a hide wagon and stood there, cradling the Fifty in his arms. At the distance, he wondered if the Indians could see it. They had faced enough of the big rifles in skirmishes with hunters to learn a healthy respect for them.

Several tribes roamed back and forth across this part of the buffalo range. From what he could see he guessed these to be Cheyennes, but tribal affiliation made little difference. Any of them would fight like hornets if that was their pleasure.

Several Indians drew together and parleyed. Shortly one made a motion with his hands, and they moved on in single file. Jeff's lungs ached. He had been holding his breath. In relief he expelled the air and inhaled long and deeply.

"By God," Gant declared with surprise, "we scared them off."

"I doubt they were all that scared," Jeff said. "Probably figured it wasn't worth what it would cost them to take us. This ain't much of an outfit if you really look at it."

Kid still crouched beneath the wagon, shaking like a dog just come out of cold water. *Well, you wanted adventure,* Jeff thought. *You can tell them when you get home about your big set-to with the Indians.* "It's all right now, Kid. They've decided to save us for a rainy day."

The Minnesota farmer was grim but not particularly frightened. "They could change their minds and come back."

"We'll double the guard tonight." Jeff doubted that anybody would sleep much. "It's high time we started back to join up with Cregar."

Gant said, "I'd almost as soon face the Goddamned Indians."

Cregar's outfit totaled five sets of hide wagons, each set made up of a lead wagon and a trailer hitched behind on a short tongue. He had sent two with Jeff and had kept three with him. Nearing the agreed-upon rendezvous point at a bend in the Arkansas River northeast of Dodge City, Jeff counted four extra sets of wagons besides Cregar's three. Cregar was an independent sort who disliked being crowded, especially by people over whom he had no authority. Jeff guessed that an Indian scare might have encouraged the outfits to move together, just as the sight of Indians had prompted him to keep these wagons moving at a deliberate pace while he performed outrider duty, watching for any attempt at surprise. The trip from the last camp had been uneventful except for Elijah letting a wheel drop into a deep hole that weak eyes had not seen. Freeing his father's wagon had required shoveling and sweat.

Gant had complained loudly, "Old man, you ain't got no business driving a Goddamned wagon. You can't see your hand in front of your nose."

Times, Elijah still showed a spark of the fire that once had burned in his belly. "I didn't have to. I was followin' after you, and I could go by the smell."

Jeff was pleased that his father could still muster that much of the old fight, but he could not let the situation run on unchecked. There was always a chance the quick-tempered Gant would disregard Elijah's age and frailty. It wouldn't take a lot to hurt him. "Let's save the fightin' in case we run into those Indians again."

They did not, nor did they see sign of any. Recounting the seven sets of wagons camped amid the trees that lined the river, Jeff saw relief in the face of Kid, who had shared a wagon seat with Gant. Gant had continued to fill his head with stories about Indian atrocities until the boy was white-eyed with fear, expecting at any moment to be overrun by a yelling horde.

"You better ease off, Gant," Jeff warned, "or we'll lose ourselves a cook."

"Damned little loss," Gant had replied, giving Kid a malevolent glance.

Someday Gant would say the wrong thing to the wrong man and get his head laid open by a singletree, Jeff thought. But Kid showed no fight. He seemed not even to perceive that Gant had insulted him.

A tall, muscular black man walked out from camp, toward the incoming wagons. Texas-raised, Jeff did not easily shake hands with black men, but Sully was a welcome exception. He leaned down from the saddle. "I see the Cheyennes ain't got your hair yet."

Sully's mouthful of perfect white teeth gleamed in an easy smile. "No sir, ain't much for them to get." He had always voiced confidence that Indians would leave him alone because his short, kinky hair would frustrate any warrior trying to take it. "I been half afraid Colonel was goin' to try to scalp us all, though. He sure ain't been in no good frame of mind, Mr. Jeff." With Sully it was always *Mister*. He would never throw off all the shackles of slavery.

"His wagons ain't stacked any higher with hides than mine are."

"He's been as cross as a sore-footed badger all the time we been out. I sure was glad to see Ol' Mr. Cephus Browder come rollin' in with his wagons last evenin'. That girl of his . . . she makes Colonel forget to holler at everybody. He prances like a stud colt."

"Arletta?" Jeff frowned. "He's old enough to be her daddy. So am I, damned near."

"He don't look at her like a daddy. The older she gets, the younger he feels."

"It's all in his head. Even Damon Cregar can't order the calendar to lie."

"Calendar don't know the colonel." The black man turned to watch the wagons coming up. "You-all didn't run into no Indians?"

"Not any that cared to fight us."

"We was lucky too. But day before yesterday we come upon three men dead, arrows stickin' in 'em to where they looked like porcupines. Wagons all burnt and the hides cut up so they wouldn't be worth nothin'. Colonel sure was made about the hides."

Jeff said, "I hope he at least buried the men."

"Oh sure, he done that. Colonel's a God-fearin' man."

"Times, I wonder if he even fears God. I never saw him back away from anything or anybody."

"I heard him pray in the war."

"In the war *everybody* prayed. But it's been a long time since I was inside of a church house. Colonel either, I expect."

Sully made a long, sweeping gesture. "This is the biggest, finest church there is, the whole outdoors. No matter whichaway you turn, you're lookin' at the Lord's handiwork. This is Freedom Church."

Sully knew more about the value of freedom than most people, Jeff reasoned. He had never weakened in his gratitude to the Lord who had willed it for him, and to the Union colonel sent to deliver him from servitude.

Jeff's father waved at Sully, and Sully jovially waved back. The quick movement of his hand startled one of the mules on the wagon driven by Kid. It jerked its head around as if expecting to be struck.

Gantry Folsom shouted, "Nigger, you trying to start a stampede and wreck us? You ought to still be wearing a chain around your neck, no better sense than you got!"

Gant often picked on Sully, probably confident that he would not fight back. A black man who raised a hand against a white, even in self-defense, was in jeopardy. It made little difference that he was in Yankee country or that Gant was a Yankee. Black was still black. Sully tried to pretend he had not heard.

Jeff did not see Damon Cregar. "Is Colonel off huntin'?"

"He's in the Browder camp, a-watchin' Miss Arletta. He's anxious to be gittin' on in to Dodge."

"Why? We don't have that many hides to sell."

"His boy Farrell is supposed to be comin' in from the east. May already be there a-waitin' for us."

Jeff had long known that Cregar had a son, living with the family of his late wife. Cregar spoke of him occasionally, concerned about his being raised soft and overprivileged by wealthy people and cushioned from the harsher realities. His son was one of the few subjects Colonel ever mentioned that were not directly related to business.

Dryly Jeff said, "One Cregar is more than enough. I don't know what we'll do with two of them raisin' hell in camp."

"We'll do what we always done . . . anything Colonel says."

A stocky, middle-aged man limped heavily out from the wagons. His face was half hidden by a misshapen, floppy-brimmed felt hat, but Jeff knew him on sight. He stepped down from the saddle to extend his hand.

Cephus Browder was missing a couple of teeth in front, but that did not inhibit his speech or his smile. "I'm pleasured to see you, Jeff. Wondered if you might've run into trouble, Indians bein' so riled and all."

Jeff didn't know why everybody called the man Old Cephus, as if he were seventy years of age. Actually, Cephus Browder probably was no older than Damon Cregar and not more than a dozen years older than Jeff. But he carried himself with the studied dignity of a man who had been everywhere worthwhile to go and had done about everything he ever wanted to do. In truth, he had never made a success of anything in his life. He had difficulty in signing his own name and had to ask somebody to read the receipts to him when he sold hides or bought supplies.

Jeff said, "The only trouble we've had was in findin' buffalo."

"I think they've drifted south."

Many people could not believe the buffalo had been killed out; it seemed improbable, as many as there had been. Like others,

Cephus Browder clung to the hope that they still existed, that the hunters need only find where they had migrated. It was as forlorn a hope as that of the Indians, who believed the buffalo were hiding safely in a hole in the ground. But Jeff saw nothing to be gained by arguing with Cephus. Everything the man owned was tied up in his wagons. An end to the hide trade very possibly meant ruin to him and was therefore unthinkable.

Jeff said, "Sully tells me you still got Arletta with you."

"She's cookin' up supper for both outfits. Bet you ain't had a good supper in weeks."

Cephus was right, but Jeff would not say so and hurt Kid's feelings. "You oughtn't to keep bringin' her out here on these plains. It's dangerous."

"Where would I leave her, in Dodge?" Cephus's sun-punished face twisted as if he had bitten into a sour apple. "That's more dangerous for a young girl than bein' out here with her pa and a good-sized outfit that can watch over her. You've seen the kind of men that gather in Dodge."

"Hasn't she got kin back where you come from?"

"None that wouldn't like as not use her for a servant. I just wish she could've been a boy. Wouldn't be as much worry to me thataway."

"Cregar's got a boy. He frets over him."

"If I knowed how to find my boy Zeb, I'd have him here with me. I wouldn't leave him back yonder someplace like Colonel's done his son. That's the only thing I can fault Colonel for."

I hope it's all you ever have to fault him for. Jeff could see Damon Cregar now, a tall man, shoulders bull-stout and broad as an ax handle, a man who could command without having to speak a word. He had only to show his stern face and motion with his hands; most men would obey him without pausing to question. Jeff obeyed him too, usually, though if he had a question he asked it.

Colonel stood beside a cook fire, where a thin slip of a girl in a faded and shapeless old gray dress was lifting a Dutch oven onto smoldering coals. Cregar did not move out to meet the wagons; people went to Cregar. He held a coffee cup in one huge hand. The other hand, balled into a massive fist, rested on his hip. His stance said all there was to say: he had been out of the army for many years, but he had never stopped being a colonel.

Jeff saw to putting the wagons in line with Cregar's and to the unhitching of the teams. Then, bracing himself, he walked up to the colonel. Somehow Cregar's presence always made him feel that he should salute, but he had never allowed himself to slip that far. Nor did he ever address Cregar as *Mister* or *sir*. He would not do that for any damnyankee, not even the one who paid him. "We're here."

Cregar's voice was strong and resonant, as if it came up from deep within his broad chest. "I can see that for myself. And I can see that you didn't bring many hides."

Jeff knew that the moment one showed the least sign of submissiveness toward Cregar, he was as good as lost. The only way to hold his ground was to meet challenge with challenge. "You want to fire me?"

Cregar gave Jeff a long stare with black eyes that seemed to bore a hole into a man and study what was inside him. Jeff stared back, putting up a stiff guard. Cregar shrugged. "Get yourself some coffee. Arletta makes it better than anybody."

The girl looked up with a smile, her blue eyes alight with pleasure over a compliment. Jeff doubted that she received many. He judged her to be eighteen or nineteen, maybe even twenty; he had never heard her or Cephus say for sure. Her reddish hair, tangled by the wind, was long enough to extend down well beyond her shoulders. Her face was browned by exposure to sun and wind. Usually she wore a bonnet for protection, but she did not have it on now. He had often wondered if she might be pretty, given a chance to pamper herself like girls in town. She would probably end up like so many women he had seen trapped in drudgery and hardship, aging before their time, burned-out old women at forty. Cephus ought to give her a better chance, except that Cephus had no better chance to offer.

Jeff said, "I brought fresh meat for the camp, Arletta. Shot an antelope this mornin'."

Her voice was soft. "I expect the men'll be right pleased. Ain't been no variety much."

Jeff made no claim to having much schooling, but Arletta had received almost none, following her father from failed farm to failed freighting business to a failing hide-hunting enterprise. He had watched her strain to read bills and receipts to her father. She could do sums, but to read a book or a newspaper was a form of physical pain.

What a waste! he thought. Cephus had struggled just to keep the two of them decently fed. Adequate schooling had been beyond her reach. One of these days some woman-starved young hide hunter or railroad hand would come a-courting, and he wouldn't ask if she could read and write. It would be enough that she was female. Pretty soon she would have a passel of runny-nose young'uns trailing behind her, no better educated than she was, doomed to scratch out a bare living with their hands as she had done, as Cephus had done. It was an endless circle, like a wagon tire going around and around.

Damon Cregar laid a big arm across the girl's shoulder. "You fix us a good supper tonight, hon, and when we get to Dodge City I'll buy you a nice dress."

She gave him a shy smile. "Ain't no need in that, Colonel. I was goin' to cook anyhow." But Jeff could see that the thought pleased her. He could read the wanting in Cregar's eyes as the big man watched the girl walk toward her wagon. Cregar had been widowed a long time.

Jeff said to him, "Sully tells me you're lookin' for your son to meet us when we get to Dodge."

Cregar had not taken his eyes from the girl. "He's stayed with those people much too long. It's time he got out of the hothouse and into the world."

Jeff picked his words carefully. "He'd be pretty close to the same age as Arletta, wouldn't he?"

"He's twenty-three." Cregar turned his head, his black eyes questioning, and cutting like a knife.

He knows damned well what I'm trying to say. "It occurs to me that the two of them might make a fittin' couple."

Cregar snorted. "I'm going to drill him like a soldier and teach him about hard work. He'll have too much on his mind to be thinking about young women."

Jeff said coolly, "That hasn't stopped his daddy."

Cregar's jaw hardened. Though he respected Jeff's competence as a hunter, he had never become accustomed to the Texan's forthright way of speaking what was on his mind with little regard to consequences. Jeff would remain a rebel to the last day he drew breath. "In the army I'd have had you court-martialed for insubordination."

"We weren't in the same army."

Cregar said, "Then perhaps you should remember who won the war."

Three

THE STEEL RAILS made a rhythmic clicking sound beneath the wheels as the train rumbled westward through the darkness. Under the light of the smoking-car's lamps, Nigel Smithwick lifted his gaze over his hand of cards and carefully studied the frowning face of the player across the table. He had learned to see much in the arching of an eyebrow, a fleeting flicker of hope or disappointment. A poker player's hunches were fine as far as they went, but they were more effective augmented by a dollop of psychology. Smithwick had practiced a great deal as card-playing had gradually evolved from a diversion to a profession of sorts.

His opponent was a heavy-browed, belligerent-looking man hunched over his side of the table, mumbling over his own cards. He growled around a badly chewed cigar, "What do you think, Englishman?" Two of the man's associates had already folded and glumly sat watching.

Smithwick prevented any sign of pleasure from showing in his face. "I think I will raise you a hundred."

The man looked pained. Smithwick wondered if it was from the cards he held or from cigar smoke burning his eyes. "Is that in pounds or in dollars?"

Smithwick sensed that the man was making idle conversation to stall while he considered his move. That meant he was uncertain about his hand. Smithwick suffered no uncertainty. "I wish it were pounds, but dollars are the legal tender in this Godforsaken country."

One of the men who had folded took immediate umbrage. He had been drinking earlier, until his flask had gone empty. "What's the matter with this country? If it ain't good enough for you, why the hell didn't you stay in England?"

The cigar chewer said, "Can't you tell by looking at him? He's a remittance man. Probably the family black sheep. They pay him to go way off somewhere so he won't disgrace his poor old father's name. Ain't that it, Englishman?"

The man was guessing uncomfortably close, but Smithwick would not allow himself to become riled. That would be poor business for a man who used his skill at cards to augment the small allowance reluctantly sent from the family estate.

The big man kept grinding. "What did you do, Englishman, kill somebody, or maybe ruin some peasant's daughter?"

Smithwick resisted making an answer. He had rather play against gentlemen, but in this raw land far from the place of his birth he accepted challenges wherever he found them, even if it had to be with such obvious ruffians. At home he would not give such men a second look, much less engage them at cards. He could never feel comfortable with a man who had black hair almost to the ends of his stubby fingers. The cigar-chewing man had said his name was Jones. The other two had introduced themselves as Black and Brown. The names in themselves had told him they were up to no good.

"Where are you men bound?" he asked, not really caring but hoping to keep his opponent distracted enough to make some mistake in judgment. The only reason these men's destinations might interest him would be in enabling him to go elsewhere. They had the rough look of men who, were they in England, might have intimate knowledge of Old Bailey. He took comfort from the feel of the derringer in one of his short-topped boots.

"Dodge City," his opponent said. "We hear business is good there for men of energy. What about you, Duke?"

Smithwick suppressed a frown, realizing the man was trying to provoke him. "I assure you, sir, I am not a duke, nor do I hold any other titles."

"I've run into other Englishmen. Just about every one of them was called Cedric, and they all claimed to be a duke or a lord or some other damned thing."

"Not I, sir. I am content to be just what you see and no more. My ancestors have bequeathed me neither title nor money beyond a pittance. I must work for my sustenance."

"Some work this is. Your hands are too smooth to hold a pick or shovel. I'll bet the heaviest thing you ever lifted was a poker deck, Cedric. Or is the name Percy?"

The baiting was beginning to arouse Smithwick's anger, but he knew that was its purpose. He refused to succumb. "We may talk, or we may play. Which is your pleasure?"

"Call." Jones's hairy fingers spread his cards, face up.

Smithwick watched the man's face fall as he laid out his hand, then reached to the middle of the table to draw in the pot. "Shall we continue, or have you *gentlemen* had sufficient recreation for the night?" He doubted that he had totally cleaned their pockets, but he had done well enough for an evening's work. He had enjoyed quite enough of their company. Part of his reason for coming this far west had been a longing for new and exotic experiences. He had not anticipated how closely it would force him into the company of so many of the unschooled and the unwashed. That closeness afflicted his nostrils.

The man called Jones chewed heavily on his cigar. His eyes smouldered with resentment. "You don't think much of us Americans, do you, Cedric?"

"I do when they play as you have played." Smithwick allowed a brief smile to flicker before he caught it. "I may never return to England." In truth, he looked forward to going back as soon as he had put away enough money to augment his family allowance and allow him to live in the manner a gentleman was due. If he could play against the likes of these every night, his stay among the colonials should not be overly long.

One of the early quitters grumbled, "I don't know why they keep lettin' these foreigners into the country. It's already hard enough for honest Americans to make a livin', what with the money panic back east."

Smithwick could not resist a barb. "If you have any thought of making your living this way, I would suggest you reconsider. Your skills are sadly lacking." He pushed back from the table and gathered his winnings. He took from his pocket a silver watch his father had worn before him. "If the railroad schedule is to be trusted, we should not be far out of Dodge City. If you gentlemen have no further desire to play, then I shall bid you goodnight. I am going to enjoy a smoke out on the platform."

Jones spoke irritably around the cigar. "Go ahead. You'll get no more of our money tonight."

He left them leaning together over the table, talking resentfully among themselves. That he had beaten these blackguards so handily gave him satisfaction, especially inasmuch as they had cheated and he had not. A gentleman never cheated, except when he had to.

The club car's air was stale from cigar and cigarette smoke and the smell of perspiration new and old. Outside, he risked catching a cinder in his eye, but at least the air would be fresher. He pushed the door open and stepped onto the narrow platform between this car and the next. The night was so dark he could barely see the prairie rushing past except that little part near the tracks where lamplight from the coaches spilled out upon the ground. The light seemed to dart and dance as it played across small bushes and clumps of grass.

Cupping his hands to shield the match from the wind that whipped between the cars, he attempted to light his cigar. The flame snuffed out too quickly. He was on his third when the club car's door opened. Turning to see, he heard a man grunt in exertion and felt something strike him hard across the back of the head. He grabbed desperately at the rail to avoid falling from the train. Rough hands slammed him against the wall and foraged in his pockets. He tried in vain to kneel, to reach the derringer in his boot, but strong hands held him. In the darkness he could not see the faces. He smelled a cigar, however, and knew the voice that cursed him.

"We'll teach you to cheat us, you foreign son of a bitch! Come west to see the sights, did you? Well, see how you like these."

Something—a gun barrel, probably—struck the back of his head again. Jones's voice said, "Under the wheels, boys."

He felt himself being hoisted up and over the protective railing, wind rushing in his face. He grabbed the steel rod, but strong, relentless hands pried his fingers loose, threatening to break them. He fell, the hard impact against the wooden ties knocking the breath from him. For a panicked, helpless moment he expected the grinding wheels to crush him. He heard the screaming of steel against steel, inches from his head, and felt the violent gale raised by the passing of the cars. But at least he had fallen clear. He rolled down what little embankment there was and came to a stop amid the weeds, listening to the *clickety-clack* of the wheels against the spaces between the rails. He pushed himself to his knees and fought for breath so that he might shout for the train to stop. Breath was slow in coming. No one could have heard him anyway.

He watched the lights of the train receding into the west. He was alone in the silence of the plains. His head pounded from the blows that had been struck. He rubbed a hand across the place and found it sticky with blood. The hand itself burned as if he had stuck it into hot coals. He had lacerated it, instinctively trying to break his fall.

For a while he did not attempt to stand up. He hurt too much. Carefully he inched a hand along his side and wondered if he might have cracked a rib. He decided he probably had not, but he would wager that daylight would reveal bruises the size of a bull-dog. He cursed the perfidy of men who would rob him and cast him away God knew how far from civilization, if indeed there *was* any this far west. He had seen but little that he considered to be civilization since crossing the Mississippi, and a wretched shortage of it even to the east.

The robbers had intended him to die beneath the wheels. They probably thought the first train to pass this way in daylight would come upon his mangled body, and his death would be regarded as an unfortunate accident. They had left nothing in his pockets, not even the watch willed to him by his father. Had he died, he could not have been identified. His family would never have known what happened to him. He would simply be another who disappeared without a trace upon the great plains of this wild and heathen West.

The thought was sobering, for he realized it could still come to pass. There was no way to know what manner of wild beasts or wild men might be roaming this wilderness, looking for just such a hapless wayfarer. He reached to his boot but found the derringer gone. The thought of being unarmed in this strange and savage land left him more alarmed than ever.

A momentary panic subsided. Reconstructing what he could remember of the brief attack, he was sure they had not reached into his boot. Probably they had not even thought of it; they were after money. Perhaps the little pistol had shaken out of his boot when he fell. He pushed to his knees and began crawling, looking for it in the dim light of the stars and a quarter moon. He felt it before he saw it, small and cold, lying a foot or so short of the wooden ties. He clasped it gratefully in his bleeding hand. It was not much, but it was the only protection he had.

He struggled to his feet in spite of the pain. His knees burned, cut like his hands. He tried walking but stumbled in the darkness and sprawled on his stomach. He heard some small animal skitter away in fright. Its fright was no greater than his own during the moment it took him to realize what had made the rustling noise.

He decided reluctantly that he should not try to move until daylight. He eased himself to a sitting position and sat contemplating his situation. Surely a train would be along tomorrow. But what if it refused to stop? He doubted that he looked the English gentleman now, his clothes dirtied and torn. He probably looked more like a potential train robber.

And what if something came along while he waited for the train? He had been told terrible stories about the Indians and the creative punishments they inflicted upon unlucky whites who fell into captivity. And the bison . . . he had seen none, but he had heard of their great stampedes, of how their sharp hooves pounded men and wagons into powder and splinters.

Coming to America was to have been his grand adventure, an opportunity to escape the monotony and emptiness of being a wayward middle son who would inherit neither land nor family business, who could stay and work as a junior under an older brother but could have little hope of ownership in his own right. The family, save for his mother, had seemed glad to see him go, weary of his aimless playing at cards, his racing of horses, his riding after the hounds. Perhaps in America, they had said, he would find enterprise worthy of his abilities.

Enterprise indeed! If fortune failed to befriend him now, his bones would bleach here on these empty plains. His whole life would come down to one good meal for a handful of prairie wolves. He stretched himself out upon the grass and pictured in his mind the Smithwick manor. He pictured his late father, his mother, his brothers. He pictured his sister Esther, who had proclaimed him a wastrel. Her dart had struck the target full on, for he had wasted the most precious possession of all, his life.

He slept fitfully, his dreams flitting haphazardly from his old home to bands of roving Indians, to a dozen rascals beating him with their pistols. He never slept so deeply that he did not feel the burning of the bruises and contusions. He dreamed his body was being used as a playing ground by a thousand biting insects. When he awoke to the half light of early dawn, he found that all of it was not a dream. He jumped quickly to his feet, brushing desperately at the ants which crawled over him. With the day would probably also come flies, drawn by the blood.

Some grand adventure, this.

His lips were painfully dry. He wished for water, tea, whiskey, anything wet. He had seen wooden water towers at intervals along these tracks before darkness had descended yesterday, but he had no idea how far it might be to the next. He looked to the east, toward the rising sun, and wished he were three thousand miles in that direction. But the wish was futile. So far as he knew, Dodge City was the nearest town, and that lay to the west. He began walking along the right-of-way, studying the horizon for any promising sign of habitation. In the spreading dawn the land looked almost flat, though he knew it gently rose and fell away, like the rolling of the Atlantic. He saw no trees that might indicate a river or creek. There was only the tall, curing grass, part brown and part green, mile upon mile of it. He remembered from a map that the railroad followed the Arkansas River to a degree but drew away from it somewhere east of Dodge City. He could not recall whether the river would be to the north or the south, or how far it might be.

His stiff legs ached from punishment taken in the fall. They limbered after a time, assuring him that he was not to be a cripple for life. Unconsciously he reached for the watch to determine what time it was, then remembered they had stolen it. That loss pained him as much as the blows on his head or the many cuts and bruises. It had been the most tangible evidence he had retained of home and family. Father would be mortified if he were still alive to know, not only for the loss but for the manner in which the loss had come about. He had been a single-minded man in the matter of duty, of proprieties, of attention to business. He would never have understood the careless ways to which his son had succumbed.

If I survive this, Father, I will never do such things again. It was a safe-enough pledge, for Father could not hear unless he were hovering about as a watching spirit. Smithwick knew it was a pledge he was unlikely to keep, if indeed he survived long enough to break it.

Lionel Smithwick had tried everything short of corporal punishment to persuade his son to enter the military service and earn a commission. It was a time-honored course for middle sons who would not inherit. But the thought of serving the empire in some distant and backward colonial land had been abhorrent to Nigel Smithwick.

India and its teeming millions seemed benign now in comparison to this wilderness.

He found himself wearying much too soon. When he took a deep breath through his mouth, his dry throat felt as if it were being sliced by a knife. He tried to concentrate on distant matters to keep his mind occupied. He thought of the three ruffians. In particular he thought of Jones, who chewed on the black cigar, and wished he could be alone with that gentleman for five minutes of bare-knuckle pugilism. Smithwick knew some tricks the Marques of Queensbury never heard of. He drew strength from his anger and kept walking.

He gasped in dismay as a gray wolf materialized from the grass. The animal was alone, so far as he could see. It circled him warily, keeping its distance. He thought it likely that the wolf had never seen a human before and was not sure what manner of beast he might be. He had heard tales of wolves hungrily attacking people, rending them apart in their desperation. A cold and elemental fear took hold of him, a fear his cave-dwelling ancestors had probably known well, living in constant exposure to wild animals of one sort and another.

He decided his best defense would be an attack. He found a long stick lying beside the track, a stick of a sort he had seen men use to punch up cattle that had lain down or fallen in the livestock cars. Taking a firm grip on his fear, he shook the stick and ran toward the wolf, shouting as loudly as his dry throat would allow. The wolf hesitated a moment, then turned and loped away, looking back at him until it disappeared in the grass from which it had come.

Smithwick's heart was a while in slowing to its normal rate. He had to sit and rest a bit before he was able to rise up and walk some more.

He had not gone far before he encountered the Indians. The wolf had been as nothing compared to this new threat. He gripped the long stick so hard that his hand hurt. He despaired of life as the half-dozen horsemen rode cautiously toward him. They might have thought at first that the stick was a rifle, but they were near enough now to see the difference. They were almost naked. Most wore feathers tied in their hair, but their faces were not painted. One led a horse with two deer tied across its back. He began to hope they were a hunting party without hostile intentions.

They stopped at ten paces and studied him as if he were some freak animal. A lone white man afoot was surely an oddity, especially one armed only with a stick. They could not see the derringer he had stuck into a pocket because it had rubbed painfully against his sore ankle when he carried it in his boot. He reasoned that in this situation it would be of little more use than the stick. To draw it would probably only make them hostile, if they were not that way already. They talked among themselves. He could tell nothing of their mood from the tone of their conversation until one of them laughed, and then another.

A horseman who appeared to be a leader put his pony into a slow walk. Smithwick's instinct was to turn and run, but he suspected that would bring them baying after him like a pack of hounds. If he was to die, he would die with dignity befitting an Englishman. He stood his ground, fighting a desperate urge to draw the derringer and shoot one of them, at least, before they overwhelmed him. But the tiny weapon was likely to do no more than inflict a painful wound. They would probably make his torture all the greater before they allowed him to yield up his final breath.

The Indian held a rifle. It was an old flintlock, its stock reinforced by rawhide wrapping, nails driven into it to form some sort of pattern. He reached out and touched the barrel to Smithwick's shoulder, then drew away, making a triumphant whoop. Another rider came up and did the same, then another except that this one touched him with a bow. Before they were done, all had tapped him with whatever weapons they carried in their hands. Smithwick held his breath, waiting for the final blow. But they drew back, talking among themselves, laughing.

It crossed his mind that in touching him they had counted some sort of score, like a player at cricket.

As abruptly as they had appeared, they rode away, crossing the tracks and passing over a low hill that lay to the south. Smithwick seated himself upon the end of a wooden tie, drained.

He did not know how long he had been there before he heard a distant sound from the west, possibly an oncoming train. He considered putting his ear to the rail but found it grimy with grease and dirt and a residue of coal smoke. He was dirty enough already. It had been his habit to change shirts daily whether he had soiled one or not, and to wipe the dust from his boots before joining polite company.

He soon saw smoke from the locomotive and stepped away from the track. He began waving his arms when the train was still four or five hundred yards away. He did not know how he would convince a conductor to accept him; the robbers had left him not so much as a farthing. But if the railroad would vouchsafe his traveling to the next city of any proportions, he could telegraph his bank in New York to transfer funds from an account he had accumulated there for emergency use. The emergency he had envisioned was more in the nature of a bad turn of the cards, not a catastrophe of present proportions.

He shouted, though no one in the locomotive could possibly hear him, and he waved his arms all the faster as the train drew near. He could not discern that it had slowed one whit. The locomotive passed him, its noise deafening and the wind from beneath it whipping dirt into his face. The engineer waved back.

The idiot! The bloody idiot thinks I am merely passing the time of day. He began to run, surprised that he had the strength, but it was in vain. The engineer was no longer watching. Smithwick shouted but knew his voice was lost in the hiss of the steam, the rumble of the great wheels. A few passengers in the coaches waved at him, not perceiving his desperate situation.

The train passed on toward the east. The acrid black smoke was like a parting insult as it settled over him. Again, as last night, he was alone on the prairie. He slumped in futility, in anger and frustration and apprehension.

Many an Englishman lay buried in foreign soils, but most had died in the cause of the empire. His own death, if it was to be here on this vast and empty expanse of grass, would be for no cause save his own recklessness in allowing himself to fall into the hands of brigands. The green hills of England had never seemed more beautiful than now, as he saw them in memory.

In a flare of indignation he imagined himself suing the railroad, of having that stupid engineer tied to a post in the city square and roundly flogged while an aroused citizenry cheered the hand that held the whip. His anger gave him strength to resume walking westward. He had no idea how many miles it might be to a water tank, a caretaker's station, or even Dodge City itself. But after the perils and indignities which he had already survived, he was determined to get there, to show them the stuff of which an Englishman was made.

Walking drew some of the stiffness and soreness from him. He gained strength, energized by his new determination and his fantasies of vengeance. This was a forbidding, hostile land to a man of his background, but he made up his mind to meet its challenge and go the extra mile, or however many miles it took to bring him to whatever passed for civilization. It occurred to him that this would make a grand story to take home, to tell someday in the drawing rooms and pubs. Mentally projecting himself into a happier future helped him cope with the thirst and his growing hunger.

The sun indicated it was considerably past noontime when he saw the wagons. At first he thought they were an illusion, for his ordeal had sent spots dancing before his eyes much of the morning. He stopped, blinking, then pulled back the skin at the corners of his eyes to bring better focus. They *were* wagons, traveling westward, paralleling the tracks but remaining north of them some little distance. He judged they were moving at a pace comparable to his own if not a little faster. To intercept them he would have to walk at an angle rather than directly toward their present position.

He managed at times to move into an awkward trot. He tried to shout, but his throat was too parched. His pinched bleat would not carry farther than he might throw a stone. Sweat set his eyes afire. He had covered perhaps two thirds of the distance when a horseman moved out toward him.

They've seen me. God be thanked, they've seen me. He stopped and waited. The strength he had borrowed all morning seemed to desert him. It was all he could do to keep from slumping to the ground. He waved his hand to the approaching rider, who slowed to look him over before he closed the last thirty yards.

The man's voice was friendly enough, though his manner indicated that he reserved some doubts. "Looks to me like you been stomped by a herd of buffalo. Lose your horse or somethin'?" He had a slow manner of speaking, an accent Smithwick associated with the South.

Words came painfully, so Smithwick wasted few. "Water? You have water?"

The man reached behind his saddle. "It ain't fresh, but I reckon it's wet enough." He handed Smithwick a metal canteen covered by canvas, stained and worn through in places by rubbing against the saddle. Smithwick turned it up and felt the blessed wetness as the water coated his throat. He gulped desperately, choking in his haste to swallow all he could. The man took hold of the canteen. "Whoa, pardner, you're fixin' to drown yourself."

Smithwick came near fighting him for possession before reason took over. The man waited until Smithwick had calmed, then returned the canteen. "Slow this time. You'll get all you want, but don't hurry it."

When the container was empty, Smithwick found voice. "My thanks, sir, and my apologies. I lost my head for a moment."

"Been in some tight spots myself, and I wasn't always thinkin' straight. How come you out here afoot?"

There would be time for a fuller explanation later, if he felt one was in order. This man might be of the same rough caliber as those who had used him so badly. He had the sun-browned face, the many days' growth of whiskers, the unkempt hair in need of a barber, the rough hands Smithwick had come to associate with frontiersmen. "I was on the train."

The rider studied him quizzically. "And you fell off?"

"With some assistance, sir."

The man seemed to grasp by intuition more than Smithwick had seen fit to tell him. "Robbed you first, I reckon?"

"They took everything I had on my person." Smithwick began to feel that he had found understanding company.

"You wouldn't be the first pilgrim who ever got that kind of welcome to this part of the country. By your talk, I take it you come from a long ways off."

"England. I am Nigel Smithwick." He extended his hand.

"Jefferson Layne. From Texas. Up here that seems about as far as England." He took his left foot out of the stirrup. "Swing up behind me and I'll take you to the wagons."

"I would be much in your debt, sir." Smithwick put his left foot in the stirrup Layne had freed. Mounting stretched muscles he had not used in walking, and pain was like a lance in his legs. "Quite a procession of freight wagons you have there."

"They're hide wagons. Buffalo hides. You'll know when we get a little closer. We're downwind."

The odor of the raw skins was an assault to his nostrils.

Layne noted Smithwick's reaction. "There's worse to be met up with in this country than the smell of buffalo hides."

Smithwick said, "I met some of them on the train."

"Maybe if you're lucky you'll never meet them again."

"On the contrary, I would meet them with great pleasure if it could be on anything approaching equal terms. That unschooled riffraff could do with a stern lesson."

An elderly man driving the lead wagon was the first to hail the two as they rode up. He sawed on the reins. "The way you rode off, Son, I thought you might've seen buffalo." He gave Smithwick a curious though silent scrutiny.

"He's no buffalo, Dad, but he's been skinned. Some highbinders went through his pockets and threw him off of the train. Mr. Smithwick, this here's my daddy, Elijah Layne."

For a man of many years, Layne had a strong grip. He made Smithwick's knuckles ache. "How do, Mr. Smithwick."

"I do much better, thank you, since your son has so kindly come to my rescue."

Elijah gave Smithwick a quizzical look. "You talk like somebody I've heard before. You a Frenchman or somethin'?"

Jeff said, "He's an Englishman, Dad."

Elijah Layne's old face brightened. "I ought to've known. Durin' the war I freighted cotton down to the Mexican border. We sold it to Englishmen and hauled back English guns. If we'd had more friends like England, the Confederacy might've won."

Smithwick said, "I wish we could have been more help." It struck him that the ruffians on the train had probably been on the Union side of the conflict, if they had been on any at all. He had detected no trace of the Southern in their speech. It was unmistakable in the two Laynes.

A big man with military bearing rode a large and splendid bay horse up the line of wagons. "What is the delay here?" he demanded of the older Layne. His gaze fastened on Smithwick, who had just dismounted from Jeff Layne's black horse. "Who are you, sir, and where did you come from?"

"My name is Nigel Smithwick. I have come from England."

The big man gave him the critical scrutiny Smithwick had seen in landed gentry when they tried to decide whether to flog an errant employee or simply to see him off of the premises. "You're a long way from home."

"I am very much aware of that, sir."

Jeff Layne said, "This is Colonel Cregar. He owns the wagons, most of them." He explained briefly how Smithwick had become stranded.

Cregar declared, "I have damned little use for any man who does not defend himself."

Smithwick bristled inside, but it would still be a long walk to Dodge City. "As a general rule I do that quite well, but they took me by surprise."

Cregar exhibited little sympathy for Smithwick's predicament. "I don't suppose you saw any buffalo while you were out there?"

"Do you mean bison? None. I must say that I was not looking for any, given my situation."

"You *would* have been if you were in *our* situation." Cregar irritably shifted his attention to Elijah Layne. "Are you going to move that team, or do you intend to make camp in the middle of the afternoon?"

Without answering, the old man flipped the reins. The wagon lurched forward as the mules took up the slack in the harness.

Jeff Layne said sharply, "My daddy's not one of your soldiers. You've got no call to talk to him thataway."

"It's my wagon, and I'm paying him to drive it, not to stand here." Cregar looked at Smithwick. "What are your plans, Smith? Are you going with us?"

"The name is Smithwick, and if it would not inconvenience you too much I would like to remain with your wagons until we reach Dodge City. When I can make contact with my bank I shall gladly pay you for any trouble."

Cregar looked him over as if he were a constable examining a prisoner. "We are not operating a charity business, but if you'll help us a little in making and breaking camp, I'll consider us even. I take it that you've had nothing to eat today."

"Not a morsel."

"You will find a young lady on one of the rear wagons. Tell her I said give you whatever she has left from our noon stop."

For all his gruffness, Cregar had the redeeming virtue of generosity, at least to a point, Smithwick thought. "That would be kind of you."

"I'd do as much for a flea-bitten Cheyenne."

Jeff Layne remained with Smithwick until Cregar was out of earshot, following the lead wagon. "Colonel forgets that he's not in command of everybody. The lady's name is Arletta. If I was you I wouldn't say the colonel *told* her to do anything. I'd just ask her real nice."

Smithwick regarded that as an indication the woman was one of those strong-willed egoists for whom any suggestion had to be made to appear their own idea. He would not be surprised to find her a snuff-dipping Amazon as well; he had seen a few of those in this raw country. He took several strides to place himself on the upwind side of the passing wagons, where the odor of the hides might be less compelling and the flies less aggressive. He studied the drivers and skinners as they went by him. They were a dirty, unshaven lot, by and large. He supposed the nature of their work made bathing and shaving seem a waste of time. Had he met them on a London street he would not have given them more than a cautious glance, and that only in the interest of self-protection. Here he found himself giving each a nod, at least.

He wondered if American notions of equality were beginning to take hold of him or if he was simply responding to his temporary condition of helplessness.

The girl was not at all what he expected. She was driving a team, a job he considered inappropriate for a woman. Especially one like this. He doubted that she weighed a hundred pounds, and she was probably not more than twenty years old, if that. It was hard to judge, for her face was half hidden by a bonnet that only partially protected her skin from the elements. The wind played with long hair of a reddish color that extended beneath the bonnet, reaching halfway down her back. She wore a common old gray dress that hung about her as loosely as a sagging tent, down to her ankles. Those were encased in rough boots that appeared never to have known blacking.

She stared with unabashed curiosity as she halted her team. "Well, I'll swun. You must've popped up out of the ground like a badger."

He had tried to become used to the Americans' many colorful ways of abusing the English tongue, but he kept encountering new ones. It was especially jarring when that abuse spilled from the lips of a young woman who seemed to have missed even rudimentary tutoring. "It is much too long a story for me to tell on an empty stomach. I have not eaten since yesterday evening."

She kept staring.

"I say, young lady, perhaps you did not understand. Would you possibly have something I could eat?"

A smile brightened her sun-browned face. "I understood you. You talk so pretty I just wanted to hear you say it again."

A portly middle-aged man had been riding horseback behind the last wagon, sort of a rear guard, Smithwick supposed. He carried a huge rifle in front of him, across the saddle. He rode up beside the girl's wagon, his gaze on Smithwick. "Anything wrong, Arletta?" His eyes were not unfriendly, but neither did they totally trust.

"Just got us a hungry stranger, Papa. There's a little antelope meat left from dinner, and some bread."

"That would do splendidly," Smithwick said, giving her a slight bow from the waist. He extended his hand toward the man. "I am Nigel Smithwick. From England."

"Cephus Browder." The portly man leaned from the saddle to shake hands. "From Ohio. These last three sets of wagons are mine. You're welcome to anything I've got." His eyes brightened. "Except my daughter. She's neither for sellin' nor givin' away."

Arletta Browder was obviously unschooled, and judging by what Smithwick could see, not often well washed.

"You need have no fear, sir."

The wagon the girl drove had no buffalo hides stacked upon it but carried cooking vessels and food supplies, bedrolls, folded-up tents and other accoutrements for extended camping. The hoops were in place for a wagon sheet to be spread over all of it in event of weather, but the wagon bed lay open except for a tarpaulin loosely draped over some of the goods to protect them from trail dust. She climbed around the spring seat and lifted part of the sheet. She dug out a tin plate, then raised the lids from two Dutch ovens. She handed him a piece of cooked meat and a couple of sourdough biscuits, all cold. "Hope you don't mind eatin' with your fingers."

"In my present famished condition I am not inclined to be particular."

"You look tuckered out. You're welcome to ride with me."

"I hope it would be no inconvenience."

"Not if you keep talkin' pretty like that."

"Some people here seem to find my speech offensive."

"Sounds like music to me. I wish I could talk that way."

"To what purpose? It would be out of place here. *I* am out of place here."

"Me and Papa, we been over a lot of country . . . farmin', runnin' freight wagons . . . huntin' buffalo. Ain't nowhere that we're out of place anymore. If a body really wants to, he can make himself at home wherever he's at."

"Not everyone. I was a misfit even when I *was* at home."

She studied him with guileless eyes. "Maybe you just ain't found your rightful home yet."

Even hungry as he was, the lingering smell of the hide wagons ahead seemed to taint the flavor of the antelope meat, and a fly appeared determined to contest him for ownership. Dust raised by the wheels left an unpleasant grit on his teeth. His head was sore from the blows struck last night, and his body ached from the fall, from the long walk.

"I assure you, young lady, this is not it."

Four

BECAUSE OF HIS WEARINESS and the monotonous, gentle jostling of the wagon, Nigel Smithwick dozed off into a half sleep on the wagon seat. He was only vaguely aware of the vehicle's movement or of the girl Arletta beside him. He came wide awake when a wheel struck a deep rut and jolted him forward. He felt the girl grab him and pull him back onto the seat.

"Whoa, Nigel. I wouldn't want to be losin' you. We just hit a buffalo trail that I didn't see for the grass."

He was not used to women—or men, for that matter—calling him by his given name on short acquaintance. That seemed a peculiarly American habit. "It felt as if you might have struck the buffalo itself." He attempted to cover his embarrassment in the aftermath of the rude awakening. "I feel the fool, falling asleep."

"After what you been through, I guess sleep is what you need most." He had told her in a brief way what had happened to him, omitting mention of the poker game. "Sleep and a good hot meal in your belly. What you fixin' to do when we get to Dodge?"

"Telegraph my bank to send me some money. And report to the authorities so they may perhaps apprehend those blackguards."

"Last time we was in Dodge there wasn't no authorities." She made a clucking sound at the mules. "Papa got robbed a couple times freightin'. We raised cain with the law, but they never done much. Just said they sure felt bad about it."

"They would not get away with such an outrage in England."

"Nobody'll ever rob Colonel Cregar. He'd burn the hide off of them. Nobody messes with him."

"He does exhibit a formidable personality."

"I wish Papa could be more like him. Once he sets his mind to somethin' he can be as stubborn as the colonel. But he just don't know how to reach out and take what he wants like the colonel does."

"And what does the colonel want?"

"Whatever's out there, I reckon."

He tried to observe her without being obvious, but her sunbonnet was in the way. "I do not understand why you are here, even with your father. It seems an odd place for a woman."

"I'm all the family Papa's got left. Had three brothers. Jim got killed at Shiloh, and Edward died of cholera from drinkin' bad water. Zeb was too young to go to war, but he hated the freightin' business after we left the farm. Drifted off out west. Figured on gettin' rich diggin' for gold in California, or maybe raisin' cattle in Texas. We never did hear from him."

"That is sad."

"Papa's never had much luck. Lost just about everything he ever had. He's just got these wagons now, and me. He keeps thinkin' maybe we'll run into Zeb someplace if we keep lookin'."

"What do you think?"

"I have a daydream that he'll come ridin' in on a fine horse, with a fine saddle and a bag full of money."

"That is a worthy dream."

"Most likely he's dead, though. This big country swallows people up, and you never hear from them again." She went silent, as if she had closed a door between them. Smithwick thought it a kindness not to try opening it.

This girl's unpolished manner carried him back in memory to a small ivy-covered farm cottage and another girl poorly schooled but of a spirit bright as sunshine. He lost himself in revery and forgot the smell of the hides.

About sundown they came upon a cottonwood-lined creek and a place used often as a camping ground, judging by the ashes and charred wood, remnants of many old campfires. Several hide wagons were already encamped there.

Arletta said, "Looks like Parson Parkhill's outfit. I reckon there'll be preachin' tonight."

"A minister, out on this Godforsaken prairie?"

"God ain't forsaken it, else why would He send Parson? Parson's a hunter of buffalo and a fisher of men, like Simon Peter in the Book."

"I suppose you've read the Book?"

"I don't read very good. Mama read parts of it to me, but she died before she had a chance to teach me much. Always wished I *could* read good, though."

Cregar was having his wagons draw into line with the precision of a military unit. Smithwick could see the big man up front giving orders, moving one wagon back a foot, another up two feet. "What could it possibly matter out here? Who's to see?"

"Colonel's to see. He's particular about gettin' things just so. That's how come he owns the wagons and all them other folks is just workin' for him."

"He doesn't own *your* wagons."

"Nope, they're Papa's . . . Papa's and mine."

"I suppose you will pull them into line with the others?"

She pondered. Somehow he had stirred a stubborn flaring of independence. "These're our wagons, not his." But she held to the mood for only a moment. "Aw, why not? Colonel sets a good example."

Smithwick did not relish the prospect of sleeping on the ground another night, though at least he should not endure the fears and uncertainties of the last one. "What may I do to help?"

"You can unhitch the team and lead it to the creek so it can water out good. Then we'll stake them to graze a spell before we tie them on a picket line for the night."

"Picket line?"

"Nothin' tickles an Indian like layin' his hands on a white man's horses and mules. The more he takes, the more they honor him."

"I have seen some corollaries in my own experience. Bankers, for example. And barristers."

He had to explain to her what a barrister was.

"Oh," she said. "Papa never had much truck with lawyers. Says they'll steal the pennies from a dead man's eyes."

After she had maneuvered the wagon into place, respecting the line Cregar had established, he set about unharnessing the mules and leading them to water. A black man helped him stake them on fresh grass not far from camp. The man had a friendly face. "I'm Sully. Mr. Jeff said maybe I ought to show you how it's done. Said you come from across the waters and you might not know."

"There is much I don't know about this country." He had been around few black people. He was unsure what his reaction should be. The other men appeared to treat Sully as if he were one of them, except for a particularly dirty and unkempt fellow whose language was as foul as his smell. He seemed to take pleasure in trying to run his mules over the black, and in Sully's haste to get out of their way. "One side, nigger. Team coming through."

Smithwick saw anger in the black man's eyes but noted that he did not act upon that anger. "How can you simply accept that? I thought slavery was over and done."

"It's just changed its clothes. Lord says justice is His. I hope He's got a heap of justice saved up for Mr. Gant." Sully staked the first mules, and Smithwick did the rest, once he saw how it was done.

Smithwick asked, "I hope the colonel treats you well."

"Me and Colonel, we been together since the war days. Traveled over a lot of country, we have. Wasn't for Colonel, I'd likely be under the ground instead of on top of it, breathin' the Lord's good free air."

"I suppose he pays you what he pays the other men?"

"I gits whatever I need. Don't need much . . . enough to eat, a place to lay my head of a night. Ain't no sense gittin' my life all tangled up in stuff I got no use for."

"So the reality is that little has changed since slave times; you belong to him."

"Me and Colonel, we belong to each other."

Sully walked to a line of trees, picking up deadfall limbs and dragging them to camp for the cook fire. Smithwick followed suit. He found Arletta giving orders to a lad who probably had never shaved; he showed a little fuzz on his upper lip and on his chin, but otherwise his face was innocent of whiskers. "If you want to be useful, Kid, you can dig me a fire pit right yonder. I'll take care of the cookin' tonight."

"Cooking's supposed to be *my* job, at least for Jeff Layne's crew." The boy sounded resentful. Smithwick supposed it injured his pride to take direction from a woman, especially one little or no older than he was.

"Colonel ain't goin' to pay you less because of me doin' the cookin'. Might even decide to promote you to skinner."

"He ain't going to promote me to nothing. Soon's we get to town, I'm leaving this country to the Indians."

She pointed to Smithwick. "Nigel there, he run into some Indians just this mornin'. All they done was count coup on him. Bet that's closer than you've ever been to a live Indian."

"It's closer than I ever intend to get."

Smithwick found the shovel. "I'll dig the pit. Show me where and how deep you want it."

She gave him a dubious look. "It ain't no job for slick hands. But I reckon you got to rough them up sooner or later." She pointed. "Right here, a foot or so deep, and wide enough to hang three pots over it." She had shed the bonnet, for the sun was too low to burn now, and she had shaken out her long hair. Her face looked less weather-punished when she smiled. "Learnin' the ways of a hide camp ain't goin' to be of much use when you go back to England."

"One never knows when a little extra knowledge may prove helpful. There is nothing painful about learning."

"Seemed painful to me. Never had much chance at school learnin'. I know my letters pretty good, but I never was much for puttin' the words together."

"It isn't so difficult. I could teach you if I had time. But I understand we will reach Dodge City tomorrow."

"I'm afraid so," she said regretfully. "If I could read books and papers I'd want to study all about the world, whether I ever seen it myself or not. At least I'd know what's out there."

Smithwick felt compassion. She was wasting her youth in this wilderness, given no chance to learn about the finer things that existed far beyond the invisible prison walls of poverty and ignorance. But perhaps it was a providential kindness that she never knew how much she was missing, for he saw little chance that she could ever rise beyond this station in life.

She did not waste time indulging in wishfulness. As soon as he had the fire pit dug she started a blaze with dry shavings, methodically building up the fire with larger pieces of wood Smithwick and Sully had dragged in. She prepared coffee beans in a grinder mounted to the side of the wagon. "These men could live on nothin' but buffalo, provided they could get coffee enough to wash it down with."

Smithwick noted the amount of ground coffee that went into the pot. What came out when the boiling was finished would be black as tar, he thought, and but little more palatable.

Elijah Layne hovered over the coffeepot, talking about good old times in Texas. When he was satisfied that the coffee had boiled long enough, he poured in a cup of cold water to settle the grounds, then dipped the cup into the open pot. He blew on it for only a moment before he began sipping. Smithwick cringed, imagining what that must do to the old man's mouth. Even while he would wish these people showed more of the civilizing graces, he conceded that they were hardy folk.

He assisted Arletta when she showed him what to do, but for the most part he felt helpless and in the way. He had not often experienced such a humbling feeling, one for which his background had not prepared him.

The boy known as Kid gave up in frustration after Arletta firmly rebuffed his clumsy attempts to help with the cooking. He stalked away and seated himself on the tongue of his own wagon, staring off in the direction of Dodge City.

Damon Cregar came to the campfire for coffee. He gave Smithwick a silent glance that judged him and found him wanting. His gaze followed Arletta as she moved between the wagon and the Dutch ovens. Smithwick could read a silent hunger in those dark eyes. He frowned, thinking it had probably been too long since the colonel had visited town. Some things were the same on the American frontier as in the more ordered societies of Europe. The girl did not seem to notice the colonel's staring. Smithwick wondered if she was too innocent to understand or if she simply chose not to acknowledge it.

Jeff Layne and the black man walked up together. They had gone out to see after the horses and mules staked to graze. Layne touched fingers to the brim of his hat as he walked by Arletta on his way to fetch an empty cup. Sully asked, "You got plenty of firewood, Miss Arletta? I'd be tickled to fetch up some more."

"Thanks, Sully. I'll holler if I see I'm runnin' short."

Layne brought his coffee over to where Smithwick stood waiting in case the girl found further chores for him to do. "You're lookin' better, English."

"I could scarcely look worse than I did when you found me."

"You might. You could've looked dead."

Parson Parkhill approached the campfire, taking a long, appreciative whiff of the frying meat before he dipped a cup into the coffeepot. "Ah," he said pleasantly, "the Lord certainly knew what He was doing when He divested Adam of his rib. There is no substitute on this earth for a woman's cooking."

Parkhill appeared badly in need of *somebody's* cooking. Though he stood six feet tall, he looked as if he might have to carry stones in his pockets to bring the scales to more than a hundred pounds. Smithwick thought him much too spare for the rigors of the buffalo range. But his eyes were lively, and he seemed eager to release a torrent of conversation that probably had been bottled up during however many weeks he had been out on the hunt. "I must say, Arletta, that you grow handsomer each time I see you."

She tried to cover her pleasure over the compliment. "Was I you, I'd see after gettin' me a set of spectacles."

"I see enough, sometimes far too much when it comes to man's perfidious and prideful ways." He turned toward Cregar. "I believe, Colonel, that I will conduct services after supper to pray for forgiveness of our sins."

For a moment Cregar looked as if he might actually smile. That, Smithwick thought, would probably break a long-standing tradition. "We have been out for more than a month. There has been no opportunity for sin."

"There has been time for *thought* of sin, and the wish that so easily becomes deed if the opportunity arises. Perhaps we should pray for forgiveness of the sins about to be committed when this company reaches Dodge City."

Cregar looked at the skinners and drivers gathering in anticipation of supper. "These men and I are not above sin, but what would you know of such things, Parson?"

"I have not always been as you see me now, and there are still times when I sin in my heart. Even Arletta, without knowing or intending it, may cause men to yield their minds to carnal desires." His firm stare indicated that he included the colonel.

Cregar looked down into his cup, his face furrowed. "Do what you want to. It was your camp before we got here."

SMITHWICK had expected Dodge City to be much more than the raw young outpost he saw from Arletta's wagon. "A city? They call this a city?"

Arletta laughed. "It's still got its diapers on. Railroad didn't get here till last year. Up to then there wasn't no Dodge City, just an army post up the river a ways. You got to give the place time."

"Time is all it has, judging by its appearance." The town, scattered haphazardly down both sides of the new railroad tracks, could easily melt to the ground and leave little trace, he thought. He saw many people bustling about, all acting as if they were involved in urgent business, but nothing had any look of permanence. The buildings were mostly of hasty frame construction. Some structures were of sod blocks, like settlers' sod shanties he had seen from the train windows. Others were not even that far off of the surface. Arletta said they were half-dugouts, cut into the ground and covered over with roofs of local timber, topped with sod. Some residents lived in canvas tents or in crude frameworks covered over by buffalo hides, a poor imitation of Indian tepees.

"Is this what the skinners and drivers were so excited about reaching?" he asked incredulously.

"It ain't buildin's that make a town, it's people. The boys just want to spend a little time where the people are."

"And the whiskey, if I am any judge."

"They been dry for a long spell. Papa don't hold with whiskey when there's work to be done, and Colonel don't allow it atall on the buffalo range."

Two women stood in front of a frame shack, waving at the wagons as they passed. Some of the men waved back, prompting one woman to raise her long skirt halfway to the knee. Arletta re-marked, "Parson sure knew what he was preachin' about last night." She gave Smithwick a critical glance. "You don't have truck with such as that, do you, Nigel?"

He was hardly innocent in such matters, but the unkempt, un-washed look of these women aroused no temptation. "You need have no concern."

"I got no call to be concerned one way or the other. You just act too refined to fall in with such as them."

"What would you know about things of that nature?"

"My mama died early, so I been mostly around men ever since. I know what they do and how they think."

Beyond the couple of blocks that passed for the main part of town, beyond the new depot and water tank, long ricks of stacked buffalo hides stretched for a considerable distance on both sides of the tracks. Smithwick had become inured to the smell of the hides on the wagons so that the increased odor almost escaped his notice. Cephus Browder had ridden beside his wagons all day, but now he loped ahead, reining in at a frame building which had known no paint but still retained the fresh pine look of new lumber. "That's Old Man Thomason's hide-buyin' station," Arletta explained. "Papa generally sells to him."

Colonel Cregar had left the wagons three hours ago to ride ahead and sound out all the buyers in town. "Wouldn't your father do better to take bids from everybody and sell for the highest offer?"

"Papa never had the patience for hagglin'. He takes what Mr. Thomason'll give him and feels grateful for the weight of a little money in his pocket. He's never had much of it at one time."

Smithwick thought he could see why Cephus Browder had not been successful at any business he had tried. Doing business was not meant to be easy and comfortable. Comfort was expensive.

Jeff Layne, riding his black horse, had pulled the Cregar wagons off to one side to await the colonel's orders. Unlike last night, when the colonel had directed their formation, he left them in a ragged line without semblance of military style. Smithwick had noted that the Texan showed little concern for appearances. He seemed content to let people follow their own natures so long as they got the job done. "I rather like that Layne fellow, even though he is a bit rough-cut."

"Jeff reminds me a little of my brother Zeb. Always seems to be lookin' off into the distance like he sees somethin' out there that nobody else can."

"He appears to have no pretensions, certainly not like Damon Cregar."

"I wouldn't be faultin' the colonel. He's got harsh ways, and it ain't everybody that likes him, but he's a good, strong man, and fine-lookin' for his age."

Smithwick thought his words over carefully. "I wonder if you are aware of the way he watches you. He is old enough to be your father, but he is a man smitten."

"I'm not blind. If he was a younger man, and he was to ask me, I'd marry him. Even like it is, I'd be a fool if I wasn't honored to have him pay attention to me."

"I am not sure honor is what he has on his mind."

Color rushed into her face. "Colonel's too proud a man to do anything dishonorable."

"For your sake, I would hope so. But there are things in a man's nature that some cannot control."

"You don't think women feel the same things sometimes? I'll bet the young ladies in England flocked around you like flies around honey, what with your pretty way of talkin'."

"There I am hardly unique. Everyone speaks more or less as I do."

"Just the same, I'll bet they flocked around. How many sweethearts did you leave behind, Nigel?"

That was altogether too much familiarity, he thought. "If you don't mind, my legs are a bit stiff. I think I shall walk a while and try to set the blood to circulating." He climbed down from the wagon. "I wish to pay my respects to Jeff Layne."

She seemed to sense that she had carried her forthrightness too far, but she offered no apology. "It's a free country. If you don't mind, you might come back and help us unload these hides when Papa gets them sold."

"That would be but small compensation for your hospitality."

Jeff Layne squatted in the shade of the wagon his father had driven, his back braced against the front wheel. Elijah's bones no longer tolerated such a position; he sat flat on the ground. The old man waved jovially at Smithwick. "Come join us, English. The shade feels good." He discoursed at some length about how hot the weather got in Texas. It seemed that whatever Elijah started talking about, the subject always shifted to Texas.

Jeff Layne asked Smithwick, "You and Arletta find a lot to talk about?"

"A bit too much, if anything. Do you find her somewhat impertinent?"

"She generally says what she's thinkin', and she's got a mind of her own. For such a little woman, she's a long way from bein' helpless."

"I would hope so. You may not have noticed, but Colonel Cregar looks at her the way a fox looks at a rabbit."

Layne removed a short cigar from his shirt pocket. He had smoked half of it before, then saved the rest. Small luxuries were not to be wasted. He lighted it, frowning at its initial bite. "Times, I'd like to stove Colonel's head in with a gun barrel. Other times, I'd follow him into hell with a bucket of water. You've got to see all sides of him before you pass judgment, and even then you're not plumb sure. He's lent money to Ol' Cephus and others. Cephus has always paid him back, but then he's had to come borrowin' again. Naturally Arletta's grateful to him."

Smithwick thought there was more to it than gratitude. He had seen young women attracted to older men. Usually it ended when the proper *young* man came along.

Smithwick tried to squat as Layne did, but his sore and stiff knees protested painfully. He had to stand up again. "I need a little loan myself, but I'd not want to ask Cregar for it. He seems to have developed a fine contempt for me."

Elijah said, "We can't have an Englishman borrowin' off of a Yankee colonel, not after the way your country helped us Confederates. Me and Jeff, we can loan you somethin'."

Jeff's expression said his father talked too much, but he asked Smithwick, "What do you reckon you'll need?"

"Enough to telegraph my bank and have some money sent to me. I will repay you as soon as it comes."

Jeff dug a gold coin from his pocket. "You look like a man who could stand a good strong drink while you're waitin' for that money. I might even join you soon's we've finished with these hides."

Concern arose in Elijah's eyes. "Son, you know the kind of trouble a man can get into when he goes to drinkin'."

"A little whiskey won't hurt me. It'll smother the stink of buffalo hides for a while."

"There's worse things than the smell of skins." A haunted look came into the old man's half-clouded eyes.

Smithwick had been watching the Browder wagons. He saw Cephus walking toward them from the frame building, accompanied by a man he assumed was the hide buyer Thomason. Cephus limped badly. Arletta had said her father had almost lost his feet in a severe blizzard the winter before. At that he had been luckier than several hunters who had frozen to death, caught unprepared on the open buffalo range. "I told Arletta I'd help unload her father's hides. When that is done, I shall be glad to have a drink with you."

He hoped the girl was through asking personal questions. It did not matter much anyway. As soon as he received his money he would catch a train out of here for a greener land. He would never see any of these people again. With luck, he might be able to put this whole unpleasant episode out of his mind.

Arletta asked her father, "Did you get them sold, Papa?"

"I done all right. Just wish we'd had three times as many hides."

The buyer was a man of about Browder's age, sporting a heavy moustache salted with gray, its edges tinged brown by tobacco juice. He wore what once had been a decent black suit, but handling buffalo hides was not clean work, or easy on clothes. "Hello, young lady. I told your papa, the market's fine when you consider the money panic back east. But nobody's bringing in many hides. I'm afraid the business is about done."

"Where are the buffalo?" she asked.

"Some think they're killed out. Others say there are still aplenty down south."

"Are we fixin' to go south, Papa?" She did not sound enthusiastic.

Cephus replied, "Army says we dassn't. Indian treaties and such. But I'm thinkin' hard about it, just the same."

Thomason nodded. "I told your papa the army talks one way and acts another. Their patrols are supposed to stop hunters from going south, but the colonel out at the post has told them not to try too hard to find wagon tracks. He said the only way to control the Indians is to kill off the buffalo. Then the tribes will have to go to a reservation. He said if he were a buffalo hunter, he'd go where the buffalo are."

Arletta said, "Papa, if them Indians have got a treaty, they won't be happy to see us comin'."

"But you heard him, girl. Colonel says he'd go where the buffalo are. And the buffalo are south." He turned to Thomason. "Show me where you want these hides unloaded."

Smithwick quickly decided that stacking hides would not be his choice for a life's occupation. The job was sweaty and hard. He worked with a pair of Cephus's skinners. One was a lanky, cheerful soul named Barney Gibson, who said he found the exercise bracing after so many hours of sitting on a wagon seat. The other was a stout and dour German, Herman Scholtz, who complained that inasmuch as the hides now belonged to Thomason, the buyer's helpers should do the stacking.

Each time they lifted a stiffened skin, the trapped odor from beneath it rose up into Smithwick's face like a London fog. He used muscles he had forgotten he had, swinging the hides up to waiting hands at the top of the long rick. As if the flies were not nuisance enough, an uncomfortable tickling sensation beneath his clothing told him he had attracted the attention of lice that had infested the buffalo and now sought a fresh host. He had seen all the skinners and even Arletta scratching themselves, often in places that were not seemly.

Gibson was philosophical. "Everything's got to live."

Scholtz had no such tolerance. "Py God, dem graybacks don't have to live on me."

Smithwick took consolation in the fact that he need not endure this for long. A bit of good whiskey to kill the stench, a bath, a fresh suit of clothes, and this humbling experience would be a thing of the past.

When the wagons had been emptied, Arletta smiled at him. "You work pretty good for a man with hands as slick as deerskin."

"I needed some exercise. And I have certainly had it."

"A little hard work is good for anybody. If you stayed around this outfit long, you'd be as healthy as a horse."

"By tomorrow I should be gone from here. I am on my way to the depot to telegraph my bank."

"I was hopin' you might be with us long enough to learn me a little more readin'."

"I am sorry, but you people belong here. I do not."

"You'll be comin' around to say goodbye, won't you?"

"I'll not leave town without doing that."

Walking away, he turned once to look back, then wondered why. He saw her standing beside her wagon, watching him. In some strange way he did not understand, he felt himself the quitter. But he owed these people nothing. He had worked enough to repay them for whatever small inconvenience he might have caused and for whatever small share of their rations he had consumed. They had no right to ask more.

At the new depot he wrote out a brief message and handed it to the telegraph operator, who counted the words, figured the charge on the back side of the paper and kept calling him "my friend." Entirely too much familiarity, Smithwick thought.

Turning away from the depot, he saw Jeff Layne walking toward him. Layne asked, "How about that drink?"

"Why not? It will be a while before I can expect an answer from my bank." They crossed the tracks to a frame structure which had the word SALOON painted in large letters on its square false front. He found the place crowded with men who looked as if they would be hunters, skinners and wagon drivers. He hesitated at the door, stiffening his resolve enough to shove his way with Jeff through the mass of idlers to the plain wooden bar.

In another time and place such men might have made him uneasy about his safety, but after riding with the Cregar and Browder wagons and associating with that sort a couple of days, he felt little apprehension. He had the security of the derringer, tucked safely into a pocket. And he had come to trust Jeff Layne, rough-looking though he was.

The saloon was some distance from the piles of dry hides, but the odor lingered on the men, blending with that of sweat and stale tobacco. Smithwick wondered if one bath would be enough to wash it away or if it penetrated to the bone.

The whiskey was no better than he expected to find in such a place, though it was priced as if this were one of the finer clubs in New York. It had all the flavor of kerosene and much of the burn. While recovering from its rough shock he turned and leaned his elbow against the bar, watching the patrons, listening to their talk. They were a varied lot, speaking in a mixture of accents. Most he could not identify, though a few struck him as Southern. Two spoke in French and a couple more in some language he was uncertain about, possibly Scandinavian. The supposed opportunities of the frontier had drawn them from all over America as well as from Europe. He wondered how and if they would ever manage to blend into one cohesive identity unmistakably American. He dismissed the question, for it was none of his affair. He would be returning home before long.

Trying not to be obvious about it, he studied the unshaven Texan who stood beside him in ragged work clothes and boots, a revolver on his hip. He wondered what they would say back home if they could see him now, in the company of such men. He had little more in common with Jeff and these others than with the Indians who had given him such a start out on the prairie. They shared a language but not a great deal more. Even the language might be debatable.

Jeff asked, "What're your plans, English?"

"I'll return east when I receive my funds."

"And do what when you get there? You got a trade of some kind?"

Smithwick felt a sermon coming, one he had heard all too often from his family. He did not need it from a comparative stranger. "I am not a tradesman, sir. However, I am considered quite good with the cards."

"That's a pastime, not a trade. A man ought to be after somethin' permanent, somethin' worth his time and labor."

Smithwick thought this frontiersman was deucedly forward to be lecturing him. "And what sort of goal do you have, sir?"

"To get a place that's my own, where Dad can sit in the shade and take his ease the rest of his days. A place where I can do as I damned please without answerin' to anybody but God, and maybe not even Him."

"Do you believe there is such a place?"

"You bet you. That's what this country is all about." Layne swallowed his drink and gave Smithwick a hard study. "A man who don't know what he's lookin' for ain't apt to find it."

"Are you appointing yourself my conscience, sir?"

"That has to come from inside you. If you ain't got it, nobody can give it to you."

It crossed Smithwick's mind that the men who had robbed him and thrown him from the train were probably somewhere in Dodge, possibly even in this saloon. Unconsciously he felt for the derringer and was reassured. He searched the faces but did not see the rascals who had called themselves Jones, Black and Brown. It also occurred to him that instead of whiling away the afternoon in a saloon he should seek out whatever law enforcement authority Dodge might offer.

Jeff asked, "Care for another drink?"

Smithwick was still a little miffed at the Texan's attempt to lecture him. "Perhaps later. Not now." The first still stirred fretfully in his stomach. It would taste no better coming back up than it had tasted going down. Surely there must be better whiskey somewhere in town, or he would be tempted to join Parson Parkhill's campaign against it.

Jeff said, "Then I'd best be gettin' back to the wagons. Colonel Cregar may be ready to unload the hides."

"Your Cregar reminds me of my Uncle Vincent, who made a career in the British army. He never progressed past major, but he was imperious, self-righteous, and not once in his life ever admitted an error. I never got along with him."

"I get along all right with Colonel. The way I do it is, I just don't pay much attention to him."

They weaved their way through the crowd and into the fresher air outdoors. The Texan set off across the tracks. Watching him, Smithwick decided Jeff meant well; he simply had an unfortunate tendency to step beyond the bounds of his own province.

A passing stranger told Smithwick the town was not yet incorporated and had no marshal, though the county was newly organized and had a sheriff. As Arletta had predicted, Smithwick's mission proved empty. The lawman explained that the offense had occurred east of the Ford County line, beyond his jurisdiction. He added, "Now, if you should happen to run across the men here in town, notify me and I'll see what I can do. But remember that you'll have to identify them to the satisfaction of a court. If you can't find witnesses, it'll be your word against theirs."

"If there had been any witnesses, they would have stopped the train."

"You see, then, how little chance you have. Were I you, I would accept this as a good lesson painfully learned and get on with my business, whatever that might be."

Frustrated, Smithwick wondered about the time and reached unconsciously for his watch, then remembered with a pang of regret that it was gone. Giving vent to his sense of irony, he thanked the sheriff for his help and walked back out upon the street. He waited for an engine to pass, pulling a string of empty flatcars to be loaded with hides, or perhaps with the buffalo bones he had seen piled farther down the track, beyond the hides. Then he returned to the depot.

The telegrapher saw him at the open window and seemed reluctant to arise from his place at the silent key.

"Has my answer arrived yet?" Smithwick asked.

The frowning telegrapher stuck a pencil behind his ear and came to the window. "Well, my friend, in a manner of speaking, it has. I'm afraid you're not going to like it."

"I can't be overdrawn. What did the bank say?"

"The bank didn't say anything. The message came back that your bank no longer exists."

"There has to be some mistake."

"I wish that were so. Your bank has collapsed. A lot of them have done that lately, what with the money problems back east, and runs on the banks."

Smithwick felt a surge of panic. "But how will I get my money?"

"I'm sorry, my friend. When a bank like that goes under, it takes everything with it. It's a ship sunk at sea with no survivors."

Smithwick clung to the window sash as his knees threatened to go out from under him. "But I am without funds, without anything."

"You needn't feel lonesome. With the buffalo gone, there are plenty of others around here in the same predicament." The operator turned away, for the telegraph key had begun clicking. "Good luck, my friend."

The bad whiskey turned over, and Smithwick felt as if someone had punched him in the stomach.

Stranded. Broke and stranded halfway around the world. What in God's name do I do now?

Five

IT COULD BE SAID that the life of the Comanche was dependent upon grass, for it was grass that sustained the two animals vital to his existence, the horse and the buffalo.

Crow Feather remembered the legends handed down through generations of his forefathers, from the time when the People walked, dragging their meager belongings on small travois drawn by dogs. He knew acquisition of the horse from the Spaniards had freed his downtrodden ancestors from the tyranny of larger and stronger tribes who had held them virtual hostage in the great mountains to the north. In a single generation the horse had transformed these hapless pawns into a mobile fighting force able to strike fiercely at old enemies and avenge years of indignities, of plunder and slavery, rape and murder.

Unrivaled in horsemanship and fighting skills, the Comanche claimed his rightful place as the master of his domain, and his domain was anywhere he wanted to be. He swept down from the mountains and annihilated or drove away all who had the temerity to stand against him, particularly the despised Apache. In a relatively few years his bold conquests had won him most of the land from the Cimarron down through eastern New Mexico and all the way into the rugged hill country of Texas. He exacted tribute from the Spanish settlement at San Antonio de Bexar. His fearsome young warriors raided Spanish ranches and towns far south of the

Rio Grande, covering themselves with glory, making themselves rich in horses and mules, stolen wives and children.

The weak had become strong, the victim the victor. Leaving a trail of blood and fire, the Comanche had become lord of the southern plains.

It was no accident that his domain included most of the lands grazed by the southern buffalo, for to him the buffalo was the staff of life and therefore a holy thing. Use of the horse made the buffalo much easier to find and kill than in the days of the People afoot. The Comanche ate the buffalo's flesh, drank its blood, sheltered himself with its skin. He did not believe in scratching the face of his mother the earth, as did the more sedentary farming tribes to the east, and the white men who turned the prairie grass wrong-side-up with their steel plows. He was a hunter, not a planter. He drifted with the migrations of his living commissary, the free-ranging buffalo, moving with the rains and the grass and the changing seasons. He was a proud man, and a free one.

The buffalo harvest had been good, and Crow Feather was content. His two wives worked the skins and cured the meat and made pemmican for the lean moons of winter. He had time to relax and enjoy the sunny days before the north wind's warm breath turned to an autumn chill. He rested for the final hunt that would come with the first deep cold, when the buffalo's hair was in its winter bloom, the best time of all for making the skins into robes. Lying in the shade of a cottonwood tree, he watched White Deer and Rabbit bent over a hide they were tanning beside their tepee. His son of five winters picked up a flint scraper and began imitating his two mothers at one end of the large skin.

Crow Feather frowned. It was not a good thing for a boy to interest himself too much in woman's work. He had seen some who spent so much time with their mothers that they became too domestic and never took their rightful places as hunters and warriors when they came of age. He must not allow this to happen to Little Squirrel.

He got to his feet and called his son. The boy, who wore not so much as a breechclout, dropped the scraper and came running. Crow Feather said, "How would you like to go for a ride?"

It was a needless question. Squirrel was always eager to climb upon a horse. Crow Feather had begun carrying the boy in front of him before Squirrel had been able to walk, so that he would grow up unafraid. Since his third summer he had been allowed to sit alone on the back of a gentle mare, though Crow Feather or one of the mothers always led it.

Crow Feather said, "This is a good day for riding. My horse needs exercise so he will not become fat and lazy."

Though he owned many horses, Crow Feather had a favorite, a bay which had carried him many times upon the war trail to the Tejano settlements and to Mexico. He always kept it staked near the tepee, for he never knew when he might want or need it. He removed the stake rope and slipped a simple bridle over the horse's head. He had a rawhide-covered saddle, modeled roughly after those of the Spanish, but he chose not to use it. A Comanche learned early to ride bareback as easily as with a saddle. He lifted the boy up onto the horse, then gripped the dark mane and swung up behind him, a horsehair rope in his right hand. His long buckskin breechclout, dyed a deep blue, hung down over the horse's side.

"Where will we go, *Powva?*" the boy asked.

"Where would you like to go?"

"To the land of the Mexicans, where we can find many horses." The boy was fond of listening to older men recount their adventures on horse-stealing trips. His bright eyes would go wide at the tales of danger and daring.

"And what would you do with all those horses?"

"I would ride them to hunt buffalo, and to fight our enemies."

Crow Feather was pleased that Squirrel was thinking like a hunter and a warrior. He should be ready to take up his responsibilities when his time came. "You must wait for a few winters yet, and grow. But I think it is well that we get you a pony of your own. You must learn to ride without someone holding you or leading your horse."

"Can I go with you to the land of the Mexicans, to get my pony?"

"You will go there soon enough. I believe we can find your pony without having to ride so far."

Even at five winters, the boy already knew something about

Mexicans, though he was as yet confused about the fact that some were friends and others were enemies. He had been once with his parents to the canyon where the Comanchero traders brought their high-wheeled carts east from New Mexico, full of wares to trade to the People for meat and hides and horses. He knew the Mexican son of Rides a Black Horse, who had been brought back as a four-year-old from a raid on a village deep in Mexico and was being raised Comanche. He knew the Mexican wife of old Many Lodges, who had been taken in a raid at the edge of San Antonio and had, after much resistance and many beatings, resigned herself to the life of the People. With time, Crow Feather knew, the boy would sort out the ambiguities and know who was friend, who was enemy.

Little Squirrel in front of him, he rode by the tepee of his uncle and aunt. He nodded to his sister, Calling Bird, who worked at the drying rack, turning strips of meat to cure in the sun. Their parents had died when she was small, brought down by a sickness carried into camp by a white captive. By custom, their father's brother had taken the two into his family, though Crow Feather had already been almost old enough to be considered a man. Calling Bird had been raised to regard her cousins as sisters and brothers. She was pleasant to the eye, and of late she had begun dressing up in a fine buckskin dress, her long black hair neatly done into long braids decorated with colored cloth. It was clear that she considered her-self ready to take on the duties and pleasures of being somebody's wife.

Crow Feather had begun considering which of the band's young men might be an appropriate husband. He should, one day soon, discuss the matter with his uncle and help him choose. Such a decision was too serious to be made by a girl of Calling Bird's limited years and inexperience.

To the south of the encampment, boys a few years older than Squirrel watched over the large and scattered horse herd as it grazed along the creek. This duty was a rite of passage. Next, when they became old enough to be considered warrior material, each in his own time would be expected to set out upon his individual vision quest. Cleansed and purified by a medicine man, he would go alone to some prominence or holy place, where he would fast for four days and nights and await the coming of some spirit guide to point the direction of his life.

Crow Feather remembered well his own quest. Day by day it had become an increasingly agonizing ordeal. Hunger and thirst had at times driven him into wild hallucinations. But he never doubted that his mind had been clear on the fourth and final night, when a great bear had visited him and had spoken to him in human tongue. The bear had thus become his spirit guide. Other young men might receive their magic from birds or small animals, but Crow Feather had been chosen by the bear to carry its *po-haw-cut*, its medicine. Few guardian spirits were stronger than the bear.

It was considered poor judgment for a warrior to speak much of his quest, for talking about the vision could weaken his medicine. But someday, when Squirrel was old enough to understand, he would tell him what he thought it was safe to relate. This would help the boy become properly receptive to whatever spirit might choose him to receive its benevolence.

Crow Feather rode slowly through the herd, careful not to stir the horses and disturb their grazing. The curing grass was important in putting fat on their ribs to help carry them through the lean, cold days of the coming winter. Horses of many owners were mixed together, but he knew all of his own and could pick them out about as far as he could see them. On those which were his favorites he knew every mark, every variation in color, every blemish, as he knew the soft bodies of both his wives.

He tested Squirrel's memory for the horses by asking him to point out which belonged to his own string. Squirrel knew most of them by sight. He also knew some which belonged to friends like Goes His Own Way, and a few of those claimed by Many Lodges.

It was a good thing that a boy develop an early affinity for horses. When he came of age his life would revolve around them. His family's welfare would depend upon his proficiency on horseback.

A dark thought intruded upon Crow Feather's feeling of contentment. He had tried to put aside what Three Bears had said about the white buffalo hunters and their threat to the People's free-ranging way of life. If they killed off all the buffalo, Three Bears had warned, no choice would remain for the Comanche but to submit himself to the white man's road, the reservation the white man had prepared to imprison the People. In such a life there would be no running of the buffalo, no riding out upon the war trail to earn a young man honor in the eyes of the band. It would be an empty world for men like Crow Feather, who had lived in the way of his grandfathers too long to change. It would be an empty life for his son, who had every right to inherit those ways and enjoy the freedoms his ancestors had earned for him with their daring and, sometimes, their blood.

He forced the image back to the dark recesses of his mind, for it was not a good thing to dwell upon negative thoughts which diminished the spirit. But it had come to him before, and he knew it would come again like a hungry wolf that refuses to be driven away from the camp.

Crow Feather located his horses and studied them one by one. At length he rode up against a grulla he had taken two years ago from a Tejano village many days' ride to the south. It was sturdy, not quite as fast as his bay but alert and quick to learn. He had hunted buffalo on it and found it to have no fear. He dropped the horsehair loop over the grulla's head and led it out from the center of the herd.

"What do you do with Gray Bird?" Squirrel asked. "Is he to be my pony?"

The grulla was much too large and spirited for a boy of five winters. "No, but perhaps he will help you get a pony."

He led Gray Bird toward the lodge of Rides a Black Horse, a warrior several winters older than Crow Feather but still a formidable force when he was on horseback. He was a man of many coups. Black Horse sat in front of the tepee, enjoying the shade while his wife cooked the ingredients of pemmican in an iron pot, to be poured into skin containers for later use. He arose when he saw that Crow Feather had come to see him. He went into his tepee and brought out a ceremonial pipe, lighting it with a small limb taken from his wife's fire.

The People did not hurry a business discussion. Each man drew smoke from the pipe and offered it to the earth, the sky and the four directions. They talked of the weather, of the buffalo, of the gossip about the youngest daughter of Sweet Water running away with a young warrior of her own choice after her father had already accepted horses from Man Who Stole the Mules. It was the kind of delicious scandal the People reproached on the one hand but enjoyed in the telling and retelling. Though Mules already had as wives two daughters of Sweet Water, he was demanding that the old man return all the horses and give him three more to pay for his embarrassment. Crow Feather smiled at the thought of the arrogant Mules setting a commercial value on his dignity.

The talk about horses gave Crow Feather the opening he sought. He pointed toward the two mounts he had tied a respectable distance from the lodge. "You have admired my grulla horse. Would you like to have him as your own?"

He suspected that Black Horse already had an inkling of what was to come, for he immediately began to discuss the animal's weaker points. "I have seen other horses outrun him. And he is no longer young."

"He is old enough to possess wisdom. Wisdom is sometimes better than speed. You have a pony that your youngest son has outgrown. He is an old pony, and not fast, but I am willing to overlook those faults. It is better that a boy like my son have an old horse and a slow one to learn on."

"You want to trade for the pony? What will you give in addition to the grulla?"

"He is close to my heart, and worth much more than the pony. I had thought you would give *me* something more in trade."

Squirrel sat quietly, trying to be invisible, for he had been taught that boys do not intrude upon men's business. But his black eyes darted hopefully from one man to another, following the conversation. The shadow of the tepee lengthened as the talk of trade continued and the boy's attention shifted back and forth. In the end, as Crow Feather had expected, the dickering led to an even trade. Black Horse could boast that he had gotten the best of it, for he had acquired a useful hunting horse in exchange for an aging pony no longer of use to him. But Crow Feather was satisfied. His son's learning was of more value than a whole band of horses. Years from now, when all these horses were dead, Squirrel would be an able hunter bringing meat to his family's lodge. He would be a warrior in his prime, a credit to all his grandfathers.

Thus had the traditions been handed down among the generations. Thus would they always be handed down, so long as the rivers ran and the People roamed free, ranging with the buffalo.

He left Black Horse rubbing down his new possession with his hands, the pride of ownership in his eyes. He rode back to the horse herd and sought out the paint pony. He used the hair rope to form a makeshift bridle and boosted Squirrel upon the pony's back. "He has much to teach you," he told his son. "It is time you begin."

He gloried in the smile that lighted the boy's brown face, the sparkle in the big black eyes.

It was a good time to be alive. It was always a good time to be a Comanche.

He did not hear the horsemen coming until they suddenly popped over the hill, four of them racing with all the speed they could coax from their mounts. With a clatter of hooves, shouting and whooping, they passed Crow Feather and Squirrel like a sudden furious whirlwind. The startled pony surged forward, catching the boy by surprise. He grabbed too late at the mane and tumbled back over the paint's rump, striking his head on a stone.

The pony ran a few paces, then stopped and turned back as if ashamed for letting itself be stampeded. The boy lay still. His heart pounding, Crow Feather jumped to the ground and dropped on his knee beside Squirrel. The boy began to gasp. The breath had been knocked out of him. Blood trickled from a gash on his head. Crow Feather pounded gently on his back, trying to help his lungs regain the breath they had lost. The boy looked confused.

The horsemen turned around, having become conscious of what happened. They were young men all, of twenty or so winters. One was named Swift Runner, and he had seemed to be winning the race when it was aborted because of the boy. Crow Feather knew him as a headstrong youth who had been on two buffalo hunts and one raid into the Tejano settlements. He was said to carry the medicine of the eagle, but Crow Feather had always doubted that he had seen any true vision. He seemed not the kind to whom the eagle would entrust such power.

Swift Runner slid from the back of his heavily sweating brown horse, which heaved for breath. Crow Feather frowned, not liking to see a horse misused. It was obvious that Swift Runner had raced him much too far.

The young man said, "Is the boy all right?"

"He bleeds where his head struck a stone. He seems not to have any broken bones."

"We did not see you until it was too late."

Crow Feather felt a tone of reproach was in order. "If some of the women and children had been out gathering wood, you might have run over them before they could move out of your way."

Swift Runner seemed unaffected by the hint of rebuke. "They said my brown horse was as slow as an old mare. I showed them."

The boy was regaining his breath. Blood still ran from the gash on his head, but he showed no inclination to cry. Crow Feather was proud for that.

Swift Runner said, "A little blood will not hurt him. See, he does not cry. A good warrior must know how to bleed."

"And have *you* bled?"

"Many times. When I was his age I fell from a pony and broke my arm. Not once did I cry."

Crow Feather let irony creep into his voice. "You are a brave warrior."

Swift Runner missed the irony. "And I will show it when we take the war trail again. I will bring home many Tejano horses, and many scalps."

He sounded much like Man Who Stole the Mules, Crow Feather thought sourly. He wondered if Swift Runner's mother and Mules's father might have slept on the same buffalo robe at some time in the distant past.

One of the other young men, more thoughtful than Swift Runner, brought a handful of moss from the edge of the river, where the water backed up into a hole well away from the current. He applied the cool moss to the boy's wound. Squirrel flinched but betrayed no other indication of his pain.

The four young men rode away, relieved to put the results of their recklessness behind them. A little farther on, Swift Runner gave a whoop and set his horse into a hard run again. The others were still trying in vain to catch up to him when they disappeared over the hill.

Crow Feather shook his head.

The paint pony grazed quietly, as if nothing had happened. When his son's bleeding had stopped and his breath had fully returned, Crow Feather walked out and caught the hair rope that had been fashioned into a bridle. "Are you ready to ride him again?"

Squirrel hesitated for a moment, then walked a little shakily toward him. Crow Feather gave him a boost onto the pony's back. "Always get back on when you fall off. Otherwise you spoil a horse."

It also spoiled the rider, he thought. He was gratified that Squirrel had not resisted.

It was difficult to tell which of the women was most distressed at the sight of the darkening wound on the boy's head, his true mother White Deer or his aunt-mother Rabbit. Crow Feather had to caution them not to make too much fuss. It was not good for a boy to learn to look for sympathy. It made him soft and weak.

While White Deer cleansed the wound and rubbed it with bear grease, Crow Feather explained what had happened. "It was the fault of Swift Runner. That boy will never be a man. He is full of talk but has no judgment."

White Deer and Rabbit looked at one another, something passing silently between them. White Deer said, "He may never become a man, but he seems likely to become your brother-in-law."

Crow Feather could not have been more surprised if she had struck him with a cooking pot. "How can that be?"

"Your sister Calling Bird. If you have not noticed, she has ripened."

Crow Feather had noticed. In his deliberations over a suitable husband for her, Swift Runner had never entered his mind. He rejected the thought now. "There are many who would be better for her than him."

"But the choice is not yours to make."

True, as her acting father, their uncle was responsible for selecting her husband. But Crow Feather had expected when the time came that he would be able to influence his uncle's decision. Some parents allowed a girl to make her own choice. Others considered that too great a risk, especially in view of the fact that a son-in-law was responsible for their welfare and should be a person they could depend upon. "I must see about this. I must stop it."

"It may be too late. He has already presented horses to your uncle."

"Where would Swift Runner get horses?"

"He borrowed them from Man Who Stole the Mules. He said he will pay Mules back when they raid the land of the Texans."

"If his carelessness does not kill him first. Surely Calling Bird does not want this marriage."

White Deer smiled. "You have not observed her closely."

It was true, he had not. Among the People, brothers and sisters kept a suitable distance from one another once they reached an age where temptation might arise. Incest was one of the most serious of all the taboos. A man had the right to kill a sister who made bold with him, though such a thing rarely happened. Crow Feather would never have considered it with Calling Bird.

White Deer said, "I have seen the way she looks at him. He has played the flute for her. I suspect she has already been in his tepee."

As a young bachelor of warrior age, Swift Runner would have his own tepee, apart from that of his parents. And because it was custom for romance to be initiated by the girl rather than the boy, it was not uncommon for a girl to slip into a young man's tepee in the dark of night. In such a way White Deer had first aroused Crow Feather's interest years ago.

It was possible that Calling Bird might already be with child, Swift Runner's child.

If that be so, Crow Feather thought angrily, he hoped the child inherited its judgment from its mother's side of the family. Yet, if Calling Bird had proper judgment she would have chosen more wisely.

His wound treated, the boy picked up a long stick and walked back to the paint pony. He led him up beside a rock and stepped upon it to give himself height. Grasping the mane, he tried three times to jump upon the patient pony's back before he finally made it, clambering awkwardly but finally gaining his seat.

Crow Feather resisted the temptation to help him. He took pride in Squirrel's determination.

Squirrel spotted a black dog which was in the habit of sneaking around camp, stealing meat wherever anyone was careless enough to leave it within his reach. He drummed his heels against the pony's ribs and put it into a long trot. Grasping the long stick as if it were a lance, he bore down upon the startled dog and thrust it at him as if he were a buffalo. He missed, but not by much.

Crow Feather smiled. The day would come when they would have to change his name. *Little Squirrel* would not do for the best buffalo hunter in the band.

Six

SMITHWICK REGRETTED the drink he had taken in the saloon, for it kept turning over and arousing moments of nausea. His money evaporated, he had no way to repay Jeff Layne, or even to continue eating beyond whatever charity he might receive from the Cregar outfit or the Browders. A Smithwick dependent upon charity! The idea was abhorrent. He stood awhile at the depot, turning back once to challenge the telegrapher. Perhaps he had read the bank's name incorrectly. The man assured him there had been no mistake. Smithwick realized that such a thought was akin to a drowning man's desperate grasping at whatever thin reed he could reach.

He might recoup enough to buy a train ticket east if he could manage a run of luck at the cards. But nothing of consequence awaited him back there, just more of the empty boredom which had driven him west. Furthermore, he lacked a stake and knew no way to obtain one short of robbery. He had committed indiscretions of which he was not proud, but he had not resorted to anything quite so alien to Smithwick family traditions. Still, he had to do *something*. It would be months before he could expect another remittance from the family business.

The Cregar wagons remained where Jeff had halted them, their cargo of hides untouched. Jeff's face was lathered, and he was shaving himself. He turned away from a small mirror propped against a wagon bed and wiped the razor on a cloth. He seemed to read the turmoil in Smithwick's face. "Trouble, English?"

Smithwick dug the change from his pocket. "Here. I remain in your debt for the rest of it." He explained what he had learned at the depot.

Jeff nodded sympathetically and resumed shaving. "I never did trust them damnyankee banks. I leave mine in the safe at Bob Wright's store here. At least if anything goes wrong I can get ahold of him and take my satisfaction out of his hide."

"I find myself at the mercy of chance, and chance has not been merciful."

The aging Elijah Layne took Smithwick's trouble as his own. "Son, it ain't right to leave an Englishman in a predicament like this. Maybe Colonel can find a place for him."

Jeff wiped his face with a wet towel. He looked much more civilized without the whiskers, though the skin was a shade lighter where they had been than on the exposed part of his face. "I ain't sure English'd be happy ridin' a hide wagon. It ain't a gentleman's style."

Smithwick suspected Jeff was subtly challenging him. "It would not be my first choice."

"Well, job or not, feel welcome to take supper with us. And after supper me and you might go have a look at the sights. Help you forget your troubles."

"I have already seen more than enough of this place."

"It'll look different come dark. Lamplight takes the rough edges off."

"I do not wish to fall deeper into your debt."

"You'd be doin' me a favor. I'm in bad need of a little entertainment. Dad don't go anymore. Too old. Kid's too young. Sully stays in camp because they killed a black feller here awhile back just for the hell of it. As for Gant Folsom . . ." He grimaced. "If you don't go with me, I'll have to go alone, and Dodge at night is too tough a place for a man to be by himself."

Smithwick knew Jeff was simply trying to be kind. "I would feel just that much worse in the morning."

"Cheer up, English. Havin' a bank go bust on you ain't half as

mean as gettin' shot and losin' a war. I've had both of them pleasures."

The conversation disturbed Elijah Layne. "I hope you boys
don't drink too much. It can sure lead to bad things." His troubled
eyes hinted at memories too dark to talk about.

The skinner Gantry Folsom had wandered up, bringing a strong
scent of buffalo hides with him, and of bad whiskey. "I wish you'd
tell me about that, old man. I always wondered why Jeff couldn't
go back to Texas. He get drunk and kill somebody?"

The hard look on Jeff Layne's face suggested that Folsom had
guessed the truth or was close to it. Worse, he was just drunk
enough to keep picking at the sore until it erupted.

"How much they offering for your head down there, Jeff?"

Smithwick saw fight building in Jeff's eyes. Hoping to head it
off, he stepped between the two men. "Texas is a long way from
here, Folsom. I would suggest that you see after your own affairs."

Anger flashed in the skinner's whiskey-reddened eyes. "Ain't you
the one to tell people what to do, a fancy-talking son of a bitch
without a cent in his pocket? Well, I ain't no Goddamned English
servant!" He brought a fist up in a wide, wild swing.

Smithwick raised his left arm to brush the fist aside, then jabbed
at Folsom's exposed chin. Folsom's head rocked back in surprise.
Smithwick hit him a second time, and Folsom went down. He
stayed down, shaking his head.

Sully's white teeth shone like ivory as the man who frequently
tormented him rolled his eyes in confusion. "That was so fast I
most couldn't see it. How'd you do that?"

"Where I went to school, the art of boxing was a part of the
curriculum. I was considerably better at that than at Latin."

Jeff did not seem pleased. "It was my place to've hit him, if it was
to be done atall."

"But he swung at me, not you."

Sully said, "He wouldn't have the nerve to swing on Mr. Jeff. He
thought you looked easier to whup."

A deep, gruff voice demanded, "What is going on here? Who
started this?" Colonel Cregar sat on his big bay horse, his face
clouded. "Have you men nothing more constructive to do than
fight among yourselves?" He concentrated his attention upon

Smithwick. "Smith, you were taken into this company out of kindness. You have a poor way of repaying it. Sully, help Gant to his feet."

Reluctantly the black man leaned down to grasp Folsom's arms. Folsom jerked free. "I can get up by myself."

Stubborn anger kept Smithwick from explaining that Folsom had struck at him first. A gentleman did not have to explain anything unless he chose to, and he did not choose to. "The name is Smith*wick*."

Cregar declared, "I have no patience with troublemakers. I want you to remove yourself from this company, Smith. Now!"

Elijah Layne started to protest. "Colonel, the Englishman didn't . . ." He stopped. Smithwick did not know if the stern look in Cregar's face had cowed the old man or if he simply realized the futility of argument.

Jeff said, "Go on, English. I'll find you tonight."

Cregar demanded, "Tonight? What about tonight?"

Jeff's voice was brittle. "Tonight's my business, Colonel. Now, we goin' to unload these hides, or not?"

Smithwick feared that if he lingered he might precipitate a fight between Jeff and his employer. The Texan did not deserve that. Walking away, he heard Cregar order the wagons moved to a hide yard owned by Charles Rath. He had probably received a better price than Cephus Browder. For that matter, he probably received a better price than anybody. Given his commanding manner, he would have accepted no less.

Smithwick found the hide buyer Thomason supervising the loading of skins onto a flatcar. "Have you seen Cephus Browder?"

Thomason glanced away from his work for only a moment. "You may find him at Rath's or one of the other suppliers. He said he is going to outfit himself for another try at the buffalo. South as far as the Cimarron, and farther if it be necessary."

"But everyone says it is hazardous to travel south."

"The greater the hazard, the greater the potential profit. A cardinal rule of business, sir. The first man into the orchard gets the pick of the fruit. Were I a younger man, and were I not tied down with my enterprise here, I would buy wagons and go south myself."

An uneasy feeling about the Browders displaced Smithwick's personal worries for the moment. He walked up the dusty street, seeking out those mercantile firms that might supply Cephus with the goods necessary for an excursion into bison country. After two tries he found the man behind a store, his cook wagon pulled up parallel to a recently built but already splintered loading dock that showed the many scars of a busy workplace. Two store employees were loading a barrel of flour into the bed of the wagon, securing it snugly against boxes and crates of other goods.

Browder greeted him with a wave of his hand. "How do, English? Come over and set a spell while the boys finish loadin' me out."

Smithwick did not see Arletta. "Where is your daughter?"

"She went off with Thomason's wife to get herself a bath and some fresh clothes. Just like her mother, always wantin' to look better than she has any need to."

Smithwick did not hide his misgivings. "I have been told you plan to take your wagons south."

"That's where the buffalo have gone. I figure to harvest me a heap of skins before the rest of the runners get down there and cause a scatterin'."

"It would seem wise to wait and go with them. The more there are, the better you can protect one another."

"Ain't no Indian raised my hair yet, and they've had some good chances. I aim to fill my wagons quick. The market's apt to break once the boys start fetchin' in a lot of hides. I even bought me two more wagons from a hunter that's givin' up."

"But surely you don't plan to take Arletta this time."

"I'd be a lot more worried what was happenin' to her here in Dodge City than out there where I can take care of her, don't you see?" He stopped to count several slabs of bacon. "I suppose you're fixin' to head east on the next train?"

"My funds did not come through. I am financially embarrassed."

Cephus gave Smithwick a long, thoughtful study. "Are you any kind of hand with a rifle?"

"I won the club trophy twice for marksmanship."

Cephus reached beneath the wagon seat and lifted out a huge thick-barreled rifle of a kind Smithwick had seen the hunters carry, probably the same one he had seen Cephus balance across his saddle. He loaded a large brass cartridge into the breech and handed the rifle to Smithwick. "Barrel's heavy. You'll need to brace it on somethin'. See that old whiskey keg layin' out yonder a hundred yards or so? Try and put a hole in it."

"Right here in town?"

"Ain't nothin' out that direction you can hurt."

The rifle was far heavier than any Smithwick had ever used. He hefted it to get the feel for it, then rested the barrel across a corner of the wagon and looked for the keg over the sights.

Cephus warned, "Hold her tight against your shoulder. She kicks like a Missouri mule."

Even warned, Smithwick was not ready for the jolt the rifle gave him, or the ear-piercing loudness of the report. Through the smoke he saw the keg jump and fall apart. Half a dozen dogs began barking, and the wagon surged forward as the team spooked. A man wearing an apron around his middle hurried out the store's back door to see what the shooting was about. He seemed satisfied when he saw nobody was killed.

Cephus settled the team and came back grinning. "You sure played hell with that keg."

Smithwick rubbed his shoulder. It would be blue tomorrow. "I don't know that I proved anything."

"You proved you can shoot. I don't suppose you'd be interested in goin' south with a huntin' outfit?"

"You are offering me a job?"

"More than a job, a percentage. My eyes ain't as good as they was. Once I show you how to set up a buffalo stand, you can do the shootin' for me. We'll earn more money than you could tote away in a sack."

Two days had given Smithwick all he cared to see or smell of bison hides. "I appreciate the offer, but it's not the life for me. I'll find something."

"What? There's men all over this town a-huntin' for work. Every train brings another load of them from back east. With me you've got a chance to make somethin'."

And a good chance of getting killed, Smithwick thought. "I'll be all right. And I do wish you would wait until you can go out with a larger party. Think of Arletta's safety if you won't consider your own."

"All my life I been pickin' up the leavin's after other men. This time I'm goin' to suck the front tit instead of the hind one. I just wish I had your shootin' eye with me."

Smithwick handed him the rifle. "I am sorry, Cephus, but I have no stomach for that kind of life."

Cephus accepted the decision with regret. "Remember us now and again when you're home in England."

"That I shall. I'll not soon forget this experience."

He turned once to look back at the farmer-become-hunter who had never made a success of anything. He had a strong feeling that Cephus would be disappointed in this venture as well. He would be fortunate to get back at all, much less to come back wealthy from the hide harvest.

Smithwick shook his head and turned the corner, walking aimlessly down the street, sidestepping horses and wagons that all seemed to have more places to go than he did. A woman with heavily rouged cheeks and a half-buttoned blouse leaned against a wall beside the door to a saloon, inviting him with her eyes and a sly smile. A drunk staggered out of a dramshop, holding a death grip on the neck of a near-empty bottle. Walking backward, the man politely begged Smithwick's pardon and bumped into a horse tied to a post. The horse kicked at him but missed. The drunk seemed oblivious to his narrow escape.

Smithwick's face twisted. He had tired of idleness among London society and had set out to search for a more vital and interesting life, but this was too much. He had to get out of this town somehow, even if he were forced to catch a freight and ride on the rods beneath.

Two women caught his attention. They came down the wooden sidewalk, moving out into the dirt street where the sidewalk ended. They did not look like the woman at the saloon, or any of her sisters he had seen elsewhere along the way. Their dresses were long, almost touching the ground. One was middle-aged, a housewife by the look of her. The other . . . Smithwick recognized the long reddish hair, the smiling, sun-browned face, freshly scrubbed.

"Arletta? Can that be you?" Her hair had been washed and

combed and brushed. She was not wearing a bonnet. Instead of the shapeless old gray work dress she wore a new one light in color, cut to a fair fit where the other had hung loosely and without form. The pointed toes of a woman's shoes peeked from beneath the flowing skirt. He had seen her only in boots.

"Sure it's me. Got cleaned up a little, is all. Mrs. Thomason, this is Mr. Smithwick. He's an Englishman."

The woman's gray eyes were pleasant. "My father was English. He had a shop in Connecticut. Are you a member of Mr. Browder's hunting party?"

"I am not a hunter, madam." He found himself compelled to stare at Arletta. He would not have thought her appearance could change so much, and all for the better. "Arletta, the clothes are a wonderful improvement. You should remain where you can look this way all the time."

"It's like drapin' flowers on a mule. He may smell prettier, but he's still a mule. You seen Papa?"

"He's around the corner, at the loading dock." He turned and walked beside the women so he could deflect any more drunks who might come staggering out of a bar.

Mrs. Thomason said, "I have tried to talk Arletta into remaining here with me while her father takes his wagons out. It would be far safer."

"Cephus does not seem to think so."

Arletta said, "I couldn't let Papa go off without me. He takes a lot of lookin' after."

Mrs. Thomason argued, "It frightens me to think of you going down into that wild country with just a handful of men. Some of it has not felt the tread of a white man's foot."

"I've been in a lot of country like that," Arletta replied. They rounded the corner, and she spied her father. She skipped toward him, proud as a schoolgirl. "Papa! Papa, look what Mrs. Thomason found for me."

Mrs. Thomason stopped and clutched Smithwick's arm. "Can't you talk to her, sir, and get her to stay?"

"I have tried to reason with her father. He can be a stubborn man. I fear I would have little more influence with the daughter."

"A stubborn streak seems to run in the family. It's a pity. She has beautiful hair, have you noticed?"

"I have noticed."

"It would be a terrible thing were it to end up hanging from some Indian's scalp pole."

The image gave Smithwick a chill. "I am afraid the only way to stop them would be to shoot Cephus. Nothing fatal, of course, simply wound him in the leg, or something."

"It might be worth the cost. I would be tempted to do it, were I a man." Her eyes were severe.

"Madam, I truly believe you would."

He gave Arletta a moment's quiet study, remembering another girl of plain speech and plain ways, a long time ago. He walked back up the street alone, killing time by stopping and looking in the windows, where there *were* windows. He noted that most of the stores seemed to be long on such frontier necessities as arms and ammunition and short on anything that might be construed as luxuries. They sold shovels and axes and skinning knives, harness and blankets and work clothes. And always there was liquor, by the drink, by the bottle, or by the keg. If neither Cephus Browder nor Colonel Cregar took liquor with them on their hunting expeditions, it was obvious that many other outfits had no such compunctions. He had been told that some who had more interest in their own profits than in the welfare of fellow hunters took whiskey along to trade to Indians for woman-finished buffalo robes.

A small stack of books caught his eye, the only books he had seen here. Curiosity carried him into the store to look at them. One was a speller, another a reader, a third *Oliver Twist*. The storekeeper sidled over expectantly after Smithwick had looked through the books. "I could let you have them cheap."

That the books had been used was obvious. Their edges showed the smudges and wear of thumbs and fingertips, and some of the pages bore pencil marks. "I fear I could not afford them at any price. I was simply surprised to find them here."

"They were my daughter's school books. She's married now and living on a farm back in Indiana. She has no further use for reading. I could let you have them all . . . say a dollar?"

"If they were but a farthing, I could not buy a page. A pity, though. I know a young lady who might profit by them."

He lingered over *Oliver Twist*, reviewing some of its well-remembered lines. "Have you ever read this?"

The storekeeper shook his head. "My ledgers give me all the reading I care to do. I do not indulge myself in idle entertainment."

Smithwick walked back out into the street, wondering at those who sought so eagerly for imagined riches that they trampled an unseen treasure lying at their feet.

And I may be the worst of them all, he thought, *for look what I left behind, and what I have come to.*

Seven

SMITHWICK HALF HOPED Jeff Layne would not find him, for he felt too depressed to enjoy the thought of spending an evening in the futile pursuit of merriment. A man who had no prospects was not entitled to such frivolity. But his pockets were empty, so he could not hide himself among a saloon crowd. He had nothing to do except walk the dusty streets, watching hopefully for something that might offer opportunity but not knowing if he would recognize it. At dusk he heard his name called and knew before he turned that the voice was Jeff's.

"Come on over to camp, English, and have some supper."

"You heard what the colonel said."

"Colonel ain't there. He's havin' his supper with a hide buyer in some fine restaurant."

Fine restaurant indeed! Such a thing was as unlikely in this raw outpost as in a Cheyenne Indian village. "I could not eat a bite of Cregar's provisions. It would stick in my throat."

"Don't blame Colonel too much. He was wrought up because he expected his son to be here waitin'. Colonel ain't used to people lettin' him down."

"Perhaps the young man had the good judgment not to come at all."

"Possible. If the boy takes after his daddy, he's probably declared his independence."

"Then I say bully for him. But I still have no wish to eat any of Cregar's rations."

"Well, then, come along to a little place that's run by an old cowboy like me who came up the trail and never went home. He ain't much for fancy, but he knows how to fix biscuits and fry up a slice of beef."

Suspicion nudged Smithwick. "Why all this interest in what happens to me?" His experience had been that such solicitude often hid some ulterior motive involving his money, or his family's.

Jeff seemed perplexed. It was evident he had not analyzed his reasons or had considered that he needed any. "Maybe it's because we're both a long ways from home, and it don't look likely that either one of us is goin' back anytime soon."

The regret in his eyes made Smithwick wish he had not asked. He used to assume that nobility was reserved for those to the manor born, but he sensed an innate nobility in this plain man who probably knew little of his antecedents. "Your invitation is accepted. With humility and gratitude."

He was curious to know more about the Texan's background, for Folsom had hinted at a colorful and probably violent past. But he had already surmised that it was impolite and possibly even dangerous to ask too many questions of people in this American West. Instinctively partisan in Layne's behalf, he felt that whatever the man had done that kept him from going back to Texas had probably been justified.

The restaurant, which Jeff more aptly described as an *eatin' joint*, was a small frame structure south of the tracks. It had a few unpainted, rough-hewn tables that rocked uncertainly on the warped plank floor. It was mostly one long room with a large cast-iron cookstove at the far end. A hind quarter of beef, or for all Smithwick knew, of buffalo, was partially wrapped in a blood-stained piece of tarpaulin and hung from a rafter. The proprietor was a paunchy man in his middle years, a fierce black-and-gray moustache sheltering much of his ruddy face. He and Jeff enjoyed a minute or so of handshaking, back-slapping and *How the hell are you?*s before Jeff got around to introducing him to Smithwick.

"This here is Cap Doolittle, from way down in Karnes County,

Texas. Cap, I want you to meet a pretty good Englishman, Nigel Smithwick."

Doolittle's grip threatened to crush Smithwick's hand. "What the hell's an Englishman doin' in my place? I don't serve no tea here, nor crumpets. All I got is coffee, beef, biscuits and taters."

"I would be in your debt for whatever you do have, sir."

"No debt accepted, just cash." The man's friendly mien belied his words. "You like your steak well done, or burned up? Jeff and most of these other old Texas boys think they can't eat it unless it's near black. Taken *me* a while to learn better."

"Prepare it as if you intended to eat it yourself."

Doolittle grinned at Jeff. "Pretty smart for somebody that didn't come from Texas. Pour yourselves some coffee while I get your supper started. Got a bottle under the counter if you'd like to doctor it a little." As he cooked, he and Jeff traded talk about what was going on back in Texas and about the decline in the buffalo. Doolittle asked, "How long you intend to keep workin' with that damnyankee colonel? It's a wonder to me that you ain't shot him by now."

"I think about it now and again. But then he'll do somethin' that makes me glad I know him. He's hard to outguess."

"Well, I'm glad he's no problem of mine."

Smithwick felt uncomfortable under Jeff's long stare. At length Jeff said, "You'd better be makin' some plans, English. You'll get damned hungry walkin' these streets."

"It is in my mind to look for the men who robbed me and recover whatever I can."

"How? They'd probably kill you. You ain't even armed."

Smithwick reached inside a pocket and took out the derringer. Jeff shook his head. "You still ain't armed."

"I have no wish to kill anyone, but this can make a nasty little wound that will not soon be forgotten."

"If I learned anything from the war, it was that the more artillery you had, the better your chance of winnin' the fight. I'll go with you."

"It is none of your concern. It was I they robbed."

"And it'll be you they kill, give them half a chance. I got nothin' better to do except visit a girl and maybe get drunk. I can do that another night." He looked up as Doolittle brought them their steak, fried potatoes and biscuits on platters. "Want to go with us, Cap, and hunt for some damnyankee highbinders?"

Doolittle hesitated only a moment, glancing toward the only other customer in the place, a lonesome-looking little man in a corner near the front door. "Why the hell not? I ain't gettin' rich in here."

BAD AS HE HAD THOUGHT the afternoon's saloon to have been, Smithwick found Dodge City had worse to offer. Accompanied by Jeff and Doolittle, he saw them all, from the east end of town to the west, on both sides of the tracks. In only a couple did he try the whiskey, for he wanted to keep his head clear. The two Texans drank somewhat more, but he could not see that it impaired their faculties. He found that both men knew many of the bartenders by their first names as well as some of the women who frequented the joints. When he commented upon that fact, Doolittle laughed. "Down where we come from, we was raised to be friendly."

"I have not seen a woman tonight who caught my fancy."

Jeff winked at Doolittle. "Stay out on the buffalo range for three or four months and you'll be amazed how much better lookin' they get."

When they had visited the last dramshop, Smithwick grimaced over the gray taste of disappointment. "I saw every face. They simply were not there."

Jeff did not share his discouragement. "Crowds change. For all we know they could've showed up somewhere just after we left." He looked at Doolittle. "You game to set up and go back the other way?"

Doolittle stroked his huge moustache. "I sure do dread it, but let's be gettin' started."

Smithwick was surprised in the second bar they revisited to come face-to-face with Colonel Cregar. The man seemed to tower over the rest of the crowd. He gave Smithwick only a passing glance but acknowledged Jeff and Doolittle.

Jeff asked, "Havin' any luck, Colonel?"

The big man shook his head. "I have inquired of every merchant in town and most of the bartenders. So many young men have come in on the railroad, looking for work, that they could all have seen him and not know it."

"Wish I could help, but I wouldn't know your son if he was to walk up and hit me between the eyes."

Smithwick pictured how Cregar's son must look. If he were as large as his father, and twenty-five years younger, he would be a formidable force to reckon with. *Just what the country needs, another Cregar to bully everybody around.*

Cregar said, "I should have made him join me the first time I heard his recklessness had gotten him in trouble. I'm afraid my wife's people spoiled him. But I'll take care of that when he *does* show up." He nodded toward the long bar. It was one of the few Smithwick had seen here that had been shipped in from a furniture factory instead of being sawed and nailed or rawhide-tied together on the spot. "I'd stand all of you to a drink."

Jeff and Doolittle accepted immediately. Smithwick held back. "Does that include me?"

The colonel grunted impatiently. "I said *all* of you." He led the way to the bar, the other patrons moving aside for him. Jeff, Doolittle and Smithwick filled the vacuum left in his wake. The bartender seemed to know him, for he reached beneath the bar and brought up a bottle that Smithwick found several grades better than anything he had tasted in Dodge.

Jeff said, "We're lookin' for somebody too. We're tryin' to help English find the men who robbed him and threw him off of the train."

The slight hint of disdain faded from Cregar's face. "Indeed?" He turned toward Smithwick. "And what, sir, do you intend to do if you find them?"

"Recover what they took from me."

"How?"

"That depends on them. They may surrender it gracefully, or I may be forced to more drastic means."

Cregar gave him an intense study. If he had any doubt, he did not yield Smithwick the benefit of it. "As a rule, Smith, I have found that men who talk about the tough things they are going to do rarely do them."

Stiffly Smithwick retorted, "Had you not asked me, I would not have said anything." He had already satisfied himself that the robbers were not in this establishment. It was probably too refined for their taste. He turned and made his way through the crowd.

Two saloons farther down the street, he found them. The three were seated at a large round table with two players who appeared to have lost heavily, judging by their downcast expressions. A considerable amount of money was piled loosely in front of the three, the largest pile belonging to the hairy-fingered cigar chewer who had called himself Jones. They must have worked fast, for Smithwick was sure it had been no more than a couple of hours since he had visited this same barroom.

He reached into his pocket and palmed the derringer. The man who had called himself Brown recognized him with a start and tugged at Jones's sleeve. The larger man blinked, the cigar threatening to fall from his mouth before he clamped his teeth back down upon it.

Smithwick declared, "Sir, I am here to collect what you owe me." He watched the man's hands as well as those of his two companions.

Jones regained his composure. "You must be mistaken, sir. I never saw you before."

"What you mean is that you never expected to see me again. Now, do you give back what you stole from me, or must I take it?"

The one called Black dropped a hand beneath the edge of the table. Smithwick shoved the derringer at him. "I would not hesitate to discharge this weapon in your face."

The hand quickly came up empty.

Jones took the cigar from his mouth and cried out to the crowd in general, "Isn't anybody going to stop this? Don't you people see he's trying to rob us at gunpoint?"

One of the two strangers who had been playing pushed back angrily from the table and looked up at Smithwick. "Have at him, friend, and welcome. I ain't been able to catch him at it, but I know damned well he's cheated us from the start."

Smithwick said, "Whatever you've lost to him, remove it from the table. It's yours."

Jones complained loudly but made no move to stop the two losing players from recovering their losses.

Smithwick pointed the derringer at him. "That watch you are carrying belongs to me. I want it."

Jones shouted to the crowd of curious onlookers gathering around, "Are all of you going to stand there and let him rob me? This is *my* watch."

"Take it from his pocket, will you please, Jeff? You will find my father's name inscribed on the case: LIONEL SMITHWICK."

Jeff lifted the watch and examined it. "That's the name on here, all right."

Jones grumbled, "I won it from him in a poker game, fair and square."

Smithwick stuck the watch into his own pocket, where it belonged. It felt comforting to have it back. "A minute ago you said you never saw me before. A liar carries a special burden. He must try to remember all the lies he has told lest the next one undo the rest." He reached for the money.

The bartender was a burly man with rolled-up sleeves revealing muscles like those of a studhorse. He pushed through the crowd and took a strong grip on Smithwick's arm. "Hold on a minute, friend. I guess the watch was yours; you identified it well enough. But as to the money, maybe it's yours and maybe it's not. That'd be up to the law to say."

A loud, booming voice overrode all the others that argued pro and con. Colonel Cregar stood there, half a head taller and broader in the shoulders than anyone else in the crowd. "Just a minute, bartender. I tend to believe the Englishman, but that is neither here nor there. There is a logical way to settle this question." He frowned at Smithwick. "I believe you said you won all the money these men were willing to gamble on the train, and they later took it from you."

"That is correct."

"Would you be willing to see if you can best them again as you did before? Then no one could accuse you of taking their money at the point of a gun."

Smithwick felt like laughing as Jones bit down angrily on the cigar. "That is a splendid idea. However, I have no stake with which to start."

"You have that watch."

"So I have. It should be worth a hundred dollars on any table. Bartender, a fresh deck of cards if you please."

Cregar turned to Jones and his two companions. He declared as if it were a military order, "Gentlemen, you will divest yourselves of your weapons." His commanding presence brooked no resistance. Jeff and Doolittle accepted the pistols and handed them to the bartender. He extended his hand toward Smithwick. "And you, sir, that cannon of yours, if you please."

Cregar turned the tiny weapon over in his hand, examining it with a bemused smile. He opened the deck of cards the bartender brought, shuffled them thoroughly and laid them on the table with a resounding thump. "Let the game commence."

For each hand the three highbinders won, Smithwick won two. His spirits rose in concert with the piles of money gradually consolidating at his end of the table. Brown was the first of the three to use up what was in front of him and declare himself out of the game.

Jeff said firmly, "I don't recollect anything said about this being a table-stakes game. Let's see what you've got in your pockets."

Brown grumbled but put out several gold coins. They were not long in moving over to Smithwick's side. In a while the one who called himself Black was cleaned out and could only watch in glum silence while Smithwick whittled Jones down to little but his clothes and what was left of a badly chewed cigar.

At length Jones threw up his hands, his face a dark shade of crimson. He glared at Smithwick, then at the men who had crowded around to watch him being trimmed. "This is robbery, and you're all accomplices to it."

Doolittle said, "I never seen the Englishman play a crooked hand. I can't say the same for you, tinhorn. If it'd been me playin' agin you, I'd've shot you before now."

Smithwick felt a soaring exhilaration as he gathered his winnings. He sorted off three gold coins and shoved one across the table at each of the losers. "I make it a cardinal rule to leave no one destitute. I wish I had a train to throw you from, but I do not, so I will say goodnight. The evening has been a pleasure."

Jones growled around the remnant of cigar, "We'll see you again, Cedric."

Colonel Cregar shook his head. "I think not. Some of the men in this room are members of the vigilance committee. If you three are still in town after the next train leaves for the east, open season will be declared."

The defeated Jones slumped in his chair, his face near purple. "Bartender, our pistols, please."

The bartender's big hands were braced on his hips. "Tomorrow, twenty minutes before the train leaves."

"Goddamn this town and everybody in it!" Jones glowered murderously at Smithwick. "Vigilance committee or no, you'll wish you'd never seen us, Cedric."

"I already wish that, devoutly." Smithwick refused to let the man's bristling hostility temper his jubilant spirit. He turned his back on the three defeated players and looked at Jeff and Doolittle. "Shall we go, gentlemen? I owe you a drink. Several drinks, in fact."

They were nearly to the door when Smithwick heard a collective gasp from the crowd and spun around. Jones had grabbed a pistol from someone's holster and was trying to cock the hammer back.

Colonel Cregar swung a Colt revolver. Its heavy barrel made a solid thud as it struck Jones's head. The cigar man fell to the floor like a sack of grain dropped from a wagon. Face down, his head bleeding, he scratched his hairy fingers against the rough plank floor, then went still.

Cregar turned to the man's two companions. Dispassionately he said, "His head felt like a melon. I may have broken it. If you have any thought for his life, you had better fetch a doctor. And if you have any thought for your own, you will leave town tomorrow, with him or without him."

The bartender knelt beside the fallen man. "It'll be without him. The son of a bitch is dead."

Smithwick felt as if all the blood had drained from his body. "Dead? Are you sure?" His mouth went dry.

The bartender said as calmly as if he were citing the price of whiskey: "If they dig him up in a hundred years he won't be any deader." His gaze sought out Jones's two companions. "You get him out of my place before he starts to stink it up."

Brown's hands were shaking. "What'll we do with him?"

"Drag him up on the hill and bury him. Been several planted up there already. There wasn't a one of them the community couldn't do without."

"But we need somebody to read over him, don't we?"

"What for? It's too late for words to bring him salvation. He's probably halfway to hell by now." Brown and Black did not move. The bartender jerked his head at a couple of acquaintances. "Drag him out the back door, will you? They can go get him when they make up their minds." He wrapped a towel around the dead man's head to keep blood from trailing across the floor, then each of the men picked up a leg and dragged Jones outside. In a minute they were back. The bartender poured free drinks for their help.

Smithwick fought to keep the evening's whiskey from coming up. Gone was the earlier exhilaration. He felt sick at his stomach and in his soul. Cregar revealed no more emotion than if he had shot a buffalo. Smithwick demanded, "Did you have to kill him?"

"I didn't intend to, but I can't bring him back to life, so I do not intend to waste any grief over him. Nor should you. He was about to shoot you in the back."

"But you don't just kill a man without at least feeling something."

"I have killed far better men than he was. They called it duty and awarded medals to me. I felt sorrow for those men, but not for this one." He shifted his attention to the bartender. "If the sheriff decides he has business with me, he can find me in his own good time."

The crowd parted to let Cregar leave the saloon, continuing a lonely search for his son. The men stared into the darkness after him as if in awe. Then they were shuffling around again, players reseating themselves at tables, drinkers at the bar. Boots scuffed through the drying blood Jones had shed upon the floor. In a few minutes it was as if nothing had happened.

Smithwick was aghast at the lack of concern. "My God! Doesn't life have any meaning out here?"

The two Texans glanced at one another. Jeff said, "Ours do, and any *good* man's. That gambler's? Not much. He tore up his ticket the minute he grabbed that gun."

"But Cregar was as indifferent as if he were going to tea."

Doolittle remembered Smithwick's derringer, forgotten in the excitement, and went to retrieve it from the bartender.

Jeff said, "Colonel's not like anybody else you'll ever know. You have to accept him the way he is or leave him be, because he ain't changin' for anybody." He pointed toward the door. "You said somethin' about buyin' us a drink. Let's go find us a quieter place."

Eight

SMITHWICK DREAMED someone was pounding on his head with the barrel of a Colt revolver, except that the Colt was as large as the Big Fifty Cephus Browder had invited him to fire. Painfully he opened his eyes. The merciless glare of daylight threatened to explode his eyeballs. He squinched the eyes shut for a minute, dreading opening them again. He heard Jeff Layne's voice.

"I do believe he's back amongst the livin'. I been half afraid we'd have to drag him up on the hill and bury him alongside that gambler."

Cap Doolittle said, "Maybe they don't drink nothin' but tea over where he comes from."

Smithwick's mouth tasted as if a rat had crawled into it and died. Or perhaps a buffalo. He turned from his back onto one side and felt the burn of bad whiskey rising all the way to his throat. It came back to him, dimly, that he had drunk a great deal last night after that disaster in the saloon. He forced his eyes open long enough to realize that he was lying on the floor of Doolittle's restaurant. He could feel the roughness of the boards through a buffalo robe someone had spread out to make him a bed of sorts. He shivered, feeling cold, though the autumn weather had been benign enough so far.

The last thing he could remember was that he and Jeff and Doolittle had been singing in some dirt-floored tent saloon where the bar had been a buffalo hide stretched across a couple of planks nailed to a row of wooden whiskey kegs. He did not feel like singing now, nor did he feel likely to sing again for a long time. He could smell something pleasant, however. "Would that perchance be coffee?"

Doolittle said, "It will be, soon's it comes to a boil. Looks to me like you'll need a gallon of it."

"Quite possibly." Smithwick dragged himself to his feet and slumped into a wooden chair. He rubbed his aching head. "What sort of poison do you people dispense around here in the guise of whiskey?"

Doolittle seemed unaffected by the prodigious amount he had put away last night. He busied himself cheerily at the big wood range, banging some utensil with reckless and painful abandon against an iron skillet. "They melt rattlesnake heads in the better stuff. The rest of it ain't that good."

A customer rattled the locked front door. It sounded like gunshots inside Smithwick's brain. Doolittle did not help, shouting, "We're closed this mornin'! For repairs!"

Jeff brought coffee to Smithwick, cautioning, "It's hot enough to scald you. I'd saucer and blow it for you, but some people prefer to do that for themselves."

Smithwick felt marginally better after downing a few swallows of the black coffee. The card game last night seemed a bad dream, and he felt instinctively for his father's watch. Its presence assured him that what he remembered was no dream. "Do you suppose that man Jones is still lying out there where they dragged him?"

Doolittle said indifferently, "Who gives a damn? Just be glad it's him dead instead of you." He brought the Englishman bacon and eggs and some biscuits left over from yesterday. "It may taste like hell to you, but you need somethin' to anchor your stomach down."

Doolittle was right about the taste. The first few bites threatened to come back up. But Smithwick managed to put away all the man brought him, and he felt steadier for it. "I don't know what came over me last night. I rarely drink much."

Jeff said, "You were tryin' to drown a bad memory. Ain't much you can do except pick yourself up, dust yourself off and forget about yesterday. Put your mind on today and tomorrow. That's what I've always tried to do."

"Does it work?"

"Usually not."

When Jeff finished his breakfast he thanked Doolittle and reached into his pocket. Doolittle waved away his attempt at payment. "Your Yankee-earned money don't spend in here. Nor yours either, English. It's been my pleasure."

Jeff looked up. "First night in near two months that I've slept under a roof."

Doolittle said, "Hope you enjoyed it. Me, I'm gettin' tired of it. I'd like to sleep out under the stars again, if they was Texas stars."

Smithwick put in, "The stars here are the same as in England. I doubt that they are different in Texas."

Jeff's voice seemed wishful. "It's not the stars, it's the place they shine on. God, what I'd give . . ." He frowned at Smithwick. "You fixin' to catch the train east today?"

"I have not been awake long enough to think about it."

"I wouldn't be in a hurry. You might wish all your life that you hadn't done it."

"Why would I wish that?"

"You'll always wonder if you could have stuck it out. You'll always wonder if you quit the loser without givin' yourself a fittin' chance. I have a feelin' you've got the backbone to make a go of this country if you'd try."

"I see no reason for you to think that."

"The way you walked right into those three crooked gamblers last night with nothin' but that little peashooter, and them all heeled? I can't say *I'd* have done it."

"It's a hard land. Last night showed me just how hard it can be."

"It's new. It'll settle down with age, like a man does."

"What would I do here? My only salable skill is with the cards. After last night all the flavor has gone from that."

"A world of things'll open up as the country settles. In the meanwhile you might find some kind of business here in Dodge. Or you might even go out on the buffalo range with us. There's worse places to be."

"I shall have to consider, once my head has cleared. At any rate, I'll not take the train today. I must buy something for a young lady."

"You don't know any young ladies here . . . except Arletta." The corners of Jeff's eyes crinkled with a hint of pleasure. "Are you gettin' notions about *her?*"

"Of course not." Smithwick felt his face flush. "I just feel sorry for her in her ignorance. I saw some books yesterday that I thought might help improve her situation."

"Arletta may not read or write very good, but cut her a-loose by herself a hundred miles from town and she'd make it back in good shape. There's a lot of men in Dodge that wouldn't get twenty miles."

"Including myself. I make no claim to be a frontiersman. But if she could combine her present knowledge with that which she could acquire from reading, she could make a place for herself almost anywhere."

"Even in England?"

"My interest in Arletta is purely one of gratitude."

"I'm glad to hear that, because Colonel has an interest in her too. I don't think gratitude has much part in it."

"He is too old for her."

"He's still much of a man, and young women get old pretty fast out here."

Smithwick made it a point to buy the books before he did anything else. The storekeeper seemed surprised, as if he might have accepted less than the dollar and been glad to get it. Smithwick also bought a change of clothes, for those he wore were torn and hopelessly stained. The books and the clothes under his arm, he sought out a barbershop, where he enjoyed the luxury of a hot-lather shave, followed by a slow, soaking bath in a metal tub to remove the sweat and grime of the long train ride, the walk and his association with the hide wagons. The bath drew away some of the accumulated soreness and left him feeling better, though it did not compromise his resolve to be moderate in any future use of Dodge City liquor.

He put on the new clothes and left the old ones to the mercies of the barber, who said he would throw them away but would probably have them washed and mended, then sell them to some transient. He walked back across the tracks to the Browder camping place. To his surprise, a stranger had claimed the site.

The newly arrived buffalo hunter scratched his bearded chin, then scratched beneath his armpit, where a louse was probably making itself known. "Browder? No, I don't know no Browder. Wasn't no wagons here when I come. Ashes was warm, though, and the tracks fresh, like somebody had just up and left. Did he owe you money?"

"No. I owed him."

"Well then, looks like this is your lucky day."

Smithwick turned away, puzzling. Cephus had indicated he was in a hurry to start south, but he had not said he planned to start this very morning. Smithwick saw the empty wagons belonging to Colonel Cregar and walked in that direction.

Jeff and the black man Sully hunkered near a small campfire, sipping coffee, laughing over some joke. Old Elijah Layne, tinkering with harness, was the first to see Smithwick. He hollered a greeting. Smithwick had had no part in supplying British arms to the Confederacy, but Elijah seemed to have given him full credit for it. Jeff pointed to the coffeepot. "Well, English, you clean up pretty good."

Smithwick glanced around uneasily, hoping not to see Colonel Cregar. "I went to deliver these books to Arletta. I found Cephus's wagons already gone."

The humor left Jeff's eyes. "South?"

"I would presume so."

Jeff said something sharp under his breath and stood up. "He must've pulled out while we were still asleep at Cap's." He turned to Sully. "Did you see them?"

"I seen wagons movin', but it weren't full light, and I didn't mark whose they was."

Elijah Layne laid down the harness. "Colonel gave Cephus a mighty strong talkin'-to last evenin'. Said it was too dangerous to be leavin' by himself, that he ought to wait."

Jeff worried, "Colonel's goin' to be mighty upset when he finds out."

The colonel's booming voice demanded, "Find out about what?" Cregar had ridden into camp unnoticed on his big bay horse.

Jeff told him what Smithwick had learned. Cregar's sharp eyes flared with anger. "The fool! The stubborn fool, taking Arletta down into all that danger. I told him not to go until the rest of us are ready."

"I reckon that's the trouble, Colonel, you *told* him. Cephus is an agreeable sort till you start tryin' to tell him what to do. He'll do the opposite just to show you."

Cregar dismounted. His fists were knotted, the veins standing out on the backs of his hands. "At the very least it would take me a couple or three days to get these wagons outfitted and ready to move. And I haven't found my son yet. I can't go off and leave here without him."

Jeff said, "I could saddle Tar Baby and go after Cephus. Like as not I could catch him before sundown."

"And do what? Bring him back at the point of a gun?" Cregar's voice crackled with anger. "No, Jeff, I'll need you to help me get the outfit ready to move. When we *do* start we'll push hard and try to catch up to him before he gets too deeply into Comanche country."

"That could take days. He won't be standin' still." He turned to Smithwick, a challenge in his eyes. "You said yourself, you ain't got anything worthwhile to do. You could go."

Cregar was incredulous. "Smith? He knows nothing of this country. He would be lost before he was three miles out of town."

Smithwick resented Cregar's abrupt dismissal of his competence. Impulsively, without taking counsel of his own doubts, he said, "I'll go."

He saw surprise in Jeff's eyes. He was somewhat surprised himself.

Cregar asked, "What would you do when you got there, *if* you got there?"

"Perhaps I can reason with Cephus, persuade him to wait until you catch up."

"You couldn't persuade the stubborn fool that the sun rises in the east if he chose not to believe it."

"I could try. And if he would not listen, at least he would have one more man and one more rifle until you do catch up."

Cregar scowled at the books under Smithwick's arms. "You look like a man who belongs in a college library, not out in Indian country. Would you know what to do with a rifle if you had it?"

Defensively Smithwick said, "I am no stranger to firearms."

Jeff put in, "Cephus told me English fired his Sharps yesterday. Told me he's a crack shot."

Cregar's face creased deeply as he looked about the camp, trying to make up his mind. "I suppose we could spare Sully to ride with him and make certain he gets there." He turned to the black man. "I wouldn't order you to go."

"You don't have to order me, Colonel. Sure, I'll go."

Smithwick argued, "I see no possibility of my becoming lost. That many wagons should leave a trail my old nanny could follow."

"You'll take Sully, and that's that," Cregar declared, as if he were giving an order to a newly commissioned shavetail lieutenant. Turning to Jeff, he pulled a roll of money from his pocket and peeled off several bills. "Take him to Rath's and get him an outfit. And buy two good fast horses."

Stubbornly Smithwick waved Cregar off. "I have my own money. I'll pay my own bills."

Cregar's eyes crackled with impatience. "You *are* an insubordinate son of a bitch."

"That is why I came to America."

Cregar jerked his head at Jeff. "Go with him anyway, see that he buys what he needs and be back here as soon as you can."

Out of Cregar's hearing, Jeff said, "I didn't really mean for you to volunteer. I figured the notion would upset Colonel so much he'd tell me to go after all."

"You do not know me very well. Sometimes I do not even know myself."

A little more than an hour later Smithwick was watching the black man throw a saddle on a long-legged sorrel horse Jeff had bought from a discouraged buffalo hunter who was selling out to return east. Smithwick had bought a sturdy dun which had a black mane and tail. The hunter had said his name was Dunny, that he could run like an antelope, go without water like a camel and find buffalo like a bloodhound. Smithwick suspected the man might lie about other things too. However, he liked the way the animal handled. Here, as in England, a man could be forgiven some exaggeration about a good horse.

Smithwick had a pistol several times larger than the derringer. He carried a well-used Sharps fifty-caliber carbine. It was shorter and lighter than the one Cephus Browder owned. He had test-fired it before buying and had smashed a jagged hole through a small wooden crate at a range of two hundred yards. Jeff had observed but said nothing. Blankets, fleece-lined coat and a change of clothes made a considerable bundle, tied behind the cantle.

He watched Sully tie a similar roll to his own saddle. Cregar pointedly gave instructions to the black man, but Smithwick suspected they were meant more for his own ears. "See if you can persuade Cephus to camp until we catch up. It could be three or four days, perhaps more. Tell him we'll be on the trail as soon as we can."

"Yes sir, Colonel."

Cregar's gaze went to Smithwick. It was distrustful. "Don't let this Englishman slow you down or lead you astray. Leave him behind if you must. The main thing is to reach Arletta as quickly as possible. And Cephus."

Sully said, "With these good horses and their slow wagons, we ought to be eatin' supper with them tonight."

"You know what to do, so be about it."

Elijah Layne surprised Smithwick a little. He was a Southern man, and Smithwick had assumed that Southern men disliked blacks. But Elijah gripped Sully's arm and said with concern, "You be watchful now, Sully. We wouldn't want nothin' happenin' to you. Or to the Englishman."

Jeff patted the shoulder of Smithwick's dun horse. "Give this country a chance, English. You're liable to like it."

Behind him, Smithwick heard the whistle of a train, one he might be boarding now had pride not crowded him into a rash decision he feared he would come to regret. "It appears that I must, whether or not I want to."

Sully set his horse into a long trot, and Smithwick followed him, south.

Nine

WEDDINGS TENDED to be perfunctory affairs among the Comanche. Despite the profound importance of marriage to the individuals involved and to perpetuation of the tribe, the wedding usually occasioned far less ceremony than, say, the buffalo-hunt dance or the war dance or the scalp dance that followed a successful venture upon the war trail.

Crow Feather was disgruntled about the one for his sister Calling Bird. After his first presentation of horses to her uncle-father, the young Swift Runner sent Man Who Stole the Mules as an emissary to speak for him. Mules took with him one more horse—the best of all—as an additional present to help her uncle-father hasten his decision. Crow Feather had tried to voice his objections to the young man, but the choice of husbands for Calling Bird was not his to make, and in the end his argument counted for nothing. His uncle was delighted with the horses. He was probably gratified as well to see Calling Bird move out of his lodge, for now he had one less mouth to feed. Watching over a girl who had advanced far into puberty and had caught the eyes of many young men was a bothersome responsibility.

After a round of congratulations and some feasting, Swift Runner took her into his tepee; that was about all the ceremony amounted to. Crow Feather suspected she had been to that tepee before, in the dark of night. Furthermore, he suspected she was already with child, for though he could not see that her stomach had begun to swell, he saw something in her eyes that he saw in White Deer's. Crow Feather's *sits-by-me* wife had finally conceived again. He had feared she had gone barren after delivering Little Squirrel.

Crow Feather was not given to lengthy analysis of his feelings, but he sensed that much of his dissatisfaction over Swift Runner grew out of the young man's affiliation with Man Who Stole the Mules. Crow Feather and Mules had been rivals for the band's admiration from the time they were boys, each trying to ride better and launch his arrows straighter than the other. Usually Crow Feather came out ahead. Mules would complain that he had cheated or that chance had intervened in Crow Feather's behalf.

Mules had never admitted that any of his failings, and they were many, had ever been his own fault. He had tried to make up in recklessness what he had lacked in ability. The results had been mixed. The People applauded courage. Recklessness, however, was another matter. It could, and did, get warriors killed without reason.

Crow Feather tried to put aside his concerns over Calling Bird and concentrate upon more important matters. It was time for the final buffalo hunt before the band moved to the winter encampment. Tonight they would perform the buffalo-hunting dance to draw the *coth-cho* up close and invoke the spirits to kindliness toward the hunt. Tomorrow he would lead the hunters out onto the prairie with their bows and lances. He had no concern about finding a herd. Scouts had located them two days ago. They should not have drifted much since because the grass was good and water plentiful. Their hair had grown dense in readiness for winter, and they had packed much fat on their frames to carry them through the moons of snow. It would be a good harvest, for which each man could thank whichever guardian spirits watched over his welfare.

Three Bears's band had not yet retreated to their traditional home farther north. They remained encamped near the band of which old Many Lodges was the nominal camp chief. Crow Feather and the others paid Many Lodges homage for his long record as a warrior and a hunt leader during the years he was in his prime, until arthritis had left him too crippled to go out with war parties or to lead in the hunt anymore. His counsel was requested and respected, though no man had more power than the People were willing to allow him. They pulled together for the common good, but they were individualists first and last.

Three Bears had tried to tell Many Lodges what he had told Crow Feather about the troublesome reports from the north, about the white hunters whose rifles threatened to leave the Cheyenne and others of that region without meat. Many Lodges had questioned him closely and had come to a conclusion that Three Bears had been listening to the wind. The buffalo were too numerous ever to be exhaustible. How ever many grown ones were taken by the People, by the wolves, by age and hard winters, there were always many times more than enough new calves to replace them.

Crow Feather began to feel a little sorry for Three Bears, for he was becoming the butt of jokes around camp. He was a man who listened to the rope-head Kiowas and the superstitious Cheyenne instead of believing what his own eyes could tell him. It was time, some said, for Three Bears to retire to an old man's place at the fire in his tepee, telling idle stories of a long-ago past and whiling away his days making arrows and points and other implements of war for men young enough and brave enough to use them.

Crow Feather was seeing to his arrows, tightly rewrapping with sinew any on which the steel points were showing sign of loosening. These points were better than the ones of flint which he had known as a boy. They were acquired from the Comanchero traders or made by the People themselves from materials they found in their raiding upon the settlements. They had discovered that the metal bands which held the white men's wooden barrels together could be filed into excellent arrowheads.

The air carried a touch of chill, but Crow Feather preferred to sit in front of his lodge. The long winter months ahead would confine him to the inside more than enough. He could watch Little Squirrel and other boys riding ponies out beyond the edge of camp, playing at war. His son was yet too small to take part in some of the more daring stunts, such as training to pick up a fallen comrade from the back of a running horse. Nevertheless, he was already showing signs that he would become a fine rider; he stuck like a grass bur to the pony's bare back. Crow Feather thought trading the grulla horse for that pony had been one of the best things he had done since acquiring his two wives.

White Deer had been to the river for water, which she carried back in a buffalo paunch. Crow Feather paused in his chore to stare at her as she walked. She was still a handsome woman in her own way, even if no longer as shiningly pretty as her younger sister Rabbit. Of the two, she was the thinker, the planner, the one he could depend upon to see that all needful things were properly done. She lacked Rabbit's quickly kindled fire, but he sensed that her emotions ran deeper. In the proper mood—and occasionally she was—she could still love him with as much fervor as she had shown when as a maiden she had first crawled under the rolled-up edge of his bachelor tepee.

"Our son rides well," she observed. He had ridden by her, shouting, as she came up from the river.

"He has the blood of his grandfather," he said, meaning Stands His Ground, father of White Deer and Rabbit.

She smiled. "And his own father." She was not one to speak often in praise of her husband, as did many wives, but when she did he knew it was genuine and not simply the prelude to a request of some kind. She seemed to have a little more glow of late, since she had finally found herself pregnant again.

He said, "Perhaps when the time comes, Little Squirrel can teach his brother."

Her smile widened. "Or his sister." She carried the water into the tepee.

THE HUNTING DANCE that night was not so much a call for the spirits to aid in finding the buffalo as simply an excuse for the People to have a good time. It did not require dressing up, though Man Who Stole the Mules came wearing the buffalo-scalp bonnet he had been awarded after participating in his first raid. He never intended for anyone to forget who and what he was. Crow Feather eschewed such ostentatious display. Everybody here knew him and what his capabilities were. They did not need reminding.

Late in the afternoon some of the young men had built a fire in the center of the camp. They had kept dragging up dry wood since so the man selected as fire tender always had plenty to burn. He built the blaze up to a size whose dancing light fought back the darkness for a considerable distance. Four drums were set up, for four was always a good number to the People, and four more men joined the drummers to help them sing. The men lined up on one side, the women on the other. As the drumming and singing began, it was up to the women to cross over the space between and select a dancing partner. White Deer and Rabbit alternated in choosing Crow Feather, though other women occasionally beat them to him. This was one time the married women were free to do a little harmless flirting, and occasionally one might do more if her husband was too busy to notice her slipping away in the darkness for a bit of variety. Crow Feather suspected some of these women were sizing up the men and offering them some hint of their desirability, looking ahead to the possibility that their husbands might be killed in war or in the hunt. In that event they would need a new husband to take them into his family. Not all marriages were as strong as his to White Deer and Rabbit.

The dance ended early, for the people would need their strength tomorrow if the buffalo harvest was to be successful. White Deer clung to his arm, her silent signal that tonight she wanted him in her blankets, not Rabbit's. He obliged, for such a signal had become a seldom thing. Perhaps in the dark hours of early morning when White Deer was fast asleep he might quietly move to Rabbit's bed, but White Deer had first claim.

The Comanche did not have the strict warrior societies that had developed in many other plains tribes, the dog soldiers who enforced discipline in the hunt. Under most circumstances each man did what he wanted, when he wanted. But in the running of the buffalo most had learned a rigid self-discipline that they did not always carry into other endeavors such as war. The men understood that success or failure of a hunt meant the difference between feast and hunger in their lodges. They worked as a team for the good of all. A man who had the poor judgment to try to get ahead of the rest and thereby scattered the buffalo prematurely might not be subject to overt punishment, but the chill the rest of the band gave him afterward would not soon be forgotten nor ever again invited.

The scouts went out ahead of the main hunting party to see if the buffalo were still where they had been seen before. They were not. The men divided and made a wide circle and came back together without finding anything more than droppings and hoof-churned ground. While part of them followed the tracks, a couple came back to report their lack of success. Crow Feather listened grimly, trying not to see Three Bears's knowing nod. "They were there three days ago," he argued. "How far can they go in three days?"

The two scouts went back out to resume their search, taking a more southerly course that would carry them into the rough breaks where buffalo liked to spend the winter. Not having heard from them by midafternoon, Crow Feather began to fret, though not aloud. He sent a runner back to camp to let the families know there would be no slaughter today, but that it was sure to come tomorrow.

Terrapin Shell, the medicine man, returned with the runner. He rode up onto a small hill, spread his blanket and sat alone, his medicine bundle between his crossed legs. He lighted sacred tobacco in the soapstone bowl of his medicine pipe and blew smoke to the sky, the earth and the four quarters. The wind carried bits of his chant down the slope to the men who waited with Crow Feather. Terrapin Shell was calling up the buffalo.

Three Bears moved in close to Crow Feather. Because he had undergone much ridicule over his notions about the white man killing off the herds, he kept his voice so low that Crow Feather had to strain to hear him. "Already it is happening here."

"We are far south of your white men," Crow Feather declared defensively. "Even if they have killed as many as you say, they are a long way from here. They have not been into our herds."

"But there is strong medicine among the buffalo. Perhaps these have heard what has happened to their brothers to the north and have gone back into the ground for safety. They know the white man is coming."

Another unbelievable story Crow Feather had heard was that the white man had a talking wire which sent messages many suns away in the time it takes a man to blink his eyes. Such a thing was impossible unless the white man had a far stronger medicine than he could imagine. And not even a talking wire would let the buffalo of the north speak to those of the south.

Yet he had to wonder at what Three Bears said. Certainly some powerful medicine must work among the buffalo to direct their seasonal migrations, their ability to know where it had rained and where the grass had greened. There must be spirits which watched over the buffalo just as there were spirits which watched over the People. There were spirits in the wind, in the grass, in the earth and the water. If sometimes these spirits took voice and spoke to men, must they not also speak to the buffalo?

Crow Feather wanted to disbelieve Three Bears. The man had a ragged scar on the side of his head which he said had been made by a stone club in the hand of a horse-stealing Ute. Crow Feather reasoned that Three Bears's mind had healed badly from the blow, as a broken leg sometimes mended crookedly and never again allowed its owner to walk the same. But a nagging doubt plagued him. He had not expected so much trouble in finding the buffalo.

His dark mood lifted late in the afternoon as several of the scouts returned, jubilant. They had located the herd. Something had possessed it to move farther westward than they had searched at first, but it was there, intact. Terrapin Shell came down from the hill, rejoicing in the strength of his medicine.

Crow Feather gave Three Bears a look that fell just a little short of reproach. Three Bears did not respond with the humility Crow Feather expected of a man who had been proven wrong. His face remained solemn while the long-quiet men around him broke into smiles and jubilant talk.

Crow Feather sent most of the men back to camp with the good news. "I will wait here for the rest of the scouts to return." He knew the buffalo-hunting dance would probably be underway again by the time he rode in. After the day's long disappointment, then its great relief, he thought he would be ready for the celebration.

Three Bears hung back, not riding off immediately with the others. The worry still clouded his eyes. "The spirits have smiled on us again today. But I say this, that the white man is still coming."

Ten

JEFF LAYNE watched with misgivings as Smithwick and Sully crossed the Arkansas River, then passed out of sight. "That Englishman talks smooth, but I doubt he can persuade Cephus to wait."

Colonel Cregar brooded. "I'm afraid I have dispatched Sully on a fool's errand. I've half a mind to send you after him and bring him back."

Jeff knew Cregar would not do that. Once he decided upon a course of action, all hell would not cause him to retreat from it, even if he found it to be a mistake. "Dad and me, we'll take the supply wagons down to Rath's and start gettin' them loaded. We'll be ready to move soon as your boy gets here."

Cregar would have preferred to give the order himself, but he accepted Jeff's suggestion. "See that you count everything as it goes onto the wagons. Rath is honest, but I don't trust a hired clerk."

Jeff looked around for Gantry Folsom. Some heavy lifting might be good for Gant's soul, if not his sour constitution. But the man was nowhere in sight. Off loafing in some dramshop below the tracks, Jeff thought, or lying up with some woman not particular about her clientele. "Want to go with me, Dad?" He phrased it as an offer. He would not give his father an order, though technically Elijah worked under him.

"I reckon." Elijah stared southward. "I sure hope nothin' happens to Sully or that Englishman."

"I'd trust Sully to the Pearly Gates. He'll take care of English."

Filling the order, merchant Charles Rath expressed much interest in the Cregar expedition south to the Cimarron and beyond. "Several hunters have already slipped away. I think most are just waiting for someone of Colonel Cregar's caliber to take the lead. Once he leaves, a dozen others will go."

"Cephus Browder has gone. Left this mornin'."

"Not many would follow Cephus, but they'll follow Cregar."

Jeff could only guess how long they might be gone. At the colonel's order, he bought three times more supplies than had been taken on the hunting trip up toward the Pawnee. Whatever might be left over could be resold to other hunters or traded for hides. Pleased, Rath said, "It would appear you intend to be out all winter."

"It's anybody's guess."

Rath mused. "If enough hunters go south, and they find buffalo, it might pay a merchant to establish a supply and hide-buying station down that way."

"Somebody like Charlie Rath?"

"Perhaps, with a partner or two to spread the risk. I'll keep an ear to the ground."

While Jeff was buying supplies, Cregar purchased several more wagons and teams from disgruntled hunters eager to brush the Dodge City dust from their boots. He hired drivers and skinners to go with them, men more afraid of going hungry than of facing whatever hostile Indians might await them beyond the Cimarron. When Jeff returned to camp with the supply wagons, he found one of the skinners trying to stir up a meal. He said to Cregar, "I know Kid left on the mornin' train, but where's *your* cook?"

The colonel said grittily, "He caught the same train, damn him. If he had been one of my soldiers I might have had him shot for cowardice."

"We can't leave here without a new belly-robber."

"I'll leave it to you to find one."

Late in the afternoon Jeff had a haircut and a bath in a barbershop north of the tracks and put on a clean suit of clothes he had left in the care of the washerwoman wife of an Irish bartender. He bought a bottle of good Kentucky whiskey and crossed back over the tracks to a shack he knew. He paused at the front step, listening for conversation inside. Hearing none, he rapped his knuckles against the door. Footsteps made the floor creak, for the small structure had been built of green lumber that had soon shrunk and warped. The door opened a few inches slowly and tentatively. He saw a woman's curly black hair, and a pair of brown eyes giving him careful scrutiny before she opened the door wide.

"Howdy, Charity."

The voice sparkled with welcome. "Jeff Layne, I heard you got into town yesterday. I kept looking for you last night."

"I was busy."

"So I heard. They had a burying on the hill this morning. That Colonel Cregar doesn't realize how heavy a gun barrel can be, laid up against a man's head."

"Wasn't much of a man that he hit. You lookin' for any company?"

"Just you. Figured you'd show up sooner or later." She took the bottle from under his arm and stepped aside. "Come on in and make yourself at home."

Charity was a slender woman, not as pretty as some he had known but of a good, even disposition and without many false pretenses. Her speaking voice fell on his ears like music. He would enjoy listening to her even if she spoke in French or some other foreign language of which he understood not a word. She used the language as if she had received some education, certainly more than *he* had. He was not good at guessing women's ages but supposed she was a year or two one side or the other of thirty. She was young enough to be interesting and old enough to know how to give a man about all the pleasure he could enjoy at one time without her seeming to do it just for the money.

She held the bottle up to read the label. "You paid right well for this." She reached into a small cabinet and brought out a couple of glasses. While she filled them, he seated himself on a narrow couch and glanced around the room. It was typical of such cribs. There was not much to see: a dresser with a narrow, cracked mirror; a small cookstove, its chimney vented out the back wall; a woodbox;

a few shelves that held a meager supply of groceries; a large
wooden trunk with steel straps that held most of her clothes; a
small high-backed tin bathtub, for she bathed every day, unlike
some of her sisters in the trade. Against the wall stood a narrow
bed with a patchwork quilt spread across it. The only things fancy
in the room were lace curtains on the two small windows and a set
of brass bedsteads. He stared at the bed, anticipating.

Charity smiled. "There's time enough. Let's not rush through a
good thing." She handed him the jigger of whiskey and raised her
own in a toast. "To better times and better places."

"I reckon we've seen both."

He had no faith that better times awaited Charity. She had been
in the business too long to put it behind her easily, yet she was
approaching an age when she must either leave it or accept a
poorer, meaner clientele and a steadily diminishing standard of
living. He had no idea where she had come from and would not ask
her. Something she had said once led him to believe she had been
married and either widowed or abandoned. He feared she might
end up fat and old before her time, drowning herself in whiskey,
perhaps ending her misery with a heavy dose of laudanum or a gun.
He did not like to dwell on such negative probabilities. He preferred to think she might yet find a good marriage with some
hunter or railroad man, or perhaps a merchant who could see a
loving woman behind the powder and rouge and bold talk.

Seating herself close beside him, she asked, "Are you in any
hurry to go, Jeff?"

"I figured on spendin' the night. Your bed's a lot softer than
mine."

She had a nice, even set of white teeth. They weren't streaked
and stained from drinking gyppy water, like some he had seen.
"Take a girl to supper?"

"I'd figured on it." He couldn't take her to one of the better
places north of the tracks. Proprietors there tended to be narrow-
minded about the company their customers kept. "How about Cap
Doolittle's?"

"Fine. Cap cooks better than I do." She put an arm around his
shoulder and let him savor a strong whiff of perfume.

They finished the drink and had another. He felt a pleasant

warmth and knew the whiskey was not solely responsible. They set the glasses aside and turned their full attention to one another. She seemed as eager as he did, though he knew when dawn came she would count the money with care.

SHE LAY on her side, playfully writing his name with her finger in the sweat on his bare chest. He caught his breath and enjoyed a cool breeze from the window she had propped open with a stick. After a bit she asked, "Who is she, Jeff?"

"Who?"

"If I knew who, I wouldn't have to ask you. I always have the idea when you're with me that you're thinking of somebody else. There must be a girl back in Texas that I remind you of."

He had heard of woman's intuition. He shifted, uncomfortable that she had touched close to the truth. "There used to be somebody, but you don't look anything like her. You're about as different as a woman could be."

"So you come to me because you think I *won't* remind you of her, but of course I do. She must have hurt you."

"When I went to war she said she'd wait forever, but forever was damned short. She married an old boy too rich to go fight. That's been a long time ago, and the scar has healed."

"You still think about her, though."

"I try not to."

She bent over him, almost smothering him. "For now, then, just think about *me.*"

CAP DOOLITTLE didn't have much business. Jeff wondered how he managed to pay for this place he rented from a saloon-keeper next door. A makeshift cotton apron tied around his middle, Cap turned away from the iron stove as Jeff and Charity entered the cafe. "Come in, folks, and set yourselves down. I'll be with you quick's I get the bread out of the oven. Ain't no meal fit to eat without there's fresh biscuits to go with it."

Jeff did not know a lot about etiquette, but he pulled a chair away from a table and offered it to Charity, sliding it beneath her as she sat down. She smiled in appreciation. Despite her questionable status in the community, she had standards. She expected her customers to come to her bathed and shaven, and she expected them to treat her with at least an outward show of the respect they would give their own womenfolk wherever they had come from. Cap had lighted a lamp against the dusk, and its glow gave Charity's face a pleasant orange hue. She placed her hand atop Jeff's on the table. Her eyes told him it was not all business with her.

Cap took the biscuits out of the oven, burning his hand and cursing with a South Texas mixture of Spanish and English epithets which seemed to possess healing powers. He came to the table, sucking at the burn on his hand. "What can I fix for you folks?"

"What've you got?"

"Beefsteak. Been no fresh buffalo meat come in. You probably had enough of it to gag a dog anyhow."

"Beefsteak, then. Nothin's too good for Charity."

"Hell, I know that." Cap returned to his stove and set up a clatter with his skillets. Jeff squeezed Charity's hand. Tomorrow she might be sitting in this place or another like it with someone else, but he wouldn't think about that. He looked into her brown eyes and enjoyed what was now.

Cap brought their supper after a time and pulled out a chair, straddling it with his considerable bulk, folding his heavy arms across its back while he watched them eat. "Ain't too bad cookin' for an old South Texas cowboy, is it?"

"Too good to be wasted in Dodge City, no more trade than you've got here. How'd you like to cook for a buffalo-huntin' crew?"

Cap's eyes widened with pleasure, then narrowed as second thoughts came to him. "There's been a lot of huntin' goin' on, but not much shootin'."

"We're goin' south, Cap. Probably all the way down into Texas."

"Texas." Cap spoke the word as he might say *Mother*. "But you can't go back to Texas."

"We won't be goin' down where the settlements are, or the carpetbaggers. We'll be up on the high plains where the only law belongs to the Comanches and the Kiowas. They've got no courts and no jails."

"Just scalp poles." But enthusiasm kindled in Cap's eyes. "How soon we . . . you gettin' started?"

"Maybe tomorrow, maybe next day. Depends on whenever Colonel finds his son."

Charity was intrigued. "Colonel Cregar's lost a son? I'm surprised he ever had one. I can't see a woman putting up with that martinet long enough for him to plant the seed."

Jeff explained that the son had been living with family back east. "He was expected to be in Dodge several days ago, but Colonel can't find a trace of him."

Charity stopped a fork halfway to her mouth and laid it back on the plate, her face furrowed. "Maybe . . . just maybe . . ." Her brown eyes lost their laughter. "I've heard something. Might be Cregar's son and it might not."

Jeff leaned across the table toward her. "Tell me."

"There's a girl, kind of new in town, came out from St. Louis with a mean-eyed gent who pimps for her. She's got a crib out close to the river. I heard she's got her painted fingernails dug deep into some young idiot from back east who showed up on the train a few days ago with more money in his pocket than was good for him. She's kept him dead drunk and laying up with her ever since."

Jeff argued, "If his money's all she's after, she could've taken it right away and drowned him in the river."

"She's not above that, from what I hear. Maybe she figures he can get more money wherever that came from, so she keeps him drunk and happy. Word is that his daddy is well fixed."

Jeff's eyes met Cap's, then cut back to Charity. "You hear a name, by chance?"

"No name. I've already told you all I know, and maybe more."

"Could you show me where that crib is at?"

Worry came into her eyes. "They say her pimp is awful handy with a knife."

Cap declared, "We'll shoot him before he ever gets close enough to use it."

Jeff resumed eating. He was unwilling to let this situation cheat him out of a rare chance to enjoy steak and gravy. "We won't shoot anybody without we need to. If we need to, then we'll kill him."

Charity pushed her plate away. "How can you talk about killing and keep on eating?"

Jeff replied, "They're two different things. We don't mix one up with the other." He thought of the Englishman Smithwick. His reaction would probably be like Charity's. If he stayed in this country long enough, he would learn.

Cap's only other customer left before Jeff was finished, so Cap blew out the lamp and locked the door as he went out with Jeff and Charity. He had strapped a pistol belt around his broad hips, beneath his round belly. He had dug another pistol out of a canvas war bag stored beneath his steel cot and lent it to Jeff, who had seen no need to carry one to Charity's.

Charity had her doubts. "You say you never saw Cregar's son. How will you know if this is him?"

"We'll just ask. Politely."

"And if nobody tells you?"

"Then I'll forget my manners. Cap never had any to speak of."

The night was dark. They picked their way with some care along a crooked trace that was more wagon trail than street. Charity stumbled and would have fallen had Jeff not held her arm. Her heels were made for style, not for walking on rough ground. They passed a couple of cribs before she pointed. "That one yonder, closest to the river."

Jeff squeezed her hand. "You'd better go back now so nobody'll know you were the one told us. You've got to keep on livin' here."

"Be careful, Jeff. You're worth more than Cregar and his son put together."

He was touched by the concern in her voice. She was an honest woman, after her fashion, more honest than the one he had figured on marrying back in Texas. He drew a roll of bills from his pocket. It was too dark to count them, so he probably gave her twice what she would have expected. "I'll be over later, if I can. If I can't, you take good care of yourself." He leaned down to kiss her and was surprised at the fervor with which she embraced him. She turned away quickly and was lost in the night.

Cap remarked, "She's a cut above the average."

"I always thought so." Jeff turned toward the river.

"How we fixin' to go about this?"

"The only way I know: straight on."

Jeff could see only the dark outline of the small shack, for clouds had covered the moon and stars. The front had no window, and lamplight was too dim through curtains on a side window to afford much help. He was within ten feet before he saw a man sitting in a chair just outside the door. The man said, "You'll have to come some other time, gents. The lady's got company."

Jeff's hand eased to the borrowed pistol in his waistband. "We've come lookin' for a feller named Cregar. Would he be the company she's got?"

"It's nobody's business who her company is. You gents move on before you get in trouble." The man stood up, his hand coming forward with a long-bladed knife. As he took a step toward Jeff and Cap, Jeff drew the pistol and swung it, striking hard against the knife hand. The man shouted in pain. Jeff swung again, laying the barrel with considerable force against the man's head. The pimp fell heavily. Jeff retrieved the knife and hurled it out into the darkness. He felt the man's pockets but found no other weapon.

Cap's voice was critical. "Colonel Cregar would've hit him a right smart harder."

"You're bloodthirsty." Jeff grasped the knob, pushed the door wide open and quickly stepped inside. In the dim light of a smoking lamp he saw a young woman slumped drunkenly in a chair, holding a half-empty whiskey glass tilted dangerously near to spilling. She blinked in confusion at Jeff and Cap. "Who are you? Didn't Andre tell you I got company?"

Her company lay on the bed, eyes shut, clothes soiled and disheveled. He had several days' growth of whiskers. His unbuttoned shirt was stained where he had thrown up on it. His trousers were unbuttoned, and he had one sock on, one off.

Jeff wrinkled his face in disgust. "My God, this place smells like a buffalo-killin' ground a week after. Open that window, Cap."

The young man was about Colonel's size, but if he bore any other resemblance, Jeff could not see it through the whiskers and the mess on his face. He demanded of the woman, "Is this Farrell Cregar?"

She tried to push herself up from the chair but slumped back. "Where's Andre? You done somethin' to Andre?"

Jeff shook the young man's shoulder, trying to awaken him. "Are you Farrell Cregar?"

All he heard was a groan. The man was in a drunken stupor and showed no sign that he might come out of it.

"Cap, we won't find out anything from these folks. You better go fetch the colonel."

"If this *is* his son, he ain't goin' to want to claim him."

"I wouldn't, but I'm not Colonel."

When Cap left, Jeff dragged the fallen pimp inside so he could keep an eye on him. If he showed any sign of fight, Jeff would tap him again with the six-shooter. He found a bottle of whiskey and poured the woman's glass full. "Drink up. It'll keep you out of trouble."

She mumbled incoherently but did as he told her.

He poured water from a pitcher into a basin and roughly set about washing the young man's filthy face. The youth brought up his hands and fought at the cold, wet rag. "Wake up and talk to me," Jeff said. "Are you Farrell Cregar?"

He received a drunken cursing but no answer to his question. Jeff found a suitcase and a clean shirt but no identification. He pulled the soiled shirt from the young man and tried putting the clean one on him but gave up after fighting the threshing fists. The underwear reeked anyway. "To hell with you. Wallow in your own vomit for all I give a damn. I hope you're *not* Farrell Cregar."

Andre began to stir. As he opened his eyes, Jeff made sure that the first thing he saw was the muzzle of the pistol, six inches from his nose. "You just lay there and act dead. I've had a bellyful of this whole damned outfit."

After a time he heard voices. For precaution he trained the pistol on the door but put it away when he heard Cregar's voice. "Jeff, are you in there?"

"Come on in, Colonel. It's all right."

He caught the disgust in Cregar's eyes as the big man strode through the open doorway. "I don't know if that's your boy or not."

Cregar took three long strides and grasped the young man by both broad shoulders, shaking him violently. "Farrell, wake up! This is your father."

The young man's eyes came half open but did not seem to focus. He mumbled a few curse words. The colonel shook him again and received the same resentful response. He stepped back, grabbed the water pitcher and poured its contents over his son's head. Young Cregar came up coughing and fighting.

The woman tried again to arise but could not. Weakly she demanded, "What you doin'? You leave my Farrell alone."

Cregar's voice was that of an officer chastising his troops. "Farrell, get hold of yourself. You're getting up from here and coming with me."

Farrell Cregar finally began to sober enough to realize who was standing in front of him. He blinked uncertainly. "Father?"

"Yes, I'm your father, but you don't look much like my son. I've never been so ashamed in my life."

Blinking hard, Farrell became aware of the girl slumped in her chair and the pimp lying on the floor, a blue welt rising on the side of his head. "What've you done to my friends?"

"Friends?" The colonel exploded. "You're not only drunk, you're a fool. These people were out to get everything they could and then murder you, more likely than not." He glanced back at Jeff. "Let's get him out of here."

Farrell swung himself to the edge of the bed and protested, "They're better friends than you've ever been a father. I'm not going!"

The colonel's huge fist came up swiftly and hard. Farrell's head snapped back, and he fell heavily on the bed. The colonel picked him up and hoisted him over his shoulder like a sack of horse feed. "Let's get away from this pesthole!"

Eleven

NIGEL SMITHWICK found that Sully watched him with quiet amusement as they moved south, beyond sight of the sprawling village that was Dodge City. "Am I doing something wrong?" he asked.

"I don't reckon, sir. It's just the way you got of raisin' up and lowerin' down every time that dun horse trots a step. Ain't seen many people do it thataway outside of soldiers."

"It's called posting."

"Looks to me like you'd get almighty tired and just want to set easy." Sully's rump remained firmly in the saddle, as had been the case with most other horsebackers Smithwick had seen of late, including Jeff Layne.

Cephus Browder's wagons had left an easy trail, their iron tires crushing the fall-curing grass to the ground. Much of it did not arise again in their wake. South of the Arkansas lay open grassland, mostly gently rolling hills that reminded him of the rise and fall of the sea. They were broken now and again by rough watercourses lined narrowly with timber. Smithwick could see for miles. He kept wanting to push harder, but Sully held his mount to a steady trot. "No use killin' the horses. We'll be fetchin' up to the wagons before the sun goes to bed."

As Dodge City fell farther and farther behind them, Sully watched the horizon, turning often to look back over his shoulder. He asked, "How's your eyes, Mr. English?"

"I've had no reason to complain."

"We've got into a country where you better use them all the time. Minute we crossed over the Arkansas, we put ourselves onto Indian treaty lands."

"We would hardly be the first, would we?"

"Already been considerable huntin' done between the Arkansas and the Cimarron, and some even further. Most folks feel like a treaty's just for Indians to keep. White man don't pay it no mind if he don't want to, and lately he don't want to."

"So if the Indians were to attack us now, they would be within their rights?"

"I reckon, if it was up to a court. But the Indians ain't got no lawyers, and there ain't no court'll take up for them."

"I have the impression that virtually all of the buffalo hunting has been in violation of one treaty or another."

"White man only gives the Indian what he don't want for himself. If he changes his mind later on, he just takes it back. Always been thataway. Ain't likely to change."

"That makes you an accomplice of sorts, does it not?"

"I was a slave a lot longer than I been free. Ain't often anybody asks me what I think, and when they do they just want me to agree with them. So I do my work and stay quiet."

The concept of slavery was almost beyond Smithwick's comprehension, one man owning another, dictating every facet of his life. On reflection, however, he realized that the hired people who worked for the Smithwick family had few more choices in their own lives. They were eternally fearful lest they do or say something to jeopardize their jobs and the wages vital to livelihood. Rarely were they asked to express an opinion on matters of importance, and even more rarely were those opinions given weight. To those who hired them, they were virtually invisible except in terms of their work.

Sully rode in silence for a while, then unexpectedly laughed aloud. Smithwick asked him what was funny.

"I was just rememberin' how surprised Mr. Gant Folsom looked when you put him on the ground. I'd still like to know how you popped him so slick."

"Perhaps I could show you something about boxing."

"Wouldn't do me no good. I couldn't afford to go hittin' a white man, no matter what he done to me."

"Not even Folsom?"

"Mr. Gant's like a louse in the seam of my shirt. I can't scratch him away, so I just put up with the itch. Sooner or later he'll turn up gone."

There could scarcely have been more contrast in their backgrounds, but Smithwick found himself liking this lanky, easy-smiling man who by tradition was supposed to be his inferior. Smithwick had always been quick to make judgments, and he had found that many were just as quick to judge him adversely by his speech or his appearance. Yet Sully seemed to accept him as he was, without judgment and without burdensome expectations. It began to trouble Smithwick's conscience, measuring himself against Sully in the matter of tolerance and coming up short.

He found himself short also in the matter of forward planning when the sun told him it was noon and his stomach told him it was time to eat. He had brought nothing with him. Prairie chickens flew up in front of him, and he raised the carbine.

Sully said, "What you need is a shotgun. That Fifty'd blow a bird all to pieces. Anyway, a shot might fetch people we don't want fetched." He reached into a canvas bag tied behind him. "I got a little grub—some cold biscuits, a little meat left from breakfast. Hope it don't taste too much like horse sweat."

It did, a little, but recent days had made Smithwick more liberal about such shortcomings.

Sully said apologetically, "It ain't like woman's cookin'. You got a woman over in England?"

"If I had, I'd not be here. What about you?"

"Had one once, back in slave times. Old master put me and a young woman together and told us in nine months he expected to see an increase in his property. Wasn't no minister had us say words, or nothin' like that. Old missus was a God-fearin' woman and said it wasn't proper. But old master said you didn't marry a stud horse and a mare. That's about all he thought we was."

"Was there a baby?"

"She birthed a boy. Had the biggest eyes I ever seen in a young'un."

"What became of your family?"

Sully shrugged. "Old missus died, and old master taken the woman into his house to do for him. Sold me down the river." He dropped into silent melancholy for a moment. "Colonel taken me down there after the war to hunt around, but old master was dead and buried and his house burnt down. Wasn't nobody knowed about my woman and the boy. They may be livin', and they may be dead. I reckon I'll see them someday when the Lord calls me home." He looked at the ground, so Smithwick could not see his eyes.

Smithwick had heard of such things but had given them little thought. Looking at this man who had lived through them, he felt his throat tighten. "I am sorry."

"That was all a long time ago. A man learns to live with what is, and not what used to be."

As the afternoon wore on, Smithwick began to wonder if they would catch up to the wagons before nightfall. He was not comfortable with the idea of two men making camp in the midst of a wild country where Indians could ride over the next hill at any moment. But Sully betrayed no misgivings. "Them horse doin's, they're gettin' fresher all the time. If we work it just right, they'll have camp made and supper fixin' before we get there. We won't have to cut wood nor fetch water."

Just at dusk the wagon tracks led them down toward a creek bottom where firelight flickered amid a stand of trees whose leaves were beginning to turn from green to autumn yellow and brown. No one stepped out into the open to meet them, but Smithwick had a disquieting feeling that they were being watched over the sights of rifle barrels.

"Hello the camp!" Sully shouted as soon as they were within hollering distance. To Smithwick he said, "It's always a good idea to let them know you're comin' in friendly. There's some nervous folks'd blow a hole through you."

Not until they were within thirty yards of the camp did Cephus Browder show himself. The bestubbled one-time farmer limped heavily to the edge of the trees and waved the horsemen in. "Light and hitch and get yourselves ready to eat supper." Smithwick saw relief in the man's blue eyes as Cephus shook hands with him first, then with Sully. Recognition had been difficult in the fading light. Cephus said, "We was afraid you was soldiers, sent to fetch us back."

"Could two soldiers have done that?"

"I've always been a law-abidin' man, at least when the law was watchin'. What brings you out so far, English? I thought you was fixin' to go back where you come from."

"Not yet awhile. We came on behalf of Colonel Cregar."

Cephus squinted one eye. "I suspected that soon's I recognized Sully. And I can guess what the colonel wants."

Smithwick looked beyond Cephus, trying to see Arletta. "He wants you to camp and wait until he can catch up with you. He thinks you take too great a risk traveling with such a small company."

Cephus snorted. "Biggest risk he sees is that I'll get to the buffalo ahead of him. If I let him catch up to me with that big outfit he's got, I'll be suckin' the hind tit again. That's how come I slipped out of town on the quiet, before the huntin' is all spoiled, don't you see?"

"I see your point, but I also understand Cregar's."

"Well, you can go back tomorrow and tell him to just worry about himself. Who knows? Time we get done with this hunt I may be as rich as he is."

"Some of the most miserable people I ever knew were rich."

"Let me get rich enough, and I can afford a little misery."

Cephus led them into camp. Smithwick spoke to men whose acquaintance he had made on the wagon journey in to Dodge City, like the skinners Barney Gibson and Herman Scholtz. Cephus introduced him to a few new men hired to go with the extra wagons he had bought. Smithwick kept looking past the men until he saw Arletta's smile. It seemed to light the camp.

She extended her hand like a man. "You're the last person I expected to see, Nigel. I thought you'd be halfway home."

"Missed the train."

"We heard about you gettin' your money back, and about that gambler."

He did not relish the memory. "I would not have wanted it at such a price."

"Wasn't you that hit him, it was the colonel, and lucky for you. Did I hear you say that he sent you out here?"

"That is not entirely the case. I volunteered. I found something in town that I thought you might like, and I wanted to deliver it." He dug the three books from his saddlebag.

Her eyes flashed with pleasure over the gift, but she made the mistake of opening *Oliver Twist* first. Her forehead creased. "I couldn't read this if I had all year to do it in."

"You can, once you've mastered the other two."

She gave those a perfunctory examination, running her finger along the lines on a page of the speller. "I know some of the words, but how will I learn the rest?"

"You can teach yourself."

"How can I teach myself somethin' that I don't know?"

"By the sounds of the letters. Perhaps I can give you a start, and you can carry on from there."

"You goin' to stay with us that long?"

He did not know the answer. He had taken this mission on impulse, reacting to Jeff and Colonel. He had not yet formulated any definite plan. "I suppose it depends upon what your father does, and Colonel Cregar."

"Don't you be in a hurry to leave us, Nigel. I've got a right smart of learnin' to do."

That, he thought, was as true a statement as he had heard.

Arletta reluctantly placed the books in the wagon and returned to her work at the cook fire. Her helper, a peg-legged man hired in Dodge City, stirred venison sizzling in a Dutch-oven bath of bubbling grease. The carcass of a freshly killed deer hung from a nearby limb. Arletta's gaze kept returning to the wagon. "What's that big book about, that *Oliver* whoever-he-was?"

"Oliver Twist. He was a poor boy in England who went through many adventures before he found his true place."

"I reckon there's a lot of people lookin' for their true place. You ain't found yours yet, have you, Nigel?"

He shrugged. "Perhaps there *is* no such place for me. I always seemed to be a misfit . . . at home . . . here . . . Nor does this seem the right place for you either. You should have a proper roof over your head, a home where you need never worry."

"Mrs. Thomason's got all those things in Dodge, but she still worries. She thinks about maybe losin' it all, about business goin' bad, about somebody killin' her husband for the money he carries. Out here the air is fresh and clean. I've got a tent of a night to keep me dry. And I'm with Papa."

"You can't live this way forever."

"Papa says this is our last trip. Anyway, I'll enjoy what I've got and not make myself miserable wantin' somethin' else. I'll trust in Providence to take care of me."

Providence might, Smithwick thought, but not Cephus Browder, nor the men she was likely to meet out here on the buffalo range.

The night carried a chill, so the men clustered around a fire of their own to eat their supper, away from the one Arletta cooked over. Arletta ate hurriedly, then seated herself on a short three-legged stool near the wagon, beneath a lantern. She read from the speller Smithwick had brought her, running a finger slowly along the lines, her lips moving silently as she negotiated the words one by one.

Cephus watched her with misgivings. "I almost wish you hadn't brought her them books. First time the men come in and there ain't no meal ready, I'll have me a bunch of unhappy skinners."

"Surely you would not deny her some small pleasure in life."

"Not if it don't get in the way of what's important."

"Being able to read is important."

"It might tell her about things she'd be better off not knowin', and set her to wishin' for things she can't have."

"What do you want her to have?"

"More'n I been able to give her so far, more'n I ever gave her mother. That's one reason I'm anxious to make this the best hunt I've ever had. I want to get enough money to buy back the farm in Ohio where we come from. I want to give her a home. I want to find her some good young feller that can work the land, that can provide for her and give her young'uns and make her happy. Ain't nothin' the matter with all that, is there?"

"It is an admirable ambition. But I agree with Colonel Cregar that you're taking too great a risk for it. If the hunting is as good as you seem to believe, a few days should make no difference."

"You ain't ever seen how a bunch of hunters shootin' in every direction can scatter buffalo, get them all skittish and hard to hold for a stand. Soon as Colonel leaves Dodge with his wagons, there'll be a dozen other outfits follerin'. No sir, I want to get there first and stake me out a good huntin' ground."

"I understand the Comanches have already staked it out."

"Ain't nobody owns the buffalo. They're God's gift to whoever goes out and takes them. If it ain't me it'll be others. I intend for it to be me."

"Do you believe the Indians will stand idly by?"

"Indians ain't keen on jumpin' an outfit this size, too many guns. And even if they did, there's enough of us to fight them off. Indians know how far these buffalo rifles can shoot."

"But you scatter while you hunt. And how many men guard the camp while the rest are out? Enough to protect Arletta?"

"Arletta's a good shot with a rifle. I'd have her doin' some of the shootin' for me if I didn't need her worse in camp." Cephus poked a stick into the fire, causing a stack of glowing timbers to collapse in a shower of sparks. "So you can ride back and tell Colonel that I appreciate him worryin' about us, but I'm goin' on."

Smithwick did not dwell long on disappointment; this outcome was no surprise. Nor was he surprised at his own quick decision. He watched Arletta. Nothing about her looked the same as that other girl, back home, but she made Smithwick remember just the same. "I may not go back. In Dodge you asked if I would come south with you. I am offering you my services if you still want them."

A smile broke across Cephus's whiskered face. "This country we're goin' to won't look much like England."

"I came to find out what the West is like. I almost gave it up after my first experience, but I have decided to allow it a second chance."

Cephus grasped his hand with the strength of a blacksmith. "Then join us, and welcome."

Long after the men had spread their blankets on the ground and gone to bed, except for one standing guard, Smithwick could see the dim glow of lantern light through the canvas of Arletta's tent, and the shadow of the girl sitting on a stool, the book in her hands.

He closed his eyes, but he was a long time in going to sleep. Old memories kept stirring. The girl's name had been Gwyneth. He had been barely twenty, she but sixteen, the daughter of a poor farmer who worked land for a neighboring estate. Like Arletta, she had little education, and her manner was as plain as her speech. But her hair had been light, her complexion fair, and she had seemed to glow in the gold of the fading sun the first time he saw her, driving cows home from the meadow for milking. He had tried to speak as she walked barefoot past him, but the words stuck in his throat. He could only warm himself in her smile.

He had found business on the meadow and in the fields often after that, until the fathers found out, his and hers. It was an impossible situation, Lionel Smithwick had declared, a thing not done. A Smithwick should remember who he was and not dally with a woman beneath his station. He could still hear his father's voice: "If you care nothing for your position, give some consideration to hers. She would soon be miserable, out of her class. There are those who would snub her or laugh at her. You think you are in love, but how long can love live in such a hopeless situation?"

In the defiant fire of youth Nigel would have faced parental condemnation and disinheritance to have married her, but the elders thwarted him. Though their meetings had been innocent, her father had feared the worst and quickly married her off against her will to a hulking lout who put her into the drudgery of a tenant farm and promptly got her with child. The last time Smithwick had seen her, the glow that had brought him joy was gone. In its place was a hopeless resignation. She was a flower that had bloomed but a moment in the springtime sun, then dried and withered away.

SULLY STOOD beside Smithwick in dawn's chill, his shoulders hunched against the autumn cold that found its way through the holes and patches in an ancient woolen coat he might have worn since slavery days. They watched the Browder outfit loading wagons, breaking camp. "I'll tell Colonel you done your best to talk Mr. Cephus into waitin'."

"Perhaps Cephus is right. Perhaps this party *is* large enough to dissuade any Indian attack."

"I wouldn't want to be bettin' this poor old scalp of mine on it. That's what Mr. Cephus is doin' with his, and with Miss Arletta's."

"You tell the colonel to hurry along. If I can persuade Cephus to slow down, I'll do so."

"I'm afraid you'd have to bust half of his wheels to do that." Sully had already said his goodbyes to Cephus and Arletta. He clenched Smithwick's cold hand. "Lord willin', we'll see one another in a few days, Mr. English." He mounted and set off northward, alone.

Smithwick watched as long as the black man was in sight, feeling a vague sense of abandonment. For a moment he regretted his rashness in volunteering for this mission. What in the bloody hell was he doing here? He should be on a train going east instead of embarked on what might prove to be a fool's errand, intruding into business that was none of his own.

He heard the shouting of the teamsters, the jingle of trace chains, the whistling of a young man driving the loose horses and mules brought along to replace any lost or crippled. Turning, he saw the wagons begin pulling away from the creek, struggling southward up a challenging grade, iron rims cutting a new trail where there had been none. Small clouds of condensation hovered about the animals as they breathed heavily of the chilled morning air. He heard a squeal of protest from a mule and the crack of a whip that responded to the complaint.

He heard Arletta's voice as she swung her team about and pulled her cook wagon into the loose formation. Behind her, the peg-legged man brought up the rear with a wagonload of camp equipment. Watching her, Smithwick put his doubts away, for he knew why he was here. He shoved his foot into the stirrup and swung upon the tall dun horse that fidgeted to join the procession. He looked northward one more time but no longer saw Sully. He turned his gaze southward and put his horse across the shallow creek, its water muddied by hooves and wheels that had preceded him. He fell in with the wagons.

He had been told that many hide outfits used oxen, sometimes as many as eight or nine spans to pull three heavily laden wagons in tandem. Cephus preferred horses and mules because they moved faster, though they were much more of a temptation to Indians than the plodding oxen would be. A stolen horse or mule was regarded as a prize to be sought at whatever risk, while an ox's only purpose to an Indian was for beef, poor meat compared to the wild, sweet, juicy flavor of the buffalo.

The early-morning cold surrendered to the warming sun. Smithwick unbuttoned the new fleece-lined coat he had bought in Dodge. This was a time of year he had always regarded with some ambivalence, a time when whatever gods were responsible for the weather seemed reluctant to bid goodbye to summer even as they embraced the first frosts of winter. Back home the gray, brooding autumn rains would probably have brought the land to a sodden mess by now. Here the sky was clear, the prairie dry, the tall grass curing to serve as standing hay for winter's grazing.

Arletta's team obediently followed the tracks left by the wagons ahead, and Arletta sat on the wagon seat, one of the books in her lap. She looked up from its pages as Smithwick pulled his dun horse in beside the front wheels. "Been through this thing three times, Nigel. I can figure out a lot of the words, goin' by the sounds like you said. But they don't always make sense. Take this one right here." She pointed to the page, but he was too far away to read it. "L-I-G-H-T. There's a picture of a lamp alongside it, so it must mean *light*. But there's a *G* in it, and an *H*. When you say it, you don't speak neither of them right out. Looks to me like it ought to be spelled L-I-T."

"That's simply the way it has always been done," he said somewhat defensively, hard put to come up with an answer to a question he himself had asked in early school days.

"Looks to me like it'd make more sense if they spelled everything just like it sounds. And take *to*. There's three ways in here to spell it. They all sound alike, so why don't they spell them the same way?"

"I haven't the foggiest idea. It's just the rules."

"The rules are wrong, if you ask me." She smiled, closing the book. "You look pretty good on that dun horse, like you'd been in this country all your life."

He was not sure she had paid him a compliment, inferring that he looked like all the other buffalo hunters and assorted frontiersmen he had encountered in recent days.

She went on, "A body wouldn't know the difference if you didn't talk. Minute you open your mouth, though . . ."

"To alter that would require far more than a change of clothing." He warmed to her good humor. "Perhaps after dinner tonight I can go through the speller with you and help you study those words you do not know."

"I'd admire to do that, Nigel." She looked up sharply, her attention caught by movement farther up the line of wagons. "Papa is motionin' at us. I think he wants you up yonder."

Cephus was too far away for Smithwick to hear him over the creaking of wheels, jingling of chains and plodding of hooves, but he was waving his floppy old hat over his head. "I'll see you in a while." Smithwick pushed the dun horse into a long trot toward Cephus, near the head of the column. The farmer was slow and awkward afoot, a result of his feet having frozen last winter. But on horseback he was the equal of the youngest man in camp.

Cephus said, "There's some rough-lookin' breaks ahead yonder. I was fixin' to scout them out and see how's the best way to take the wagons through. Also need to be sure there ain't no Indians waitin' to do us mischief. I could use your good eyes if you'd be of a mind to go with me."

"Let us be about it, then." It surprised Smithwick that he felt little apprehension. Somehow these rolling prairies had lost much of their early strangeness and threat. They had taken on a certain familiarity since his frightening experience of being afoot and defenseless beside the railroad tracks. He attributed the difference to the comfort of a good strong horse beneath him, and the feeling of security afforded by the Sharps carbine.

Normally talkative, Cephus held silent while they rode together far past the wagons. At length he said, "I suppose you figure me for a foolish and stubborn old man, comin' out here against all the best advice."

Smithwick had to consider his answer, because Cephus was not far from the mark. But it would serve no useful purpose to offer insult. "Mr. Thomason in Dodge said the first man into the orchard picks the best fruit."

"I'm glad you decided to stay with us. Ever since I seen you fire my rifle and hit that keg, I knew you'd be a good man to have

along. You ain't the only Englishman I've seen with a huntin' outfit. I've seen English, I've seen Irish, I've seen Germans and
Swedes . . . good men, most of them. It don't matter where you
come from as long as you can fit in wherever you're at."

They came to the breaks Cephus had seen from a distance. The
timber was small and scraggly and the watercourse dry. Evidently it
was only a wet-weather creek, running for a short time after a rain,
then drying up. A large pothole held a remnant of water, enough
perhaps for the loose stock but not enough to justify unhitching
and watering all the teams. They had not been overly long without;
they could wait.

"A little steep here for the wagons," Cephus observed. "I'll ride
a ways west. You go east. One of us is bound to find a gentler
place."

Smithwick did, about three hundred yards from the water. He
rode up on a point and waved his hat. In a little while Cephus
came, pushing his horse in a gentle lope. The old farmer approved
of the site. "We oughtn't to have much trouble puttin' the wagons
across here." He stared off into the distance, his jaw dropping a
little. "Yonderway, English. Tell me what you see."

Smithwick saw nothing at first. Then he discerned a lone horseman in the edge of scrub timber perhaps four hundred yards to the
east. Heartbeat quickening, he squinted, trying to bring the figure
into better focus. "Your eyes are not so weak as you pretend. I
almost missed seeing him."

"You wasn't lookin' for him, but you'll learn to. People like me,
we're *always* lookin' for him."

Smithwick went more by instinct than by what he could actually
see. "An Indian?" The horseman held still, watching the two men
even as they watched him. "I see no others. Do you think he is
hostile?"

"Wouldn't you be, if you seen a bunch of people comin' to take
what you'd always figured belonged to you?"

Smithwick was surprised to detect even that hint of sympathy in
Cephus. "If you feel that way, why do you go into their country?"

"If it wasn't me it'd be fifty others. Like it or not, the Indian is
fixin' to have this country taken away from him. He can go to the
reservation easy, or he can go hard. One way to help him go easy is

to kill off the buffalo to where he's got no choice. There won't be as many Indians die that way."

Smithwick suspected that was the way many hunters rationalized what they did. "And besides, it is good business?"

"It is, for a fact." Cephus's face wrinkled. "Come on, we'd better go see about his intentions. If there's to be a fight, we don't want it sprung on us by surprise."

The Indian drew away. By the time Smithwick and Cephus reached the place where he had been, he had disappeared. Tracks indicated that he had been alone.

Cephus said, "Just scoutin' us. But sooner or later we're liable to see him again, and not by himself."

Twelve

NIGEL SMITHWICK found that he was enjoying the trip more with every day that passed. The freshness of the open plains, the knowledge that he was traversing land seen by relatively few white men, aroused a sense of adventure beyond any he had ever felt. He had seen no Indians since the lone scout he and Cephus had encountered. Neither had he seen any buffalo as the string of wagons rolled steadily southward.

The only excitement of note had come when Arletta's peg-legged camp helper found the small supply of whiskey Cephus had brought along for medicinal purposes. He had carried the liquor out of camp a little way and proceeded to become gloriously drunk. When found the next morning he was as stiff as a man three days dead. Only Arletta's sympathetic intercession had prevented a disgusted Cephus from leaving him there to find his way back to Dodge afoot. A disabled veteran of the war deserved better, she pleaded.

"Wasn't the war that cost him his leg," Cephus declared. "He got drunk and fell under a freight wagon." But he asked Smithwick and one of the skinners to pitch the man into an empty vehicle. "If he ain't recovered by tonight, we'll go off and leave him. He'll damned sure sober up walkin' back to Dodge."

Smithwick suspected that some of the crew had left home for good reason, either as hapless alcoholics like the peg-leg or as perpetrators of various and sundry offenses who found anonymity

in a new land beneficial to their health. He had heard an unsub-
stantiated rumor that the dark-humored Herman Scholtz had
caved in a fellow worker's head with a shovel on an excavation job
in Pennsylvania. Considering the vast difference in their personali-
ties, he wondered why Scholtz had teamed with sunny-natured
Barney Gibson. Barney often seemed lost in a private world of
pleasant reveries that sometimes caused him to laugh aloud, star-
tling those around him.

Cephus would ordinarily talk until a listener's ears hurt, but as
the slow miles passed beneath the broad iron tires of his wagons he
said less and less. His eyes seemed to pinch a little more each day.

"Perhaps we shall have no Indian trouble," Smithwick offered as
they rode several hundred yards in advance, watching for game
that would enrich their supper, and for obstacles to the wagons.

"Ain't the Indians that bother me. It's the buffalo. Where are
they at?" The voice carried a hint of desperation. Smithwick
sensed that Cephus lived with the chilling specter of yet another
failure, another bankruptcy.

Some of the skinners had advanced a theory that sounded plausi-
ble. They said this was the area into which the Arkansas River
buffalo customarily migrated for the winter, and that herd had
been decimated by the hide hunters' guns. They theorized that the
Texas buffalo herd, which might range this far north in spring and
summer, had already migrated much farther south.

Cephus refused to accept that the Arkansas buffalo were gone.
"They're down here someplace," he argued. "They've got to be.
We'll keep lookin' till we find them."

Nights, after supper, Smithwick would sit with Arletta beneath
the lantern and go through the speller with her, helping her learn
the words that she found difficult. When she tired of that, he
would read aloud from *Oliver Twist*. Several of the wagon drivers
and skinners would gather around to listen, for they had heard
each other's stories time and again. They eagerly welcomed this
fresh narrative from a faraway land. Barney Gibson would smile,
even at the unhappy parts. Herman Scholtz complained that it was
a waste of time to read stories that were not true. He would draw
away, but not so far that he could not hear.

The plight of the boy Oliver aroused Arletta's sympathy. "That

London must be a coldhearted place. Not even Dodge City would let a bunch of little boys go hungry and cold thataway."

"It's only a story," Smithwick argued. "In any case, things have improved since the times Dickens writes about."

"Makes me glad we live where we do. We wouldn't let such a thing ever happen in this country."

"Has it not occurred to you that in killing off the buffalo you are probably consigning Indian children to hunger?"

He sensed that he had touched a vulnerable spot, for she seemed to withdraw into herself a little. "I've thought about it. But like Papa says, somebody's goin' to do it whether it's us or not. Government's tryin' to get the Indians to go to reservations where it'll feed them, where they won't go hungry in the wintertime and where white men won't be killin' them on sight. It'll be for their own good."

"Will the government take care of them once it gets them to the reservations? Or will it simply rejoice that they no longer roam free and leave them in neglect and despair?"

"They promise they'll take care of them. The government wouldn't lie, would it?"

"I cannot speak for your politicians, but I know mine. If it suits their purpose, they will lie."

"At least you was raised rich. Your folks could pay them off if you needed somethin' from them."

He had never thought of his family as rich. They were property owners, but by the standards of their class they received hardly more than a casual tip of the hat from the London bankers. Or from that parasitic class of London politicians who toiled not, nor did they spin, and whose price was too high for the Smithwicks to pay. "You overestimate us. As for the Indians, they have neither money nor vote. They will be easily forgotten."

"I'd like to think you're wrong."

"So would I. Ask me again in ten years."

"I wish you'd still be around in ten years, Nigel. But like as not you'll be back across the waters, and you'll forget that you once knew a girl so ignorant you had to read to her."

"I will not forget." He wanted to reach over and clasp her hand but denied himself the liberty. "I shall remember that it pleased me very much to read to her."

It was Arletta who did the touching. She took his hand and squeezed it, and for a moment she laid her head against his shoulder. He warmed, remembering the girl named Gwyneth.

The next morning Smithwick and Cephus rode far ahead of the wagons, as had become their custom. They came to a dry watercourse, much like the one in which they had seen the lone Indian. Cephus pointed with his chin. "I'll go down yonder. How about you ridin' up thataway?"

If Cephus's main concern was buffalo, Smithwick's was Indians. Carbine across his lap, he set Dunny into an easy trot. He rode a mile, finding a couple of places where the wagons should be able to cross without difficulty. Turning, he saw Cephus waving his hat in excitement. His first thought was that Cephus had seen Indians. He touched spurs to the horse and set him into a lope, his right hand clutching the carbine.

Cephus did not wait but turned and moved back in the direction he had originally taken, his horse moving in a long trot. Before Smithwick could catch up to him, Cephus dismounted beside a long stretch of shallow water, a remnant from the last rains some weeks ago. His eyes danced with delight as he pointed toward the ground. "Looky there!"

Smithwick looked in puzzlement. "At what?"

"Them droppin's. Don't you see?"

"I never found cause to become excited about manure."

"Them's buffalo doin's, and fresh. Been a herd waterin' here. The tracks lead off yonderway." He raised his arm, indicating a southwesterly direction.

A smile crept across Smithwick's face. "I have a lot to learn about manure."

"Sometimes the Lord sends His blessin's in small things. I'd've froze to death in that big blizzard last winter if it hadn't been for buffalo chips. I got taken by surprise where there wasn't no timber. Built me a big pile of dried chips before the snow covered them up. Come nigh losin' my feet, but them chips kept me alive."

These had brought fresh vitality into eyes haunted by memories of past failures. Cephus said, "I'd commenced to worry about them buffalo goin' into the ground, like the Indians say."

Smithwick shared some of the farmer's elation, tempered by an element of caution. "Where there are buffalo, are there not likely also to be Indians?"

"Every rosebush has got thorns on it." Cephus led off in the direction of the tracks, which meandered but held in general to a southwesterly course. Ten years seemed to have lifted from his shoulders. He sat straighter in the saddle, alternately humming a discordant tune and talking about his plans to make this final big hide harvest and then leave it to return to the life of a farmer. A *gentleman* farmer, he said.

They came in a while to a cleft in the hills. Ahead Smithwick saw half a dozen dark shapes peacefully grazing. A few more buffalo had already taken their fill of the cured grass and were lying down out of the wind, contentedly chewing cud. The sight of them gave him a tickle of excitement.

He half expected Cephus to dismount and dance a jig. The hunter's voice quivered with delight. "Main herd's probably on past that gap in the hills. The wind favors us. If it blowed the other way they'd be on their feet and runnin'."

"If we can see them, can't they see us?"

"Buffalo eyesight is weak to start with, and their winter coat of hair sometimes gets down over their eyes, like blinders on a mule. But just the same, it don't take much to spook them into a run."

Cephus started a wide circle, *taking roundance*, he called it, working to the far side of the hill. He dismounted before reaching the top. Smithwick silently followed his example. He had found that the dun's previous owner or owners had trained the horse to stand where the reins were dropped. Cephus crouched low to cover the last few feet. He spoke just above a whisper, but his voice crackled with delight. "What I been tellin' you, English? I just wish you'd looky yonder."

The sight made Smithwick catch his breath, for he had seen nothing of its like before. A chill ran along his back in response to a feeling that he and Cephus might be the first of their race who had looked down upon this narrow valley, where buffalo were scattered thinly for a mile or more between the grass-covered hills—cows, bulls, reddish calves darkening with the growth of winter hair. He could hear the chuffing and snorting and watched a big cow turn suddenly, lower her horns and charge at another which had crowded her. Startled, the smaller cow gave way, not quickly enough to avoid taking a horn in her ribs. Most of the animals were grazing, but some already took their ease. The cured grass was plentiful; it must have been no challenge to fill their bellies.

Smithwick's initial awe began giving way to a troublesome doubt. He had heard stories about herds so huge that they blackened the ground for miles and, on occasion, held up the passage of a train for hours. Against such accounts, this bunch seemed modest. "How many would you estimate there are?"

Cephus was a while in answering, his hand pivoting from side to side as he took a silent count. "Some shy of a couple hundred. Ain't much to a lot of herds I've seen, but it's a startin' place. Bound to be a lot more farther on."

"I hope so." Still, Smithwick wondered. His brief experience in this country gave him little basis for opinion, but he assumed these were remnants of the Arkansas River herd, migrated south for the winter. By most accounts that herd had been shot to pieces. How many such remnants might still survive? He did not communicate his concern to Cephus, for he did not want to compromise the man's euphoric mood. "What do we do now?"

"Find a good place to camp the wagons. Come mornin' we'll be up here on the hill, makin' ourselves rich."

From fewer than two hundred head, even if we were to get them all? Smithwick asked himself. *What if this is all there is?*

Cephus could not restrain his jubilation as he approached the wagons. He spurred ahead, waving his hat, shouting "Buffalo!" Smithwick did not try to keep up with him, letting the dun horse hold to its gentle trot as Cephus rode all the way down the line, passing his happy message. Following, Smithwick could see anticipation in the faces of the skinners and wagon drivers and a shooter known as Illinois Ike. Earlier, they too had begun to doubt, their hope flagging.

He found Arletta's face aglow. "Did you see them, Nigel? Was there really a lot of buffalo?"

"I do not know how many makes *a lot*. Cephus thought there might be near two hundred."

A little of her glow faded. "We used to find them by the thousands."

"Perhaps we will again, a little farther on." He hoped the words did not sound as hollow to her as they did to him. But he saw one reason to feel relieved. If they stopped a few days to work this area, Colonel Cregar should catch up.

On their return from the valley where the buffalo grazed, Cephus had followed a tiny creek to its head and found a clear, small spring that would make a good camping place. He directed the company to it. The men formed the wagons into a wide circle as a precautionary measure in an unfamiliar country and began setting up camp with an energy and a purpose Smithwick had not seen in days. He found himself caught up in its contagion and managed to put his doubts aside.

Cephus walked over several acres of reasonably flat ground just south of the campsite. "We could stake down a thousand hides here and not be crowded for room."

Smithwick smiled thinly. "You're a man of infinite hope."

"Been times that was all I had, just hope. It helps you forget an empty belly."

Smithwick did not read long from *Oliver Twist* that evening. The men's minds were not on the story, nor was his own. Cephus silently cleaned his rifle and greased cartridges as he listened half-heartedly. Arletta put the book back into her wagon. She said, "It's hard for anybody to think about anything now except the buffalo."

"Do you look forward to the killing?"

"Not the killin', but what it can bring us. Papa promises this'll be his last hunt. We'll get us a farm and live like we used to, in a house and not out of a wagon."

"He has told me he wants to help you find a good man and see you settled and happy."

"I reckon I could find my own man if I decided to. That's one place I wouldn't need Papa's help." She gazed anxiously at him as if she feared he might misunderstand. "But I'm not sayin' I'm lookin' for one right now."

"You will, sooner or later. It is in human nature."

"How about you, Nigel? What about *your* nature?"

He did not answer immediately, looking for Gwyneth's face in the campfire. "There was a girl once, in some ways quite like you. But it was an impossible situation."

"Did you ever find another?"

"Not one I was ever that serious about. A lady I later considered marrying turned me down."

"Must've been somethin' the matter with her."

"The fault was with me. What do I have to show for my life? The little money I have in my pocket came from besting other men at cards. I have done nothing of benefit to anyone."

"You came to help us."

"A spur-of-the-moment decision. Had I taken more time to consider, I might very well have caught the train."

"But you followed your first feelin's, and they pointed you in the right direction. You're a better man than you know, Nigel Smithwick." Her voice sharpened. "Don't you be talkin' about yourself like you were some no-account. I won't listen to any more of it." She leaned over, grasped his arms and kissed him. Then she strode toward her tent, leaving him staring after her in surprise and puzzlement.

HE WAS IN the midst of a dream that carried him back to England when he was awakened by a firm hand shaking his shoulder. Cephus Browder was a dark form hovering over Smithwick's sleeping place on the ground. "Sun's fixin' to catch you in bed."

Smithwick saw little danger of that. Folding back the tarp that protected his blankets from the frost, he found not so much as the first light of dawn on the eastern horizon. "It does not take long to spend the night in this camp."

Cephus's voice was jubilant. "Not when there's buffalo waitin' for us. I've got a feelin' we'll get all the men can skin today."

Most of the men slept in their clothes, but to Smithwick that seemed hardly civilized. He dressed beneath the blankets, for the morning carried a chill that made him shiver. As he pulled on the boots he had kept dry beneath the tarp, the smell of cooking reached him. Arletta and her one-legged helper were preparing breakfast. That gave Smithwick an incentive to hurry. This trip, the long days on horseback in the clean prairie air, had had a salutary effect on an appetite jaded by endless night hours hunched over card tables in poorly ventilated barrooms, coughing against the pervasive cigar smoke, sipping whiskey of an indifferent to sometimes malevolent nature. Shaving, he had noticed that his skin was taking on a darker and healthier tone.

A few more weeks of this and his own family might no longer recognize him.

He heard ill-natured squealing and stirring of the mules as wagon drivers caught and harnessed their teams before breakfast. Arletta called out, "It's ready."

While he sat on a wagon tongue and ate from a tin plate, Arletta put a hand on his shoulder. "I wish you'd kind of watch out for Papa. He's so excited about the buffalo, I'm afraid he'll forget to watch out for himself."

Smithwick was acutely aware of her hand and its pressure. "I shall do what I can, but he is supposed to be teaching me."

"You can learn from one another."

From the commotion made by the mules, Smithwick would have thought every wagon in camp was being readied to move, but he found that only two teams had been harnessed, each hitched to a single wagon without its trailers. Cephus said, "Barney and Herman'll follow us in their wagon. The Fulcher brothers'll follow Ike."

Illinois Ike was a brooding, taciturn war veteran who kept his own counsel. Smithwick had not heard him say a dozen words in succession and for a time had wondered if he might be a mute.

Cephus handed Smithwick a thin forked stick, whittled from the branch of a tree. "Tie this on your saddle. You'll be needin' it."

Daylight was barely more than a faint promise as the three horsemen left camp. Smithwick hunched a little, cold despite the heavy coat. Humming to himself, Cephus led off in the direction where they had seen the buffalo yesterday. Two wagons rattled along behind them. Mules snorted, braced by a night's rest and the predawn chill. The frosty morning air magnified the sounds. Cephus said, "Damned noisy, ain't they? Liable to run the buffalo off if we let them get too close."

Smithwick looked back once at the warm campfire receding in

the distance, then turned up the collar of his coat. Cephus alternated between pushing his horse for more speed and holding back to conserve its strength. His excitement was almost as visible as his condensed breath, hanging in front of him like smoke. At length he reined up and turned to wait for the wagons. "Wind's out of the north, what little there is of it, so they won't catch the scent. Ike, you take your wagon and make a big swing around them hills yonder. Some of the buffalo ought to still be in the valley just to the north of them. Main thing is to stay far enough apart that we don't get in each other's way or run off one another's buffalo."

Ike appeared to be an experienced hunter who needed no instruction but had the grace to nod as if he appreciated it. He signaled to the driver of the second wagon, and they rode off as Cephus had indicated. The crisp air carried the sound of their passage long after they had gone out of sight.

Cephus turned to Barney Gibson, who drove the remaining wagon. "You and Herman stay here. Build a little fire if you want to, but don't put out a lot of smoke. We wouldn't want it to make the big shaggies shy away."

Barney smiled. Anything seemed to suit him. "Sure, Cephus."

Herman grumbled. "Too cold my feet are for a *little* fire."

Cephus seemed not to hear. He beckoned Smithwick with a nod. "I've seen how you can shoot a whiskey keg. Let's go see how you can shoot buffalo."

The sun had come up but for a time seemed only to intensify the cold. Smithwick saw that they were near the place where they had found the herd. Cephus ascended the hill, stopping short of the top to dismount. "We'll leave the horses here."

Crouching as they made the last few yards to the top, they saw the buffalo several hundred yards farther up the valley. Steam seemed to hover over the animals as they grazed, some of the calves pitching and playing, butting heads. Cephus scooped up a handful of dirt and turned it loose, noting the direction of its drift. The buffalo moved slowly, grazing into the gentle north wind.

Cephus said, "We'll need to get a mite closer. A good shooter like Ike can take them at five or six hundred yards, but for my old eyes a hundred or two hundred yards is better. I like to see them get a bellyful of grass and be feelin' contented before I start shootin' into them. They're less apt to run off. We'll give them an hour or two."

"An hour or two? I could have slept that extra time."

"Fact is, I been layin' awake all night thinkin' about this bunch. I'd've got up even earlier if I hadn't thought it might cause a mutiny in camp." Cephus's faded blue eyes twinkled. "Anyway, there's somethin' unhealthy about sleepin' too much. I've seen more men die in bed than with their boots on."

"If any of yours die in bed, it will be in the dark."

Cephus pulled up the collar of his coat and stretched out on his stomach in the brown grass. "I'm beginnin' to feel a little drowsy. Wake me up when you see them shaggies start layin' down to chew their cud."

Despite being so excited earlier, Cephus was able now to drop off to sleep. Smithwick sat on the ground, his legs crossed, flexing his toes in a vain effort to defeat the cold that penetrated the heavy boots and woolen socks. After a time he retreated back down the way he had come and walked briskly in circles to stimulate circulation. He envied Gibson and Scholtz their small fire.

Between the exercise and a gradually warming sun, he managed to find some comfort. He returned to the hilltop better able to appreciate the grandeur of the scene below. He rough-counted upward of a hundred mature buffalo scattered over an area perhaps three or four hundred yards square. Far beyond them, in the general direction Illinois Ike had taken, he saw more, probably the remainder of those he and Cephus had observed yesterday. They seemed oblivious to the threat of the guns that would shortly begin bringing them down.

Two gray wolves skulked through the grass between the two hunters and the grazing animals. A cow raised her head and watched them. Several more buffalo looked up in response to her warning snort, and they faced around. The wolves circled wide, respecting those short black horns.

As the sun continued to press away the morning chill, Smithwick unbuttoned his coat. One by one the buffalo began lying down to soak up the warmth, their early-morning appetite appeased. He heard a distant rifleshot, a heavy boom which echoed up the valley. Ike had begun his work. Smithwick expected to see the buffalo run, but they paid no noticeable attention to the sound. Gently he shook Cephus's shoulder. "It would seem to be time."

Cephus sat up and yawned, studying the valley. Again he let a handful of dust drift. "Wind ain't changed. Let's go back to the horses."

They rode some three hundred yards and dismounted again at a low gap between the hills. Cephus lifted a heavy canvas pouch from behind his saddle, brass cartridges inside making a metallic rattling sound as he slung the pouch across his shoulder. He untied a forked stick similar to the one he had given Smithwick. Carrying his heavy Sharps Fifty, he motioned to Smithwick with a silent jerk of his head. Smithwick followed, carrying his own sack of cartridges, the stick and his carbine.

In the gap, Cephus dropped to one knee and gave the valley another long study before he pointed to a shallow ravine. "We can use that to get closer." Most of the buffalo were four or five hundred yards away. "From here we'd miss some. *I* would, anyway. The closer you get, the better you can call your shots."

Bending low, they traveled along the ravine until it shallowed. Smithwick surmised that the ravine, cut diagonally across the plain, was an old buffalo trail eroded by rain and wind. Cephus said quietly, "This is far enough." Cautiously he reached out to bend some clumps of grass that obscured his view. Most of the dried stems broke and stayed down. He opened the canvas pouch and spread a dozen or so greased cartridges out in front of him, careful not to let them touch dirt. Using both hands, he pushed the pointed end of the forked stick into the ground a couple of feet beyond the edge of the shallow ravine. He opened the breech block and inserted a cartridge.

"Now," he said in a voice barely above a whisper, "in any bunch like this there's a leader, one the rest of them'll follow. It may be a bull, or it may be a smart old cow. That's the one you've got to bring down first, or it'll take off runnin' with the rest right behind it."

The nearest of the animals was no more than fifty yards away, others as much as two to three hundred yards. Smithwick studied them intently. In the military, leaders like his Uncle Vincent wore insignia or even uniforms that marked their rank. One of these buffalo looked about the same as another to him except for differences in sizes and ages. "How do you discern which are the officers?"

"It's mostly just a feelin' you get. But generally there'll be one that's a little to the outside of the main bunch and watchin' for anything that might mean trouble. If a wolf moves, or even a rabbit, the leader'll be the first one to jerk its head up and look. And if it sees somethin' to spook at, it'll be the one that breaks and runs. That's why you've got to shoot it first and bring it down clean."

From the distance came the deep booming of Illinois Ike's rifle. Most of the animals seemed not to notice, but Smithwick saw that one cow looked up and around at each report, trying to determine where the unaccustomed sound was coming from. She was suspicious and increasingly nervous.

"Is that the one?"

"Like as not. Another shot or two and she'll start movin'. I'd best be bringin' her down."

She was no more than fifty yards away. Smithwick said, "It should be easy to hit her in the heart."

"They're harder to kill than they look like. Hit one in the heart and it's liable to run a hundred yards, bellerin' like Satan. That'll set off a stampede. No sir, you want to hit them in the lungs. They'll drop where they're at. With a little luck, the rest of them'll just mill around tryin' to figure out what the trouble is. You can keep shootin' into them until somethin' finally sets them to runnin', don't you see?"

Cephus stretched himself out on his belly. "Lots of runners like to shoot from a sittin' position, but my old bones won't take that anymore." Lying against the slanted side of the ravine, he rested the barrel of the big rifle in the crotch of the forked stick, adjusted the front sights and drew a careful bead. He took a deep breath and held it while the age-spotted skin stretched across the gnarled knuckles of his right hand. Even expecting it, Smithwick was jarred by the deafening roar of the rifle. A black cloud of powder smoke followed the flash of fire from the muzzle.

A puff of dust marked the point of impact just behind the last rib. The cow's hind legs collapsed. For a moment she seemed to sit on the ground, her forelegs braced while she tossed her head in confusion, blood streaming from her nostrils. Then she went down heavily on her side, her legs kicking up dirt. The nearby animals flushed at the sound of the rifle but did not run. Several began to gather around the fallen cow as if trying to see what was the matter with her. A bull, more frightened than the rest, began to move away in an awkward trot. Cephus drew another bead and put a bullet in the same place he had hit the cow. The bull tumbled forward, almost turning a somersault.

"Had to stop him next," Cephus explained casually, "or he'd've led them away."

The rest of the buffalo began moving in a circle, bewildered. Smithwick was surprised that they did not run.

Cephus said, "Looks like we've got us a stand goin'. Find you a good spot and let's see what you can do."

Smithwick trembled a little at the prospect, unsure whether to be thrilled or repelled. The shooting he had done in the past had been for sport. He saw little sport in this, shooting these confused, frightened beasts while they milled helplessly. It was a business, pure and simple, and he had committed himself to it. He moved twenty yards back up the ravine where the report of Cephus's rifle would not deafen him or the drifting black smoke choke him. He shoved the forked stick into the ground, loaded a cartridge into the breech and picked a bull which walked in a circle, tail switching in anxiety. He aimed for the spot where he had seen Cephus's bullets strike. His hands trembled, and he had to lower the weapon for a moment. Buck fever, he had heard deer hunters call it. He waited until he had calmed a bit, then aimed again. The carbine was lighter than the big rifle Cephus carried, but it kicked hard against his shoulder. Through the smoke he saw the bull run a few steps, knocking two cows out of the way, then fall hard.

Cephus said, "That's the way, English."

Smithwick's mouth went dry as he watched the bull in its death throes. He remembered his boyhood exultation as he had felled his first deer in the forest. He felt some of that exhilaration now, a sense of competence, of power.

Cephus called, "You're doin' fine. Keep on shootin'."

Smithwick reloaded. He took a long, deliberate aim and fired again, this time at a cow starting to move away, showing the beginnings of panic. He brought her down. His spirits rising even higher, he shifted the sights to a third and a fourth. He lost track of time, immersing himself in the challenge of the task at hand. He had to stop, finally, because the carbine became too hot. He feared it might jam, or even split open. Herman Scholtz, who always had a negative story to relate, had told him of a shooter who let his rifle heat so much that it exploded and crippled his hand.

Cephus held out, the thicker barrel of his Fifty allowing him to keep firing longer. After a time, however, he stopped, unbuttoned his trousers and urinated on the rifle. The sound was like bacon sizzling in a pan. Smithwick watched askance. The wind had picked up and carried the sharp odor to him. "That smells abominably."

"A man makes use of whatever Nature provides."

Thirteen

IT WAS THE HARVEST TIME of year known in Tejano settlements and northern Mexico as the Comanche Moon. It was the time just before deep winter when Indian ponies were strong from summer's grass, when war-painted warriors rode hundreds of miles south from the high plains to sweep away horses and mules. If it came handy and not at too great a cost in their own blood, the raiders also garnered Tejano and Mexican scalps to parade before the People beneath the high and sheltering canyon walls of their winter encampment.

Since his coming of age, Crow Feather had relished this annual final foray before the bitter blue winds, the stinging sleet and deep, wet snows forced him to winter's long idleness at the fire in his tepee. He had missed but once, nursing a leg broken in a horsefall during the autumn running of the buffalo. That had been the longest winter of his life.

This time, though both legs were sound, he would reluctantly miss that great sport again. Three Bears, hunt leader of the visiting band from the north, had stoically endured the ridicule of those who regarded him as an alarmist, given over to wild imaginings. He had convinced Crow Feather that he should travel north and see for himself what the white hunters had wrought upon the once-great buffalo herds of their sometime-allies, the Cheyenne. Like most of the others, Crow Feather had maintained a strong doubt, for it was beyond reason that any force was great enough to kill all the buffalo. They were as many as the grains of sand.

"Surely," he had argued, "they have gone back into the earth to wait. They will come out again when the white man has gone."

"So I have thought also," Three Bears said, "but I have held council with the Cheyenne. They tell me that where the white man's thundersticks speak, nothing remains but bones. When they have killed all they can find in the north, they will come for ours and yours, and the children will cry in hunger."

It was well known that the Cheyenne, and for that matter the Kiowa, had peculiar ways and peculiar beliefs alien to those of the People, the True Human Beings. But after the long day in which it had seemed his hunting party would not find the buffalo, Crow Feather had decided it would be wise to see for himself, or at least to counsel with the Cheyenne and be satisfied that they had indeed fallen victim to their own gullibility.

So he watched Man Who Stole the Mules boastfully preparing to ride south, smoking to the moon for success on his horse raid. He was to lead a contingent of restless young warriors keen for adventure. Some had not yet tested their courage against the guns of the Tejano settlers and the Mexican *hacendados*. They were eager to prove themselves, to taste the honors that attended the return of a successful raiding party to the sanctuary of winter camp. Some hoped to acquire horses and mules they might present to prospective fathers-in-law to earn their blessings for a marriage. If they could prove their bravery through daring deeds and the counting of coups, that was worth even more than horses.

Crow Feather owned many horses, so his sacrifice in missing this raid was not so great as it might once have been. He had ridden the war trail many times. He knew the obscure camping sites, the secluded watering places, the secret trails where it was possible to hide tracks and confuse any of the enemy bold enough to pursue. He would miss the excitement of the moonlight raids, but there would be compensating adventure in the trip to lands he had never seen, lands known to his forefathers as they had gradually drifted southward from the great mountains. He doubted he would go as far as the white man's iron road, if such a thing truly existed, but he would see for himself if there were white men enough to kill off all the buffalo.

His sister's new husband Swift Runner was to be a member of Mules's raiding party. Crow Feather had assumed from the beginning that he would go. Swift Runner seemed always to have had more respect for Mules than for his brother-in-law. Perhaps it was that he felt more of a kindred spirit in the loud and boastful Mules, whose temperament was closer to his own. By Comanche standards Crow Feather was already in his middle age, no longer so lithe, a little more inclined to meditation than to rash action.

He watched, hiding his envy as Man Who Stole the Mules led his procession out of the camp to the encouraging shouts and cheers of the band. Calling Bird was there, waving, proud of her man. Crow Feather thought his sister's stomach might be swelling a bit, which was no surprise. He had become convinced that the seed had been planted before the horses had been given that sealed her marriage. Such a thing was not considered a disgrace among the People, though they did not encourage it. It was a law of nature that young people be drawn together, just as it was a law of nature that fruit become ripe in its own good time. Babies were always welcome. The people had little concept of illegitimacy. The child of any was a child of all.

He found Rabbit standing just behind him, her eyes a-sparkle with excitement. She said, "I have everything ready. We need not wait longer."

He had held silent counsel with himself over the advisability of taking one of the women. He had rationalized that the trip would be long and lonely and the nights cold. White Deer would be best at making camp for him and cooking, but she was pregnant. Anyway, Rabbit was better at keeping his blankets warm. He had chosen Rabbit. It was better that White Deer remain in the winter encampment and care for the two children, her own and Rabbit's as well. The women's mother and Stands His Ground, their father, would see that she and the children wanted for nothing during the absence of Crow Feather and Rabbit.

Saying his goodbyes to White Deer, he saw no resentment in her eyes over his taking her younger sister. It was custom among the People that a woman dutifully accept her husband's wishes, though not all did so without loud and unpleasant complaint. He suspected White Deer was more than content at not having to go, not having to endure the many long days of riding, perhaps into the freezing breath of a winter norther. White Deer would enjoy the comfort of the warm tepee while Rabbit endured whatever hardships the journey might impose. Perhaps Rabbit would also be pregnant by the time she returned. Cold nights and the trip with Crow Feather would provide ample opportunity.

Crow Feather took his children into his arms, first the girl, then the boy, admonishing them to pay heed to what their mothers told them, and their grandparents. Rabbit's eyes brimmed with tears as she hugged her daughter and handed her into White Deer's waiting arms. Crow Feather was confident that White Deer would not show favoritism just because the boy had been born to her and the girl to Rabbit. That was not in her nature. He touched his hand against White Deer's cheek and said a quiet farewell. *"Mah-rib-ba."* He turned to the split-eared brown horse that was to be his mount for the trip.

They took three, two to ride and a third to pack their camp necessities. Crow Feather would have traveled much lighter had he gone on the war trail with the young men, but with Rabbit along he saw no reason to sacrifice all comfort. They found Three Bears's band had already broken camp and taken the trail, so they followed the tracks, biding their time. It was good for a change to be alone with Rabbit. They stopped to rest the horses beside a small spring at midday and took full advantage of the unaccustomed privacy. Though Comanche custom provided for wives to share a tepee and a man, Crow Feather had never felt fully at ease taking his pleasure with one woman while the other lay nearby. He relished those rare times when White Deer found business elsewhere, when he and Rabbit could enjoy one another without inhibitions.

They caught up to Three Bears's band late in the afternoon. Three Bears showed surprise that Crow Feather had brought a wife along, but he indicated neither approval nor disapproval. Among the People a man was free to do almost anything he wished so long as it was not at someone else's expense or endangerment. Rabbit was no threat except that perhaps her youth and beauty might cause some of the men to become discontented with older, plainer wives.

Rabbit put up a modest buffalo-hide tent at the edge of camp. A full-size tepee would be impractical for the journey. While Rabbit gathered dry wood and built a fire with flint and steel traded from the Mexican Comancheros, Crow Feather went to Three Bears's lodge. They smoked together and talked of old victories. Old defeats were disregarded. Crow Feather savored the smell of buffalo meat boiling in an iron pot while one of Three Bears's two plump middle-aged wives stirred it with a buffalo rib. He watched children playing about the camp. They no longer looked hungry as when he had first seen them the day of the big hunt. Momentarily he felt a tug of regret over leaving his own children behind and reexamined his wisdom in making this journey. But had he not come with Three Bears, he would almost certainly have gone south with the raiders, leaving the children in either case. A man could not allow himself to become too content with domestic life, for duty and custom would inevitably call him away.

Three Bears invited him to bring Rabbit and share meat, for there was plenty, and the buffalo from which it had come rightfully belonged to Crow Feather's people anyway. Crow Feather knew Rabbit was probably preparing a meal for him, but he would not refuse hospitality freely offered. He would remain at Three Bears's fire later, when all had satisfied their appetites, and share stories of wonder and war with the men of the band while the women withdrew to their duties.

Many days of leisurely travel brought them to the winter encampment of Three Bears's people along a narrow river which snaked like a castaway ribbon along a broad floodplain of reddish sand. High hills on the northern side would buffer the icy winds. Scrub timber offered additional protection as well as wood for the fires that would keep the lodges warm. Kindred bands had arrived earlier. Families already settled helped the newly come women raise their lodgepoles and cover them with buffalo skins that would provide shelter through the long, cold season ahead. Many reunions would be celebrated at night, many stories told and retold, so that Three Bears was in no hurry to continue the pilgrimage northward into Cheyenne lands. Crow Feather controlled his impatience and tried to put a full heart into the camaraderie. Having Rabbit with him made the wait tolerable.

Rabbit was enjoying herself. An outgoing young woman quick to laugh, she easily cultivated friends among the women despite the beauty that could as easily have caused them to be jealous. That made it less difficult the night Three Bears said he would be ready to go when the morning sun entered his lodge, and Crow Feather had to tell Rabbit she must remain behind.

She mourned, "I thought we were to travel together."

"We have, this far, but the rest is for men. We cannot be certain about the Cheyenne. Usually they are friendly, but not always. And if we should have a fight with the white men, I would not want one of their bullets to find you. Our child would cry for its mother."

"But if a bullet should find *you?*"

"Then you will go back to our people. You will be safe there. They will never allow the white man to take the land that is ours, or the buffalo that are ours."

She accepted with sorrow in her dark eyes. Her hands roamed with some urgency over his shoulders, his back, as if she thought she might somehow hold him here. He promised, "I will not let a bullet find me, or an arrow." She pulled him down upon their buffalo-robe bed, and he was reminded, though he needed no reminder, why he must come back.

Three Bears had chosen two young men, already tested in battle, to accompany them. Four could travel rapidly and give a good account of themselves should the need arise, yet were not enough to be perceived as a threat by any distrustful Cheyenne. One of the two was his son, whom he said proudly was probably the best horse thief in the band. Once some Comanchero traders had brought a long train of oxcarts out upon the plains, heavily laden with goods to swap for buffalo robes and for horses the band's warriors had taken from the sedentary eastern tribes the white men called *civilized*. Three Bears's son had led two untried young men to trail the traders back almost to their homes in New Mexico, far enough that no one could be certain who had done the deed. They had managed to steal back most of the horses in the dark of the moon. For this audacious accomplishment he had been renamed Fools the Mexicans.

Three Bears had laughed in telling the story, for the same horses were later traded to another group of Comancheros. These were allowed to return home unmolested, lest too many such incidents discourage continued commerce with the People.

Three Bears set a much steadier pace for this journey than for the leisurely movement of families from the buffalo hunt to the winter encampment. Here he was not hampered by the burden of women and children. Traveling, he pointed out landmarks to Crow Feather, telling him the names the People had given to the creeks and the rivers, to the better camping grounds. Crow Feather carefully committed them to memory the best he could, reinforcing that memory by drawing rough maps in the sand each night and studying them until he could call up their images on demand from the eye that was in his mind.

They came, in time, to a region far north that Three Bears said he had visited only once. That had been many years ago, when Fools the Mexicans had been hardly more than a toddler, practicing with tiny bow and short arrows against birds and rabbits that had the poor judgment to venture within his range.

They came upon a small hunting party of Kiowas and paused to share a night's camp with them. They conversed in the *maw-ta-quoip*, the language of the hands, for it was a point of pride with most Comanches to speak no tongue except their own. No language was as good, certainly not that of the rope-head Kiowas, so-called by the People because they interwove long braids of horsehair to the ends of their own natural hair, to a point that the braids sometimes dragged the ground if they did not drape them across their shoulders.

The Kiowas bore out much of what Three Bears had said about the white man killing off the buffalo. Many Cheyennes had been forced to drift south into Kiowa hunting grounds in search of meat. This in turn had caused some Kiowas to range farther south than was their custom, infringing upon lands traditionally held by the People. It had occasioned some hard feelings. Only the fact that they had long been allies had prevented there being war with some of the less tractable Comanches.

Crow Feather remembered how eager Man Who Stole the Mules had been to attack Three Bears's band without bothering to establish their identity. Had the interlopers been Kiowa instead of Comanche, Mules would probably have slaughtered them, or made the effort, despite the long alliance.

Three Bears was more proficient than Crow Feather in the language of the hands. Living farther to the north, he had more frequently encountered other plains tribes. When Crow Feather found himself unable to comprehend all that the hands were saying, Three Bears explained, "Long Walker says he knows many of the Cheyenne well. He offers to travel with us to see that we do not come to harm at Cheyenne hands."

Crow Feather had never felt totally comfortable in the presence of those who were not of the People, but concern over the white man's encroachments was forcing him to consider a higher level of tolerance. He was beginning to acquire some inkling that those not of the white man's race must put aside old enmities and stand together instead of fighting among themselves as they had done since the times of all his grandfathers. It was a concept difficult to accept in the light of ancient hatreds, and it might be impossible to convince some who had shed the blood of traditional enemies or had lost blood to them. But Crow Feather sensed a greater challenge, a much larger fight than the old quarrels with neighbors over hunting grounds. There had been an element of blood sport in intertribal warfare, but the conflict with the white man was moving beyond any such concept. From his conversations with Three Bears and from what the Kiowa said, he was beginning to see this developing as a question of survival—not simply his own but that of his wives, his children, of all his people.

When they broke camp the next morning, Long Walker and one other Kiowa split off from the hunting party to accompany the Comanches northward. They were now four, and half again four as the Comanche counted. They moved into a land more open than most of his own home country, the hills gentler, broken now and again by gullies and narrow watercourses. Timber was scarce and confined mostly to the banks of creeks and streams. The grass was taller and denser than most he had known, and it was brown now because autumn had blown a frosty breath across it. This should be a grand country for buffalo, he thought. The Kiowa said this was a region into which the northern buffalo had always retreated to spend the winter, but Crow Feather had seen only a scattered few. The scarcity lent strength to what Three Bears had told him about the white man's wasteful slaughter.

The second day after Long Walker had joined them, they saw a rider paralleling them at some distance. When they tried to approach him, he disappeared. "A Cheyenne wolf," Three Bears said. *Wolf* was a term applied to those who scouted ahead of hunters or war parties; they were the eyes of the larger band. "We will soon see the others."

Their shadows had not lengthened more than a little before many horsemen appeared from a ravine in front of them. Crow Feather counted three times four. Several carried rifles, in contrast to the bows of the four Comanches. Of the Kiowas, only Long Walker possessed a white man's firearm.

Long Walker handed his rifle to the other Kiowa and motioned for the party to wait while he rode out alone to meet the Cheyennes, his right hand raised without weapon. It became obvious that he was known to some of the party, for the mood turned immediately from distrust to friendly acceptance. Crow Feather watched them parley with the hands for a few minutes before Long Walker turned his horse and rode back with the Cheyennes. He was glad Long Walker had come along. Without him the Comanches might not have convinced the Cheyennes of their peaceful intent. It could have been a fierce fight, and a short one.

They all dismounted and went through the ceremony of passing the pipe to establish friendship and peaceful relations. The smoke had a flavor much to Crow Feather's taste. One of the young Cheyennes told him in sign that it was white man's tobacco, acquired through trade in buffalo robes. Not all of the white man's things were bad, the Cheyenne said; he also liked the white man's firewater. An older warrior sternly reproached him. Crow Feather did not understand the words, but the tone of voice left no doubt about their meaning.

The visitors followed the Cheyennes to their camp. It was small compared to the winter encampments of the Comanche, but it was meant to be. The thinning of the buffalo herds made it difficult to sustain a large encampment. A small camp was easy to move in search of game or to evade the military. The pony soldiers seemed to regard any large encampments as a threat and tended to raid them as a precautionary measure. The Cheyennes said there had been many such raids, either unprovoked or in retaliation for some offense by other bands or even other tribes.

Both white man and Indian tended to take revenge upon those of the other race who happened to be nearest at hand, whether they were the perpetrators or not. They regarded the guilt of one as the guilt of all.

Though the plains tribes differed in many of their ways, hospitality to visitors was one custom widely shared. A visitor who came peacefully into camp would be treated with generosity so long as he remained there, though, as was occasionally the case, he might become fair game as soon as he left. Crow Feather no longer felt apprehension. He sensed that the Cheyennes accepted the visitors as allies against a common threat. It had not injured the Comanches' cause, of course, that the Kiowa Long Walker had ridden with them. The Cheyennes treated them to more roasted meat than they could comfortably eat.

His belly hurt, but Crow Feather did not want to seem ungrateful by refusing any part of the Cheyenne hospitality. Later, despite his distress, he joined in the hand talk around the council fire. He understood most of it, and Three Bears clarified the rest. The Cheyenne reinforced what Crow Feather had first heard from Three Bears about the wholesale slaughter of buffalo, their hides hauled away on the iron road. Where the Cheyennes camped now was land guaranteed to them by the great treaty council at Medicine Lodge six years earlier. The white man had agreed not to encroach south of the Arkansas River. But now that he had killed most of the buffalo to the north, he was breaking his word. He was venturing south, a few here, a few there. If these early ones were not turned back, the Cheyennes said, the rest would soon invade like a flood bursting over the banks of a stream. Yet, any action taken against them would probably bring punitive expeditions by the military, which seemed to turn its eyes away from white men's violations but did not tolerate the red man's attempts to defend his land and his treaty rights.

Clearly, the white man had two sets of laws, one for himself and another for everyone else.

Firelight dancing in his face, Three Bears gravely turned to Crow Feather. "You know now that what I have said to you is true. The Tejano settlements in the south are as nothing against the numbers of white men who live to the north and east. They will soon be upon us like the swarms of grasshoppers that eat all the grass and leave the ponies to starve. We must join with the Kiowa and the Cheyenne and make war against them."

"I have heard much talk here about the white man, but I have seen none."

Three Bears relayed the statement in sign talk. A Cheyenne known as Horse Catcher responded. He would take Crow Feather and any of the others who might still doubt. He would show them white men. It should not be a long journey, for there had been reports of buffalo hunters well south of the Cimarron.

Crow Feather signaled agreement. He would go. They would all go.

The sun was high the next day when he heard the distant sound of guns. The party included all four of the Comanches, the two Kiowas and eight of the Cheyennes. They reined up and waited to discern the direction, for sometimes on these plains the echoes were misleading. Satisfied, Horse Catcher set the pace. Without discussion, it had been agreed tacitly that he was the leader, or would be so long as it suited the others. Among most plains tribes a leader acted only with the consent of those being led. If they doubted or if he displeased them, they were free to go their own way. They could choose another leader or no leader at all.

Nearing the source of the shooting, Crow Feather listened intently. The guns had a deeper, more powerful sound than any he had heard in the hands of the Tejanos. One of the Cheyennes told him the hunters carried strong-medicine rifles, with an effective range so great that they could shoot today and kill tomorrow. The Indians along the Arkansas and the Republican rivers had learned by bitter experience the folly of challenging these weapons head-on, for their own rifles were no match, nor was their marksmanship as keen as that of the hide men. One had to take these hunters by surprise or from good cover.

The party followed a dry creek bed and its thin stand of scrub timber. Horse Catcher silently motioned to Crow Feather and

Three Bears. He dismounted and climbed a low hill afoot, crouching as he neared the top, dropping to his belly and crawling the last few feet. The two Comanches followed his example.

Below them, in a long valley, Crow Feather saw a small herd of buffalo, perhaps ten times four. They moved about in nervous confusion, several sniffing suspiciously at some of their number which lay on the ground, dead or kicking in their death throes. A buffalo cow jumped, then fell, her hindquarters out of control. She tried for a moment to drag herself on her forelegs, slinging blood from her nose, then went down on her side, legs thrashing. A heartbeat after the animal's fall, Crow Feather heard the report from the rifle. He saw the hunters then, two of them, lying prone at the crest of another hill where they had an open field of fire into the herd.

Crow Feather wondered why the buffalo did not take fright and run instead of milling stupidly, leaving themselves open to continued slaughter. Three Bears said, "This is the way the white man likes to hunt. He does not run with the buffalo as we do. He strikes from a hidden place, like a snake."

Crow Feather turned to survey the ground. "We could go around and come up from the other side of the hill. They would not see us until we are almost upon them." He repeated in sign for the Cheyenne.

The Cheyenne replied that killing just two hunters was like killing two ants from an ant bed. But perhaps it would cause others to take fright, to retreat across the Arkansas. He inched backward on his belly until he was far enough down the hill not to be seen. He arose and returned to the waiting warriors, Crow Feather and Three Bears beside him. The plan was stated in a perfunctory manner, more as a request than an order, but all agreed to it. The warriors shed their equipage except for weaponry and stripped down to no more than breechclouts and moccasins so they would have unhampered freedom of movement.

Because of the range of the hunters' guns, surprise was essential if none of the warriors was to be killed. But any chance at complete surprise was thwarted. As the party rode around the back side of the hill where the hunters were, they came unexpectedly into the view of two white men who waited with a wagon. One of the men fired a quick shot. The slug snarled past Crow Feather like an angry hornet.

Ignoring a shout from Horse Catcher to pull back, several of the younger Cheyennes charged up the hill toward the hunters, firing their rifles. But the two white men had been alerted by the shot from the wagon, and the big buffalo guns boomed. In a minute the warriors were retreating down the hill, two carrying a fallen comrade between them. The rest of the party withdrew into the cover of scrub brush and carried on a desultory fire against the two men at the wagon. Crow Feather saw a loose horse running down the hill. In a moment a dun-colored horse followed, one of the hunters bent over in the saddle and holding the second man.

Several Cheyennes fired at him, but their bullets kicked up harmlessly in front of or behind the rapidly moving target. The rider reached the wagon and took cover behind it. He lowered the second hunter into the arms of the two waiting white men. It was clear that the man he had carried was wounded. The two men placed him in the wagon, then jumped up into it and set their team into a hard run.

Whooping, the party set out in pursuit, futilely sending arrows that fell short of the wagon and firing rifles that had no better effect. Good aim with a rifle was difficult from running horses. Periodically the hunter on the dun horse would stop, dismount and quickly level his rifle across the saddle. Each time he fired, he hit a warrior or a horse. It was soon evident that the party must drop back or face decimation at the hands of this man and the devil-gun he carried.

The Cheyenne leader decided to do as the hunter did. When the hunter stopped to take aim, Horse Catcher followed suit. He fired as the hunter started to remount. Crow Feather saw the man jerk and suspected the bullet had struck him.

The Indians trailed the fast-moving wagon at a respectful distance. One of the wagon men kept firing back with no more effect than the warriors' own guns had accomplished. The hunter on horseback no longer dismounted to shoot.

Crow Feather saw a camp with many wagons, and many men moving behind them. Long before the warriors came within good range, the white men were firing in their direction, trying to cover the retreat of the hunter and the men in the wagon.

Horse Catcher signaled for a halt. He spoke first in the Cheyenne tongue, then turned to the Kiowas and Comanches. In the language of the hands he said the camp was too large and too well defended with the great buffalo rifles. They had drawn blood from the white man but had lost blood of their own. There would be other days. This did not seem a good day to die.

Three Bears turned to Crow Feather. "Is it not as I have said? Must you also see the iron road?"

Crow Feather grimaced as if he had tasted gall. "No, I am satisfied. We have no choice but to fight. Fight we will, and kill until they stop coming!"

Fourteen

THE BUFFALO Nigel Smithwick and Cephus Browder had been shooting broke into a run at last, raising dust as they moved rapidly away from the two riflemen. They left behind them a considerable number of dead and dying on a hundred or so square yards of killing ground. Cephus began to count, his fingers making a poking gesture toward each fallen animal.

"Makes it a lot easier on the skinners when they don't get scattered too bad." He finished his count. "Between us we killed forty-two head. A pretty fair stand. I expect near half of them are yours." He studied Smithwick. "Are you all right, English?"

Smithwick trembled in the aftermath of excitement. "I do not know that I ever experienced anything quite so stimulating."

"You done fine. This is about as many as I'd expect Barney and Herman to skin before dark. It's just as well we leave the rest for another day. Second-day skinnin' ain't no pleasure, and I don't want to listen at Herman bitchin' about it. Besides, the wolves are liable to chew on them durin' the night and spoil the hides. Nothin' I hate worse than seein' somethin' wasted." He began gathering his empty cartridge cases to be reloaded in camp. "I'll pick up yours, English. How about you goin' and fetchin' the wagon?"

Smithwick walked back to the dun horse, then led the wagon and skinners to the gap. Barney maneuvered carefully to skirt the ravine while Herman lectured him in heavily accented terms about the dire result if he let a wheel drop off the edge. Smithwick suspected Barney went closer than he had to, for he grinned like a Cheshire cat, enjoying making Herman nervous.

Cephus had retrieved and mounted his horse. "The boys don't need us for what they've got to do. I ain't heard Ike's rifle in a spell. Let's go see how he's done."

It was the better part of two miles to a broad opening where Illinois Ike had set up his own stand. Smithwick and Cephus found him there, standing beside his coarse-haired gray horse, watching his skinners begin the job. Cephus rode among the motionless black and brown shapes lying in the grass, their blood already drying in the sun's late-morning warmth. His hand moved up and down as he counted. "I make it thirty-one head."

Ike said, "My count too."

Cephus said, "English, would you mind stayin' here and keepin' a watch over the skinners while me and Ike go scout out more buffalo?"

The shooting was the satisfying part, but the skinning was likely to be something else. Nevertheless, Smithwick assumed this was part of his education. "I am at your disposal." He watched the two men ride away in the direction Ike's buffalo had run when his stand had broken up.

The two skinners were Kentucky brothers, Ab and Eb Fulcher, who looked enough alike to be twins. Smithwick was unable to tell which was the dirtiest and bloodiest. They had already made a start on the animals Ike had shot. Three rolled hides lay in the wagon, and three stripped carcasses glistened white in the sun except for streaks of pink and red where the knives had sliced a bit deep. Only the heads were left unskinned.

Smithwick watched as Ab drew the sharp edge of a blade across a young cow's vulva to be certain she was dead. He used a ripping knife to make the first cut from the lower jaw down the neck, straight across the belly and out to the tail. Next he cut laterally from the first incision down the inside of each leg. He and Eb then used curved knives to reach beneath the hide and cut it free around the neck, down the sides, along the legs.

Smithwick stood close enough to receive the full impact of the warm, sweet smell that arose from the carcass as the hide was peeled back. It was not to his liking. Ab brought a horse he had unhitched from the wagon. He looped a rope around a roll of the neck hide, then led the horse away, tearing the uncut portion of the hide loose from the body. The animal's innards made a gurgling sound as the carcass was turned partway over.

"She ought to be tender," Eb said to his brother. "Let's take the hump and hams for camp meat. And the tongue. We'll take all the tongues."

"All the tongues," Ab echoed.

"What about the rest of the carcass?" Smithwick asked. "It seems a waste to leave it here."

Eb, his arms bloody most of the way to the shoulder, pointed his crescent-shaped knife toward gray figures crouched a couple of hundred yards away. "The wolves don't think so. They'll have a feast soon's we leave. You'll hear them tonight, calling their cousins in from miles around."

"From all over," Ab agreed.

The skinners rolled the hide, and Ab carried it to the wagon, stooping under its weight. Eb said, "When we get to camp we'll spread them apart and stake them out to dry. After a few days in the sun they'll weigh maybe half what they do now. They won't be near as much of a load to handle." He took a butcher's steel from his belt and sharpened a fine edge back onto his skinning knife while his brother proceeded to the next carcass and began the same ripping process as before.

Smithwick had been surprised at their speed in removing the hide. The two worked together with precision and skill, wasting few motions.

"You seem to have had a great deal of practice," he observed to Ab.

"We've been following Cephus and Ike for two years. Between them and us, we've probably skinned out more than ten thousand buff. Wouldn't you say so, brother?"

"I'd say so."

"Ten thousand buffalo that didn't feed Indians so they could go out and butcher white folks. I'd reckon that as a service to the country. Wouldn't you say so, brother?"

"I'd say so."

At least the Fulchers seemed to have no quarrel with one another, which had not always been the case for Smithwick and his own brothers. He found the skinning process distasteful and backed away from it. "I shall go up on that hill and look around."

The brothers grinned at one another. Ab offered, "We've got extra knives in the wagon if you'd like to join in."

"I would just be in your way." He could hear them chuckling as he mounted the dun and rode up the hill from which Illinois Ike had done his shooting. At the top he was grateful for the breeze which carried the smell away from him. He could see all the way to the other set of skinners. Beyond lay the camp, hidden behind a hill.

Dismounting, he ran a patch through the barrel of the carbine to dislodge the residue of black powder. Under heavy use a weapon could foul to a point that it would no longer be accurate and might even suffer permanent damage. He seated himself on the ground and rubbed his shoulder, already sore from the many times it had absorbed the recoil.

After a time he heard the boom of a rifle in the direction Cephus and Ike had taken. Thinking of Indians, he pushed to his feet and rammed a cartridge into the carbine. But the shots were methodically spaced, as they had been earlier in the day. The two men had found more buffalo. In a while he saw Ike returning alone on his gray horse. Smithwick rode down to meet him.

Ike said, "I'm going to fetch another wagon and a couple more skinners. We didn't intend to take any more hides today, but Cephus thought they were too handy to let them go. Have you eaten anything, English?"

Smithwick had some bread and cold venison that Arletta had given him to put in his saddlebag, but the excitement had kept him from feeling hungry. "I have not wanted anything."

Ike said, "You look tighter than a fiddle string. Lots of men do, the first time or two they make a kill like you did today. Be glad it's just buffalo, and not men. Buffalo won't cost you any sleep."

"What do you mean?"

Ike's eyes pinched as if he had looked straight into the sun. "In the war they assigned me to be a sharpshooter. It was my job to pick off rebel officers and artillerymen. Now sometimes they wake me up in the middle of the night. They stand at the foot of my bed and stare at me until the sun comes up." It was by far the most Smithwick had heard the man say. Ike left, riding in the direction of camp.

Near dark, Smithwick led the two wagons in. Cephus and Ike had not yet returned with the third wagon, so he had taken it upon himself to serve guard duty for the first pair. The other men in camp, except for Arletta's peg-leg helper, came out to assist in unloading the hides, spreading them on the ground with flesh side up. The men who had remained behind had not been idle. They had been cutting sharp pegs which they used to stretch the hides and pin them to the ground, a dozen to two dozen pegs per hide. One man followed the others, spreading an arsenic poison lightly over the skins to kill any insects that frost had not already eliminated. Cephus had told Smithwick that amateur hunters often let most of their hides be spoiled by insect damage and poor handling.

He watched awhile, learning the basics of the process, then walked to the campfire, checking to see if a coffeepot was on. Arletta anticipated his need and gave him a tin cup, letting her hand touch his for a moment. "Ike said you done right well for your first time."

"I must say, I rather enjoyed it."

She seemed not quite to believe. "Enjoyed it? But they just stand there helpless and let you kill them."

"I cannot explain it. I suppose I should feel disgusted with myself, but I do not."

"I never heard Papa or Jeff or Illinois Ike ever say they enjoyed it. They do it because it's a livin'."

"I cannot account for my feelings, or control them."

Her blue eyes softened as she stared at him. "I've been havin' trouble controllin' mine too, Nigel. I've had feelin's lately that never came over me before."

He raised an eyebrow, hesitant to ask her what sort of feelings.

She said, "I've always been one to speak my mind. When you sit with me, helpin' me read, I want to drop the book and put my arms around you. I want to touch your face with my hands. I want to kiss you." She tiptoed and gave him a quick kiss on the mouth. "Like that." She did it again, harder. "Or like that. See there? You enjoy it too."

He looked around quickly, wondering if anyone had seen. "Arletta, you shouldn't."

"If we both feel like doin' it, I don't see the harm."

His face heated. "It might carry us to a point that we could not stop. At least that *I* could not."

"I wouldn't let it go that far. Even if I did, what would be the matter with it if we both wanted to?"

"Given a bit of bad luck, we could find ourselves forced into a marriage that wouldn't be right for either of us."

She drew back as if he had slapped her. "You're sayin' you wouldn't want me."

"I *would* want you, but I should not. A gentleman simply does not let himself . . ."

"I suppose a *gentleman* would be ashamed of me."

"It is not that. I *am* drawn to you. But we are so different . . . our backgrounds are a world apart . . ."

"The truth is, you *would* be ashamed of me. I don't talk good like you do. I'd never fit in with your kind of folks. I'd stand out like a mule amongst the Thoroughbreds."

"That is not it, Arletta." But it was, and he knew that she sensed it. She turned away from him. He caught her arm. "Arletta . . ."

She did not look at him. "I'm sorry, Nigel. I had a notion you felt the same way I do. I can see I made a mistake." Her voice broke. "I promise you I won't let it happen again." She pulled free of him and hurried to her tent, drawing its flap down behind her.

The coffee had turned bitter. He poured it out.

HIS EAGERNESS satisfied by the first day's success, Cephus waited much later before leaving camp the next day. He gave the morning sun a couple of hours to compromise the chill and allowed the buffalo time to graze. He and Ike had come into camp after dark with twenty-three more fresh hides, Cephus singing as if he had dallied too long in a Dodge City saloon. Morning found him calm and contemplative. Sitting on a log, sipping his third cup of coffee, he scratched figures in the sand.

"Ninety-six hides we got yesterday. Even at just two dollars a head, that's nigh onto two hundred dollars. Ten days like this and we'll have two thousand. Give us a month . . ." He shook his head as if he could not believe the fortune that awaited him.

Arletta *didn't* believe it. "Every day won't be like yesterday, Papa. After you finish this bunch, what if you can't find another?"

Cephus's confidence refused to be shaken. "They're out there, aplenty of them. We'll have so many skins that our wagons won't haul them all. We'll have to get freighters to come down from Dodge and help us carry them back." He looked up at Smithwick and Ike. "You-all ready for another big day?"

Ike had reverted to his silent self, only grunting assent. Smithwick nodded. He had slept but little, remembering the injured look in Arletta's face, and his stomach was uneasy. Arletta had avoided looking at him through breakfast. He wished she would glance his way so he could tell her, at least with his eyes, that he was sorry, that he had not wanted to hurt her. She came up beside him, finally, as the men were saddling their horses. He said, "Arletta, I did not sleep last night. I have wanted to tell you . . ."

She gave him no time to finish. Quietly she said, "Please try to stay close to Papa. He gets so wrapped up in the shootin' sometimes that he forgets to watch out around him. And his eyesight ain't what it ought to be."

"It seemed good enough yesterday. You saw how many hides he brought in."

"But he had to get up close enough to smell their breath. He oughtn't to even be out there."

"I'll keep my eyes open." He tried again. "Arletta . . ."

But she turned and was gone.

The three rode by yesterday's first killing ground, where the skinned carcasses took on a ghostly white sheen in the morning sun. Several wolves pulled back suspiciously at the approach of the riders, then returned to their feeding when the horsemen had passed. By tomorrow, Smithwick thought, these dead animals would be ripening and sending up a stench that might even turn away a wolf. It was too late in the year for buzzards, Cephus said. That was probably a good thing, because buzzards in large numbers might bring Indians to investigate.

Smithwick asked, "Do you not think they already know where we are? They have probably been watching us all along."

"I ain't seen but one, back yonder to the north."

Smithwick looked to Illinois Ike. Ike had no comment, but he was watching in all directions.

Just beyond the valley where Ike had made his stand the day before, they rode through a stand of brush along a wet-weather stream bed and saw buffalo grazing in knee-high grass along a gentle slope beyond. They were fewer than yesterday's bunch that had milled so long under Cephus's and Smithwick's guns. Cephus stuck his finger in his mouth and wet it, then held it up to check the direction of the wind. He pointed to a nearby hill, bald of any vegetation except grass. "Ike, that'll be a good place for me and English to see how many we can get. I wouldn't be surprised if you find another bunch a ways farther on."

Ike silently turned back toward the two wagons that trailed a hundred or so yards behind. He beckoned, and the Fulcher brothers followed him. Cephus signaled for Barney and Herman to remain where they were, the brush screening them from the buffalo. Smithwick followed Cephus up the hill on the side opposite the animals. They dismounted a little short of the hilltop and finished the climb afoot, carrying their rifles and their bags of brass cartridges.

Cephus pointed. "They're a little farther away than them yesterday. I sure wish I had me one of them telescope sights like Colonel's got. They cost more than a good wagon, but they bring a buff up to where you can almost touch him."

The range appeared to be mostly three to four hundred yards. That was little challenge to most good marksmen, but Cephus tugged at the corners of his eyes, trying to bring the buffalo into better focus. Smithwick offered, "I can do the shooting if you would prefer."

"I'd be obliged. If I hit one wrong I could spill the whole bunch. Here, take my Fifty. It's got more range than your carbine. With a hundred and ten grains of powder, this old poison-slinger can knock a bull down at six or seven hundred yards . . . if you've got good eyes to aim with."

Smithwick took the Big Fifty. Although he had fired it once in

Dodge City, he was still surprised at its weight. It was by a considerable margin the heaviest rifle he had ever had in his hands, almost like a small cannon. Keeping low to minimize the chance of the buffalo seeing him, he pushed the forked stick into the ground to support the heavy barrel and spread more than a dozen greased cartridges within easy reach. He settled down onto his stomach and adjusted the rear sight.

Cephus let a handful of dirt slip between his fingers to gauge the wind. "It's blowin' a little harder up here than down there where the buffalo are. You'll need to make allowance."

Smithwick could not decide which animal was most likely to lead the bunch away. Cephus said, "Sometimes you just got to put a round into the easiest target. Then watch and shoot the first one that acts like it's fixin' to run off."

Smithwick found his hands shaking a little despite the warming sun. He felt the same rising excitement that had carried him through yesterday's shoot. He flexed the hands a few times while he chose a bull that had grazed its fill and seemed about to lie down. Holding his breath, he sighted behind the last rib and carefully squeezed the trigger. The big rifle pushed hard against his shoulder as flame and black smoke belched from the octagonal barrel. The buffalo went down as if it had been hit by a train.

He put another cartridge into the breech. A cow began heading out. He took less time in drawing a bead, for stopping her was urgent. She tossed her head and bellowed as her hindquarters collapsed. Snorting blood, she dragged herself in a half circle before she flopped down on her side, kicking. The nearby buffalo shied away but did not run. Like those yesterday, they seemed more bewildered than frightened. A pair ventured up to sniff around the dying cow. One began bawling. Smithwick put a bullet into her lest she stir the others into a frenzy.

Cephus said, "You're doin' fine, English. Don't let yourself get in a hurry. Just keep layin' them down, slow and deliberate. Make them skinners earn their keep."

The skinners more than earned their keep. Smithwick had just brought down his third bull when shooting broke out below the hill. Cephus jumped to his feet, grabbing up the carbine Smithwick had left lying across his saddlebags to keep it free of dirt.

"Indians!" he shouted. He ran for his horse.

Smithwick had the presence of mind to snatch up the unfired cartridges and jam them into his pocket as he hurried toward the dun. He heard yelping behind him. Half a dozen warriors pushed their horses up the hill in a run. Rifles cracked, and arrows swished past him. Cephus triggered the carbine. Smithwick dropped to one knee, swung the Fifty's heavy barrel up and fired at the nearest rider. The bullet slammed the warrior back over his horse's rump. He tumbled to the grass, limp as a rag doll. The others flushed to one side or the other, startled by the Fifty's savage impact. Smithwick reloaded quickly.

Cephus had one foot in the stirrup when an arrow drove into his side. Crying out, he fell heavily against his horse. The animal jerked away from him and stampeded down the hill, the stirrups flopping. Cephus stumbled and went to his knees.

"Cephus!" Smithwick ran toward him. A bullet pierced his fleece-lined coat and burned a shallow cut across his ribs. He wheeled and fired again, bringing down a horse. The Indians wavered and turned back. That gave him time to get an arm around Cephus and lift him to his feet.

Cephus seemed disoriented, but he managed to hold onto the carbine even though he was unable to put it to use. Smithwick swung into the saddle and dragged Cephus most of the way up on the horse's left side. "Try to hold onto me. I'll do my best to hang onto you." He put the dun horse into a run, risking a fall as they rushed wildly down the hill.

The two skinners fired from behind their wagon, holding back upward of a dozen Indians armed mostly with bows and arrows. Cephus's riderless horse instinctively ran toward the wagon and the two mules hitched to it. Barney Gibson caught it while Herman kept shooting.

Smithwick clung desperately to the weakening Cephus but could feel him slipping from his precarious grasp. He shouted, "Cephus is hit! Get ready to grab him!"

Barney turned Cephus's horse loose and ran out to meet Smithwick and his burden. Herman fired a couple more shots, then rushed to help. The two men took hold of Cephus and relieved Smithwick of his weight. Barney shouted, "Into the wagon with him. Let's get the hell away from here!" The carbine slipped from Cephus's fingers.

While the two lifted the groaning man into the bed of the wagon, Smithwick turned to face the Indians. The barrel of the Big Fifty seemed to weigh a hundred pounds as he brought up the front sight. It was not meant to be fired from horseback. His bullet went wild, but the rifle's power made the warriors hesitant about pressing too closely. Their arrows fell short. Bullets from their rifles whispered harmlessly by. The Indians had no more luck than Smithwick, firing from horseback.

Herman picked up the fallen carbine and jumped into the wagon bed with it, dropping onto his stomach beside Cephus. Shouting something in German, he tried to fire but found that Cephus had not had time to reload. He retrieved his own rifle and set it to smoking. Barney jumped upon the seat and flipped the reins. The gunfire had excited the mules; they were more than ready to run. He gave them their heads and shouted, applying the whip. *"Hyahhh! Hyahhh!"*

Smithwick drew in beside the wagon as it bounced across the prairie. The Indians immediately gave chase. He reloaded the Fifty and turned in the saddle. The barrel bobbed up and down. He realized he was as likely to hit the ground ten feet behind his horse as to send the bullet anywhere near the Indians.

"Keep going!" he yelled, and reined the dun to a sudden stop. He jumped to the ground, leveled the barrel across the saddle and fired. An Indian pony went down. Dunny lunged against the reins. For a moment Smithwick feared he would lose him. He managed to get a foot into the stirrup and pull back into the saddle. The Indians had reined up and dropped down low on their horses when they saw what he was about to do, but now they came again in full cry.

The wagon had pulled fifty yards ahead of him, the frightened mules running with all the heart they possessed. He drummed his bootheels against the dun's ribs but made little gain. The Indians were too far behind for their arrows to reach him, but he knew he was within range of their rifles. He reloaded the Fifty, stopped the dun and again stepped down to fire across the saddle. A warrior fell. Smithwick remounted, reloading as he rode. A third time he stopped and fired while the wagon lengthened the distance. As he swung his right leg up over the horse's rump, a bullet grazed a fiery trail across his back. Momentarily numb, he grabbed at the horse's mane. He would have lost the rifle had he not bent across it and pinned it to the saddle.

Dunny bolted. Smithwick gave him his head and let him run, following the wagon. He heard firing ahead and knew the camp was aroused. The men were providing cover for the incoming wagon and for him. He tried to look back toward the Indians but could not see them. His eyes burned with tears brought up by the wind. The dun jumped over some obstacle Smithwick did not see, and he felt himself falling. He struck the ground hard, face first, taking a mouthful of dirt, losing his breath. His ribs ached, for he had fallen upon Cephus's Big Fifty. His back burned where the bullet had etched a mark.

Strong hands grabbed him. An anxious voice shouted, "Help me get him in there behind the wagons." Other hands took hold. He felt himself lifted up and carried, his toes dragging on the ground. By the time they set him down, he had begun to regain his breath. "I am all right. See to Cephus."

Someone declared, "Looks like they're backing off." The rifle fire dwindled away.

Smithwick could not see. His eyes were afire, full of dirt. He managed to ask, "Cephus? What about Cephus?"

Herman Scholtz's voice was strained. "He von't make it, English. That arrow, in his lung he got it."

He felt his coat being removed. A firm hand pressed cloth against the burning place high on his back. A voice declared, "Damn that peg-leg, drinking up all the whiskey. We could sure use some of it to wash out this wound."

Barney declared, "He didn't get it all. He didn't know I got a jug hidden in my war bag."

"Against Cephus's rules?"

"I've got my own rules. One of them is to never be caught without a little whiskey." Barney brought the jug. Smithwick clenched his fists and tried not to cry out as the raw whiskey seared his flesh. Tears washed enough dirt from his eyes that he was able to see the men hovered over him. Barney said, "It's shallow and a long ways from the heart, English. But it's apt to get pretty sore."

"It already is," Smithwick wheezed. "What about Cephus?"

"Barely alive. Arletta's with him."

"I want to see Cephus. This can wait."

Barney and Herman lifted him to his feet. Shakily he made his way across camp to where Cephus lay atop a tarp-covered bed on the ground. The arrow's shaft still protruded from his side. Pulling it out would cause him needless agony. Arletta's eyes were dulled by shock. Tears glistened on her cheeks.

Cephus's eyelids fluttered, and he tried to focus on Smithwick's face. His voice was raspy and weak. "English? That you, English?"

"I am here, Cephus."

The old farmer raised his hand. Smithwick took it. "I am sorry, Cephus. I should have seen them earlier."

"They was on us too quick. Thanks for not leavin' me. They'd've chopped me up."

"You would not have left me."

"I might've." Blood ran from the corner of his mouth. Her hand trembling, Arletta wiped it away. Cephus coughed up more blood. "English? Do somethin' for me?"

"Anything in my power."

"Watch over my girl. Help her sell the outfit. Help her get back to where we come from. Don't leave her till she's set and safe."

Smithwick could read nothing in Arletta's eyes except grief. He had no idea how he could keep the promise, but he said, "I will see to it."

Cephus turned his head, trying to find his daughter. "She's a good girl. Like her mama Rebecca was." His voice faded as he repeated the name. "Rebecca . . ." He took a sharp breath and did not breathe again.

Barney Gibson gently closed Cephus's half-open eyes. "I'm sorry, Arletta."

She held a while longer to her father's hand, then laid it across his chest and brought the other hand over to join it. "Please, leave me with him for a little while."

Smithwick said, "Arletta . . ."

She made no response.

Smithwick got to his feet. Herman said, "You bleed a little, English."

Smithwick knew a certain amount of bleeding would help in cleansing the wound, but the skinners gave him another fiery treatment from the whiskey jug to be on the safe side.

Barney said, "It's not much of a wound, but a man can still get blood poisoning."

Herman recounted a case in which inadequate treatment of a wound had caused a man's jaws to lock shut. "He could not eat, even. Starved to death, poor fellow, that he did."

Smithwick heard hoofbeats and the rumble of a wagon. The two Fulcher brothers were racing in from the hills, Illinois Ike close behind them on his gray horse. Half a dozen Indians trailed at a distance, respecting Ike's buffalo rifle. Several men hurried to the edge of camp, ready to provide cover if the Indians threatened to press too close to the wagon. The mules were lathered with sweat and so wrought up that they threatened to run through camp and out the other side before the skinners could bring them to a stop. Ike reined up, his rifle smoking, his face flushed with excitement. His gaze went to Arletta, kneeling alone beside her father at the far edge of camp. His voice was strained. "Cephus?"

Barney spoke sorrowfully. "Dead."

Ike wiped a coat sleeve across his sweaty face. "I wish we had gotten here sooner."

Smithwick said, "It would have made no difference. Cephus had no chance."

"I see they hit you too."

Smithwick shrugged and wished he had not, for the gesture set fire to the wound. "They missed the heart."

The Fulcher brothers managed to get their mules calmed and solemnly walked across the camp. They gave a moment's silent attention to Arletta and her father, then came over to see about Smithwick. Ab asked, "Reckon what we'll do without Ol' Cephus? Turn back to Dodge?"

Eb answered, "That'll be up to Arletta, when she's in condition to decide."

"We ain't never worked for a woman, brother."

"If we had to work for a woman, I'd sooner it was Arletta than just about any I know."

Defensively Ab replied, "A woman ain't strong enough to run an outfit like this, brother." He looked at Arletta, weeping quietly at her father's side. "There's Indians all around us. We ought to start breakin' camp and head for Dodge right now."

Ike looked at Smithwick. "What do you think, English?"

"I am new here. It is not my place to make a decision for Arletta."

"You have the right to decide for yourself. That is what this country is all about."

Scholtz said, "The blood poisoning you must watch, English. Once I knew a man whose jaws they locked together . . ." He let a grimace tell the rest of the story.

Presently Arletta came to stand beside the men. Her hands were clasped tightly, her eyes glazed. "I want to thank you, Nigel."

"I wish I could have saved him."

"You could've left him there to save yourself. There's some that would."

"I take no credit. Had I had time to think, I might have done differently."

"No you wouldn't." She reached out to touch him but pulled her hand back. "I'm sorry. I almost forgot I made you a promise. I won't forget again." She wiped her sleeve across a tear that ran down her cheek. "I'm done with my cryin' now. There'll be no more of it." Her voice firmed. Her gaze swept over the crew gathering around her. "How many buffalo did you and Papa kill before the Indians came?"

Smithwick tried to remember. "Eight, I believe. Perhaps nine."

She turned to Ike. "How many did you leave out there?"

"Five. I was a little longer in setting up a stand."

"I want those hides. Ike, I'd like you to take a wagon and half the men. Bring them back."

Ike looked stunned.

Smithwick stared in disbelief. "Don't do it, Arletta. There are no more than thirteen or fourteen. You would be fortunate to get thirty dollars for the lot."

"It isn't the money they'll fetch that counts, it's what they've already cost. Papa paid for those hides. He paid all he had to give. I want those hides for Papa."

Ike frowned. "If you're sure . . ."

Gone were her tears. A solid determination took their place. "Papa's always been the boss. Now, till we finish his work it's my place to take charge. I want you to go, Ike, and bring in those hides."

Ike touched his hat brim and beckoned to the Fulchers, then turned without a word. Several men followed, some looking back toward Arletta, shaking their heads.

Smithwick demanded, "Arletta, are you sure you know what you are doing?"

"Papa came on this trip to get buffalo hides. Well, Nigel, this outfit is mine now, and we're goin' to get buffalo hides!" She went back to kneel beside her father.

Barney said, "You oughtn't to look so surprised, English. Old Cephus had a big streak of stubborn in him when somebody tried to tell him what to do. Arletta's her daddy's daughter."

Fifteen

BY THE TIME the Cregar wagons had lumbered from Dodge City to the Cimarron, Jeff Layne had stretched the limits of his patience with Damon Cregar's son Farrell. He had not heard the young man open his mouth except to complain about the treatment he was receiving at his father's hands, and the crew's. At Colonel's request, Jeff and Cap Doolittle had dragged Farrell to a Dodge City barbershop and held him under cold water in a metal tub until he showed signs of shedding the many devils that had crawled out of the Dodge City rotgut. The barber had shaved off several days' growth of whiskers while Farrell described the man's antecedents in pungent detail. Without remorse the barber extracted payment in blood, scraping his razor hard against the bruised and swollen spot where Colonel's fist had connected with his son's chin.

Colonel had burned all of Farrell's clothing except for a hat, a belt and a serviceable pair of boots. The clothes had been fouled during Farrell's several days and nights with the crib girl, and Colonel suspected they might contain tiny crawlers more tenacious even than buffalo lice. Sturdy work clothes were more appropriate anyway, Colonel declared. He intended to give his son plenty of work.

Sick from his excesses in Dodge City, Farrell lay in the bed of Elijah Layne's wagon most of the first day on the trail. Jeff's father patiently allowed the verbal abuse to roll off like rain from a slicker, unacknowledged. Jeff threatened to add a second knot to the one Farrell already bore on his chin, but Elijah waved him away. "Boy'll be all right soon's he gets all that bad liquor sweated out of him. Young feller's got to sow some oats."

"I don't remember you havin' that much patience with me."

"You was mine."

Elijah had been a stern father in those long-ago days when Jeff had been growing up. He had worked hard and expected his son to work hard, for they were never but a step or two ahead of the wolf in those hungry times after Texas gained statehood. Jeff had run away once when he was twelve, certain that a better life must await him somewhere beyond his father's authority. It had been a sobering, dream-shattering experience. He had found that the rest of Texas was also dirt-poor, at least the part of it he saw before desperation drove him back to the family farm. Wisely, Elijah had not punished him. He had rightfully figured that experience was a better teacher in this case than the rod or a willow switch. And it was, for Jeff had learned that his father's strict attention to work and duty was what kept the wolf at bay. Where that kind of dedication was missing, he had seen families in actual hunger, children hollow-eyed and skinny.

The experience left a lifelong impact on Jeff. He worked hard so long as there was work to be done. Fun and leisure came only after the work was finished. On those rare occasions when he could indulge himself, he enjoyed the opportunity to the hilt.

He tried to find pleasure in the work itself, but it was hard to find much pleasure in killing buffalo.

By the second day Farrell's health seemed to have improved even if his attitude had not. Colonel had black Sully lead out a bay horse he had bought in Dodge, one resembling the big bay Colonel himself liked to ride. Colonel said, "Farrell, this was the best horse I could find for sale. Take care of him and he'll take care of you."

Farrell offered no thanks, or words of any other kind. Mounting, he set the bay into a hard run, testing its speed, heedless of possible prairie-dog holes. Sully turned to Jeff, speaking quietly so Colonel would not overhear and be upset. "What if he falls? That poor horse is apt to bust a leg."

Jeff thought Colonel needed to be upset, if he wasn't already. He spoke loudly enough that Cregar had to hear. "That boy's got about as much judgment as a wood rat."

Colonel stalked away, glaring toward his errant son, who still raced across the prairie.

Jeff thought Farrell was probably expressing his resentment for his father by abusing his father's gift. It was a damned poor way to treat a dumb animal.

Elijah said, "Farrell looks a lot like Colonel. With them both ridin' the same kind of horse it'll be hard to tell them apart at any distance."

"*I* can tell." Jeff suspected Colonel had looked much like his son at Farrell's age. Farrell was about the same height and lacked but a few pounds coming up to his father's weight. However much they might resemble one another in most ways, the eyes were different. Colonel's reminded Jeff of a hawk on constant watch for prey. When he spoke to a man, he stared a hole through him. Farrell seemed to look past a man's shoulder, never meeting the eyes and holding.

Jeff heard Colonel speak of Cephus Browder several times, always in conjunction with the term *damnfool*. Cregar's voice softened when he spoke of Arletta. He regretted the days he had lost in Dodge, allowing Cephus a long head start. The farmer's trail was easy to follow, however, for the wide iron tires had crushed an indelible mark of their passing in the cured and brittle brown grass.

Early the afternoon of the second day they came to a narrow, timbered creek which still held a remnant of standing water from summer rains. Busy seeing that the wagons did not bog in the deceptively deep mud, neither Colonel nor Jeff missed Farrell until the train was strung out southward, the creek behind it. Jeff was riding beside Elijah's wagon when Colonel brought his bay horse up in a fast trot. His eyes were troubled. "I don't find Farrell anywhere. Did you see him cross the creek?"

Jeff turned to look peevishly toward the rear wagons. "I was givin' my attention to *important* things. You sure he's not back there?" But the colonel never said anything without being sure, and Jeff sensed where Farrell had gone.

Cregar gave voice to Jeff's suspicion. For a moment he was not the military commander; he was a distressed father. "I think he took advantage of the timber to slip off. He's probably on his way to Dodge. I'd like you to go and bring him back."

Jeff gritted his teeth. He was a shooter, not a nursemaid. "He won't want to come. I might have to get rough."

Colonel's voice went deep with anger and a sense of betrayal. "Use whatever measure you deem necessary short of killing him."

Resentfully Jeff set Tar Baby into a long trot until he had passed the wagons, then loped him to the creek. There he searched until he found a fresh set of horse tracks leading eastward through the timber, breaking out into a narrow dry tributary that would have hidden horse and rider in a northward course long enough to be clear of the wagons. *Devious son of a bitch*, he thought. The depth of the tracks indicated that Farrell had run his horse for a considerable distance. A bad mistake, should he happen to encounter Indians and need the mount fresh enough to extend itself. Jeff held Tar Baby to a steady trot that could eat away miles without running him into the ground.

Fatigue had dissipated much of Jeff's initial anger by the time he saw the bay horse about half a mile ahead of him. He pushed the black to an easy lope and closed much of the distance before the fugitive looked back. Farrell spurred into a run.

Jeff resisted a temptation to make a horse race of it. *You damnyankee idiot, you'll be walking and leading him before long.* He held to a steady trot, knowing that sooner or later the bay would have to slow down.

At length he saw Farrell draw the horse to a stop. Young Cregar glanced back at Jeff, then looked forward again. Jeff saw two horsemen probably half a mile beyond Farrell.

Farrell waited, his gaze fixed on the distant riders. As Jeff rode up, Farrell asked with some anxiety, "Indians?"

Jeff knew these horsemen were white by the way they rode. More than likely they were scouting ahead of a buffalo-hunting party following Colonel Cregar's lead toward Texas. But he would not tell Farrell that. Instead, he said, "Who else would be out here?"

Farrell chewed his lip, contemplating the problem. "I'm known as a good shot. I could probably get them both."

Jeff made no attempt to hide his disgust. "You might. But where you see one Indian, or two, there's usually a bunch more close by. How many do you want to kill?"

Farrell turned upon him with hostile eyes. "What is Father paying you to bring me back?"

"Nothin'. I'm doin' it as a courtesy to him. For me, I'd as leave see you go back to Dodge and drown yourself in whiskey. Or go back to those *friends* of yours who likely figured on cuttin' your throat when they got through milkin' you like a farmer's cow."

"Do you think you're man enough to take me back if I don't want to go?"

Farrell was younger, taller and broader of shoulder, and he didn't have an old war wound making his hip hurt. Despite that, Jeff leaned forward, hands clenched tightly on his saddlehorn. "Hell yes, but I've dirtied my hands on you all I intend to. If you're bound and determined, then go. If you get to Dodge alive, see how much whiskey you can swill before it strangles you to death. I'll tell Colonel he oughtn't to've bought you such a fast horse." He turned Tar Baby around and started south.

Presently he heard hoofbeats and knew Farrell was following him, but he did not deign to look back. Young Cregar trailed a length behind for a mile or so, like a sullen dog that has felt the sting of a whip. At length Jeff said testily, "We're not Indians that we've got to ride in single file."

Farrell pulled up beside him, his jaw set hard.

Jeff demanded, "How come you've got to act like a snot-nosed four-year-old?"

"Wouldn't you, if you had a father like mine?"

"I don't know. Mine's not like yours."

"Then there's no way you can understand." Farrell clenched a fist, the knuckles going white. "Sometimes I wouldn't see him for two or three years. And when he *did* come he would curse and find fault and make me feel a foot high. He wasn't a father, he was a regimental commander."

"Colonel said somethin' about you gettin' in trouble back yonder." He did not articulate the question, but it lay there bold and open.

Farrell sidestepped it. "I didn't want to come here in the first place, but my grandparents are old and ailing. They said it was time I go. I didn't have anybody else to live with."

"You're old enough not to need anybody to live with. You could muster the guts to find work and go on your own."

"The fact is that I don't know how."

"Then it's high time you learned." Jeff had felt self-sufficient by the time he was fourteen or fifteen. Boyhood was short in South Texas. He spoke no more to Farrell the rest of the way back to the wagons. Farrell fell in behind the last one, keeping a respectable distance from Colonel.

Jeff rode up beside his father's wagon. Elijah studied him but asked no questions.

Colonel Cregar pulled back from the front of the line. "You appear none the worse for wear. Did you have any trouble with him?"

"No trouble. But if he tries again, he can go to hell."

"I can see that you don't have much regard for my son."

"You've got good eyes."

"I love him because he's my son, but I can't say that I like him much. I know now why his mother's people let him go." Cregar returned to the head of the line without riding back to speak to Farrell.

Jeff said to Elijah, "Colonel made a mistake in sendin' for him. If he'd left him to find his own way, he might grow up."

Cap Doolittle shouted from the wagon behind, "Colonel's biggest mistake was in not stayin' a bachelor." Cap turned to look at Farrell, trailing far behind. "On second thought, maybe he *did.*"

THE TWO HORSEMEN Farrell had taken for Indians had been white buffalo hunters, but the half dozen who appeared just short of the Cimarron crossing were not. Jeff was scouting in advance of the wagons when the Indians appeared a quarter mile to his left. They were the first he had seen south of Dodge City, though he had been watching, expecting them sooner.

Colonel Cregar came up in an easy lope, buffalo rifle balanced across his saddle. "I see just six," he said without betraying any excitement. "Hardly a force to attack the train."

"They've likely got brothers and cousins enough if they're of a mind to do it. These'll just take our measure. Indians know how to count, same as we do."

"I have little concern about our measure. But I worry about Arletta and that damnfool Cephus."

"They've got a good outfit. And the Englishman is with them. Cephus told me he's a crack shot."

"A useless remittance man. How often I have wished I had sent you to the Browder wagons instead of him."

The Indians halted two hundred yards away, demonstrating a healthy respect for the buffalo guns. One moved forward after handing a rifle to a companion. He rode with both hands high, one holding the reins, the other open, palm forward to demonstrate that he was unarmed. Jeff had learned to identify most of the plains tribes if he saw them close enough. This one was Cheyenne. The warrior stopped two lengths from Jeff and Colonel. He was middle-aged, gray streaks in his braided black hair. Anger darkened his face. Though Jeff did not understand the harshly spoken words, he understood the gesture when the warrior pointed northward and made a pushing motion with both hands.

He said to Colonel, "He's tellin' us to go back."

"I can see that for myself." Colonel shook his head and pointed south. The warrior's voice became louder and angrier. He made several threatening gestures and whipped his horse around, putting it into a long pacing stride, rejoining the other five. They waved rifles and bows at the interlopers, then retreated over a hill and were gone.

Jeff said, "I can't say I blame them much."

"Nor do I. But it is the destiny of civilized man to take over this land and convert it to higher use. It is the destiny of the savage to yield. Have you ever read much of world history?"

"I always been too busy tryin' to make a livin'."

"The pattern has been set since history began. Civilization has always advanced, and the wilderness has always given way. The strong and forward-looking have prevailed over the weak and backward of the world. It has been so in Asia and Africa and Europe. It is so in this country as well. We are tools of destiny."

"Maybe you are. I'm just tryin' to make a livin'."

He had expected the Indians; they were no surprise. By this time he had also expected to encounter buffalo, and their absence *was* a surprise. He had anticipated that where they found buffalo they would also find Cephus Browder. That at least would ease the relentless drive that caused Colonel to pass up a well-sheltered campsite on a running creek to make one more hour's progress before nightfall and settle for a dry camp on the open prairie. Jeff had become reconciled to the fact that the buffalo along the Arkansas were virtually wiped out. But surely, he had thought, there must be a herd south of the Cimarron in No Man's Land, or a little farther, in northern Texas. The only indication he could see of buffalo was a scattering of dried and disintegrating chips, probably several weeks old.

He calculated that the Cregar wagon train had probably crossed into the northern extremity of Texas. He stared wishfully at a distant range of hills, so far away they looked the deep blue of a late-evening sky. Far, far to the south lay the home to which he could not return. But he could tell himself that at least he was in Texas. He imagined he could see a difference, feel a difference, smell it in the wind that ranged southward toward the land from which he had come. His heart ached with homesickness, and with knowing that he dared not travel that far.

This was the *Llano Estacado*, the Staked Plain. It was so named, he had heard, because early Spaniards had staked trails across it lest they become lost and unable to retrace their steps. There were no markers, no way to tell where the boundary lay at the southern edge of the neutral ground. This was so far north of the state's settled regions that it could as well have been another country. Travelers had long moved in a generally eastward or westward direction along the old Santa Fe Trail, but few white men had ventured south of that trail into the heart of the Texas Panhandle except for occasional military and trader expeditions.

Boundaries would become important only when people began to settle here. Jeff's observation of this open grassland, rolling beyond him as far as he could see, led him to guess that the first bite of the farmer's plow might yet be decades away.

In midafternoon a fragment of sound caught his attention. Though it came from the south and was broken badly by a brisk north wind, he thought it to be a gunshot. Riding three hundred yards ahead of the wagons, he reined up to listen. He heard it again, a single shot. The wind made it difficult to judge the distance.

He rode back to Colonel Cregar, who sat on his bay horse alongside the lead wagon. The creaking wheels, the trace chains and the plodding hooves would have masked the sound from him.

"I think I heard a buffalo gun, Colonel. The way the shots're spaced, it sounds to me like a hunter has got him a stand goin'." The sound came again. Cregar heard it this time, for the wind had dropped.

Jeff did not often see Colonel excited. He was excited now. "That has to be Cephus Browder's outfit. Thank God we've caught up to them before the Indians. The thought of that girl . . ." Cregar's face contorted. He turned to the driver of the lead wagon. "You keep following the tracks. They should lead you to the Browder camp. Jeff and I are going to see about that shooting."

Farrell rode up in curiosity to hear the last part of the conversation. Uninvited, he followed two lengths behind his father and Jeff. They had traveled a mile or more, the wind at their backs, when Jeff heard the sound of running animals. Twenty or so buffalo broke out of the frost-denuded gray brush that marked a meandering draw. Stampeding into the wind, they rushed by the horsemen in a dusty clatter of dewclaws and cloven hooves.

Jeff said, "Looks like the shooter lost his stand."

As the dust settled behind the frightened buffalo, a horseman rode up the draw in their wake. Jeff knew him only as Illinois Ike, a solitary sort who hired out to whomever offered the best pay for the use of the big rifle that lay across his lap. Another rider trailed close behind him, carrying a smaller weapon. Jeff sensed that he was along as lookout and guard for the shooter.

The red-bearded Ike nodded civilly at Jeff and Colonel but offered no conversation. Jeff said, "Howdy, Ike. We just passed your buffalo, headin' north."

Ike gave the three men a moment's quiet scrutiny. "We've been shooting into the same bunch for most of a week. Those are all that's left, and they're too skittish to hold for long."

Cregar demanded, "You're with Cephus Browder, aren't you?"

"*Was.*" Ike's eyes narrowed. "Indians killed him."

Cregar spurred his bay horse in closer, his face like a building storm. "For God's sake, man, tell us the rest of it. What about his daughter?"

"She's all right. They shied away from the camp."

The colonel expelled a long breath.

Jeff knew most of Cephus's crew. "Anybody else hurt?"

"Nothing serious. An Englishman carried Cephus away from the Indians and took a grazing shot across his back. He's on the mend."

Jeff refrained from reminding Colonel that Smithwick was a braver man than he had figured him for. Colonel wouldn't be satisfied if Jesus Christ Himself came riding up.

Cregar demanded of Ike, "With Cephus dead, why haven't you started back north?"

"Arletta doesn't want to."

Cregar leaned forward, his eyes challenging. "You should *make* her go."

"Make her?" Ike snorted. "You've spent too long giving orders to men, Colonel. You don't know much about women. That woman, anyway."

"I'll talk to her."

"Won't do you any good." Ike jabbed his thumb westward. "Camp is yonderway. We'll follow the buffalo and see if we can get a few more." He jerked his head at the guard and rode north.

Farrell had been silent, listening with interest. Now he said to his father, "I always liked stubborn women. They give a man a challenge."

Colonel turned on him fiercely. "I heard about your woman trouble back east. You will stay away from this one!"

Farrell gave his father an ironic smile that offered no promises.

"You heard me," Colonel declared, and tapped spurs to his horse's ribs.

Jeff caught a faint smell of woodsmoke before they saw the wagons, formed together in a circle amid timber at what appeared to be the head of a narrow creek. The colonel's train had not yet arrived. A peg-legged man chopping wood spotted the three riders and broke into an awkward run, evidently fearing they were Indians.

Jeff waved his hat over his head. "Hello the camp!" He hoped his voice would carry. Several people ventured beyond the wagons. One wore a gray skirt that flared with the wind. "She looks all right, Colonel."

"No thanks to her damnfool of a father."

"It does no good to speak ill of the dead."

"It did damned little good to speak to him when he was alive."

Arletta stepped forward a few paces, several of her men beside her. Missing was the smile that usually lighted her face when company came. "We been expectin' you, Colonel."

Relief rushed into Cregar's face, relief and something more. He dismounted and swept her into his strong arms, embracing her with a violence that startled Arletta as much as it amazed Jeff. Ordinarily Cregar was a man of iron control, over himself as well as others. He declared, "Praise God you're all right."

Farrell's surprised expression yielded to one of quiet calculation as a flustered Arletta freed herself from Colonel's arms and stepped back.

I'd give a dollar to know what's going on in Farrell's head, Jeff thought. *I doubt that it's anything good.*

Colonel said, "I'm sorry we could not have arrived much sooner. Perhaps things would be different."

"But you didn't, and they ain't. Papa's dead."

Cregar spoke with a softness Jeff had seldom heard from him. "Your shooter told us. At least we're here now to protect you."

"We've done all right protectin' ourselves. I send extra men to guard the shooter and the skinners when they go out. We've seen Indians a time or two, but they ain't pressed us. We're gatherin' hides." She pointed to what must have been a couple or three hundred staked out to dry on the level ground south of the creek, where the prevailing north wind carried most of the smell away from camp. Some had the flesh side up; others showed the dark hair.

Jeff made a rough count. It was not a particularly good showing by the standards of earlier times on the Arkansas and the Republican. But those flush times were gone.

Colonel motioned toward the two men who remained on horse-back. "You know Jeff. This young man is my son Farrell."

Arletta spoke to Jeff. Surprise flickered in her eyes as she nodded at Farrell. Her gaze went from him to his father and back again. Jeff guessed she was intrigued over their looking so much alike. *Whiskey and water sometimes look alike too,* he thought. *But, God, what a difference.*

Farrell reciprocated her stare.

Colonel said, "You've done well, Arletta, but this is no place for you. I am going to buy your wagons and your hides so you can return to civilized country."

She shook her head. "Thanks, but I'm not sellin'. I'll go back when I've got these wagons loaded."

"I'll pay Dodge City prices."

"No. I'd sooner we hadn't come, but now that we're here I'm finishin' what Papa set out to do."

Cregar was distracted by his wagons, appearing on rising ground to the north. "We'll talk some more, Arletta."

She spread her feet a little wider. "It's a free country. But I've got nothin' for sale."

Cregar rode to meet his train. Farrell held back a moment, his gaze fixed on Arletta. Jeff felt relieved when Farrell finally trailed after his father. "Ike said English got shot. Where's he at?"

Arletta motioned for him to follow her. "He's still too sore to fire a rifle, so he's been restin' in camp."

"Colonel means well, Arletta. He's fretted about you ever since your daddy snuck this outfit out of Dodge."

She stopped, facing him defensively. "You fixin' to start in on me too, Jeff? I'll tell you what I told Colonel."

"It ain't for me to argue with you. You're a grown woman. You can make up your own mind."

"I am, and I have. Papa never had much luck, but at least he never let anybody tell him what to do." She looked a moment toward the two departing Cregars. "So that's Colonel's son. Favors him a right smart, don't you think?"

He could see that Farrell had piqued her curiosity. "If a mule favors a Thoroughbred."

She led him to a small tent, its front flap open to catch some of the heat from a small fire built just far enough away to minimize the chance of the canvas taking flame.

Smithwick lay on a bedroll, a buffalo robe doubled beneath him to serve as a mattress. Jeff demanded, "Do folks in England laze around in bed all day?"

Smithwick blinked in recognition. He pushed cautiously to his feet, extending a hand. "I am glad you are here. I wish you had arrived a few days earlier."

"So do I. Maybe Colonel can spare a wagon to take you to a doctor in Dodge."

"No need. The healing has begun. It itches as if a hundred ants were crawling on me." He grimaced. "It was the first time in years that I tried to do something useful, and look at me."

Arletta walked away, leaving the two men alone in the tent. Jeff waited until she was beyond hearing. "Colonel wants real bad to send her to Dodge. Maybe if you went she'd feel like she ought to go and take care of you."

"She would see through that. This is nothing more than a nuisance wound, and she knows it."

From a distance Jeff heard the deep roar of a rifle. Illinois Ike had caught up to the remnant of buffalo.

Smithwick said, "There cannot be more than a few left. She has already said that when those are taken she will move farther south. Nothing Cregar can say will change her mind."

A gust of north wind popped the tent's canvas. Jeff said, "Looks like it's fixin' to be a long winter."

Smithwick carefully stretched his arms, wincing as the wound pulled tight. "You will think I am crazy, but out there . . . while everything was going on . . . I loved every minute of it."

Jeff was incredulous. "In spite of what-all happened?"

"In spite of that. I have never known such excitement, such a feeling of pure exhilaration."

"I agree with you. I think you're crazy."

Sixteen

COLONEL CREGAR'S WAGONS made considerable disturbance, pulling in downstream from the Browder camp. The wagon drivers shouted and cursed at the mules. Cregar's strong voice boomed orders like a regimental commander. Smithwick frowned in the big man's direction. "I suppose I should go and report to him."

Jeff said, "He ain't the one that's been shot. Let him come to you." He could see that Smithwick's wound, though not of a threatening nature, still caused pain. "You probably lost some blood. You need to be eatin' a lot of liver."

"The Fulchers and Barney Gibson say I should take a heavy diet of buffalo meat, as nearly raw as I can tolerate it. Herman Scholtz says I need a lot of pork. I am afraid hogs are somewhat scarce here."

"Liver, that's the thing. Get the skinners to fetch you plenty of buffalo liver."

Arletta stood at the edge of camp, observing the Cregar wagons as they pulled into a circle of their own. Jeff noted the intensity with which Smithwick watched her. His own interest in Arletta was largely one of friendship. He was attracted to her in the casual way that a man might be drawn to any young woman, but he recognized this as nothing more than sexual attraction, slight enough that he could easily put it aside. He would guess that just about every man in camp felt much the same way. But he sensed that Smithwick's feelings had become something more.

Colonel Cregar paused in forming up his wagons. His gaze fastened upon Arletta until a struggling mule became tangled in the traces. He turned to give both driver and mule a military dressing-down.

Smithwick said, "Cregar will have a harder time with Arletta than he has with his mules. Her mind is firmly set."

"Arletta's no ordinary girl. I might get interested in her myself if I was a few years younger . . . say, about your age."

Smithwick's face took on color. "Am I to regard that as an offer of advice?"

"I generally try not to give advice unless it's asked for. Now, if you was to ask me . . ."

"I do not." Smithwick studied her, his eyes pinched. "Can you imagine her in England, trying to fit in? She would be humiliated, even if everyone tried to be kind. And of course there would always be some who would make sport of her."

"I can see you've done some thinkin' on it."

"A bit." Smithwick seemed reluctant to make the admission.

"She may not talk like a schoolteacher, but she knows stuff you'd never learn out of a schoolteacher's books."

"It would be a cruelty to put her through that. I realize I have many shortcomings, but I would never be cruel to her."

"She's too good a woman to have to end up with some mule skinner and stick her feet under a poor man's table all of her life. Or some no-account who'll take advantage of her till he's used up everything she owns, then go off and leave her."

Farrell Cregar walked from his father's wagons toward Arletta's. Broad-shouldered and straight of back, looking like a young Colonel, he no longer appeared the wreck Jeff and Cap had found in the Dodge City crib. His clothes were new and relatively clean, and he had shaved early in the morning. Smiling, he tipped his hat to Arletta and made a slight bow from the waist. "Miss Browder, it will be awhile before our camp is set up and supper prepared. I would give ten years of my life for a cup of coffee."

Coffee! Jeff thought. *He'd probably give twenty for a glass of whiskey.*

Arletta stared. "You're the spittin' image, all right. A one-eyed mule could see that you're Colonel's son."

Jeff muttered so that only Smithwick would hear, "Son of a *bitch* would be a better way of sayin' it."

Farrell said, "I did not have the opportunity earlier to express my sympathy about your father."

Arletta kept staring. "Thank you. Thank you." Flustered, she turned to face back into camp. "There is coffee at the cook wagon. I keep it on the fire all the time." She moved in that direction, looking back over her shoulder. Farrell followed her. She took a cup from a box, filled it from the steaming black coffeepot and handed it to him. Fragments of the conversation floated to Jeff, enough that he could tell Arletta was asking Farrell about his life back east.

He responded to the concern that arose in Smithwick's eyes. "Looks like he's sparked her curiosity."

Smithwick only nodded.

"He may not look like much to me and you, but if I was a woman, I'd probably figure him handsome." Receiving no reply, he said, "Any time you want my advice, English, all you got to do is ask for it."

He doubted that the pain in Smithwick's face came entirely from the wound.

As soon as the Cregar wagons had been situated and the teams unhitched, Jeff's father hurried over to the Browder camp. Elijah was gratified to find Smithwick not seriously hurt. "I'll get the boys to save you a good bait of buffalo fat. That's what you need to build your strength, is buffalo fat."

Despite Arletta's warning that argument would get him nowhere, Colonel Cregar tried. Sitting at her campfire after supper, he enumerated the hazards he could foresee and speculated on some he could not. He kept reaching out, touching her hand, touching her arm. "No woman should subject herself to the hardships and perils of this wild country. I want you to go back."

Arletta did not weaken. "You told Papa the same thing."

"With all due respect, I don't believe your father ever grasped the full danger of coming down here. That failure cost him his life. I would not want it to cost yours."

"If I was to leave now, his dyin'd go for nothin'.""

"If you are trying to make his death worthwhile, how many hides would you have to collect? A thousand? Ten thousand?"

Arletta turned in frustration to Smithwick. "You've got the words, Nigel. Tell him so he'll understand."

Smithwick was slow to reply. Jeff sensed that he wished he were back in England at this moment instead of being drawn into an argument almost certain to prove futile.

"She means it is more than the hides. Cephus came here with a goal. He gave it all he had. She feels that if she did less she would betray him and the sacrifice he made."

Cregar scowled. "You have just borne out my reservations about your judgment, Smith. How can you support her in this dangerous folly?"

"I believe I understand the way she thinks. That does not necessarily mean I agree with her."

Arletta turned on Smithwick, hurt in her voice. "Are you against me too, Nigel?"

"I am not against you, I just mean . . ." Smithwick looked trapped. He turned toward Jeff for help, but Jeff concentrated his attention on poking a fresh stick of wood into the fire. The Englishman risked alienating both sides in an argument not his own. Jeff saw no point in jumping off the cliff with him.

Farrell Cregar had been listening from the edge of the firelight. He stepped to Arletta's side and took a protective stance. "Father, the lady is capable of making up her own mind."

The colonel snapped, "This is none of your business!"

"Nor yours. She appears to be of age. She has a right to do whatever she chooses."

Arletta gave the younger Cregar a look of surprise that quickly turned to gratitude. "That's what I've tried to tell all of you." She pushed to her feet. "Ike says the buffalo here are played out. We're movin' south in the mornin'. Colonel, you can follow along or go your own way. Now, goodnight."

Colonel Cregar watched in frustration as Arletta passed beyond the flickering light of the campfire. Sharply he said, "Farrell, we have some things to talk about." He stalked off toward his own camp.

Farrell remained, facing into the darkness where Arletta had disappeared. "Am I to understand that this entire outfit belongs to her?"

Jeff considered young Cregar with suspicion. "It does, since her father's death."

"And she has no man to take care of her?"

Jeff waited a moment to see if Smithwick would say anything, then declared stiffly, "Every man in this camp watches out for her."

From the darkness came Colonel Cregar's demanding voice. "Farrell!"

Farrell made a thin smile. "She's a bit plain, perhaps, but all in all not a bad-looking young lady. My father seems to want her rather badly."

Neither man replied.

Farrell said, "He is used to getting whatever he wants. It might do him good to be disappointed for once."

Colonel Cregar reappeared in the firelight, fists clenched. "Farrell, are you coming or not?"

Farrell's voice was stubborn. "Father, you are no longer in the army, and I am not a soldier."

"As long as you are with my outfit, you will do what I say!"

"And if I should choose not to remain with your outfit, what would you do about it?"

"You have nowhere else to go. You don't even know how to work and support yourself. But by God you're about to learn! Even if it kills you, you're going to learn." Mumbling to himself, the colonel turned back toward the firelight of his own camp. Farrell's thin smile returned. "Tell the young lady I said goodnight." He followed his father but took his time.

Jeff stood up. "Need help back to your tent, English?"

"No, thank you. I can manage quite well for myself."

"You haven't managed this situation too damned well."

BREAKING OF CAMP was delayed by the necessity of moving the many buffalo hides Arletta's crew had staked out. They were in various stages of drying. Farther north, on the Arkansas, they might simply have been left with a man or two to watch over them and turn them until they were sufficiently dried. But in this unexplored region with its unknown hazards, such a course was risky for men as well as for the skins. Cheyennes had sometimes slashed hides to make them worthless. If they could not stop the slaughter of the buffalo, they might at least take the profit out of it. Such an idea was likely to appeal to Comanches as well.

Arletta would not ask for help, but Colonel Cregar sent most of his wagon men and skinners to assist her crew in loading the hides. Arletta protested that her own men were capable of doing the work. Cregar dismissed the notion with a wave of his hand. "The sooner finished, the sooner we can all leave."

"You can leave any time you're ready," she countered sternly. "I'm not holdin' you here."

"But you are, young lady. It took us several days of hard traveling to catch up with you. I would not think of moving now without you."

When Cregar was gone, Jeff said apologetically, "Colonel's got a head like a rock, but he means well."

Her voice softened. "I know he does. So does everybody else. But I'm a grown woman, and I don't like people tellin' me what to do, any more than Papa did." She turned to observe Farrell Cregar helping load the cook and supply wagons, a job he had chosen for himself. Approvingly she said, "The colonel's son doesn't feel like he's too good to work."

Jeff observed dryly, "What he's doin' won't get his clothes as dirty as movin' hides, and there's not as much heavy liftin'."

She seemed to miss his sarcasm. "He's got a nice smile."

Smithwick could not furnish much assistance. When he tried picking up and loading a few of the camp implements, he stretched the healing wound and flinched in pain. Arletta bade him find a seat on a wagon tongue. "I thought you didn't agree with what I'm doin', Nigel."

"It's your choice to make, not mine. I just want to be of some help."

"Biggest help you can be is by not addin' to my work. You will if you tear that place open again."

"I feel useless, an unnecessary burden."

"You wasn't useless when you brought Papa down off of that hill.

For that I'm grateful. Now I'll be more grateful if you'll set yourself down and stay out of our way."

Jeff had wondered a little about the Englishman's rightful place. He had come to the Browder company on a mission for Colonel Cregar, but so far as Jeff knew Colonel had not invited him to move to the other camp or offered to pay him for his time. Cregar would probably treat him like an errant private anyway. He was better off staying in the Browder camp.

Just before the wagons moved, Arletta paid a last visit to her father's grave. Jeff went with her, along with Elijah, Smithwick, Illinois Ike and most of her crew. Sully and Farrell came over from the Cregar wagons. Colonel Cregar did not.

Arletta's blue eyes were sad but resisted tears. "I'll come back someday and put up a stone."

Sully asked, "How you goin' to find the place, Miss Arletta?"

The grave was unmarked lest Indians dig it up to mutilate the body. Wood had been piled over it to be set ablaze so it would appear to be the site of a burned-out campfire, not a man's final resting place.

"I'll know. I won't forget, no matter how long it takes me to get back here."

Smithwick gave Jeff a doubting look, but Jeff knew Arletta could do it. She might read books poorly, but she could read the land like an Indian scout.

Colonel Cregar used up his patience. He rode over with his back as straight as a ramrod. "The wagons are ready." He did not seem to direct the statement to anyone in particular. "The day is wearing away."

Jeff flared at his employer, "For God's sake, show some respect." Cregar glared back at him but did not reply.

Arletta turned. "Colonel's right. We can't do anything for Papa by standin' here. Jeff, would you mind settin' the fire once we get the wagons to movin'?"

Cregar said, "Jeff should be out front, scouting."

Jeff replied sternly, "I'll catch up."

Cregar's dark eyes gave him silent rebuke for his insubordination, but the colonel rode off without saying more.

Smithwick walked to Arletta's cook wagon. He was about to

climb up when Farrell Cregar dismounted from his bay horse and tied it to the back of the wagon. Farrell said, "I'll drive for you, Miss Browder."

Arletta said, "I can do it myself," but she looked pleased.

"You have other burdens. It would be my privilege to take this small one from your hands."

Arletta gave Smithwick an apologetic look and said to Farrell, "All right, if you think Colonel can spare you."

"I am sure he will not miss me in the least." Farrell gave Arletta a boost, holding her arm longer than necessary, then climbed up beside her.

Smithwick's face took on more color. He moved toward the wagon immediately behind Arletta's. "I'll ride with Barney."

Jeff said, "The advice is still available, any time you want to ask for it."

Smithwick's eyes showed pain. "No advice."

The wagons moved away. Jeff carried a couple of burning branches from the cook fire and shoved them beneath the dry wood stacked on Cephus Browder's grave. Not until he saw flames lick to the top of the pile did he mount Tar Baby and set him into a gentle lope in the wake of the train.

Colonel Cregar's wagons led the procession. It was not Colonel's way to trail behind anyone. Jeff held Tar Baby to an easy trot, in no hurry to face Colonel's rebuke for not hopping like a frog at his order. That rebuke might be verbal, in the best military fashion, or it might be silent, a blistering gaze. One was as onerous as the other.

Jeff had enough money saved up that he was free to tell Colonel to go to hell if the notion struck him. He had considered it in the past but had liked the way the Cregar pay kept adding to his account at Wright's store. His savings, along with whatever he might earn on this venture, should allow him to buy a little land, a little livestock and become independent. Land was available in Kansas, lots of it. Texas would have been his choice, but because of what had happened down there it was out of reach. Kansas would probably have to do.

He rode up even with Barney's wagon. Barney had a captive audience in Smithwick, telling him more than he probably wanted to know about his experiences as a buffalo skinner. Smithwick sat hunched, stoically accepting the jolting of the wheels against the rough ground. The wagon bed sat flat upon the runners, and the wagon seat was simply a plank secured across the two sideboards. There was no semblance of springs to absorb shock.

Jeff asked, "The ride hurtin' your back, English?"

Smithwick's pain was evident. "A little suffering is good for the soul."

"But damned hard on the innards."

Arletta's wagon, just ahead, had a spring seat and would have been easier on Smithwick, but Farrell Cregar occupied half of it. Farrell seemed to be telling Arletta the whole story of his life, and she appeared to hang on every word. Jeff was disgusted enough to tell Farrell that a hurt man needed the seat more than he did, but that would wound the Englishman's pride. He probably would not accept the place even if Farrell gracefully offered it, an unlikely proposition in itself.

A man could get in enough trouble just minding his own business without courting more by intruding in other people's affairs.

Arletta gave Jeff a tentative nod as he passed her wagon. Farrell continued his monologue and did not acknowledge him. Jeff moved on up to the Cregar wagons. Sully looked back over his shoulder. "How's Mr. English bearin' up?"

"He'll be glad to see sundown."

"He'd be mighty welcome to come and ride with me, but I don't expect this rough old wagon would be any easier on him."

It was not just the jolting that was giving Smithwick pain, Jeff thought. English was riding behind Arletta's wagon, where he could watch Farrell Cregar sitting with her, filling her head with all kinds of unlikely tales.

He asked, "Sully, what do you think of Farrell Cregar?"

Sully looked backward and forward before he answered. "He puts me in mind of a horse that's always lookin' for a bigger haystack, the kind of horse you can't drive away from the barn."

"How'd you ever learn to judge people so good?"

"I've spent a lot of time with horses."

Jeff found an impatient Colonel riding at the head of the line. "You took your own sweet time."

Jeff tried to return as stern a stare as he received. The Confederacy might have lost the war, but Jeff had never conceded. "Illinois Ike has already searched out the country we'll cross this mornin', and he didn't find any buffalo."

"You won't find any, either, straggling along with the rear wagons." Colonel looked over his shoulder. "I haven't seen Farrell since we broke camp. Are you sure he's still with us?"

Jeff suspected his answer would give Colonel a jolt. "He's back yonder, ridin' with Arletta."

Cregar's square jaw dropped. "With Arletta? What for?"

"You ought to know what for. He's young. She's young."

Cregar turned his horse half around to look back down the long line of wagons. Those toward the rear were obscured by rising dust stirred by the hooves and the wheels. He muttered something under his breath. "Go tell Farrell I want him up here."

Jeff suspected Farrell's attentions to Arletta were calculated to heap aggravation upon his father. If that was so, the ploy was working. "He's your son. *You* go tell him." He touched spurs gently to Tar Baby's sides and moved on in a brisk trot. He could see Illinois Ike riding a quarter mile or so out in front, dwarfed in a broad vista of open, treeless grassland that stretched toward a far-distant line of blue hills.

Ike properly belonged to the Browder outfit, but inasmuch as the two companies had joined for the trip south, he had taken it upon himself to move well forward and be the eyes for both. Like Jeff, he carried a carbine rather than the heavy fifty-caliber he would use for shooting buffalo. The lighter, shorter rifle would be more useful in a running skirmish. Even if they found buffalo today, they were unlikely to shoot into them. They would set up camp and make preparations first.

As Jeff came abreast of him, the red-bearded shooter gave a silent acknowledgment. From what Jeff had seen of him in the past, Ike was alone even in the midst of a crowd. He had observed him reading a Bible last night in the Browder camp. He respected the man's private ways and did not attempt to initiate conversation. Ike settled back, unreachable, in a somber world of his own. Jeff surmised that in some personal way Ike continued to fight the war in his mind. He had seen many men unable to turn it completely loose. Of those he knew who had been in it, not one had escaped without scars of some kind, including himself.

At length Ike looked up at the sun. "We've moved into country I've not seen before. What say I go there . . ." He pointed southwestward . . . "And you go yonder? Maybe one of us will find buffalo."

"Good. We'll cover twice the ground." Each would be alone if they happened upon Indians, but together or separately, such an encounter would likely end in a horserace back to the wagons anyway. Tar Baby could travel fast when pushed to it. Jeff had not seen Ike's big gray run. "Meet you at the wagons about sundown. Sooner if we see feathers."

Ike angled off. He appeared still immersed in his thoughts, but Jeff saw his head jerk as a jackrabbit hopped up from behind a clump of dry grass and skittered away in a zigzag pattern. Illinois Ike would not be caught asleep.

Far to the south, Jeff could see the blue front faces that marked a string of hills. He had been looking at them since early morning but seemed little closer now than when he had started. He thought it reasonable that if buffalo were to be found, they would be in hills and canyons and along timbered creeks where they had water and shelter from the bitter winter storms that soon would howl down out of the north.

This was Texas—it had to be—but this high plateau land was vastly different from the South Texas he had known, a land of sand and mesquite and chaparral, a land of short and usually-benign winters. It was a land of small farms, of long-horned cattle, of log cabins and adobe houses and Mexican *jacales* built from brush and mud. It was a land where a generation had grown up without seeing an Indian. But it had faced trouble enough of its own, trouble that wore blue uniforms or came carrying carpetbags and tax bills and eviction notices. It had seen blood spilled in dirt streets and in the loneliness of the brushy rangelands. It had become a region beset by greed and prejudice, factional hatreds and fear.

Yet it was a land he ached to see again. He longed to ride once more amid its chaparral, to chase a *ladino* steer through the brush and bring it to the ground with a rawhide reata like the Mexican *vaqueros* with whom he had sometimes worked. He wished he could sit in the little adobe farmhouse of his youth, staring into a fireplace at blazing dry mesquite, watching the changing images wrought by the bright red flames, building dreams that had eventually gone to gray ashes like the wood he had chopped and burned.

He thought of a woman he had once been convinced that he loved but who had married someone else soon after he joined the Confederate army. Odd, as badly hurt as he had felt at the time, he could hardly remember anymore what she looked like. When he tried to conjure up her image, more often than not Charity came to mind instead. He wondered sometimes what Charity would think about South Texas, though of course he could not take her there. Statutory limitations did not apply to a killing.

He came suddenly and unexpectedly upon a place where the level grassland seemed to fall away just in front of him, where a wrong step might plunge him down from a ragged edge onto a steep jumble of broken-off rimrock and red clay and black earth and finally into the floor of a canyon perhaps a hundred feet below. He stared in wonder, for he had been unaware until he was almost upon the brink. It had appeared that the plain would stretch on and on, to the eastern horizon and beyond.

The north wind carried a chill despite the sunshine, and a gust of it lifted Tar Baby's black mane. Jeff suspected that in the bottom of the canyon the air was still. He dismounted and led the horse to the rim. The old hip wound made walking painful, but he had to see. He watched his footing, knowing how easily the ground could break away under his weight to send him and the horse sliding, tumbling down that rough, steep wall.

At this point the canyon was probably two to three hundred yards wide, though it looked much wider to the south. This was but a narrow finger of it, a fracture in the plain. On the other side the plain continued, though he saw evidence of other fingers, other fractures. He reached back in memory for what he had heard about this part of the country. It was not much, for white men had never been welcome here. He reasoned that he had approached the eastern edge of the Staked Plains, that from here the land rapidly fell away.

He had heard different versions. Some said the great plateau had risen above the ground around it. Others said the lower country was but a remnant of what had been a far larger high ground. They said the land to the east had broken and sunk, that time and wind and rain had eaten it away until it was hundreds of feet lower.

The Indians probably had a more interesting story for it.

He stood and marveled, for this was as grand a sight as he had ever seen, grander than he would have imagined could exist in the same state where he had spent his youth. He saw a dozen colors and shades in the horizontal patterns of the canyon wall, as if it had been a many-layered cake, some layers ragged and broken as if set in place by a careless cook.

"Damned pretty scenery," he said aloud to the horse, "but this ain't findin' us any buffalo."

If there were any, he suspected they would be in that canyon, for the sun glinted upon a narrow stream farther south, down on the floor. He rode along the edge, looking for a way to descend. He found it after a while, a narrow old buffalo trail picking its way down a place where the canyon wall angled back, less steep than where he had first encountered it. The trail was packed almost as hard as a macadam road. He guessed that generations of buffalo and other grazing animals had used it for access to the high grass above, the water and shelter below. Walking, leading Tar Baby down, he saw dried droppings which indicated that buffalo had passed this way. His confidence began to rise.

The horse snorted as a startled deer leaped from a motte of brush and fled in a springing, bounding gait along the narrow creek, disappearing into a stand of small timber.

A good place for buffalo to spend the winter, Jeff thought. Or Indians. He slipped the carbine out of the military-style boot on his saddle and carried it in one hand. At the bottom of the trail he stopped to look around, to burn into memory the landmarks that would lead him back. He suspected that as he rode south the trail would disappear from view. In event of pursuit he could not afford to waste time hunting for the way out.

He rode north first, to the head of the canyon. It narrowed and closed within a few hundred yards. Above him towered the ragged wall, the rimrock jutting out at the top. Years of rain and wind had gradually eroded the supporting earth from beneath its edge, caus-ing the exposed rimrock to splinter and break off in pieces under its own weight. Shards lay scattered all the way down the slope. Near the bottom, water seeped from between layers of rock, enough that a tiny gurgling rivulet began at the head of the canyon and meandered southward. Here it was so narrow he could step across it. Other seeps and springs would augment it until it became a full-fledged creek farther along.

Beneath the sheltering wall he did not feel the chill north wind that had been at his back all day on the plain above. The sun felt warmer. The floor had a good cover of cured grass. He saw signs that it had recently been grazed, and a scattering of buffalo chips to show what had grazed it.

People claimed that buffalo were stupid, a belief supported by the fact that they would so often mill in confusion while a shooter killed them one by one. But Jeff reflected that they were intelligent enough to find a sheltered place to overwinter and not leave themselves exposed to the brutal extremes of the open plains.

He had been brought up to be a farmer and a stockman. For a few moments, turning and looking southward down the long canyon, he reflected with a stirring of excitement on what a fine place this would be to graze cattle, *his* cattle. But he dismissed the idea as impractical, at least for the foreseeable future. The buffalo would present formidable competition for the grass, and of course there would be the Indians. Even if he were somehow to acquire the land rights on paper, the Comanches held first claim by the force of bullet, arrow and lance. He had no idea how long they had been here, or who might have been here before and had yielded the land to their superior force. What mattered was that they were here now, and they would not relinquish it without spilling much blood.

Anyway, his present mission was not to look for grazing lands, it was to find buffalo. He followed the creek southward. As he had expected, it grew larger and wider as rivulets ran into it from seeps in the sides of the canyon. He watched the west wall for other trails that would lead to the top. He found several. He also found buffalo, a scattered few at first, then more and more as the canyon widened. It was now a mile across and looked wider farther on.

The buffalo exhibited no particular fear of him. Some already lying down and chewing their cud would not even arise until he came close enough to have thrown a rock at them. Those still grazing would move aside with a grunt of protest as he approached, but they did not stampede away. After he had passed, they would resume grazing. It was obvious they had not been fired into by white hunters, and it had probably been a while since they had been chased by Indian horsemen. They would be easy, for a time.

One thing would not be easy: bringing the wagons down into this canyon and taking them back on top once they were loaded with hides. After riding several miles and seeing no trail up that was fit for a wagon, Jeff explored a small side canyon and found a place where the west side was not a wall at all but a long and gentle slope. If necessary they could double the teams in going out, moving the wagons in relays.

On top, he stopped to study again the tranquility below, a broad canyon floor dotted with clusters of grazing or resting buffalo, brown, black and the shades between. A side of him took pleasure in the prospect for the wealth in which he would share. Another side enjoyed the scene for its beauty and regretted the carnage that his discovery was to bring. Once the guns began their talking and the skinning knives started their work, this peaceful place would be transformed by destruction and waste, death and decay. Never again would it look as he saw it now. He tarried, staring, wishing he might leave it as it was, a secret all his own.

But that was a futile wish, for more hunters followed behind the Cregar and Browder wagons. If his group did not claim this canyon and take these buffalo, others would. Colonel Cregar would say they were but the instruments of history, doing what had to be done for the manifest destiny that dictated the taming of the land, the conversion of the wilderness to the needs of civilized men.

Gazing down upon the contented animals scattered as far as he could see, visualizing the slaughter that awaited them, he did not feel civilized.

Seventeen

NIGEL SMITHWICK sat on his dun horse halfway up a game trail, watching Arletta Browder crouched behind a boulder just above the canyon floor. She steadied her father's old Sharps rifle across the top of the rock and fired slowly but consistently into a frightened cluster of some forty buffalo. One by one they fell to her marksmanship, kicking out their lives in spasms against the dry earth. Farther up the canyon, screened by a stand of small timber, Barney Gibson and Herman Scholtz waited with their wagon to start the skinning when Arletta finished this stand, or lost it.

Smithwick had tried firing the heavy rifle, but its violent recoil threatened to tear his wound open again. He contented himself with standing guard while Arletta did her own shooting. Illinois Ike was farther up the canyon. Smithwick could hear the distant echoes of his rifle, evenly spaced, methodical, as if Ike were some kind of killing machine. The hide-drying ground had expanded considerably.

Smithwick's gaze frequently searched from north to south, but he had seen no sign of Indians since they had arrived here and set up a semipermanent camp on the creek, near the protective canyon wall. Cold northers had begun shrieking down across the plains with discomforting regularity. Jeff had assured him this was a good thing because it kept the Indians fairly confined to their winter encampments, wherever those might be. In that respect, bad weather was the hunter's friend.

The storms were much less severe down here than up on top, the reason the buffalo had come to the canyon. Now, however, their refuge had become a trap. The hunters had blocked the game trails with timber and rocks so the animals could not scale the walls and escape. The Browder and Cregar camps were set up side by side for mutual protection against the Indians. It had been agreed that Arletta's company would hunt north of the camps and Cregar's to the south.

It disturbed Smithwick to watch Arletta manage a stand. Though shooting had exhilarated him, he wondered how a woman could calmly keep squeezing the trigger and taking the lives of these huge, bewildered beasts. She must find it distasteful, he thought, but if so she managed to cover her feelings. He remembered with some irony that when he had first met her he had assumed she was a simple country girl. She had proven to be a complex woman with contradictions difficult to reconcile.

One point that frustrated him was her growing interest in Farrell Cregar. Jeff had offered an explanation of sorts. He said Arletta had long admired the colonel, though in a fatherly role rather than as a potential lover. "Then along comes Farrell, who looks like the colonel except a hell of a lot younger. It's only natural she'd give him a good lookin'-over."

He had hinted at something else. He had suggested that Smithwick himself might have awakened dormant female urges which, rebuffed, sought fulfillment in the next eligible young man who came along. "You put a bull in a pen across from a heifer and she'll come into heat even if he can't reach her. She'll be ready to take the first bull that comes along."

Smithwick was put off by the indelicate comparison but realized the plain-speaking Texan was interpreting the situation in terms of his own cattle-country experience.

He tried to tell himself that Arletta's future was none of his affair; he had nothing to offer her. To take her to England was out of the question; she could never be part of his circle there, not if she tried for twenty years. Still, he wanted her to have a better life than she had experienced up to now. Her father, though he tried, had brought her many disappointments. He feared that Farrell Cregar offered nothing more.

True, Farrell was young, and he was handsome enough. It was to be expected that he might turn a lonely woman's head. Still, Smithwick sensed something less than handsome behind the facade. The mouth smiled easily, but the eyes did not. Farrell seemed to him like a pleasant painting hanging on the wall, all illusion because it was flat and cold to the touch. Turn the painting around and the back side was empty.

Jeff had told him about finding Farrell in a Dodge City crib, and about the antagonism that smoldered between father and son. He had not told Arletta. Perhaps Smithwick should, for she seemed to have little or no inkling of it. But how could he? How could he articulate his suspicion that Farrell was toying with her to torment his father? She would probably reject the suggestion, as she had rejected all advice about turning back to Dodge City, and resent him for telling her.

Smithwick had not helped her with the speller or the reader since the skirmish that had killed her father. He had tried once to read *Oliver Twist* to her, but an invisible wall of hurt had risen between them. He had seen that her mind drifted elsewhere, perhaps to the buffalo, perhaps to Farrell. The London of the Dickens story seemed a million miles away, and a thousand years.

Arletta slowed her shooting, then stopped. She carried with her a small canteen so she could run a wet patch of cloth down the barrel and cool it. The remaining buffalo continued to mill for a bit, then a cow set off southward in a trot. The others followed her. Smithwick rode down to where Arletta sat on a small rock, running the wet patch through for a third time. He remembered how her father had cooled the same rifle. He wondered if she knew. It was not something a gentleman would tell her.

He asked, "Don't you think you have killed enough?"

"When all the wagons are loaded with hides, that'll be enough." Her gaze followed the escaping animals. "How's the back?"

"About healed. I should soon be able to take over this job for you."

"I'm doin' all right. Papa taught me a long time ago how to shoot."

"Did he teach you how not to see the blood?"

Her eyes narrowed critically. "He taught me that some things die so that other things can live. That's nature. It's been goin' on since the Creation."

"But this is not the place for a woman."

"That's what everybody keeps sayin'. And just what do you think a woman's place is? In a kitchen, settin' food on the table for a man? Been years since I've lived in a house. I haven't had a kitchen *nor* a table. Maybe when this hunt is over I'll have those things. Maybe I'll live the way you think a woman's supposed to. If it's to my likin'."

The impatient snap in her voice took him aback. He said, "I just want what your father wanted, for you to have the best life you can. This is certainly not it."

"What will you care whether I get all that or not? You'll be on the other side of the water, doin' whatever it is that Englishmen do."

"I'll care. That is why I brought you the books. I wanted you to take pleasure from what reading can bring you."

"Someday I *will* learn myself to read books like you do, and I'll learn how to write a fit and proper letter. I might even write to you in England and tell you how I'm gettin' along. But before I can do all that I'll need a lot more buffalo hides."

Gingerly she felt the barrel. "It's cooled down considerable. I wish you'd go tell Barney and Herman they can start the skinnin'." She mounted her horse and set out in the wake of the scattered buffalo.

He watched her and felt empty.

AS HE HAD PROMISED, Colonel worked Farrell like a mule in the daytime, keeping him skinning or pegging out or turning skins, chopping firewood, reloading cartridges, whatever would keep his son's back sore and his hands raw. But Farrell was never so exhausted that he failed to visit Arletta in the Browder camp at night, every night.

Colonel came over one evening a while after Farrell arrived. He bade his son to leave. "I want to talk to Arletta."

Farrell retorted, "*I'm* talking to her."

Cregar pointed toward his camp. "Go, I said!" His voice brooked no argument. Farrell glared at his father, but he retreated, looking back over his shoulder.

Arletta stood beside the campfire, her eyes resentful over Colonel's imperious manner. "What do you want to talk to me about?"

Smithwick and several other men sat nearby. Colonel surveyed them critically. "I would prefer we speak in private."

"This is about as private as it gets around here. Secrets don't last long in a camp like this anyway."

Colonel gave the men a dark frown. "It's Farrell. I want you to tell him to stop coming over here."

"He's your son. You talk to him."

"I've tried. He hears only what he wants to."

"He's grown. I'm grown. He wants to come see me, and I don't mind it, so what's the wrong in that?"

Reluctantly Colonel said, "There are things you don't know about him. I am ashamed to say it, but he's not good enough for you."

Arletta's eyes flashed. "I guess I'm old enough to decide who's good for me and who isn't."

Colonel seemed to realize he had overstepped himself. He became almost apologetic. "I am thinking of your welfare, Arletta."

"No, you're tryin' to run everybody's lives includin' mine. You've got no claim on me. Nobody has." She cut her gaze to Smithwick for a moment, then turned toward her tent, leaving Colonel standing there red-faced and frustrated.

EVEN BEFORE the lanky Parson Parkhill appeared one evening to share supper and offer his good offices with the Lord on behalf of anyone needing his intercession, Smithwick knew other hunting parties had made camp in the area. He had heard the boom of their rifles in the distance. It was custom among veteran buffalo runners that first claims to a herd be respected, though eager greenhorns had sometimes broken up a hunter's stand by firing into a herd he had staked out as his own. Himself and Farrell excepted, Smithwick thought it unlikely that many greenhorns had yet ventured this far south of Dodge City.

Newly arrived hunting parties had settled in other branches of the canyon, or in other breaks and canyons where interference between them would be minimal. Any resentment over competition for the buffalo was largely offset by the feeling of safety in numbers. Hunters took comfort in knowing they were not completely alone, that in event of trouble others were near enough to hear and, they hoped, hurry to their aid.

Parkhill was distressed to learn of Cephus Browder's death and offered to hold a memorial service for him after supper. "His body may have been left buried on the prairie, but it is only clay. His spirit is what matters."

Arletta said gratefully, "Papa was a good man, and I expect he's got to heaven on his own. But I'd be obliged for any good words you might want to say."

What started as a funeral service developed into a lengthy prayer for success in the present hunting venture and for protection of God's servants from whatever dangers might lurk in this trackless wilderness. Smithwick wondered at the propriety of asking the Lord to deliver up buffalo for wholesale butchery inasmuch as they were also His creatures.

Parkhill covered that unspoken question: "Only when the buffalo are gone will the heathen yield up this land so that it may know the blessings of civilization and serve the needs of those who know and fear Thee. On this delivered ground we shall build churches to proclaim Thy glory, and towns where Thy servants may live in peace and piety and prosperity."

Towns like Dodge City? Smithwick wondered.

Farrell Cregar stood next to Arletta during the service. Smithwick noted that Colonel Cregar's critical gaze never left the pair, not even when all heads were bowed except his own. Colonel did not join the *Amen* at the end of the long prayer. He seemed impatient to be about other business, though it was night and there was no urgent business to be done. When Arletta went to her cook wagon, Farrell trailed after her.

Colonel motioned Parkhill toward a large cottonwood log that had been dragged into camp for a seat near one of the campfires. "Parson, you seem to have a great deal of persuasive power with the Lord. How much of that power would you have over a young woman who stands badly in need of counsel?"

Parkhill looked toward Arletta's wagon. "I know you want her to return to Dodge City. But with these two combined camps, you have a great deal of defensive strength. Arletta is in less danger here than in a smaller party caught out on the trail."

"I can see other dangers besides Indians. She is a lone woman in a camp with many men."

"I know most of these men. Some are given to drink and to gambling and to consorting with harlots when they are in town. But I doubt that there is one who would take advantage of a decent woman like Arletta. On the contrary, I believe they would defend her to the death."

Colonel stared darkly into the fire. "Would you at least talk to her?"

It was the first time Smithwick had heard Colonel Cregar make a request in a tone of supplication. He had not thought the man had it in him.

From a distance came Farrell's voice. Smithwick strained to make out the words but could not. He heard Arletta's quiet laugh.

Parkhill looked in that direction, then back to Colonel. His expression in the firelight indicated that he understood what Cregar was trying in an oblique manner to say. "I'll not tell her what to do, but I shall pray for her to make the right decision. And I shall make the same prayer for you, Colonel."

Parkhill went to Arletta's wagon, and Farrell came to the fire. Father and son did not look at one another. The preacher returned after a bit. "She remains adamant. For now, Colonel, I think you had best leave her be."

Farrell went back to Arletta. Smithwick could hear their voices in low and private conversation. Sully led Parkhill's horse up from the picket line. Parkhill thanked him, swung into the saddle, then shouted to all within hearing, "Should any of you feel a need for the Word, or just for a cup of the strongest coffee south of Dodge City, you are welcome in my camp." He rode into the winter darkness.

Sully moved up to the fire to warm his hands. "That there is a mighty fine gentleman. He listens to the Lord."

Gruffly Colonel Cregar said, "I would hope so, for I do not believe he listened to me." He moved toward his tent.

Smithwick sat looking into the flames. A few snowflakes began falling, dancing in the campfire's rising heat, most evaporating before they could die in the blaze. Jeff Layne sat down beside him and began whittling idly on a stick. He said, "I've been lookin' for a storm to start just about any time."

"We have not had much snow yet."

"I was thinkin' about a different kind of storm. You still standin' guard over Arletta while she shoots?"

"I have not let her go unprotected."

"Are you sure?" Jeff looked toward the cook wagon.

Smithwick followed his gaze. It was dark there; he could not see Arletta or Farrell. "She's of age to make her own decisions . . . whether to stay or to go . . . who to like and who to turn her back upon."

"I remember once when I was a boy down in South Texas. There was a deep hole of water in the river that went through our place, and a big fish that I sure did want to catch. But I kept puttin' it off, thinkin' he'd always be there when I got ready to take him. Then along come a feller with a cane pole, and first thing I knew he was walkin' off with my fish."

Jeff pitched the stick into the fire and folded the pocketknife. He held out his hand to catch some snowflakes. "Enjoy your tent tonight. I'll be wishin' I had one if I have to shake six inches of snow off of my tarp in the mornin'."

Smithwick called, "Wait a minute." He followed Jeff into the darkness where nobody could overhear. "What could I do? I have no claim on her. I have told you why I could not take her to England."

"So now you're finally askin' for my advice?"

"I suppose I am."

"This is her country. Here she don't have to change, don't have to be anybody but herself. Why would you have to take her somewhere else?" He held out his hand and caught more snowflakes. "I've met Englishmen that learned to like it here so much they wouldn't ever go back. Why do you figure you have to?"

The snow fell harder, but Smithwick was not ready for his blankets. He brushed away that which had fallen upon the cottonwood log and sat down again, leaning toward the fire. He waited alone until Farrell came by on the way to his own camp.

"Farrell," Smithwick said, "we have never had a real conversation. Would you care to sit for a minute?"

"In the snow?" Farrell had but little snow on his shoulders. Obviously he had been inside Arletta's tent. "It's not getting any warmer out here."

"You seem to like Arletta."

"Any reason I shouldn't?"

"That depends upon your intentions."

"Her father is dead. Have you appointed yourself to take his place?"

"I made a promise to him. But the main thing is that I consider myself her friend. I would not want to see her hurt."

"Then you keep watching her in the daytime so the Indians don't get her. When evening comes, *I'll* watch out for her."

"You know what I am trying to say. Do wrong by her and you will answer to me."

Farrell stiffened. From where Smithwick sat, looking up at him, he appeared seven feet tall. "She's my business, Englishman. Don't you meddle in my business, or I just might hurt you."

As Farrell left, Smithwick leaned down to pick up a small stone from between his feet. Without thinking better, he hurled it into the flames. It struck the burning wood and raised a shower of sparks. His shoulder grabbed him like a meat hook and made him gasp in pain.

INEVITABLY buffalo numbers thinned to a point that the daily hunts yielded scarcely enough hides to busy the skinners for more than a couple of hours. The only time Smithwick saw Arletta's face light up with the kind of smile she used to display was when Farrell Cregar came to visit the camp each evening.

Colonel Cregar looked more and more like a thundercloud about to hurl a lightning bolt at whatever offended him. He came with Jeff Layne to the Browder camp one night after supper to confer with Arletta. Smithwick was not invited to be a party to the conversation, but he was already sitting at the fire. He chose not to get up and leave.

Cregar told Arletta, "Jeff and I agree that we need to find a new camp. We've about wrung this one out."

"I'm afraid you're right."

Jeff said, "Me and Ike can start scoutin' south in the mornin'." He turned. "English, do you feel up to a ride? Liable to take a couple or three days."

Surprised at being asked, Smithwick said, "It might be good for me."

Arletta appeared dubious. "Are you sure you're up to it?"

"Yes. I am only concerned that you might not have someone to watch over you while you shoot."

"I don't really need watchin', Nigel. I've just humored you so you wouldn't feel like you didn't earn your keep."

His face warmed with chagrin.

Colonel said, "I would ask that you take Farrell along." He glanced at Arletta, then cut his gaze away. "He could learn something from you men."

Jeff's frown indicated that he had rather carry along a sack of snakes. "Ain't no tellin' what we might run into."

"He needs seasoning. A little hardship, a little danger might have a salutary effect. And I give you my permission to administer corporal punishment if he fails."

Arletta said, "I'll speak to Farrell. He won't be givin' you any trouble."

Jeff glanced at Smithwick, then gave Arletta a doubting look. "You sure he'll pay attention to what you tell him?"

She smiled. "He has so far."

They set out shortly after daylight. Farrell had put up no resistance against riding with the others to look for a new hunting ground. It was a chance to escape the back-breaking camp labor for a while. He trailed a length behind the other three until Jeff declared, "Bad things can happen to stragglers in this country."

"We haven't seen an Indian since before the Cimarron."

"That don't mean they haven't seen *you.*"

Farrell caught up, riding abreast of the others but remaining well on the outside. He was with them, yet alone.

Smithwick had tried to be objective in analyzing his instinctive distrust of the colonel's son beyond the obvious fact that Arletta seemed attracted to him. He had been slow in recognizing one factor: Farrell had been reared to privilege, not having to work if he did not so wish. Smithwick gradually came to see in him some reflection of his own past, a reflection that was becoming increasingly distasteful. His family had called him a wastrel. They had accused him of having no sense of commitment, of directing his life solely toward pleasure. Now that circumstances had forced him to accept responsibilities, he realized with regret that his family had been right on all counts. He wondered if Farrell would ever come to a similar conclusion.

The four men's search for a new hunting ground carried them by a couple of camps established after their own. Exploring a likely-looking branch of the broadening canyon, they found Parson Parkhill had already settled in for what he hoped would be two or three weeks of good shooting. The tall, lanky preacher said, "It is not like the Garden of Eden we found on the Republican, but we rough-counted upward of a thousand head grazing along this branch. The Lord continues to provide. Would you gentlemen care to break bread with us?"

Jeff accepted for the group. "I've been curious to see what kind of cook keeps you so skinny. You wouldn't dress out sixty pounds with the liver and lights left in."

"The cook is fine. The Lord has chosen to leave me skinny so that I do not tempt young maidens to the primrose path."

Smithwick noticed that Farrell seemed hungriest of them all, eating a second plateful. The hard work the Colonel imposed upon him had given him a strong appetite.

Finished, Farrell asked Parkhill, "Are you truly a minister?"

"I am, sir. I served as a chaplain in the late unpleasantness."

"In which army?"

Parkhill looked first at Jeff, who had fought for the Confederacy, and then at Illinois Ike, who had worn the blue. "At this late date, sir, I do not see that it makes a difference. We are all one again in the sight of the law, and all mankind is one in the sight of the Lord. Even the heathen Indian."

Smithwick thought that if Parkhill ever tired of the ministry he probably could find a place for himself in politics. And politics could certainly stand an infusion of religion.

Riding farther south under Jeff's leadership, they found the canyon broadening into a fertile valley several miles wide. Its steep walls fell away to the east and west and became benign.

Jeff was enthusiastic. "I wish you'd look at the grass. This ought to be good buffalo country if somebody ain't beat us to it."

The deep sound of a buffalo rifle brought the riders late in the day to a small camp half hidden in scrub timber beside a stream so narrow that Smithwick could have jumped across it with a running start. This was a single-shooter outfit, with one man in camp reloading cartridges and starting supper. Once he determined that his prospective visitors were not Indians, he set down his rifle and waved them in with his hat. "You-all come and give them horses a rest. We'll have supper after awhile, when the bunch gets in."

Smithwick saw nothing notable about the camp except that the canvas stretched over the wagon hoops was a rusty red instead of the usual gray or dirty white. The man looked like just another of that anonymous horde of hunters and skinners he had seen in Dodge City, but Jeff and Ike knew him. They called him Tug. They exchanged pleasant greetings, almost the only time all day that Ike had spoken half a dozen words in succession.

Jeff asked, "You still tendin' camp for Archie Grosvenor?"

Tug said, "Ain't nobody else'll put up with that Englishman. Him and his skinners'll be draggin' in for supper directly."

Smithwick felt a surge of interest. "You say the man is English?"

Tug gave him a quizzical look, recognizing the accent. "Damned country's gettin' overrun with them, looks like. If you want any tea, you'll have to fix it yourself."

"I have become reconciled to coffee, among many things."

While Jeff and Ike sat with Tug to visit about the prospects for buffalo, Smithwick noticed that the pile of wood was low at the cook fire. He decided to make himself useful. He searched along the creek for deadfall timber and started dragging it up in small amounts that would not tax his healing back. Farrell was taking no part in the conversation. Smithwick suggested, "If you are bored, you could help me."

Farrell was far from his father's iron discipline now. "I'm tired," he said.

Daylight was fading when Grosvenor and his two skinners returned to camp with their wagon. Jeff and Ike shook hands with the middle-aged hunter whose hair and beard were mostly white. Jeff introduced him to Smithwick. "English here is a countryman of yours, only he ain't reformed yet like you have. I wish you'd tell him that this ain't a bad country."

"Indeed it's not," declared Grosvenor, grasping Smithwick's hand with strength and gusto. "How long has it been since you left the old fogbank and came to the sunshine?"

"A bit more than six months. And you?"

"Seven years. You could not pay me enough to make me live there again." He stepped back to observe Smithwick with a certain bemusement. "A fellow Englishman and prospective convert to the new world. This calls for something more than coffee. Gentlemen, I believe I might unearth a bottle if I explore deeply enough into the supply wagon."

Jeff said, "We'll help your skinners unload and stake the hides first. English has got a sore back, so why don't you and him set and visit?"

Ike and Jeff pitched in with Grosvenor's skinners. Farrell stood back and watched. "Now sir," Grosvenor said to Smithwick, motioning for him to be seated by the fire, "tell me how things were the last time you saw merry old England." For an expatriate who expressed no desire to return, he seemed highly interested in hearing about what he had missed.

After the visitors shared biscuits and buffalo hump and coffee with the small crew, Grosvenor broke out the promised bottle. Not all hunting outfits were as scrupulous as Colonel Cregar about liquor in camp. While the bottle was on its second round, Jeff inquired about Grosvenor's knowledge of the country below. The white-bearded shooter said, "So far as I am aware, there are no companies to the south of us. I purposely negotiated a wide circle around the other camps so we would not find ourselves in one another's way."

Jeff promised, "We won't crowd you."

"I would appreciate that. We have not found enough bison that we can afford to share and still show a profit on the trip. I fear that for the hide trade the best times are gone."

Jeff agreed. "It'll pretty soon be time to start lookin' for another business or learn to live without eatin'. Ever thought about raisin' cattle, Archie?"

"The idea has occurred to me. But I would need a partner who knows something about them. You have had some experience, have you not?"

"Growed up with them, south of here. Way south." Jeff gazed off into the darkness. Sadness came into his eyes.

Farrell held control of the bottle most of the evening, accounting for half of its contents by himself. He sat a little apart from the others, making no attempt at conversation. Between asking questions of Smithwick and telling him how much he enjoyed life in this new country, Grosvenor would not have given Farrell much of an opening anyway.

Grosvenor said, "I might go for a visit—I still have family there, you know—but I would feel suffocated were I forced to remain. I tell you, Nigel, my coming to this country with its open plains and its open opportunities was like being granted a new life. I am free of stuffy conventions, free to do and be what I want, not burdened by what is expected of me because of my ancestors."

"You have no regrets?"

"Only that I waited so long. I have lived more in these seven years than in all my previous life. Were I to knock on the golden gates tomorrow and St. Peter were to ask me which part of heaven I wished to enter, I would request that it be such a place as these plains. I don't suppose you understand what I mean."

Smithwick smiled. "I have gained some inkling."

JEFF AWAKENED him early, and they saddled their horses at daylight. Smithwick stretched his goodbyes, reluctant to break up the association with his newly found countryman.

Grosvenor placed a hand on Smithwick's shoulder. "Jeff told me about the young lady. I say if you want her, find yourself a home here and forget what those back in England would think. It is your life, not theirs."

As the four riders continued south, the canyon walls continued to fall away until Smithwick saw them no more. He sensed that he and his companions were gradually descending to lower ground. They rode toward a line of broken hills, where he saw a scattering of buffalo, then larger and larger numbers, groups of fifty to two hundred apiece. Like those they had first encountered in the canyon, these exhibited little fear of the horsemen. They warily moved aside but quickly resumed grazing.

Jeff observed, "Looks like they ain't been shot into."

Farrell replied, "Not yet." Eagerly he brought up his carbine.

Jeff leaned to lay a firm hand on the barrel. "Not now. You'd just spook them up before there's any purpose in it."

Farrell protested, "They tell me the Indians run them when they hunt. There would be some sport in that. The way we do it, we'd just as well be shooting someone's milk cows."

Jeff's voice was stern. "You ever find yourself afoot with one of them buffalo snortin' into your pockets, you'll *think* milk cow. This is not supposed to be sport. It's a mean and bloody business. Run them and you wouldn't get half as many hides. What's more, the skinners would have to travel all over hell and half of Texas for the buffalo you *did* shoot."

They found a suitable campsite on a creek wider and swifter than the one where they had headquartered in the canyon. Its timber was taller and thicker, which would help make up for the loss of the protective canyon walls if a harsh winter storm bore down upon them.

Jeff turned to Smithwick. "You heard any shootin' today?"

"Not a shot."

Ike simply shook his head.

"Well then," Jeff said, "Colonel's goin' to be right pleased. Looks like we've come upon a virgin ground."

Farrell declared, "I always liked that word: virgin."

Smithwick knotted his fist but had nothing to say.

Eighteen

JEFF AND IKE looked over their shoulders often, not only watching for danger but fixing landmarks in their minds so they would have no trouble finding their way back here. It went against Jeff's cowboy upbringing to explain his every move. He expected a man to discern things for himself by observation.

Smithwick asked no questions, but Farrell failed in the discernment department. "You keep looking back as if you expect Indians to attack at any minute. I don't believe there is an Indian within a hundred miles."

Jeff scowled at him. "No? Then maybe you'll take a look over yonderway." He jabbed his thumb in a westward direction.

Farrell squinted. "Where? I don't see a thing."

"*You* wouldn't," Jeff said sharply, letting the matter drop. He was running a bluff, trying to jolt Farrell to a higher degree of awareness. He succeeded, because Farrell kept watching for whatever it was that Jeff had seen or pretended to see, then turning to look behind him. He no longer straggled.

Jeff said in a satisfied voice, "I don't believe we'll need to use any corporal punishment."

Smithwick seemed to see through Jeff's ruse. "That is a bloody shame."

Jeff made it a point to stop again at the Grosvenor camp, giving Smithwick another chance to visit with his countryman and Gros-

venor further opportunity to argue the merits of Smithwick's remaining in this country. He thought he could see Smithwick weakening. At Parson Parkhill's they availed themselves of another
cooked meal, better than they would have prepared for themselves
on the trail. Parkhill was eager to know about the new hunting
ground they had found. Ike said nothing. Jeff was purposely eva-
sive, simply tilting his head southward. "It's down yonder a ways."
Smithwick had the good judgment not to comment, and Farrell
was too busy eating to talk.

Riding away from Parkhill's camp, Jeff muttered, "Even a
preacher ain't above jumpin' the claim on a good buffalo ground.
He can always say the Lord led him to it. Him and the Lord'll have
to find this one without any help from us."

As canyon walls closed in, Jeff knew they were nearing camp.
Even cold weather could not stop the carcasses from stinking, and
they lay in various stages of decay. Smithwick looked disturbed.
Jeff said, "It ain't all waste. Come back a year from now, and
everywhere that a shaggy has died you'll find the grass taller and
greener. He fed on the grass, and now the grass feeds on him. The
Indians say everything moves in a circle."

"Grass would seem to be of little use if no buffalo remain to eat
it."

"Grass is good for its own sake. It helps hold the earth together.
I used to wish for grass like this down in the South Texas cow
country. The buffalo is cousin to the cow, you know."

"They are cloven-hooved, and they all chew cud. I see little
other resemblance."

"You ain't seen those wild Longhorns runnin' in the deep brush.
They've got lots of the buffalo's habits and ways. They ain't yard
pets, that's for damned sure."

He began to hear distant shots, the measured firing of a buffalo
rifle. "Colonel's. I can tell by the sound."

As they approached the killing ground he saw two men in a
wagon, moving out among a dozen or so scattered black and brown
carcasses. The pair were too far away to recognize, but he assumed
they were a couple of Colonel's skinners, ready to do their work.
One man climbed down and approached a fallen buffalo while the

other took the wagon farther toward the center of the killing area. The man afoot bent to make the initial slit along the lower jaw.

Suddenly the buffalo rose up hind end first and shook itself. Even at the distance, Jeff imagined he could hear its bellow of rage and the frightened cry of the skinner as he stumbled backward, then turned to run. The bull charged after him, its huge head down, its short tail twitching.

The potential was deadly. Jeff spurred his black horse, Smithwick's dun and Ike's big gray but half a length behind him. Farrell brought up the rear. Jeff saw little chance of reaching the skinner before the buffalo caught him. The man ran hard, dodging like a rabbit trying to escape a wolf, but the bull stayed on his heels, lifting its black head in swift jerks, trying to impale him on its sharp horns.

The wagon driver swung the mule team around and vigorously applied the whip. Jeff was near enough now to hear him shouting at the mules and the other man desperately crying for help. Fighting the team, the driver forced them to cut between the man and the bull. A black horn slashed viciously at the near mule, which tried to jump over the traces and threatened for a tense moment to flip the wagon. The driver regained control and kept the wheels rolling. He motioned wildly to the running man. "Grab on! Grab on!"

The skinner clutched the tailgate and tried to swing aboard but was too exhausted to make it. He clung to the wagon, his feet dragging in the dry grass. He shouted in panic while the driver laid the whip to the mules and pulled away. The bull stopped, pawing the ground, shaking its head in anger and pain. Blood and mucus streamed from its nose. Jeff stepped down from the black horse, carbine in his hand, and dropped the animal with one shot to the lungs.

His excitement ebbed. "Colonel must've knocked the bull down but missed the vitals. I did that once myself. Still got a scar where the horn gouged my ribs."

The winded and frightened skinner was Gantry Folsom. He had dropped to hands and knees in the brittle grass. Wheezing for breath, he shook like a leaf in the wind.

In relief now that the danger was past, Smithwick let a laugh bubble up. "It would appear that the ribs were not the part most in jeopardy for Mr. Folsom."

The wagon circled and came back. Sully sawed on the lines to halt the excited, trembling mules. "You all right, Mr. Gant?"

Folsom, still on hands and knees, slowly looked up through the dust, first at the four horsemen, then at the black man. He tried to speak but could not. Mouth open, he continued to struggle for breath.

Sully got the mules quieted, then jumped down and fetched Folsom a cup of water out of a wooden keg tied to the sideboard. Folsom gulped it, choking a little. When he finally was able to speak, his first words were, "Goddamn you, nigger, where were you at? You like to've got me killed."

Sully's mouth dropped open, but he did not reply.

Smithwick exploded, "He saved your life, you stupid son of a bitch!"

Jeff blinked in surprise at the Englishman's unaccustomed outburst.

Folsom's glare swept from one of the men to another, settling on Jeff. "And where the Goddamned hell were *you?*"

Jeff said, "We were too far away. If Sully hadn't done what he did, we could've thrown your hide in the wagon with the rest of them. He saved your neck, and that's a mortal fact."

Folsom scowled at Sully and continued to tremble in the aftermath of his narrow escape. Sully stared at him in silence, bewildered by the man's hostility.

Jeff said, "The way you're shakin', Gant, you'll cut those hides to ribbons. You'd just as well go back to camp."

Sully argued, "But we got all that skinnin' to do."

"I'm no greenhorn with a knife. I'll stay and help you." He jerked his head at Folsom. "You can ride Tar Baby. You better treat him like he was a basket of eggs, or I'll bust a singletree over your head."

Folsom mounted stiffly and awkwardly. He was about to ride away, but Smithwick took hold of the bit. "There is one thing remaining. I did not hear you say *thank you* to Sully."

Folsom growled, "You can go to hell. And him too." He drummed his bare heels against the black horse's ribs and set off

toward camp. Ike shook his head and followed twenty yards behind. That was close enough, given the fact that the wind was out
of the north and Folsom had neither bathed nor changed clothes
since God knew when. Farrell put his bay into a long trot to catch
up. Smithwick remained with Jeff.

Jeff said, "You'd just as well go to camp too, English."

"I would not be much help at skinning, but I can stand watch."

"Suit yourself." Jeff turned to Sully. "I don't savvy why Colonel
sent you out with Gant, knowin' how hard he treats you."

"Mr. Gant's skinnin' partner slipped and cut a gash in his hand.
Colonel said I'd best take his place for a few days. He told Mr.
Gant that if he done me any hurt he'd tie him to a wagon wheel
and roast him like a pig."

"That'd be one stinkin' fire."

Sully looked puzzled. "I didn't expect Mr. Gant to hug my neck
or nothin', but I didn't look for him to act like it was all my fault."

"He owes you. The longer he studies on that, the worse it'll dig
into his craw. Of all the men in this outfit, you're the last one he'd
want to be in debt to."

"Because I'm black?"

"He's white trash, and he knows it. He ain't been able to hold
himself better than any man in the outfit except you. Now he owes
you, and he'll hate you for it."

Sully's eyes were troubled. "It don't make sense."

"The last time the world made sense, I was a barefooted kid in
South Texas." Jeff set out across the killing ground. "I'd better see
if I can find the knife that Gant dropped."

Daylight had given way to dusk as the wagon rumbled into
camp, its load of fresh hides quivering to the jolting of the wheels.
Jeff, on the wagon seat, saw that the drying grounds were almost
bare. The earlier hides had been taken up and loaded on wagons.
Both camps had been prepared for moving.

Elijah Layne hobbled up, relieved to see Jeff. "It gave me a start,
Son, when I seen Gant come ridin' in on your horse. I was afraid
somethin' had happened to you."

"Nothin' ever happens to me. Did you hear about Gant's little
foot race?"

The old man's eyes sparkled. "Farrell told us. The boys been hoorawin' Gant till he's about ready to bite a snake."

Jeff turned to Sully. "He'll blame you for that. You should've let the bull get him. Nobody would've faulted you."

"The Lord would've seen, and I'll have to face Him one of these days."

Colonel Cregar strode to the hide wagon, his back as straight and stiff as a ramrod. "There's no point in unloading those hides. We'll break camp at sunup." He put a huge hand on the sideboard. "You did some quick thinking out there, Sully."

Sully smiled uneasily, his eyes looking for Gantry Folsom. "Thank you, sir."

Colonel turned his attention to Jeff. "Farrell appeared none the worse for wear. Evidently you did not have to use corporal punishment."

"It never did come to that."

"A pity. A good whipping might do a great deal for that boy."

Jeff said ruefully, "I ain't sure I'm big enough to do it."

As Cregar walked away, Jeff looked across into the Browder camp. He could see Arletta at the cook wagon, where she and the peg-leg were preparing supper. Farrell sat on a log, sipping coffee from a tin cup.

Jeff looked at Smithwick. "Farrell didn't waste any time. You ought to've come to camp when I first told you."

Smithwick shrugged. "It probably would have made no difference."

"I let another man take a girl away from me once. But at least I had a war for an excuse."

Smithwick did not answer. He led his dun horse toward the other camp.

Farrell did not come to his father's wagon for supper, taking his meal with Arletta instead. Jeff walked over there after he finished eating. Arletta arose from the wagon tongue, where she had been sitting beside Farrell. She said, "Ike and Farrell talked like you saw a lot of buffalo. Enough, you think, to finish out our wagons?"

They appeared two-thirds full already. Jeff said, "Like as not."

She seemed pleased. "I've been tellin' Farrell that if we get all the hides the wagons can carry, and if they fetch as much in Dodge as they ought to, I plan to sell the outfit and go back to Ohio like Papa wanted. I should have enough to buy a little farm like the one we lost. Maybe even the same place."

"You couldn't farm a place by yourself."

"I may not always be by myself."

Jeff felt a tingle of apprehension for her and for Smithwick. The Englishman was looking down at his feet. Farrell continued to sip his coffee as if he had not heard. Jeff tried to picture him with his hands on a plow. The picture refused to come together.

Presently he saw Arletta and Farrell stroll off together in the winter darkness. He poured himself a cup of coffee and sat down by Smithwick. He sipped and shook his head. "Coffee tastes a little bitter tonight."

Smithwick's voice was sad. "I thought so too."

Colonel Cregar came over after a while. His gaze searched the men seated around the fire. "I want to talk to Arletta about tomorrow's move. Has she already retired?"

Barney Gibson offered, "Maybe so. I saw her and your son together a while ago. I guess he's gone back to your camp."

Suspiciously Cregar said, "No he hasn't." He moved out of the firelight toward Arletta's tent beyond the cook wagon. For a minute there was silence, then an explosive, "Farrell, you come out of there!"

Jeff heard a surprised cry from Arletta and an angry response in a voice he knew was Farrell's. Jumping to his feet, he made out the vague form of Colonel Cregar in a half crouch as he held back the tent flap to peer inside. Farrell emerged. The two big men faced one another, Colonel advancing, Farrell backing away with his hands up in a defensive posture.

Colonel's voice snapped like a bullwhip. "You sorry whelp! Taking advantage of an innocent girl . . ." His right arm moved in a blur, and Jeff heard the fist connect with Farrell's chin. Farrell stumbled backward and fell.

Colonel stepped forward. "I thought you might've learned something from your trouble back home. Get up from there! Get up and take the whipping of your life!" As Farrell pushed himself from the ground, that huge fist hit him again. Farrell staggered but this time did not fall.

Arletta moved beyond the tent flap, her dress in disarray. "No!" she cried. "No!" She grabbed Colonel's arm. He jerked free and advanced on Farrell. He swung his fist again, but Farrell managed to duck under it, then step in quickly and bring up his own fist from near the ground. The colonel shuddered at the impact. He rubbed a big hand against his chin, then roared and charged again. He did not swing but spread his arms to grapple with Farrell, trying to throw him to the ground.

The men who had ringed the campfire began shouting, most for the colonel but one or two for Farrell. Hearing the commotion, men hurried over from the Cregar camp.

Smithwick said, "We'd better try to stop this. They could hurt one another."

Jeff gripped the Englishman's arm to hold him back. "Leave them alone. There's two damnyankees that deserve one another."

The Cregars were still on their feet, arms locked, each trying to throw the other off balance. Stumbling, staggering into the flickering reddish firelight, they looked like two awkward dancers, one leading for a step or two, then the other. The onlookers scattered, yielding them room.

Arletta shouted futilely, "Stop it! Both of you, stop it!"

The colonel's bull strength seemed to gain an advantage, and he pushed Farrell back several steps. Then Farrell planted his feet solidly on the hard-packed ground and reversed the direction. Off balance, Colonel gave way. He stumbled backward into the fire, drawing Farrell into it after him. The burning logs rolled out from under them. Sparks leaped like fireflies.

The heat forced the two men to separate, both pausing to stomp away the sparks and tiny coals that clung to their boots. The colonel rushed but met Farrell's fist head-on and staggered. His hesitation gave Farrell time to punch him again, a sidewise blow that glanced from his jaw. Colonel's mouth was bleeding, but so was Farrell's nose. Colonel came back with a punch to Farrell's ribs, and Farrell lost most of his breath.

The two men faced off, trading punches, grunting from the exertion, crying in anger and frustration and pain. Jeff wondered how they managed to remain standing.

Arletta moved to put herself between them. Jeff pulled her back.

Gently he said, "You'll only get yourself hurt. It's been weeks a-buildin'. Let them beat it out of their systems."

It took an excruciatingly long time. Colonel was the first to go to the ground, heaving for breath. Farrell swung at him, lost his balance and fell. Both were on their knees, faces and fists bloody, clothes torn and powdered with dry dirt except where their sweat had caked it into mud. They pummeled one another, but the blows became slower and weaker until they made no impact. The only sound was the wheezing and grunting and groaning of father and son, exhausting themselves in one terrible release of old disappointments, old quarrels that had compounded over the years until they finally erupted in an explosion of pent-up resentment.

They fell forward at last, one against the other, neither able anymore to raise a hand or clench a fist. Arletta moved in, taking Farrell's right arm. Her voice was near breaking. "Somebody help me with him."

Sully, face creased in sorrow, caught Colonel under both arms. "Here, sir. Let me raise you to your feet." Jeff went to his aid. Smithwick turned to assist Arletta with Farrell, but Ike had already taken that responsibility. The two supported young Cregar to Arletta's tent and lowered him onto her blankets. She lighted a lantern and knelt over the young man, touching her hand gently to his face. "Ike, would you please fetch me some water?"

Sully and Elijah Layne helped Colonel Cregar back toward his camp. Jeff rejoined Smithwick at the campfire. Both men looked toward Arletta's tent, where she was washing Farrell's face with a wet cloth.

Jeff said, "Looks like it's too late for any more advice."

"It would seem so." Smithwick shuddered. "I thought they might kill one another."

"Your luck ain't that good." Jeff grimaced. "Farrell growed up with a lot of anger in him. His daddy left his raisin' to other people like what he was doin' was more important. And Colonel must've built up a lot of grand notions about what he could make of the boy. But he waited too long. What they both got was a lot less than it ought to've been."

"You have a way of seeing through the smoke to the flame beneath. In England they would regard you as a philosopher."

"I thought a philosopher had to be an educated man. I never read six books in my life."

Jeff walked to Arletta's camp at daylight to see how long it might be before she was ready to move. By her weary look, he suspected she had sat up all night, watching over Farrell. The younger Cregar emerged shakily from the tent, his face puffed, splotched with black and blue marks, red where his father's knuckles had cut the skin. His eyes were swollen almost shut.

Jeff's only sympathy was for Arletta.

A harsh norther had blown in, popping tents, intermittently spitting sleet and snow. The men in both camps huddled around their fires, unusually quiet while they ate their breakfast. The fight dwelt heavily on everybody's mind, as gloomy as the change in weather. The last of the camp equipment was being loaded on the cook wagon and its trailer when Jeff rode up to Smithwick on his black horse. The Englishman's shoulders were hunched against the cold.

Jeff said, "Colonel's wagons are ready to roll."

"How is the colonel?"

Jeff eyed Farrell, who was trying to eat but having little success. His lips were cut and enlarged to twice their normal size. "See one Cregar and you've seen the other." He watched Arletta beckon a reluctant Herman Scholtz to help Farrell up onto her wagon.

When Farrell was set, Arletta came to Jeff and Smithwick. Her eyes were dull with worry and hurt and loss of sleep. "I won't say good mornin', Jeff. There ain't much good about it."

"No ma'am, the weather's sure taken a turn for the worse."

"Will our route carry us by Parson Parkhill's camp?"

"It can if you want it to."

"I want it to."

Jeff felt uneasy. "You got some prayers you want said?"

"Somethin' like that. Tell the colonel to start when he's ready." She turned toward her wagon.

Jeff awkwardly shifted his weight from one foot to the other. "Well, hell, English, don't look like there's anything more to be said, is there?"

Smithwick shuddered. Jeff suspected he felt a chill not altogether caused by the new norther. "Not that I can see."

◻ ◻ ◻ ◻

PARSON PARKHILL had done his shooting for the day and was eating a belated midafternoon meal when Jeff and Smithwick rode into his camp, the wagons trailing behind them. Parkhill was affable, as always. "You boys light and fetch yourselves something to eat. Coffeepot's fresh."

Jeff dismounted, looking back at the wagons. "Much obliged." Smithwick stretched his legs, his arms. He claimed that most of the soreness had gone from his back, but Jeff wondered if he was simply tired of the invalid treatment.

Parkhill said, "I'm surprised that you folks decided to visit me. Is this not out of your way?"

Jeff said, "You'll be surprised again when you see Colonel's face, and his son Farrell's. Was I you, I'd act like I didn't notice."

The tall, skinny minister-hunter appeared to sense the situation. "I could smell tension between them. When I gave the memorial service for Cephus I touched upon the Biblical admonition to honor thy father."

"I doubt as Farrell was listening."

The wagons did not circle, for it was too early in the day to make camp. Cregar's remained in a line. Arletta's pulled up parallel to them. Coionel was one of the first to walk to Parkhill's fire, or rather to limp there. Sully strode protectively by his side. Whatever the minister's thoughts about Colonel's battered face, he covered them well. "Come on up, sir, and warm yourself. One of the Lord's greatest blessings is friendship, and a blazing fire on a cold day."

Cregar thanked him but said no more. Sully dragged a log up close to the fire and helped Cregar seat himself upon it.

Arletta came presently, arm in arm with Farrell. If anything, the younger Cregar looked worse now than at breakfast. His face had a blue cast, and he shook from the cold. Jeff still mustered no sympathy.

Parkhill took Arletta's hand. "Jeff tells me you especially wanted to see me. I am blessed."

Arletta brushed past the pleasantries. "Can you marry us, Parson?"

Jeff had half expected it, but nevertheless he felt as if she had struck him a blow. He whispered, "English, you goin' to say somethin'?"

Smithwick held silent, his face cold.

The minister stammered, staring first at Arletta, then at Farrell, then back to Arletta. "I am vested with the power, yes. But are you certain? Have you thought this through, and prayed over it?"

"I have," she said, her defiant gaze settling on Colonel Cregar, who painfully pushed himself to his feet. Cregar's swollen mouth hung open in dismay.

She said, "We've got no license."

"The Lord gives you all the license you need. This will satisfy Him. When I am next in Dodge City I shall register the marriage at the courthouse. That will satisfy Caesar. Do you have a ring?"

She said, "No sir, we don't."

"Well, that also can wait. The ring is only an outward symbol. What matters is in your hearts."

Colonel Cregar lurched forward, putting himself between the minister and the young couple. "Parkhill, I forbid this. I forbid you to perform this ceremony."

Parkhill was taken aback. "These young people are of age, are they not? That is all the law requires, or the Lord. Surely you do not put yourself above both law and the Lord."

The words had no more effect upon Cregar than the cold winter wind. "I forbid you!"

"I suspect that this ceremony may only sanctify what has already occurred, sir. Now, unless you intend to shoot me, I would ask that you stand aside." He went to his wagon and returned with an old black Bible, carried so long that its cover was ragged and torn, many of its pages dog-eared, much of the red edging worn away by his fingering through it year upon year. "If you will please join hands . . ."

They did it carefully, for Farrell's swollen hands looked like ground meat.

Colonel said darkly, "Arletta, you don't know what you are doing."

Arletta's voice was crisp. "That's not for you to say. It's for me to decide, and nobody else."

The men from both companies gathered, hats in their hands, listening solemnly as Parkhill recited the ceremony, holding the Bible open but not looking at it. He knew the Scriptures by heart. He reached the part that said, "If there is anyone present who knows any reason why this man and this woman should not be joined in holy matrimony, let him speak now or forever hold his peace."

Jeff settled an expectant gaze first on Smithwick, then on Colonel Cregar, who had walked partway to his own wagon but had stopped to listen, his back turned. Sully held to Colonel's arm, steadying him. Smithwick looked at the ground. Jeff punched him with his elbow, but the Englishman said not a word.

Parkhill concluded the service. "I now pronounce you man and wife. Farrell, you may kiss the bride."

Farrell flinched at the pain when his cut lips met hers. Arletta stood on tiptoe and kissed him on the cheek.

Jeff muttered to Smithwick, "If it's any consolation, it won't be much of a honeymoon for him tonight."

Smithwick's eyes were bleak. He did not answer.

Nineteen

IN ONE RESPECT, Crow Feather's mission to the north had been successful. Rabbit was with child. In another respect, though he had become convinced that the white hunters were indeed the threat Three Bears had warned him they would be, he was unable to convince most of his band. They still believed, as he once had, that the buffalo were too many ever to be reduced seriously by any natural force.

That those to the north had gone temporarily into a hole in the ground to escape the white man was consistent with the buffalo creation legend common to the plains tribes. It was well known that the original buffalo had emerged from such a hole to populate the earth. It was logical that they might retreat into one for their own preservation, to reappear when the spirits were ready and the medicine right.

Man Who Stole the Mules was the most vociferous. He had never reconciled himself to the fact that Crow Feather had been besting him in one competition or another since they were boys. He regarded anything Crow Feather said as a challenge to himself, to be met by another challenge.

A dozen men sat in a circle around the fire in the council lodge, which smelled of Mexican-trader tobacco in the pipe they had passed before beginning the argument, and the deliberations. A cold wind tugged stubbornly at the flap and tried to force its way in. Looking for support and finding it, Mules said sarcastically,

"You speak of the iron road that carries away the buffalo skins. Did you see the road yourself?"

Crow Feather had to admit, "I did not travel that far. But the Cheyennes say it is there. They have seen it, and the iron horse that travels on it. They say it can carry more than all our horses and all our travois."

"The Cheyennes," Mules snorted. "We all know how they are. They see monsters in every shadow and believe in all manner of foolish things. They are not True Human Beings."

"At first I did not believe what they said about the hunters. But then I saw for myself the buffalo killed for nothing but their skins. There were more of them than all of us together can count. Everything I saw was as the Cheyennes said it would be. I must believe that the other things they told me are true."

"Then let the white man come. We have always found him as easy to kill as the buffalo. Easier. The more that come, the more we can kill. We shall count many coups."

Provoked by Mules's derision, Crow Feather demanded, "Have you ever tried to kill all the wasps from a nest? The Cheyennes say the white men are like wasps, and the nest they come from is so large they never stop."

"How many white men did you see with your own eyes?"

Crow Feather could discern in the doubting glances of the others at council that his argument with Mules was futile, for he had not actually seen a great many. He could bear witness to the hunter camp his mixed party of Cheyennes and Kiowas had attacked. He had spied upon a couple more wagon trains that moved along in their wake. There had been, by his rough count, perhaps ten times four altogether. Hardly a wasp's nest. The rest he had accepted on faith. The People had a tendency to disbelieve most of what was told them by outsiders. If a Comanche had not seen it, it probably did not exist.

He was remorseful now that he had not gone far enough north to see the iron road for himself, and even the big white-man village from which the hunters came. But Three Bears had been convinced without having to see them and eager to return to his own winter encampment. And Crow Feather would admit to himself if to no one else that he had felt ill at ease in a country so far from his own. His mind had dwelt much upon young Rabbit, waiting for him in Three Bears's encampment. He regretted the weakness that allowed thoughts of a woman to distract him from seeing his mission through all the way to the iron road. It would not have happened when he had been Swift Runner's age and eager to prove himself as a warrior. In the questioning eyes of those seated around the fire, he could see that this weakness had brought him to failure.

Many Lodges was the eldest of those at council. He had led more buffalo hunts than anyone in the band, more raids on the Tejanos and the Mexicans, though his legs were now stiff and his joints so afflicted by arthritis that he had to be content to remain in camp and watch the younger men ride out without him. His advice was still sought and usually heeded by those who asked. When many eyes turned to him, he stared into the fire for a time, then solemnly spoke his mind.

"This is what I say. I have found that the word of the Cheyenne is not always to be trusted, or that of the Kiowa, for they are given to wild imaginings. Their medicine is not true like ours. It may be that Crow Feather has believed too much.

"But when they talk of the white man's greed I must listen, for I also have seen that his stomach is never full. I have found him foolish and wasteful. He listens to the voices of bad spirits and drinks the water that makes men crazy. You say he takes only the skins and leaves the meat. That sounds like the white man. Though it does not seem reasonable that they could kill all our buffalo, we should not let ourselves fall asleep.

"So I say this, that we should wait until the grass is green and the ponies are fat. Then, if what Crow Feather says appears true, we should seek out the white men and drive them from our land."

Crow Feather chafed. It would be a long time before the grass was green and the ponies fat. The white men were coming even now. He had observed that the older men became, the more cautious they were, and the more patient. Many Lodges was old. He saw, however, that most of the council agreed with Many Lodges. There was no hurry. How many buffalo could a few white men kill in winter, when the north wind made the ponies tremble and snow blanketed the old grass? Nobody liked to fight in the cold. Spring would be time enough.

He said, "Many Lodges has seen many more battles than I have, and killed many more buffalo. I will not quarrel with his judgment. But I would like to take some of the young men and see what the white man is doing now. At least we will know."

The council members talked awhile and finally approved his suggestion. He suspected they were compromising to get him out of camp a few days so that their ears would not hurt, listening to him press his argument.

Mules said, "I will be glad to go with Crow Feather. I have never seen a white man who gave me fear."

Stiffly Crow Feather declared, "I am not afraid of any one white man, but I am afraid of what a great number of white men can do. I have seen enough to believe."

Mules gave him a look of disdain. "I say the more white men who come, the more scalps we can take. I welcome them."

Given his choice of warriors to ride with, Crow Feather would put Mules among the last. He would concede that Mules was a willing fighter . . . too willing, if anything. His recklessness had added to his honors, but it had caused at least three deaths among those around him, deaths Crow Feather thought could well have been avoided. And after the deed was done, there came the incessant bragging. It was acceptable for a warrior to boast of his victories, but Mules abused that custom.

It bothered Crow Feather more than a little that his brother-in-law, Swift Runner, was quick to declare, "I go with Mules. Mules and I are not afraid of white men."

Crow Feather's sister had chosen poorly, he thought. It would have been better to have let her elders choose her husband, the conventional way, than allow her to do it herself. A young woman's head was too easily turned. He could only hope that his nephews, when they came, would lean toward their maternal blood.

Crow Feather carried his disappointment into his own lodge. White Deer saw it first; she had always been the most discerning of his two wives. "They did not listen to you," she said. It was a statement, not a question.

"They listened. They did not believe."

Rabbit was the one who moved to him first, her soft arms offering sympathy and support. White Deer, much the farthest along in her pregnancy, was less generous with her physical tenderness, though he could see in her eyes that she empathized with his distress. She said, "They will believe when the white man spreads across the land like a thunderstorm out of the north."

"By then it may be too late. I wish one or two more had traveled with me and Three Bears. Goes His Own Way, perhaps. Or Many Lodges, if he were a few winters younger. He would have seen for himself."

"So, what will you do now?"

"Go again, but not so far this time. I will see if white men have come into our hunting grounds and report to the council."

Rabbit clutched his arm. "Will you take me again?" Her adventuresome spirit had gloried in the last trip, seeing country she had never seen before, meeting people she had never known and, perhaps most of all, not having to share her husband with her sister White Deer.

"No, there might be a fight. This will not be for women."

"Other women have gone on raiding journeys."

"And when the medicine was not right, some have died. You are with child. This time you must remain behind." Seeing the disappointment in her eyes, he resolved that he would share blankets with her tonight, though it was her sister's turn for his attention. White Deer probably would not be all that disappointed. Sometimes when she was not feeling particularly receptive, she suggested that he go to Rabbit.

White Deer came close to him now. "I can feel the baby moving."

He placed his hand flat upon her belly. He could feel it, a strong kick that to him indicated another boy baby, a brother for the son White Deer had already given him. He would wish that it be so, for a good son could bring much honor to a father. But there was something to be said for a girl baby as well. If she were comely, some warrior would give him many horses one day to bless their marriage. And it was custom among the People that a son-in-law see to the welfare of his wife's parents in their declining years, as Crow Feather saw now to the needs of Stands His Ground and his wife.

"I should not be gone many days," he said, kneeling, beckoning his son to come to him. "The white man's wagons leave big tracks. If they are there, they will not be hard to find."

Rabbit's eyes were fearful. "And if you find them, what then?"

"If there are many, then the council will know I am right. If there are not, Mules will have a big laugh."

White Deer might not always be keen on her husband's lovemaking, but she was protective of his dignity and reputation. "If he laughs, I will put the dogs on him."

It was not a thing a Comanche woman would ordinarily do, but White Deer was not an ordinary woman. She had the spirit to do it, and the will. It was right that her babies be sons.

He put his arms around the two women he claimed as his own, and he was no longer sure with which he should share his pleasure tonight.

SIX OF THEM rode northward at daybreak from the winter encampment, robes wrapped around their shoulders, their breath like smoke in the winter air. All had volunteered. Three, like Goes His Own Way, were men Crow Feather would have picked had the choice been his instead of Many Lodges's. Man Who Stole the Mules and Swift Runner were the exceptions. Mules had declared from the beginning that he would go along to prove his contention that Crow Feather was jumping at shadows. The others might reserve judgment, but Mules had already made up his mind.

It was a pity that his mind was such a small one.

They rode at a leisurely pace the first day, finding several scattered small herds of buffalo which appeared normal. They found few dead. One cow had become bogged in mud and evidently had been attacked by wolves while she was helpless to defend herself. The remains of an old bull also had received attention by the wolves, but enough of the skin remained to indicate that hide hunters were not involved in his death.

Mules took these early findings as sufficient support for his viewpoint. "Where are your white hunters? Have they turned into wolves? I think we should go home."

"We have not yet traveled far enough," Crow Feather replied.

Goes His Own Way chided Mules, "We have barely gone beyond the smoke of our own camp, and already you are tired. Go back if you wish. You will not be missed."

Goes His Own Way was three winters younger than Crow Feather, but they had been good friends since boyhood. Crow Feather had appointed himself brother to Goes, who had many sisters but no brothers, and whose father had been killed by the black-faced buffalo soldiers in an ill-fated horse-taking trip to the Tejano settlements. Like other brothers, they had not always agreed; Goes had strong opinions, as his name suggested. But he was a firm ally on a raid or a hunting trip, or in an argument with such empty-headed ones as Mules.

Mules said, "I will still be riding when the rest of you are begging to return to your wives. If we do find any white hunters, we will kill them all ourselves, Swift Runner and me, while you stand back in safety and watch. Their scalps will hang in our lodges."

Swift Runner joined in a disdainful echo.

Crow Feather said, "You sing a fine song, but it will not be so pretty when your arrows go against a hunter's rifle that shoots on one hill and kills on the next. The Tejanos you have fought have never had such a rifle."

"My medicine is strong. I have ridden through bullets that fell like hail, and they missed me every one, even while other men were falling around me."

The spirits sometimes show mercy to fools, Crow Feather thought.

They camped at dusk in a place he knew well, where the high north bank of a creek shielded them from the force of a cold wind that bent the dry grass and drifted the light snow into half-moon patterns across the open plains. They had fresh meat, for Goes His Own Way had brought down a fat, barren buffalo cow after first apologizing to her for taking her life. Crow Feather regretted that it was too far to carry the extra meat back to the winter encampment, but the men packed what they could for their own use and blessed the rest to their brothers the wolves, who prowled watchfully nearby, looking hungry.

Crow Feather dropped off to sleep while Mules was still recounting his exploits in the fall excursion to the settlements, one Crow Feather had missed because of his journey north. Mules had killed and scalped a Mexican man and boy and had dragged the man's woman back to the encampment as a slave, assuaging to a degree his disappointment over the elopement of the girl he had intended to be his third wife. Crow Feather had a pleasant dream in which a horse dragged Mules through a river of fresh buffalo dung. He was disappointed at dawn to realize that it had not really happened. He held to a hope that his benevolent bear spirit had brought him this as a vision of an event yet to come.

At midmorning they halted abruptly, for the north wind had brought them an unaccustomed sound. Crow Feather recognized it at once as a rifleshot.

Goes His Own Way turned to him, his black eyes intense. "I have heard many rifles, but not one which sounds like that."

Crow Feather listened for confirmation before he spoke. In a moment he heard it again. "It is the kind I told you about, the one the white man uses to kill buffalo. It is very large, and it carries death as far as it can see."

Mules was ready for action. "I would like such a rifle. I will kill the hunter and take it."

Crow Feather scowled. "If he sees you, that rifle will kill you before you are near enough to know the color of his coat. We are on this journey only to observe, and to tell the council what we have seen."

They rode cautiously, taking cover where it existed, following a stream lined with scrub timber that would mask their movement. They came to a killing ground several days old, where naked buffalo carcasses lay scattered, stinking in decomposition despite their north sides being covered by banked snow. The stench was as formidable as an armed enemy. Crow Feather tried to count by fours but lost his way, for there were many. He saw shock in the others' faces. "This is what I have been trying to tell you. Where the *teibo* hunter makes his tracks, he leaves nothing alive."

The men around him murmured in anger at the waste. Only Mules offered dissent. "This was but one small herd. We saw many times more buffalo than this just yesterday. All alive."

Crow Feather lashed at him. "We will see more places such as this. The white man is like the grasshoppers that devour the last blade of grass."

The rifle continued to boom. Actually, there were more rifles than one, the reports sounding from other locations. Mules demanded, "Should we not kill this hunter before we move on?"

"There will be time enough. Let us first see how many there are. The council will want to know."

The hunter camp was larger than the one he had attacked with the Cheyennes and Kiowas. He could see many wagons, and many white men busily moving about. Below the camp, hides too numerous to count were spread out on the ground, drying much as the women of the People dried them except that here he saw no effort being made to work them into robes or to scrape away the hair and flesh so the leather could be converted to lodge skins or other such useful goods. Many of the wagons were already loaded with dried hides, stacked one atop the other and tied down.

He spoke to Goes His Own Way, but his message was meant for Mules. "It would be foolish for our six to attack such a large camp with so many men in it, and so many guns. None of us would live to reach the wagons."

Goes recognized the logic. "What do you think we should do?"

"We should keep traveling. This is but one camp. I fear we will find many more, but it is best that we see for ourselves, then return to camp. We should let the council decide."

Mules was obstinate. "I say we should kill one hunter, at least."

"That would only alarm the others and make them harder to find. We can kill hunters after the council has heard us."

It did not take long for Crow Feather to win over all except Mules and Swift Runner. The farther north they rode, the more skinned buffalo and the fewer live ones they saw. Where the first day the men had talked and joked and even sung among themselves, they were now quiet, their faces solemn, their eyes smoldering in silent rage. They lay belly-down on a hilltop and watched a white-bearded hunter bring down animal after animal out of a small herd that milled in bewilderment.

Goes His Own Way said in a choking voice, "He does not spare even the calves."

In the distance, from a camp on the creek, Crow Feather could see a wagon approaching, two men riding in it. They would be the skinners, on their way to steal the hides from the People's buffalo.

He thought it good that the warriors watch the skinning. The council would not be able to ignore their anger as it had dismissed his warning.

Mules had never known restraint. Before Crow Feather could move to stop him, he was on his horse, charging down the hill toward the hunter. Swift Runner followed but was left hopelessly behind. The white man's back was turned and his attention fastened on the buffalo. He did not hear Mules's horse until too late. He turned quickly, raising the big rifle, but Mules drove an arrow into the man's chest. The hunter fell back, dropping the rifle, grabbing at the arrow with both hands. Mules gave him no chance. He put a second arrow into him, then was on the ground with his knife, slicing, gouging, tearing away the scalp while the dying man screamed. Mules raised the white-haired scalp over his head and screeched in triumph as Swift Runner reached him.

The remaining buffalo broke their milling pattern and stampeded southeastward.

The two men in the wagon had dropped below a rise and had not seen. Goes declared, "They will kill Mules and Swift Runner if we do not kill them first."

Crow Feather would not have wept over Mules, but Mules had wives and children who would. And he had no wish to hear the lamentations of his sister over Swift Runner. He said, "We can go around that hill and surprise them as they come up. We must not give them time to use their rifles."

The job was swiftly done. The two wagon men froze in fear for a fatal moment at the unexpected sight of the Comanches who swept upon them with a whirlwind's fury. They died without firing a shot, one with an arrow from Crow Feather's bow, the other's head crushed by a blow from Goes's stone ax. The two warriors backed away to let the others count coup, though a lesser one than their own. Goes's honor was the highest because he had struck a death blow from his own hand, not from the distance of an arrow's flight.

Crow Feather looked down upon the dead men without pity or remorse but only with concern over the fact that this killing was likely to cause other hunters to be more wary, harder to surprise. It was right that they die, as the buffalo died.

Each of the skinners had a rifle. Crow Feather took one, Goes the second, along with a handful of cartridges. The other men divided what little else of value they found in the wagon. Man Who Stole the Mules rode up leading the shooter's horse and carrying the big rifle as his trophy. Swift Runner cut the two mules loose from the harness and led them away from the wagon.

Crow Feather frowned at Mules. "The other hunters will be expecting us now. They may even come out looking for us."

Mules refused to accept criticism. "What difference does it make? These white men were easily killed. Let the others come. They will be as easy."

Crow Feather despaired. There was no talking to a fool. He turned to the others. "You can all give witness. You have seen for yourselves the skinned buffalo. You have seen how the white man kills all he can reach. You can tell the council that I spoke the truth."

Goes His Own Way said, "I did not doubt you, not from the first. They come upon us like a sickness." The Comanches had experienced many kinds of strange sicknesses since the coming of the white man, maladies their forebears had never known, scourges against which their guardian spirits and medicine men seemed helpless.

Mules ran his hand approvingly along the neck of the horse he had taken from the hunter. "The more white hunters, the more scalps and more horses for us."

Swift Runner agreed, whooping as he lifted the leather reins of the two mules he had taken.

Crow Feather had a taste in his mouth as if he had eaten spoiled meat. Mules did not see the point. He probably never would until his children were half dead from hunger.

Mules said, "These men came from a camp." He pointed in the direction from which the wagon had approached. "There will be more horses and mules and rifles for us to take."

Crow Feather frowned, disturbed by Mules's greed. "We do not know how many men are in the camp. We are not enough to fight a great number."

Mules raised the heavy buffalo rifle. "I am not afraid. I have the white man's medicine gun." Without waiting for the others to counsel, he set off in a lope, backtracking the hide wagon. Swift Runner followed but was burdened by the two mules he led.

For a second time it became the duty of the rest to try to spare Mules the price of his folly. With a sigh of resignation, Crow Feather set out behind him. Shortly he saw the camp. It was a small one of only three wagons, two hitched together and already loaded with a considerable number of dried hides. One wagon was covered with canvas of a reddish color. A lone white man ran for the cover of timber, a rifle in his hand. He had seen Mules coming. Any opportunity for surprise was lost.

Mules, well ahead of the others, let go of the horse he was leading and whooped in exultation as he charged after the fugitive. The big buffalo rifle bobbed up and down in rhythm to his horse's gait. He gave a loud screech and fired.

Mules's timing was lamentable. The heavy barrel dipped just as he jerked the trigger. His horse went down head first, his rump end cartwheeling up and over. Mules hit the ground rolling, the horse's flailing hooves barely missing him. Dazed, Mules tried to crawl away. A puff of dust lifted a hand's span from his head as the frightened white man in the timber shot at him.

Goes His Own Way gave Crow Feather a look of disgust. "Should we leave him?"

Crow Feather was tempted, but to abandon a fellow warrior to the enemy was disgraceful. "We cannot." He and Goes handed their bows, quivers and trophy rifles to others so they would not be encumbered. Dropping down on their horses' sides to present a poor target, they put the mounts into a run. As they neared the fallen Mules they parted, one on each side of him. Mules raised up enough that they were able to grasp his arms. Crow Feather shouted, and they dragged Mules out of harm's way. It occurred to Crow Feather that the white man in the timber had a splendid chance to shoot all three of them, but he held his fire, perhaps from fear, perhaps from fascination over the daring of the recovery.

They did not release Mules until they had him behind the hide wagons. They dropped him unceremoniously and let him roll, without dignity. The other warriors joined them there, keeping the wagons between themselves and the lone surviving white man. The fall had knocked the breath from Mules's lungs. Crow Feather watched him struggle to breathe and wished for him to choke.

Goes His Own Way asked, "Should we go after the hunter?"

"No," Crow Feather replied. "He is well hidden and might kill one or two of us before we get him. There will be others, when the council hears what we say."

Mules regained his breath and looked anxiously at the men gathered around him. "My rifle. Did you get my medicine rifle?"

Crow Feather's smile was cold. "If you want your rifle, go and get it yourself." That would make Mules an excellent target for the white man. "You had best leave it behind. It was bad medicine for the hunter and bad medicine for you."

Goes snickered. "We should no longer call him Man Who Stole the Mules. We should call him Man Who Kills His Own Horse."

Crow Feather added sourly, "There is no need for us to kill the white man. He will probably laugh himself to death."

Twenty

THE KILLING of Archie Grosvenor and his two skinners sent a shock wave rippling through the buffalo-hunting camps scattered across the upper Texas plains. Though most had been on the lookout for Indians and were puzzled by the long period of quiet, the deaths had a sobering impact. They invoked a cold dread.

The camp tender named Tug had remained hidden in the timber until darkness, fearing the Indians might be waiting to ambush him when he showed himself. Because they had driven away the horses and mules, he had walked southward all night. He stumbled into the Browder camp at daybreak, his legs near buckling.

Arletta was visibly shaken. "We've gone so long without trouble . . ." Her eyes bored into the exhausted Tug. "You're sure they're dead?"

"The Indians had Archie's horse and the mules. And one of them had Archie's rifle. Damned good thing for me that he didn't know how to use it. He shot at me and killed his own horse."

Smithwick felt cold inside, remembering the jovial Englishman who had expressed so much love for this new country. He shuddered at the realization that it could have happened to Arletta had fate not led the Indians to someone else's hunting ground. Since her marriage to Farrell Cregar, she and Farrell had been riding out together to shoot buffalo. She declared that she did not need Smithwick's protection. His wound healed, he had begun finding his own buffalo, setting up his own stands. He worried about Arletta, however. He was not convinced that Farrell could or would protect her. At least Arletta appeared the happiest he had seen her.

But tears glistened in her eyes as she listened to Tug relate what had happened. Smithwick sensed that she was remembering the death of her father. She leaned against Farrell. Young Cregar just stood there, slow in putting an arm around her, and even then seeming to do it as an afterthought.

Smithwick took the news to Damon Cregar and Jeff Layne. The colonel had spoken to neither his son nor Arletta since the wedding, though the two outfits camped within a hundred yards of one another. Cregar was unmoved by sentiment. He ate breakfast in a businesslike manner as he listened. "What was the man's name? Grover?"

"Archie Grosvenor!" Jeff declared with agitation.

Smithwick put in, "He was English, like me."

"Whatever his name was, he is dead. Our primary concern now must be to see that the same thing does not happen to any of us. I want to talk to this man Tag."

"Tug," Jeff corrected him. His agitation seemed to grow.

Cregar started toward the Browder camp. Smithwick and Jeff had to push hard to match his purposeful stride. Elijah Layne trailed behind, not even trying to stay up. If Cregar gave his son a glance, Smithwick failed to see it. The colonel looked at Arletta a moment, his face darkly disappointed, then turned to the weary Tug. He gave him the piercing stare of a battlefield commander taking a report from a lieutenant about a lost engagement. "How many Indians were there?"

Men often exaggerated the threat they had faced, but Tug was a realist. "I saw six."

"Only six?" Cregar seemed to disbelieve. "That is hardly a decent war party."

"It's more than enough when you're all by yourself."

"I assume they were Comanche?"

"I didn't ask. The one that came after me had blood all over his hands. I didn't want him spillin' mine."

"Obviously you did not go to the aid of your fellows."

The colonel's attitude began to irritate Tug. "The only shootin' I heard was Archie's, killin' buffalo. First I knowed, they was comin' at me and the camp. Wasn't hard to figure that they had already got everybody else."

"Where did the Indians go?"

"How the hell should I know? I wasn't even sure they'd left. That's why I didn't try to move till dark."

Cregar could have been dressing down a soldier. "For a man who was there, you are a damned poor source of information."

Cregar's manner caused Jeff Layne to snap, "He would be a poorer one if he was dead. You can see what he's been through. Why don't you leave him the hell alone?"

Colonel's face flushed as it always did when he encountered insubordination. "I am attempting to determine the facts."

Jeff appeared near mutiny. "There are three good men dead, friends of mine, and they need buryin' before the wolves get them. That's facts enough. English, you want to come with me?"

Elijah pleaded, "Son, you be careful."

Cregar stepped in front of Jeff. "Two men will not be enough if the Indians are still skulking around there. We shall take a stronger party." He stated it as a matter of fact, not a recommendation. Given his stern tone, not even the independent-minded Texan challenged the authority Cregar had assumed for himself.

Smithwick said, "There are other camps to the north of us. Parson Parkhill's for one. They should be told."

Colonel did not gladly suffer unsolicited advice. "I was about to take care of that. Once the burial detail has completed its work, you may divide up and visit the nearby camps. Each of them can send people to notify others."

Arletta declared, "A lot of them were friends of Papa's. I'd know them. We can go, Farrell and me."

Cregar curtly rejected that proposal. "The risk is too great for a woman. Your place is here where you can be protected. And it is your husband's place to help provide that protection." He said *your husband* with a heavy and sarcastic emphasis. Not *Farrell*, not *my son*, but *your husband*. The colonel managed not to look at Farrell.

Jeff said, "This could just be a stray party that found an easy target, or it could be the first shots of a war. We'd best be doublin' our guard."

"Do you think I have not already seen that for myself?" Cregar demanded. "If any man has forgotten the need to be watchful, let this incident remind him."

Half a dozen well-armed riders set out as a burial party, Sully carrying a shovel across his saddle. They saw no sign of Indians. Wolves had already visited the three dead men. Fury welled up in Smithwick, and he galloped ahead, firing his pistol at a couple that still nosed around the body of Archie Grosvenor. They fled past several other wolves which fed on a dozen or so buffalo dropped by the Englishman's rifle before the Indians had stopped him forever. All the wolves retreated a short distance, then waited, watching, unwilling to give up their bounty.

Looking upon the mutilated body, Illinois Ike went crimson. "I once shot a rebel who directed artillery fire down on us. For two days while we were stalled there, I had to watch the buzzards strip him to the bones."

Jeff Layne's lips drew inward against his teeth, and he cursed beneath his breath. He and Grosvenor had shared bottles more than once.

Smithwick could not look a second time at what remained of his countryman. He and Sully rode toward a wagon a little way to the west. They found the two skinners, their bodies in the same condition as Grosvenor's. Smithwick shuddered.

Sully took off his battered old hat. "They've traded their wagon for a golden chariot."

Jeff wanted to bring Parson Parkhill to read over the men before they were buried. Colonel Cregar impatiently insisted that the party had more important things to do. "These men are already on their way to heaven or hell, and it is doubtful that anything Parkhill could say will change their course. He can come and read over them afterward, if that be his wish."

But Illinois Ike, who often read his Bible at night in camp, had brought it in his saddlebag. Defying Cregar, he read aloud while the rest of the men stood with hats in their hands, heads bowed. They buried the three men together in a single wide grave where the skinners had died. Smithwick had seen or heard little to indicate that Jeff gave much thought to religion, but he heard the Texan say "Amen" to Ike's prayer.

No particular effort was made to hide the grave as had been done for Cephus Browder's. Jeff said the Indians would probably not be interested enough to dig up the bodies. They and the wolves had already done a thorough job of mutilation.

He gave Smithwick a long, probing stare that carried a hint of accusation. "Still look like a grand adventure to you, English?"

Smithwick had no answer. His stomach was turning over.

The Grosvenor camp was eerily silent except for a north wind tugging at the reddish tarp spread over the hoops of the abandoned cook wagon. Cregar examined the buffalo hides, those already dried and loaded on a wagon and those still staked to the ground. Tug's defense had prevented the Indians from damaging the skins, if that thought had even occurred to them. Cregar said, "We can pick these up when we start to Dodge City."

Jeff's eyes narrowed in suspicion. "You wouldn't be figurin' on takin' them for yourself, would you, Colonel? I'd say these belong to the heirs of Archie Grosvenor, if he's got any, and to Tug if he don't."

Cregar looked annoyed. "I would remit the proceeds, minus a suitable fee. After all, we will have to furnish teams for the wagons."

Smithwick bristled with indignation. "Arletta has extra mules that are not earning their keep. I am sure she would not charge a dead man for their use."

Annoyance turned to anger in Cregar's eyes. Stiffly he mounted the big bay horse. His tone was crisp. "Anyone who wants to carry the message to other hunting camps may go ahead. I am returning to see to the protection of my own. Come along, Sully."

Sully gave Jeff and Smithwick an apologetic shrug, then mounted, carrying the shovel.

Jeff had picked up Grosvenor's buffalo rifle beside the body of the Indian horse shot by its rider. He extended it to Smithwick. "I feel like Archie would want a fellow Englishman to have this."

Mindful of Jeff's attitude toward the hides, Smithwick said, "But not as a gift. I'll pay a fair price to his estate."

"I wouldn't've thought otherwise."

Smithwick and Jeff set out northward to carry the news to Parson Parkhill's camp. Ike and Barney Gibson slanted northwestward to seek out another, so that the news could quickly be spread and all camps be put on their guard.

Smithwick broke a long and brooding silence. "This helps me to understand, I think, how some people have come to hate Indians so much."

Jeff shook his head. "I've shot Indians when I had to, but I never let it be a personal thing. They're doin' what's natural to them, same as those wolves back yonder. We've come to take their land away from them, startin' with the buffalo, like they took it from whoever who was here before. Takin' is in human nature. White or red, we've all got the human failin's."

Smithwick gave Jeff a long study. "There is something else I shall never become used to."

"What's that?"

"The way you have of seeing both sides of a question. Life must be more difficult for you than for someone like Colonel Cregar, who never once doubts that he is right."

"The last time I swore I was right, a Yankee soldier put a bullet in my hip."

ALMOST OVERNIGHT, the buffalo seemed to disappear. Smithwick and Jeff and Ike scouted for two days without finding more than a scattered few, hardly worth the distance, time and effort to bring in their hides. Ike said, "This reminds me of the Republican and the Arkansas. Maybe they're farther south."

Jeff's voice had a bitter edge. "Maybe they're not even there. Give us men enough and guns enough, and we could kill off every creature that walks, crawls or swims."

Smithwick thought it was high time Jeff left the buffalo range and found some less sanguine form of endeavor. "The wagons are already beginning to sag. What would we do with more hides if we had them?"

They rode way around a killing ground several days old. It sent off a stench that could knock a man out of his saddle. Jeff said brittlely, "That was a stand of mine. Killed fifty-seven head without changin' position. At two dollars apiece, a hundred and four-teen dollars. Doesn't seem like much money for all that blood."

Smithwick asked, "How much money would be enough?"

"Sometimes I wonder if there's enough in the world."

After dark Arletta approached Smithwick, who sat on a log near the cook wagon, eating his supper from a tin plate. She said, "We've got about all we can carry without breakin' the wagons down. Soon as the green hides are dry enough, we'll head north."

That came as no surprise to Smithwick. "Have you talked it over with Colonel Cregar?"

"I've got nothin' to say to Colonel Cregar. You've seen how he treats Farrell."

When the colonel could not avoid Farrell completely, he looked through his son as if he were a pane of glass. "I suspect Colonel will be ready to leave whenever you are."

"If he's not, we'll go without him." She returned to the cook wagon where Farrell stood with a cup in his hand. Farrell turned away from her. Smithwick wondered if the two might have had an argument. Arletta put an arm around her husband's waist and leaned to him, saying something Smithwick could not hear. He did not want to. He looked away.

When he turned back the couple were gone, probably into their tent. He saw no lantern glow through the canvas. He tried not to think about what they might be doing, but the mental image was persistent and disturbing.

It had been a point of pride for Colonel Cregar that his company always led off. Arletta thwarted him, riding past him with cold satisfaction as her wagons rumbled out of camp in single file, headed northward. Farrell rode his bay horse past his father. He pointedly avoided giving the older man even a glance. Frustration darkening his face, the colonel shouted at his crew to hurry up and get their wagons ready to move.

Smithwick drew rein beside Jeff Layne. He asked, "Did you not tell the colonel we were leaving this morning?"

"If Arletta wanted him to know, she'd've told him herself. It won't hurt him, breathin' her dust for once."

"He will be a holy terror, trying to catch up."

"Colonel's been a holy terror all his life."

They put their horses into a trot, moving toward the head of the line. As they passed Arletta, Smithwick saw that she still held a grim look of satisfaction for her small victory over Colonel. Farrell was not riding beside her; he trailed considerably behind her wagon.

Arletta sternly held the lead all the way to the first night's camp. Her cold smile appeared again when Cregar pulled his wagons past hers before ordering them into a circle. Smithwick observed, "He is setting himself up to establish the lead tomorrow."

"He can have it," she said. "I just wanted to show him how I feel about the way he treats my husband."

Coming up out of the canyon onto the high country above was a bigger chore than had been hoped. Jeff and Smithwick led the wagons to a place where other outfits had worked their way down to the lower ground on a reasonably benign grade. Even so, it became necessary to unhook the trailers from the hide wagons and make the ascent one at a time. Colonel did a great deal of shouting and browbeating of men and animals to get his wagons up the slope, as if he were competing in a race. Only Elijah Layne escaped his bullying. Smithwick supposed Cregar did not want to stir Jeff to rebellion again, defending his father.

When the last of his train was on top and his men were reattaching the trailers, Colonel came back down and started to repeat his performance with Arletta's.

Arletta walked up to him with a purposeful stride. Farrell kept his distance. "Colonel, you have enough to do just takin' care of your own outfit. My crew can manage these wagons perfectly well, thank you."

Colonel forgot himself and looked for his son, his black eyes flashing indignation. He quickly corrected his error. "Very well. I shall leave you to see after your own affairs, Miss Browder."

"It's Mrs. Cregar," she corrected him sharply.

Colonel put his horse up the slope without looking back. Triumphant, Arletta glanced around, seeking her husband. Farrell had hung back, remaining clear of the quarrel. Though he was the basis for it, Arletta was the one who stoked the fire.

A couple of times Smithwick thought uneasily that he glimpsed something moving at a distance behind the wagons. When he focused his attention, it was gone. "It is probably imagination," he told Jeff, "after seeing what happened to Archie Grosvenor and his skinners."

Jeff's brow furrowed. He gazed intently in the direction to which Smithwick had pointed. "Maybe, and maybe not. It might be a good idea if you followed behind the wagons and spent a lot of time lookin' over your shoulder."

Smithwick saw the logic. A sudden attack from the rear could allow the easy killing of a few drivers and let the Indians escape before the rest of the train had time to organize a defense. He dropped back, waiting until the last wagon moved a hundred yards ahead of him before he took up the trail. He felt alone and vulnerable, yet he also enjoyed a glow of satisfaction. After an aimless life without purpose or plan, he at last had a sense of responsibility. He felt capable. He carried the carbine—Grosvenor's heavy Big Fifty was in Arletta's wagon—and he felt equal to whatever challenge this uncharted land might offer.

Ahead, at the bottom of a long decline, he saw what appeared to be a creek bordered with scrub timber. Wagons were drawing out of the line of travel to pass an obstacle, then pulling back once they were clear of it, working their way up the gradual slope beyond like a slow-moving snake. As he neared, he perceived that two sets of wagons and their trailers had stopped. Gantry Folsom and Sully were unloading hides from one of the lead wagons, which leaned precariously in the dry creek bed. Its left rear wheel was crushed, the spokes sticking out in all directions like broken ribs in a buffalo skeleton. A good wheel lay on the ground, a wagon jack beside it.

Questions were unnecessary. He said, "It would appear you could use some help."

Sweat rolled down Folsom's face and soaked his shirt beneath the armpits. So far as Smithwick had seen, he had not changed that shirt once since leaving Dodge City weeks ago. It was hard to tell which smell was the strongest, his or the hides'.

Folsom cast the black man a hard look. "I could've used some help a while ago to keep this damned nigger from crowding his wagons up close behind mine. Made my mules so nervous they hit that rough ground too fast."

Sully protested, "Mr. Gant, I was a long ways behind when

you . . ." He broke off. Argument with Folsom was futile. If anything, Folsom was probably trying to goad him into it so he would
have an excuse to abuse him. Sully looked up at Smithwick. "Colonel told me to stay and help Mr. Gant fix his wagon. It was too
heavy for the jack, so we've had to unload a lot of the hides."

Smithwick took a quick look up and down the creek bed. It was
crooked, bending away a short distance in both directions. The
timber, though not tall, would provide cover enough for anyone
who wanted to come close without being seen. He felt a vague
uneasiness. The last wagon in Arletta's string had already moved a
considerable distance. "Perhaps you have taken off enough weight
now. I suggest you try the jack."

Folsom challenged him with angry eyes. "Why don't you get
down off of that horse and help us? Or are you afraid to get a little
grease and dirt on them Goddamned slick English hands?" He
picked up a wrench. "We better loosen the wheel nut before we
jack up the wagon." Instead of using the wrench himself, he
handed it to Sully. "Here. Your hands are already as black as they'll
ever get."

Sully's eyes told Smithwick he knew Folsom was still trying to
crowd him into an angry mistake. They also indicated that Sully
was not far from the edge. Smithwick dismounted and dropped the
reins. Removing his coat, he reached for the wrench. "Here, let's
see how black a pair of English hands can get." He grunted with
exertion, nearly losing his footing when the nut suddenly broke
free and turned. Sully set the jack under the axle and labored over
the handle. The wagon began to rise.

Folsom showed no inclination toward helping. He said, "That's
enough. The wheel's clear."

Smithwick finished removing the nut, then he and Sully slipped
the broken wheel from the hub. Folsom stood back, watching. It
was just as well. The farther away he was, the less irritating his
odor. They fitted the good wheel into place, and Smithwick tightened the nut. It would need a finishing turn when it was off of the
jack. He drew a sleeve across his forehead to wipe away the sweat.
"I never knew how much satisfaction a man might derive from a
bit of honest manual labor."

Sully smiled. "Then the Lord has been mighty good to me, because He's given me that kind of satisfaction all my life."

Smithwick heard something that sent a tingle of foreboding along his spine, a rustling in the brush, or perhaps a rising of the wind. Turning, he glimpsed sudden movement. Folsom exclaimed, "Godalmighty damn!"

Half a dozen Indians came rushing along the dry creek bed, barely a hundred yards away.

Twenty-one

SMITHWICK FROZE for a few seconds, dry-mouthed, his body tingling with a burst of excitement. It was the hilltop all over again, where Cephus Browder had taken his mortal wound. Forcing down his dread, he made three long strides to grab the carbine he had set against the front wheel of the first trail wagon. He whirled to grab Dunny's reins, for the Indians would try to take the horse even if they got nothing else.

He was too late. Gantry Folsom was swinging up into Smithwick's saddle, his black-whiskered face twisted in fear. He shouted, "I'll go get help!" Folsom put the dun into a hard run toward the wagon train, abandoning Smithwick and Sully to fend for themselves.

Sully started toward his own wagon but turned back, for he would not have time to make it. He jumped onto the front of Folsom's wagon and lifted the skinner's rifle from beneath the springless seat.

Smithwick dodged around the corner of the wagon and braced his carbine against the stiffened hides. The Indians were so close he could see the colored figures painted on their buffalo-hide shields and the tassels and feathers which rimmed their edges. He heard the swish of an arrow and a solid thump as it plunged between two hides inches from his head. The Indians were too chancy a target; he aimed for a larger one, the chest of the nearest horse. Through the black smoke he saw the horse pitch forward, sending its rider rolling in the grass.

Sully fired once. Feathers flew from a hardened shield as the bullet glanced off. Sully tried to lever out the spent cartridge, but the rifle jammed. His eyes went wide in desperation as he fought vainly to clear the chamber. "This rifle is as dirty as Mr. Gant hisself. It's the Lord's mercy it didn't blow up in my hands."

Smithwick was marksman enough to bring down an Indian at this range, but he stayed his hand. Those were men in his sights . . . savages, perhaps, but men. Well, not altogether. The warrior whose horse he had brought down appeared to be little more than a boy, probably trying to prove his manhood by rushing out in front of the others.

The charge was blunted. Two of the warriors reached down to pick up the one who had lost his horse. The others loosed arrows, which thumped into the hides still stacked on the wagon. One warrior left the rest and engaged Gantry Folsom in a hard chase toward the wagon train. Smithwick halfway wished Folsom would lose, but he knew the Indian would almost surely capture Dunny and lead him away.

He heard distant shots from the wagon train. Just when it appeared Folsom might be caught, the Indian abandoned the effort, unwilling to ride into the heavy rifle fire. He turned back to lend the others a hand against the two men at the crippled wagon. His fellow warriors had begun retreating toward the timber. They had lost the element of surprise as well as a horse. They continued loosing arrows. One stopped to fire a rifle.

Smithwick heard a dull thud and a groan. Sully swayed, then fell backward from the wagon. The rifle clattered to the wooden plank that served as a seat. Smithwick tried but could not reach Sully in time to catch him. The black man struck the ground and lay trembling, his eyes wide in shock. He raised a hand as if to point but lost the strength to hold it and let it fall. Hit hard, he gasped for breath. Smithwick grasped his hand. "Hold on, Sully. Help is coming."

But he knew instinctively that no help would save Sully. Blood pumped from a hole in his chest, and it bubbled over his lips.

Five horsemen raced from the wagon train. Smithwick recognized Colonel Cregar's big bay in the lead, Jeff and Farrell Cregar not far behind. Trailing were Ike and a young man who customarily drove the loose stock for Arletta. They were the only ones who would have been a-horseback, other than Folsom.

Colonel Cregar reined to a sliding stop, Jeff barely a length behind him. Cregar's anxious eyes sought out the black man. "My God! Sully!" He swung to the ground and came running, letting go of his horse. He took a black hand in one of his own and raised Sully's head, cradling it on his arm.

Smithwick was not prepared for the sight of tears welling into the big man's eyes. Cregar's broad shoulders shook with a silent sobbing.

Sully's voice was almost too weak to hear. "Colonel?"

"I'm here, Sully."

"Colonel . . . thank you, sir."

"For what? For letting this happen to you?"

"For givin' me freedom . . ."

Tears rolled unashamed down Cregar's cheeks. "You hold on. Don't you go off and leave me by myself."

"A man ain't ever by hisself, not when he's got the Lord." Sully's eyes rolled back. Smithwick thought he was gone, but the black man's lips moved once more, in a whisper. "Colonel . . ." His hand came up from his chest, reaching, then dropped back. He shuddered and was still.

The other horsemen had dismounted and stood around Colonel and the fallen Sully. Farrell removed his hat only after seeing Jeff and the others do it.

The Indians had disappeared in the timber. Farrell broke the awkward silence. "We're letting them get away."

No one paid attention to him.

Colonel remained on his knees, holding Sully, his shoulders shaking. Cregar crying was something Smithwick would never have expected to see.

Farrell looked on in disbelief, and perhaps resentment. "Father never showed me half the concern he gave that ragged old nigger."

Jeff said tightly, "Sully was the only person who gave Colonel all he had and never asked for anything back." He motioned toward the hides lying on the ground. "Let's get these loaded so we can carry Sully in. Ike, would you ride down yonder a ways and watch out that the Indians don't hit again?"

The wagon's axle was still on the jack. Jeff helped Smithwick lower it while Farrell stood watching his father and Sully, his eyes unreadable. They tossed the skins up to the young stock handler, who stacked them. With irony Jeff asked, "About to get enough adventure, English?"

As easy as it had been to dislike Colonel, Smithwick would concede that Cregar had charged out in front of the others in coming to help. In his grief over Sully he had finally betrayed what Smithwick considered an unabashed human emotion.

The job done, Jeff went to the Colonel's side. "The wagons are ready. We'll put Sully on one of them and take him in."

Cregar vigorously shook his head. "On top of those stinking hides? No sir, he's going in on horseback, as befits a man."

Jeff and Smithwick carefully placed Sully across the stock handler's saddle, face down. Cregar rode alongside the horse which carried the burden, his big hand holding Sully to keep the body from sliding off. Smithwick fell in behind him, driving the first wagon, the handler the second. Jeff and Ike and Farrell followed, providing a rear guard.

The train had halted, waiting. Arletta walked out from her wagon, holding her long gray skirt. She watched anxiously, at the distance probably unable to discern who was being carried across the saddle. Her eyes were grim as the riders neared her. She brought her hands to her mouth, recognizing Sully. She lifted her gaze to Smithwick on the lead wagon. "Nigel, I was afraid it might be you."

Farrell rode up in time to hear and gave Smithwick a hard study.

Arletta moved to Colonel Cregar. Whatever animosity she might have felt for him was gone, at least for the moment. "I'm sorry about Sully."

Colonel gave only a nod in acknowledgment. "Where is Gantry Folsom?"

She did not reply in words but jerked her head. Smithwick saw his dun horse tied behind Cap Doolittle's cook wagon. The look in Cregar's eyes brought him a chill. He climbed down from the hide wagon and walked ahead of Cregar, who had dismounted and handed his reins to Jeff.

Folsom was on the far side of Cap's wagon, leaning against a wheel. Vomit was drying on the front of his shirt.

Cregar's voice cracked like the popper on a bullwhip. "Folsom, come out here!"

Folsom hesitated. He reminded Smithwick of a whipped dog with its tail between its legs. Reluctantly he moved out from behind the wagon, his eyes downcast.

Colonel demanded, "Look at me!" Folsom raised his eyes, but not his chin.

"I said *look!*" Cregar closed on him, a quirt in his hand. He lashed Folsom about the head and shoulders. Folsom cringed, covering his face with his arms and whimpering like a hurt pup.

Smithwick exclaimed, "Good God, Cregar, what do you think you are doing?"

Cregar barked, "Somebody give Folsom a gun!"

Jeff moved in, grabbing Cregar's arm. "Colonel . . ."

A wild rage surged into Cregar's eyes. "A gun, I said! Give him a chance before I kill him, a better chance than he gave Sully." Breaking free of Jeff, he raised the quirt and lashed Folsom again. Smithwick and Jeff grappled with Cregar. It was like wrestling an angry bull. In a moment all three were threshing on the ground. Cregar strained hard, but the two managed to hold him. He gasped for breath, the fight slowly leaving him as the burst of fury burned itself out.

Jeff said, "We're fixin' to let you up, Colonel, but you've got to get control of yourself."

"I'm all right," Cregar wheezed. He waved off Smithwick's attempt to help him to his feet, pushing to a stand by himself. His seething gaze cut back to Gantry Folsom, who cowered against the cook wagon, welts rising on the side of his face. The skinner raised his arms defensively.

"Folsom, whatever belongs to you, get it. You'll not spend another night with this train."

Folsom lowered his arms and raised his head, not quite believing. "You're setting me afoot?"

"I am."

Folsom trembled. "But what'll I do?"

"You may join some other outfit, if you can find one that will have you. Or you may walk to Dodge City. But if you try to rejoin this train I'll kill you!"

Folsom's eyes pleaded. "There's Indians out there."

Cregar was unmoved. He dug a roll of bills from his coat pocket and peeled off several. "That should be as much as you are owed." He dropped the money on the ground so Folsom would have to stoop to pick it up. He walked away unsteadily, his broad back marking an end to the conversation.

Farrell had watched in silence. Jeff said harshly, "We could've used some help with your daddy."

"I could have used some help with him years ago."

Elijah Layne moved to Jeff's side. "All this fightin', and a good soul layin' yonder not even cold yet."

Pain was in Jeff's voice. "We didn't make the world. We just live in it and do the best we can."

Smithwick dug Folsom's filthy blanket roll and war bag from under the wagon seat and pitched them to the ground. He handed Folsom the rifle Sully had not been able to unjam. "If I were you, I would give this weapon a thorough cleaning before I did anything else. You may need it."

Colonel Cregar sent a skinner from farther up the line to take charge of the wagon and trailers that had been Folsom's responsibility. The lead wagons began to move, and the skinner pulled these into line when Folsom finished retrieving the little that belonged to him. Smithwick untied his dun horse from Doolittle's wagon and inspected him carefully for any sign that an arrow might have touched him.

Doolittle said, "He's all right. I looked him over good."

Smithwick patted the horse on its neck. He motioned toward Folsom, who knelt beside his pitiful pile of belongings. "He will get terribly hungry out here by himself."

Doolittle frowned. "Let the son of a bitch eat rabbit." He climbed upon his wagon and set it into motion.

Smithwick waited for the train to pass slowly by, then resumed his rear-guard position behind the last of Arletta's wagons. He kept looking over his shoulder but did not expect to see Indians again, not so soon. He saw only Gantry Folsom, shoulders slumped, a forlorn figure standing alone on the open plain. After a time, Folsom picked up his blankets and war bag and began to trudge along far behind the wagons.

Smithwick shuddered, remembering when he had been thrown from the train and set afoot. He told himself Folsom had it coming, but that was not enough. This would test the courage of a brave man, and Folsom was a coward.

They buried Sully at dusk on the open plain. Colonel stood quietly while Illinois Ike read from his well-worn Bible, and he dropped the first spadeful of earth atop the blanket-wrapped body. He stood back in anguished silence and watched as the grave was filled in. Today was the first time Smithwick had ever had reason to feel sorry for the big man.

Colonel lamented, "He was the only true friend I ever had. He deserved a place in a churchyard, not out here alone on the prairie."

Jeff made a sweeping motion with his hand. "He used to call this *Freedom Church*. These plains are open and free, and he liked that."

Supper was a somber ordeal. Smithwick walked to the edge of camp and stared at a tiny fire flickering perhaps half a mile away. It was an open invitation to any Indian who might be watching, a sign of a straggler, an easy target. Folsom should know better, he thought. But the night was cold, and freezing probably seemed as much a danger as the Indians.

Arletta's voice startled him. "You know Folsom stands a big chance of dyin' out there, afoot and alone."

"I know no way I can help him."

"You can take him a horse and saddle. I would lend him Papa's to keep him from bein' on my conscience."

"It was Colonel Cregar who cast him away. I see no reason he should be on your conscience."

"I'd know I could've helped him and didn't. I realize you've got no reason to feel sorry for him, but would you do this . . . for me?"

"Why not send Farrell?"

"There's already been too much trouble between him and his father."

Smithwick shrugged. "I suppose I have nothing to lose. Colonel Cregar can't even remember my right name."

He caught his dun while Arletta saddled a horse Cephus had ridden some. She tied a sack behind the cantle. "There's food in there, maybe enough to get him to Dodge. Tell him I'd appreciate it if he'd leave the horse and saddle with Mr. Thomason. The saddle at least, because it was Papa's."

"You seem to have a weak spot, Arletta, toward outcasts and derelicts like me, and like Folsom." He could have added Farrell to the roster but did not.

She seemed to sense the thought, nevertheless. "I know you've never approved of Farrell, and God knows he's got his weaknesses. But he's all I have now."

She deserved more. "Do you think you can make a farmer out of him?"

She said, "I can try."

Smithwick remembered a vicar's sermon about the faith of the mustard seed. He wished he could have had that faith about Arletta, faith that he could make her happy despite the difference in their backgrounds, faith that he could stand strong beside her and defy anyone who might disparage her lack of sophistication.

He had that faith now, but it was too late.

He approached Folsom's little camp with care. He suspected the man was frightened enough to shoot at anything that moved. A hundred yards out, he called, "Folsom, I am coming in."

Hearing nothing, he rode closer and called again. He heard Folsom's voice out in the darkness, well away from the small campfire. "Who is it?"

"Smithwick. I brought you a horse."

Folsom appeared, carrying his rifle. "I thought you was the Goddamned Indians. I built me a fire, but I been afraid to stay with it. I warm myself a little and go back out again." His voice hardened with suspicion. "How come you bringing me a horse? I got nothing you'd want."

"It was Arletta's idea. This is her father's horse and saddle."

The suspicion lingered. "I don't see why she would give a damn what happens to me. Nobody ever done me a favor without they wanted something."

"She wants the horse and saddle back. She would like you to leave them at Thomason's hide yard."

"That's all?" Disbelief was in his voice.

"That is all. She has a good heart. If I were you I would get started now. I would ride by night and hide by day, at least until I was out of Comanche country."

"I still don't understand. Nobody ever gave much of a damn whether I lived or died. People always said I was shiftless and no-account, till I didn't see no reason to be otherwise."

"The same things have been said about me."

"I know I oughtn't't've run off the way I done, but I was scared. And I'm sorry about Sully. He was a good man, to be as black as he was."

"I never understood the way you treated him. You fought in the Union army to free the slaves."

"It wasn't because I wanted to. They conscripted me to go and fight for them black heathens that never done a speck of good for me or mine. Family lost what little land we had because I wasn't there to work it. And when I got home I couldn't even find a decent job. They was hiring freed niggers so cheap they didn't need a white man."

"So you vented your spleen on poor Sully."

"There wasn't no other around."

Smithwick returned to the train in a dark mood, wondering if he should have left Folsom to the Indians. After unsaddling Dunny he walked near Arletta's and Farrell's tent on the way to his own. He heard Farrell mumbling angrily, and Arletta's sharp reply. "I said *no!* Now go to sleep!"

Smithwick crawled into his blankets, but he did not sleep much.

AFTER THE SKIRMISH that cost Sully's life, Smithwick took it upon himself to assume a rear-guard position. The next to last day before they reached Dodge City, Farrell stopped and waited behind the last wagon until Smithwick came up. He reined in beside him, a brooding look in his face. After a time he demanded, "How well did you know Arletta before I came along?"

Smithwick studied his reply. "Not so well as you seem to suspect."

"She says you were teaching her to read. Are you sure you weren't teaching her anything else?"

Smithwick flared. "If you are inferring . . . that is an insult to her and to me."

Farrell's eyes hardened. "You didn't teach her very well. I've had it better from an upstairs maid."

Smithwick clenched his fists. "If it is a fight you want, I am at your service!"

"I could whip hell out of you, Englishman, and you know it. So you'd better remember who she belongs to . . . who this whole outfit belongs to." Farrell spurred the bay into a long trot toward the wagons, leaving Smithwick to stew in silence.

He remembered his promise to Cephus about watching out for Arletta's welfare. He had done a damned poor job of it.

At supper he sensed a quiet tension between Arletta and Farrell. When Farrell walked out into the darkness to answer a call of nature, Arletta beckoned Smithwick with a quick movement of her head. Standing behind the cook wagon, she said quietly, "I gather that you and Farrell had a few words."

"Very few."

"I know I disappoint him, but he should've realized I'm not one of those Dodge City crib girls."

"He is a spoiled, half-grown boy in a man's body. Do you still think you can turn him into a farmer?"

She did not answer.

SMITHWICK RODE beside Jeff as the outfit entered Dodge City. The town appeared less hectic than last time. Its dirt streets carried less wagon traffic, and fewer horses were tied to the posts and rails along the streets that paralleled the railroad tracks. The arrival of the long train of hide wagons brought out a considerable number of spectators, plainly glad to see prospects of new business. Colonel Cregar, much subdued since losing Sully, halted his wagons and proceeded alone to talk to the hide buyers.

Arletta drew her wagons into line a short distance from Cregar's and called the crew to gather around her. Though Jeff was not involved, he followed Smithwick.

She declared, "I'd like everybody to stay close till Farrell and I get the hides sold. Then we'll pay you, and you can go out and get drunk and visit the girls if you want to." She gave Farrell a questioning glance. "Most of you, anyhow."

Farrell frowned. "Why do I have to go with you?"

"This outfit belongs to both of us." Smithwick thought she lacked enthusiasm. She said, "Nigel, would you kind of watch over things while Farrell and me go take care of business?"

Farrell protested, "All day long I've been tasting that first drink."

Her eyes snapped with annoyance. "And probably the tenth as well. Come on, Farrell."

The couple walked in the direction of Thomason's hide yard. They moved along a little apart, not locking arms as Smithwick had seen them do before. Jeff glanced at Smithwick, his eyebrows lifting in a silent question.

Barney Gibson walked up while they watched the couple enter Thomason's frame office. "Herman and me, we think the honeymoon is already over. Arletta had better keep her eyes on him. He could grab a train and leave her."

Jeff mused. "That might not be the worst thing that could happen." He gave Smithwick a suggestive glance and rode back toward the Cregar wagons.

Smithwick helped unhitch the teams, feed and water them. He noticed Arletta's peg-legged helper sneaking away toward a dramshop on the south side of the tracks. He dismissed any notion of going after the man; the departure was an improvement to the camp.

Arletta returned in an hour or so, the hide buyer Thomason walking beside her. She led the horse she had lent to Gantry Folsom. Smithwick did not see Farrell. Arletta said, "Mr. Thomason is buyin' the hides."

She should have been smiling over that, Smithwick thought. She was not.

Thomason wore the same stained old suit Smithwick remembered from before. The buyer said pleasantly, "I have always prided myself on being a businessman, but I am glad I don't have to contend with hard bargainers like this young lady every day. I would not remain in business long."

Arletta commented, "I had to get a good price if I'm goin' to buy that farm."

Smithwick blurted the question. "Where is Farrell?"

Arletta looked down. "He'll be along."

Thomason said nothing, but his eyes told enough. He changed the subject. "If you men will bring us a wagon and its trailers one at a time, we're ready to start counting and stacking hides."

Smithwick moved to Arletta's side. "Do you want me to bring Farrell back?"

"No. He'll come when he's ready. *If* he's ready."

Smithwick took the reins from her hand and patted the horse's shoulder. "I had little faith that Folsom would actually return your horse and saddle."

"But he did. If any of you happen to run into him around town, tell him I'm grateful."

"It is he who should be grateful. You probably saved his worthless life."

"Nobody is worthless. The Lord put everybody here for some purpose."

Smithwick wondered about Farrell's.

She touched Smithwick's arm, then drew away. Her lips pinched tightly. "If you should happen to see my husband somewhere, tell him I've taken a room for us over at the hotel. I think he might appreciate a roof for a change, and a good soft bed. Tell him I'll be waitin'."

Smithwick did not intend to go out of his way looking for Farrell. He had released the horse into the loose bunch and was watching Arletta at her wagon when Jeff returned.

The Texan seemed to read his mind. "When I was a kid I had the prettiest little paint pony you ever saw. Man came along and offered to buy him. We was in deep need for money, so Dad had no choice but to sell. I had to stand there and watch that feller lead my pony away. It hurt like hell, but I had to give it up."

"You are being a philosopher again."

"You know what you need, English? You need some real sippin'-

whiskey, and the company of a good-lookin' girl. I'll bet Charity'll know just the one for you."

Smithwick felt embarrassed. He tried an uneasy smile but could not hold it. "I do not think so."

"I do. I'll see to it that you have a good time tonight if it kills you."

Twenty-two

JEFF HAD NEVER SEEN Colonel Cregar so quiet as he was after the burial of Sully, all the way to Dodge City. It would have been in his nature to ride constantly up and down the line, cursing mules and men, pushing hard for an extra couple of miles before the day ended. Instead, he plodded along near the last of his wagons in the long line, his head down, his thoughts far away. Jeff wondered if he would grieve as much for his own son as he grieved over the former slave who had been his helper and companion for so many years.

"It's kind of spooky," Cap Doolittle commented from the seat of his cook wagon. "It's like watchin' a dead man ride. I'd almost rather see him the way he was."

"It'll pass. An old badger like him won't stay in his hole for long."

Cap looked back southward, from where they had come. "Reckon we're out of Texas by now?"

"I expect so, but the Comanches haven't put up any signposts."

"Didn't it seem to you like the air was sweeter back yonder? Didn't it seem like you could smell home?"

"Main thing I smelled was gunpowder and dead buffalo."

Cap's eyes had a wistful look. "I was sore tempted to leave this outfit and ride on south, back to where we come from. You might say it was imagination, but I'd swear I could hear it callin' to me."

Jeff felt a quick sadness, remembering the same feeling. He had tried to force it out of his consciousness, but he had awakened some nights thinking how near he was to home. He would ache to go, and he would not sleep anymore, remembering.

Damn those thieving carpetbaggers, and damn the gun that killed them!

Cap said, "I've been thinkin' maybe when we finish this haul I'll take the cattle trail south. I wish you and your daddy could go with me."

The wanting was like a sore that would not heal. "You know we can't."

"How long a memory do you reckon the law has got?"

"Long enough."

Cap shrugged. "Anyway, we can throw us a remember-Texas celebration when we get to Dodge, get drunker'n hell and do somethin' we'll worry about plumb into next summer."

"Maybe later. I've got somethin' planned."

"Charity?" Cap sighed. "She sure beats hell out of *my* company."

One way Jeff helped take his mind off Texas was to think about Charity, to let his imagination carry him into her willing arms. He hoped she was still in Dodge. Women in her line of work tended to move around, especially if they got wind of a boom somewhere. Having been isolated so long on the southern buffalo range, Jeff had no idea what was happening anywhere else. For all he knew, Dodge City could have died on the vine like an overripe melon, replaced by some newer place farther down the tracks.

But the first sight of the town was reassuring. It was still there, so probably Charity was too.

NO MATTER how late he had been up, old habits usually seemed to awaken him by sunrise if not earlier. He lay awhile, wanting to leave the bed and fix a pot of coffee but not wishing to disturb Charity. She lay facing him, her hand on his arm. In the dim light of morning she looked small and delicate, and so pretty he had to summon considerable resistance not to lean over and kiss her eyes, her small nose. He would wait until she awakened in her own good time. While he waited, he could look at her, at least, enjoying her soft woman smell and indulging himself in whimsy about the pleasure of waking up beside her every morning for the rest of his life.

He wondered if it would work. A woman should have a home,
and he had none to offer, at least not yet. Beyond that, in Charity's
case there was the fact of her occupation. It was one thing to accept
her favors on an occasional basis, realizing all along that theirs was
basically a commercial relationship regardless of the pleasure it
yielded to them both. It would be another to live with her and daily
confront the reality of her past. He was honest enough with himself to know that even though he would profess otherwise, all those
other men might sooner or later rise up between them like a phalanx of malevolent ghosts. And he felt that she would be honest
enough to tell him so, should he ever be so reckless as to suggest
that they marry.

Her eyelids fluttered as the sun began to pierce the thin curtains
on the east window. For a moment she seemed confused to find
him lying beside her, then a smile lighted her eyes. Her hand
moved up his shoulder to the back of his neck and summoned him
to lean across and kiss her. "Been awake long?"

"A while."

"Why didn't you shake me?"

"I enjoyed just lookin' at you. Figured you needed your sleep."

"I can sleep after you're gone."

"I may not sleep for a week, just thinkin' about you."

She kissed him for the compliment. He reached for a half-empty
bottle on a stand beside the bed and tipped it up for a long, bracing
swallow. He offered it to her, but she shook her head. He said, "I
wonder how English and your friend Prairie Rose made the
night?"

"He's a man. She's a woman. I imagine he'll be sleepy all day."
She raised up. "I'll start a fire in the stove and fix us some breakfast."

He pulled her back down beside him. "Not yet awhile."

Prairie Rose occupied a cabin little different from Charity's. After they had breakfasted together, Jeff and Charity walked to it,
arm in arm. Jeff knocked on the door. "English, are you still
alive?"

Hearing no answer, he knocked again. He heard the creak of

bedsprings and a tread of feet across the floor. A pair of sleepy blue eyes blinked into the morning sun as the door opened cautiously. The young woman yawned. "You-all lookin' for the Englishman?"

Jeff said, "I thought he might be ready to go back to camp."

She yawned again. "He went back hours ago."

Some people didn't know how to get their money's worth, he thought. "Didn't you two get along?"

"He talked real pretty. That's all he done, was talk. Talked about England, about the buffalo, and after he had drunk a right smart he got to talkin' about a woman name of Lettie or somethin'."

"Arletta?"

"That's it. Talked about her like I've heard men talk about wives that died. We never even turned the covers down. You reckon he's sick or somethin'?"

"Or somethin'."

He found Smithwick alone, bent and poking into a campfire amid Arletta's empty wagons. A coffeepot hung from an iron cross-bar set over a couple of forked steel rods driven into the ground. Smithwick said, "My coffee-making abilities are limited, but fetch a cup if you feel brave."

Jeff's first swallow told him bravery was not enough. "What you goin' to do when Arletta sells her wagons? One thing you *won't* do is hire out to be a cook."

"I have not decided. There does not appear to be much going on here in Dodge."

"Colonel's likely to be hirin' on. Half his crew has talked about quittin' him."

"I had rather sweep out saloons than go with Cregar."

Jeff tried a second swallow of the coffee. It had not improved with age. "What did you think of Prairie Rose?"

"She was a good listener."

"So she told me. You didn't give her a chance to show what else she can do."

"I told you last night, I really was not interested. I will admit that temptation crooked a finger at me, but I could not bring my-self to it."

"Arletta?"

Smithwick's eyes gave the answer.

A movement drew Jeff's attention toward the hotel. "Yonder she comes now. Her husband's not with her."

The two men stood up as Arletta approached the campfire, trouble in her expression. "Have either of you seen Farrell?"

Smithwick said, "No. What time did he arise?"

"He never came to the hotel." Her voice was strained. "I haven't seen him since yesterday afternoon."

Jeff slowly expelled a breath between his teeth, suppressing a few words he thought descriptive of Farrell. "You want us to go find him?" He remembered where he and Cap had found Farrell the last time. He was probably there again, or in some place like it.

She shook her head. "He knows where I am." She leaned against the cook wagon, her back turned. Jeff looked at Smithwick. If the Englishman ever intended to play his cards, this would be the time. But Smithwick just stood there, looking as if a horse had kicked him.

Jeff muttered, "For a man who speaks the language like it came right out of the book, you can be as silent as Illinois Ike sometimes. If I was you, I'd go to her right now."

"What could I say? She is married to him."

A man in a neat brown suit came riding up on a pacing horse of very nearly the same color. He dismounted a suitable distance from the fire to avoid raising dust. He gave his reins a quick wrap around a wagon wheel and walked directly to Arletta.

"Mrs. Cregar? You *are* Mrs. Cregar, are you not?"

Arletta wiped her eyes before she turned. "Yes, I'm her."

The man glanced briefly about the camp. "My name is Wilbur Daniels. Has your husband spoken to you about me?"

"Not as I recollect."

"I do not see your husband." Daniels put it more as a question than a statement.

"He's not here right now. You got business with him?"

The man appeared ill at ease. Jeff and Smithwick moved closer, sensing that he did not bear good tidings. "The fact is, Mrs. Cregar, that I have already done business with him. He sold me these wagons and teams last night."

Jeff felt a tingle. "What's that?"

The man, running more to paunch than to muscle and finding

himself facing two men who displayed no friendliness, sputtered for a moment. "I said he sold me this outfit."

Arletta was stunned. "He couldn't! It's mine!"

"I regret to differ with you, madam. If he is indeed your husband, then by law he may dispose of the property as he chooses. It is mine, bought and paid for."

Jeff's hand dropped to the pistol on his hip. "You don't touch as much as a horse collar till we talk to Farrell."

The man drew himself to a defensive attitude of wounded innocence. "I doubt that will be possible. He said he had a train to catch."

A train. Jeff swore to himself. He could read the bitter thought that raced through Arletta's mind: Farrell had left her and had taken her money with him. His hand was still on the pistol. "You got a receipt?"

"I have." Daniels started to reach inside his coat. Jeff brought out the pistol, suspicious that the man might be going for a gun. Daniels blanched, his hands freezing in place.

Smithwick extracted a paper from Daniels's fingers. He read it quickly, frowning. "It appears to be as he says."

Fear raised Daniels's voice to a higher pitch. "I hope we may handle this situation amicably, without recourse to the authorities."

Arletta sank down upon the wagon tongue. For the moment she was not the strong-willed young woman who had taken over command of the Browder outfit after her father's death. She looked like a forlorn little girl who had just lost family and home. "I was goin' to sell the wagons and everything, put that with the hide money and try to buy back the farm Papa lost."

Smithwick said, "You still have the money from the hides."

"It won't be enough." She stared at the ground, wiping her eyes. Shortly she squared her shoulders. When she stood up the tears were gone. She was a determined woman again. "Do you intend to use the wagons yourself, Mr. Daniels?"

"No, I plan to resell them. I understand Colonel Cregar is in the market."

"You can just as leave sell them back to me as to him."

Alarmed, Smithwick stepped in front of her. "Arletta, you are not returning to the buffalo range."

"It looks like I have to. I'm just afraid the hide money won't buy all the wagons and teams back."

Smithwick said, "You are welcome to what money I have."

She gripped his arm. "Thanks, Nigel, but I couldn't ask you to loan me anything. You know why it wouldn't look right." She was slow to withdraw her hand.

Jeff frowned, solemnly studying the pair, then the empty wagons. It took him a minute to decide he really wanted to speak the idea that ran through his mind. "You need a workin' partner, Arletta. For a long time now I've been savin' up a stake and wonderin' what to do with it. I'll buy in with you, fifty-fifty."

She regarded him at first with disbelief, then a light of hope began shining in her eyes. "You know the risk we run, goin' back down there."

"I ran away from home when I was twelve. Startin' with that, everything I ever done was risky."

She grasped Jeff's hand and shook it, trying to be businesslike but unable to restrain her delight. "I wish I knew how to thank you."

"It's a business proposition. Me and Dad, we'll be lookin' for a profit on this deal."

She turned to Smithwick, hugging him in joy, then flushing and stepping back. Smithwick reddened.

Jeff asked, "What about Farrell?"

The harsh look in her eyes was more of an answer than any words she could have spoken. "Come along, Mr. Daniels. Let's go to the Thomason office."

Daniels led his horse because it would be awkward to ride while Arletta walked. Jeff and Smithwick followed several paces behind. Jeff said quietly, "I put up the money, English, but she hugged *you*. In your place, I wouldn't let her get away this time."

"I have already let her get away. I will not be going with you, Jeff."

Jeff missed a stride. "You're givin' her up?"

"I lost her by default. To stay would only prolong the agony." He turned and walked toward the wagons.

Thomason was distressed about Arletta buying back her outfit. "I shudder at the thought of you going down into that wild country again," he told her. "Colonel Cregar is a man of means and stature. Surely he would stand good for his son."

Arletta's voice was clipped with hurt. "I would not ask him to, or take his money if he offered it."

"Pride," Thomason said critically. "In small measure it can be a blessing, but sometimes it seems that those who can least afford it are most prideful of all."

"There's been times that pride was about all Papa and me had. But we always came out, somehow."

As Arletta had predicted, the hide money was not enough to buy back all the wagons and teams. Jeff turned to Daniels. "I'll meet you at the Long Branch in an hour or so and pay you what you've still got comin'."

"That would be my pleasure." The chunky man paused. "We might even indulge in a friendly game of poker, if you would like." He retreated from Jeff's hostile glare. "I suppose not."

Jeff watched his hasty departure, muttering under his breath. "Arletta, how about me takin' the wagons out and you stayin' here in Dodge, where you'll be safe?"

"When was anybody ever safe in Dodge?"

"Well, then, how about you goin' back to Ohio? When we finish the hunt I'll send your share to you, and you can buy that farm."

"The farm doesn't seem like such a good idea anymore."

Jeff argued, "There has to be someplace that you can wait and be safe."

"This outfit is all I have. I've got nowhere else to go."

Thomason had watched Arletta with concern. "I hoped you would decide otherwise. But I can see your mind is set, so I will tell you something that may be of help. Fred Leonard and Charlie Myers are planning to set up a trading post somewhere down on the Texas buffalo range. They are offering to pay hunters to haul goods south in their empty wagons. That should cover part of your supplies."

Jeff felt a quick elation. "Sounds like this partnership may be off to a good start. Let's see if we can make a deal."

As they walked together she admitted ruefully, "I made a mistake, Jeff. Marryin' Farrell was the worst thing ever I done."

"I never could understand why you did."

"Fact is, I was right taken with Nigel. He set somethin' to stirrin' in me, and it hurt when he said nothin' could ever come of it. Then Farrell showed up. He had a way about him, and a pretty smile . . . When the colonel tried to make me come back to Dodge, Farrell took my side. Nigel didn't. And nobody ever paid attention to me like Farrell did." She paused. "I don't reckon you can understand any of this."

"I might."

"If you do, you've got me beat. I don't understand it at all." Her eyes seemed almost to plead. "I'm afraid it's too late for me and Nigel."

Jeff knew what Smithwick would say: she was still a married woman. But he replied, "It's never too late, not till they nail the lid on the box."

"You're a good man, Jeff." She squeezed his hand, then released it. "You go on to Leonard and Myers. I'd best find our crew before they hire out to somebody else. They don't know they've still got a job."

He found Colonel at Myers's, talking about hauling supplies south for the new trading post. He noticed a hole in Cregar's left sleeve, and a dark stain that looked like dried blood.

"What happened to you?"

"Some damned fool. Drunk probably."

Myers said, "The colonel had a narrow escape last night. Somebody fired a shot at him."

Cregar shook his head. "I know some people don't like me, but I doubt that anybody hates me this much. It was probably some careless drunk who didn't know his rifle was loaded."

"Did you see who it was?" Jeff demanded.

"It was dark. Just some drunk."

Jeff almost blurted out Gantry Folsom's name. He doubted that Colonel knew Arletta had furnished the skinner a horse to come into Dodge. He decided against telling. Colonel might search out Folsom and kill him. As he had said, it was possible the shot had been accidental, fired by somebody loaded with rotgut. "Just in case, Colonel, maybe you'd best not be out and about after dark while you're in town."

"It was nothing." Colonel shrugged off Jeff's concern. "I want you to buy Arletta's wagons and teams for me if the price is right. I doubt that she would sell to me directly."

"Arletta's goin' back out for another hunt."

Cregar's jaw went slack with dismay. "Did you try to persuade her otherwise?"

"Fact is, me and Dad are leavin' you, Colonel." He hesitated. "I hate to tell you this, but it's Farrell's doin'." He explained about Farrell selling the wagons and teams. "Looks like he taken a train and got off with Arletta's money."

Colonel's face fell. "I knew he had his shortcomings, but I did not believe he would sink that low." He slammed a hand down on the counter. The whole store seemed to shake. "I'll make up Arletta's loss."

"You'll never talk her into it. She's got too much pride. She reminds me of you."

Cregar turned away. He seated himself upon a stack of folded blankets, his broad shoulders slumped. He brought his right hand up over his eyes. Losing Sully, and now having to face the harsh facts about his son . . .

Jeff found himself in the uncomfortable position of feeling sorry for him.

Twenty-three

NIGEL SMITHWICK was on the street to watch the departure of the caravan from Dodge City on the early March morning. Jeff had tried one final time to talk him into going. "What have you got better to do?" he had demanded.

"I don't know. I shall probably work my way back east. I might even return to England."

"You need her, English, and she needs you."

"But she is tied to Farrell." Smithwick felt cold. Jeff seemed able to look through him all the way to the core. "I should have listened to your first advice. It is painful to be near her all the time and know she belongs to a man who does not deserve her."

"More painful than bein' away from her?"

"Only time will answer that."

Smithwick's gaze sadly followed the caravan's leaders as they set out toward the Arkansas River crossing. It was one of the largest wagon trains the town had ever seen. Some were regular freight outfits, but most were hunter companies, their wagons loaded to capacity with building materials and tools and supplies for the proposed trading center. The plan, such as it was, called for establishing a post near the Canadian River, in the center of the buffalo-hunting range on the Texas high plains.

It was projected to be more than just a hide-buying station. It was to have a large store handling rifles and ammunition and all kinds of groceries and other camp needs, a blacksmith shop to shoe hunters' animals and repair their wagons, a restaurant to feed them while they visited to trade, a saloon to see that they did not thirst. Though it would curtail the necessity for hunters to return to Dodge City, at least Dodge was its supply point and would profit by its existence. No Texas town of any commercial significance lay as near the new hunting grounds.

Smithwick raised his hand to Elijah Layne and Cap Doolittle as their wagons passed by him. They were with Arletta's and Jeff's outfit now. He felt a discomforting mixture of pleasure and despair as Arletta stopped her wagon and climbed down. He had wanted to see her one last time, yet he had dreaded the pain the *goodbye* would bring him.

She blinked rapidly. He knew it was not just from the dust raised by the wheels and the hooves. She said, "There's still time for you to change your mind."

"You know why I had best not."

A tear escaped despite her strong effort. She embraced him, pressing her cheek against his. "I'll never forget you, Nigel."

"Nor I you." He held her arm as she climbed back upon the wagon. He watched her for a time, but she never turned to look over her shoulder.

Jeff stood beside a woman whose only name, so far as Smithwick knew, was Charity. He heard Jeff tell her, "I'll be back one of these days."

She replied, "I'll be here, or someplace else."

Jeff kissed her, gave Smithwick a final wave and rode away on his black horse. Smithwick approached the woman. He thought she was rather comely though beginning to show the lines and strains of her occupation. He said, "I fear you gave him a most noncommital answer."

"It's the best answer I had. Jeff's as good a man as I know, but there's no future for us together. The past would stand in the way." Her voice indicated regret. "I believe you have reason to understand such things."

He winced. "I do."

"Jeff left half a bottle of good whiskey at my place. Would you care to join me? We can make it a wake of sorts."

"I don't believe . . ."

"I know you're a friend of his. It'll be just a drink, nothing else."

"In that case, why not?" A strong drink might help lift the weight from his shoulders. He walked with her, pausing for a final look at the long caravan stringing out to the river and beyond. Dodge City might never see another of its size. He suppressed a strong urge to saddle Dunny and join it. He had battled that urge for the last two days, leaning in one direction a while, then the other.

He saw little in Charity's room different from Prairie Rose's. His gaze went unbidden to the bed. In his mind he saw her lying there with Jeff Layne. The mental image changed, and it was Arletta he saw, with Farrell. He swallowed the whole glass of whiskey Charity poured for him.

He had an uncanny feeling that she read his mind. She said, "Colonel Cregar never did find out where his son is, did he?"

"It was our understanding that he took the train east."

"I could have told him otherwise, but I thought it was best to leave well enough alone. The way Jeff feels about Farrell, I was afraid it would come to a fight. Maybe worse than just a fight. I didn't want Jeff in trouble."

"You know where Farrell is?"

"He's been hiding out up the tracks with a girl I know, waiting for the hunting outfits to leave."

Smithwick's eyes opened wide. "Do you think he might still have the money?"

"Whatever part he hasn't spent. But it won't last long. Money melts like ice around this place."

Smithwick pushed to his feet. Charity said, "The bottle's not empty yet. Don't you want the rest of it?"

"I just want you to tell me how to find Farrell Cregar."

THE PLACE was nothing more than a tent, its sides boarded up to a height of about three feet to ward off the worst of the winter cold. Smithwick considered announcing himself as he would in approaching a hunters' camp but decided surprise might be a good ally. He tied the dun horse to a post. He could see smoke rising from a chimney and heard the clanking of a pot or pan against what he assumed was an iron stove. His chore might have been easier if he had caught Farrell asleep, but he would take things as he found them. He opened the tent's flap and stepped inside with pistol in his hand.

Farrell stood at the stove, holding a coffeepot. A woman sat on the edge of the bed, buttoning her dress. Both gave him a moment's surprised stare before Farrell demanded, "What in the hell . . ."

"You swindled Arletta. I have come for her money."

"She's my wife. Whatever is hers is mine."

"This is not a courtroom, and I am not interested in the niceties of the law. I just came to get her money."

Farrell scowled. "Did she send you?"

"No. She thinks you took a train east."

"That's the best way to leave it. You'd better remember she is a married woman."

"I remember. You are the one who seems to forget. Now, the money."

Farrell's arm moved. The coffeepot sailed toward Smithwick, spilling coffee across the dirt floor. Instinctively he raised his hands to deflect it. The pistol fired, blasting a hole in the pot. Black gunsmoke filled the tent.

Farrell was on him in three long strides, twisting the hand that held the pistol. A sharp stab of pain caused Smithwick to loosen his grip, and the pistol fell to the floor. Farrell attempted to knee him in the groin, but Smithwick turned aside. He brought his left fist up and struck Farrell on the nose. Startled, Farrell released Smithwick's wrist. Smithwick stepped back and went into a boxing stance. Farrell brought his hand away from his nose and appeared surprised by the blood on it. Enraged, he swung wildly.

Farrell was taller and broader, and Smithwick had hoped to avoid a fight. He had seen little chance of beating him in any kind of head-on contest. But he felt a glow of satisfaction now as he realized that Farrell knew nothing about the art of boxing. Moreover, he had been drinking. Smithwick stepped under the swing and came up with a sharp double punch that set Farrell back on his heels. He kicked the pistol under the bed, out of reach.

Farrell appeared dazed. This was not to be the wade-in-and-knock-him-down kind of battle he had had with his father.

Smithwick danced back and forth, side to side, stepping in to punch, then stepping back to avoid the angry sledgehammer blows Farrell attempted in reprisal.

Farrell quickly wore down, cursing in anger and frustration as his hard-swinging fists missed Smithwick or glanced off his guard. Each time Farrell opened himself up, Smithwick's darting fists caught him on nose or chin or in the stomach. Farrell had fought his father to a standstill with brute force, but that force meant little against an opponent who bounced around like a ball and avoided most of what was thrown at him.

The woman saw Farrell was losing and came to his aid, swinging the punctured coffeepot. Smithwick dodged, then maneuvered to get Farrell in front of her. He struck the hardest blow so far, sending Farrell staggering back against the woman. She fell to the floor, striking her head against the iron bedstead. She sat up whimpering, rubbing the place that had taken the impact. She made no more effort to join the fight.

Smithwick felt his strength leaving him. It was time to finish. He struck Farrell two hard punches to the chin and stomach. Farrell fell, doubling up on the floor. Smithwick bent over him, feeling his pockets. He saw a wallet lying on a small washstand. He extracted most of the money. "I am leaving you thirty dollars," he said, breathing heavily. "I would suggest that you find honest work, and quickly."

He pulled the bed away from the tent's wall and retrieved his pistol. Farrell reached out for something upon which to pull himself up and touched the stove. With a shout he jerked his hand away, bringing it to his mouth and sucking at the burn.

Smithwick said, "Your father had hopes for you, Farrell. I would not be surprised if he renounces you now."

Farrell said bitterly, "He renounced me when I was a boy. I don't owe him a damned thing."

"You owe something to Arletta, something more than this money. You owe her her freedom."

One of Farrell's eyes was beginning to swell shut. The other narrowed. "That would suit you just fine, wouldn't it? Well, forget it. What's mine *stays* mine."

Smithwick had already won the fight; he saw no gain in an extended argument. He left the tent and mounted the horse. Farrell stood at the tent opening, holding onto a pole for support. He shouted, "You'd better remember, she's married to *me!*"

Smithwick put the horse into an easy trot. He ached in several places where Farrell had managed to strike him, but somehow it was pleasant pain.

He caught up to the caravan as it neared its first-night camp on Crooked Creek. Jeff Layne was riding rear guard. His wide grin was as welcome as sunshine after a London fog. "Never expected to see you again, English, except maybe in a nightmare." His grin disappeared as he saw the bruises. "Some of them rough boys run you out of Dodge?"

"I found Farrell."

"I hope he looks worse than you do."

"I rather think he does."

Jeff said, "I'll ride to the wagons with you. Arletta's been lookin' like her dog had died. I want to watch her face light up."

Smithwick received a greeting from Barney Gibson and Herman Scholtz as he passed their wagon, then Cap Doolittle and Elijah Layne. He looked ahead, searching out Arletta. She rode along with her head down, the wind lifting and playing with the long reddish hair that extended far beneath her bonnet. She straightened up, seeming to sense something. She turned, blinking as if she could not believe. "Nigel?" He thought for a moment she might cry. She caught herself and made a weak laugh instead. "Couldn't stay away from Cap Doolittle's cookin', could you?"

"Among other things."

She stopped the team and patted her hand on the vacant side of the seat. He tied Dunny to the tailgate of the trailer, then climbed up beside her. She clasped his hand tightly, her eyes glistening. As the wagon moved again, she murmured, "I didn't say much of a goodbye to you this mornin'. I been frettin' all day, thinkin' of a hundred things I ought to've said."

"You can save them." He reached into his pocket. "I have something for you." He gave her the money.

"What's this?"

"A gift from Farrell."

"I don't understand . . . or perhaps I do. I wasn't goin' to say anything about those bruises."

"Mine will heal before his."

She leaned against him and squeezed his hand.

When all the various outfits had made camp and fires began to blaze along the bank of the creek, Colonel Cregar came seeking Smithwick. He critically studied Smithwick's bruised face. "Word has come to me that you found Farrell. Is there anything you want to tell me?"

"Nothing that gives me any pleasure."

Cregar's eyes showed pain. "It has been a long time since anything having to do with Farrell gave me pleasure."

Smithwick made it brief. As much as he had initially disliked Cregar, he shared the big man's regret.

Cregar's face colored. "I had resigned myself to the fact that Farrell is a wastrel and a drunk and a chaser after women. I had not thought he might also become a thief."

Smithwick wanted to spare Cregar's feelings as much as he could. "In his mind the property was as much his as Arletta's."

Cregar flexed his hands, making fists and loosening them. "I will send a runner back to Dodge City tomorrow with enough money to buy him a train ticket east."

"Out of sight, out of mind?"

"Out of sight, yes. Out of mind? That he will never be." The big man's voice was heavy with despair. He stared at something far out across the darkening prairie, or perhaps at nothing.

Elijah Layne approached Cregar hesitantly. "You all right, Colonel?"

"No, but you are, Mr. Layne. You have a son you never need worry about."

"Colonel, a father worries every day of his life."

Smithwick fondled the old watch he carried and thought of his own father, who would have had more than sufficient reason to turn his back upon a wayward son but never quite did. He wondered which of the Cregars was the most unfortunate, and which was most to blame.

Considering its extraordinary length, the caravan made good time, camping its second night on the Cimarron. The evenings were festive, for an air of high adventure seemed to permeate the ambitious undertaking. There was no lack of groceries upon which to feast. The music of fiddles and French harps drifted on the sharply cool breeze. At one campfire, men danced on a dry buffalo hide. To Smithwick's surprise, Arletta went. She danced with several hunters and skinners she knew. She danced also with Smithwick, her face glowing.

The heavily laden wagons had to pull hard through the rough, sandy terrain, but little concern was felt about attack. Most Indians were probably still snug in their winter encampments, Jeff said. Even if some were roaming about, it was unlikely they would assault a force of this size. At most they might try to pick at the fringes, to catch a herder inattentive and run off some of the loose stock.

In contrast to the trip last fall, when Cephus Browder had made his own trail, these wagons followed ruts deeply cut by months of iron-rimmed traffic. By hunt and find, hit and miss, hide men had eventually settled upon a reasonably direct route, whereas Cephus had meandered in his search for buffalo.

One day Arletta crooked her finger and beckoned Smithwick to pull his dun horse in beside the wagon she drove. "We're missin' the place where we buried Papa." She tilted her head. "It's yonderway, not more than a few miles."

Smithwick had long recognized Arletta's strong feel for the country, an instinct he was trying with only partial success to cultivate. "You would be a better judge than I."

"I want to visit Papa. Would you catch up my horse?"

He felt misgivings about her riding away from the caravan. "I shall get Jeff and a couple of others to go along."

"You'll be enough, Nigel. I'd rather Jeff stayed here in charge."

They set out toward the southwest, Arletta's leg crooked across a sidesaddle. At first Smithwick wondered what landmarks might have led her to decide this was the place. Then he began to discern a familiar pattern in the landscape. He recognized a valley where he and Cephus had successfully set up a stand. Buffalo bones lay bleached and white, stripped by scavengers and the winter elements.

The crew had purposely masked Cephus's grave by smoothing it over. Timber had been burned on top of it to make the spot appear a campfire site. Warily Smithwick rode a wide circle through the brush to be certain it concealed no Indians before he followed Arletta to the place where her father lay buried. Charred wood still remained on the bare, fire-blackened patch of ground. The ruse had been successful, for the earth had not been disturbed since the day they had ridden away.

Smithwick helped Arletta down from her horse. She was solemn, but he saw no tears. He stood back, holding the horses, letting her walk the final few yards alone. She took off her bonnet and stood with head bowed, her hair lifting in the soft breeze. Looking down upon the dark bit of bare earth, she said quietly, "Papa, things didn't work out like you hoped. I reckon nothin' much ever did." She knelt, picking up a handful of the ash and dirt mixture, letting it sift slowly through her fingers. "It's goin' to, though. It may not be just the way you saw it, but it'll be all right. I'll *make* it all right."

She remained on one knee a while. When she started to arise, Smithwick hurried to help her to her feet. For a moment, clasping her hand, he wanted desperately to fold his arms around her.

He said, "I made a promise to your father. I told him I would take care of you, protect you until you got home. I fear I have done a poor job of it."

"There was a limit to how much you could protect me against my own foolishness." She looked once more toward the grave, then turned her back on it. She held his arm as they walked toward the horses. Abruptly she stopped and faced around, her chin upturned, her hands on his arms. "Nigel, I wish . . ." She did not complete what she had started to say, but her eyes said the rest, asking him.

He drew her into his arms and pressed his lips against her open mouth. Her arms went around him, pulling hard. He felt a surge of warmth, of wanting, and sensed her strong response. They broke for breath, then came together again, their hunger fierce.

Smithwick brought a hand up to the side of her face and found her cheeks flushed red. He felt his inhibitions burning away like a blaze in dry grass. He had to stop now or there would be no stopping. "Arletta, you are a married woman."

"A married woman should have a husband. Where is mine?"

"Wherever he is, you are still tied to him."

"It would be awful easy right now to forget that."

"For the moment, but we would remember it afterward. It would shame us both."

Despair crept into her voice. She pulled away from him a little. "You're right, of course. I just wish you weren't always so damned right."

"I was not right when I said we could never make a life together. We could have. I realized that when it was too late."

Again she clung desperately to him. "Nigel, what're we goin' to do?"

"I wish to God I knew."

He helped her onto her horse. They rode in silence a long time. At last she said, "I didn't think you looked like much the first time I saw you. You were all weak and pale and washed out. You've turned into a right handsome man. You've got a good sunburned color, and you've fleshed out some."

"This country agrees with me, I suppose, more than I ever thought it would."

Hopefully she asked, "You're not still studyin' on goin' back to England, are you?"

"Less and less all the time. I have been looking for a good reason to stay."

"I wish I could be that reason."

He felt his throat tighten. "I wish so too."

"It's a big country. We could go someplace that nobody would know us."

"*We* would know."

A sense of melancholy came over him like a cold, damp fog. "I wish it had not taken me so long to realize what I truly wanted."

BY THE FIFTH DAY the caravan began encountering scattered hunting outfits, camped wherever they could find water, wood and game. Buffalo were scarce, the hunters said, and occasional rotting carcasses told why. The rifles and skinning knives had done their work too well.

Scouts for the long wagon train found what they regarded as a suitable site for the trading post on an open meadow just north of the sandy-bottomed Canadian River. Smithwick remembered riding over the place once when he was scouting with Jeff Layne and Illinois Ike. They had come across a crumbling set of adobe walls, which Jeff had guessed were a remnant of a much earlier trading post for the Indians. Three creeks, tributaries of the Canadian, bordered the wide meadow and provided natural subirrigation to its rich cover of tall grass. That grass would make excellent hay for the animals.

The merchants chose a spot about a mile north of the old ruins, in the center of the meadow where they had a broad field of vision in all directions. Most of the hunters, eager to be after the buffalo, quickly unloaded the merchants' wares from their wagons and scattered in several directions. Those in less of a hurry, and several artisans employed directly by the merchants, set in to cutting timber along the nearby creeks and spading up blocks of grassy sod. These would be used to construct buildings and corrals for which the merchants stepped off and staked the perimeters.

The post quickly acquired a name from the ruins just to the south: Adobe Walls.

Though Leonard and Myers were willing to pay for their help in building the facilities, Jeff and Arletta agreed that their mission was to hunt buffalo, not to act as carpenters or pick-and-shovel labor. As their wagons departed the place, workers were digging a deep trench and standing cottonwood logs in it to form a large corral. Even the most skilled of Indian horse thieves would find it difficult to remove stock from that sturdy enclosure.

Smithwick did not know if the crew could sense the strong attraction that had surfaced between himself and Arletta. The two tried not to let it show. They avoided eye contact with one another as much as they could. He wondered if their effort not to draw attention might be so obvious that it countered their purpose. No one said anything, not Jeff, not Elijah or Cap or any of the skinners. If they knew, they showed no sign of making judgment.

The buffalo proved elusive. Elijah Layne lamented, "I can remember when we used to find them in bunches of two and three hundred. Now they're in bunches of four and six and eight."

Cap Doolittle remarked dryly, "And some bunches don't have any at all."

Though Smithwick and Jeff and Illinois Ike ranged out for miles in all directions from wherever the wagons waited, they found but few. It began to look as if the trip was doomed to financial failure, not just for Arletta's and Jeff's partnership but for other hunters whose paths they crossed. Smithwick wondered what losses Leonard and Myers must be risking through their heavy investment in the trading post at Adobe Walls. They were not alone. James Hanrahan had built a saloon there of sod blocks and stocked it liberally. The merchants depended upon bartering supplies to the buffalo runners in return for hides. From all reports, business was slow.

Arletta began to show the stress, watching wagons and shooters go out day after day and come back with little to show for their effort. Only a few dozen hides were staked down to dry beyond the camp. Though the skinners were paid by the day rather than by the hide, the Fulcher brothers, Herman Scholtz and Barney Gibson were becoming restless and discouraged. Cap burned the biscuits and oversalted the beans.

Sitting at the campfire after supper one night, Arletta apologized to Jeff and his father. "I'm sorry I let you invest your savin's just to help me out. Looks like we all bid fair to go broke."

Elijah tried to ease her worry. "Me and Jeff, we been broke most of our lives. It ain't like it was the first time."

Jeff said, "If the war taught me one thing, it was to never let myself be scared of anything small. Losin' my scalp, that would be somethin' big. But losin' my money . . . hell, there's more where I got that from." He stood up and looked southward, into the darkness. "The buffalo are still out yonder. Some folks say the southern buffalo graze south clear down to the Concho River in the wintertime. They'll come driftin' north one day soon, as the spring grass rises."

And that was the way it turned out.

Smithwick was awakened just before sunup one morning by an unfamiliar sound, something distant, like a faraway roll of thunder, felt more than heard. He sat upright, throwing aside his blankets and reaching for the rifle he kept covered to protect it from frost or dew. His first thought was of Indians. He saw Jeff, already awake in the pale predawn light, standing in his long underwear, peering off toward the south.

The muffled sound continued, rising and falling. Now and again Smithwick heard something besides the faint rumble. He saw no clouds that might indicate thunder. "I say, Jeff, do you know what that is?"

Jeff turned, his eyes shining with pleasure. "It's buffalo. We'd best be gettin' dressed. We don't want to go meet them without our britches on."

In a few minutes the whole camp was aroused. Cap Doolittle started breakfast. Arletta emerged from her tent, a coat over her shoulders. Her eyes were joyous. "They're comin', aren't they, Jeff?"

"Like spring flowers after the winter snow. You know what the Bible says, everything comes to him that waits."

"And we've waited long enough." She threw her arms around Smithwick and hugged him with all the strength she had.

Cap hammered a pothook against a Dutch oven. "Chuck!" he shouted. "Come and get it or I'll throw out the whole mess!"

Arletta made no move toward the cook wagon. "Nigel, would you please saddle my horse? I want to ride out and see them."

Smithwick turned to comply. Jeff put a hand on his shoulder. "You-all better eat breakfast first."

Arletta demanded, "How can you think of eatin' when the buffalo are comin' in?"

"Easy," Jeff replied. "The Indians say to always eat anytime you get a chance, because you never know how long it'll be before the next chance comes. We may not be back before supper." He watched with satisfaction as Arletta hurriedly wolfed down bread, venison and black coffee. "Our partnership's lookin' better now, ain't it?"

They saddled their horses. The Fulcher brothers, Herman Scholtz and Barney Gibson hitched teams to a pair of hide wagons. Barney demanded good-naturedly, "Herman, what if these southern buffalo don't understand your way of speaking English?"

"Then my knife the talking will do, and maybe it will skin one loafer who laughs too much."

Arletta, Jeff, Smithwick and Ike rode out of camp, moving toward the continuing sound of a herd on the move. The wagons followed at a respectful distance. Smithwick began to hear bellowing.

"Bulls," Jeff said. "It's the breedin' season."

The sound of animal movement and the combative challenges of rutting bulls became stronger. Smithwick started to ride upon a hill for a look, but Jeff cautioned, "Where there's buffalo there may be Indians. Chances are the Comanches have broken up their winter encampment to follow the migration."

The four riders took rising ground to a place where they came in view of a broad valley. Smithwick looked down through a thick rising of dust at more buffalo than he had ever seen, thousands plodding along ancient trails, following a primal instinct which had brought them and their ancestors upon this route at each spring's greening for generations beyond counting. Some passed within fifty yards of him. He listened to the chuffing of their breath, the rattle of hooves and dewclaws, and over it all, the calling of the bulls.

Jeff commented, "The Indians say they come up out of a hole in the ground. It must be one hell of a hole."

If Arletta had been a kitten, she would have purred. "What a beautiful sight! Too beautiful to spoil by shootin' into it."

Smithwick's hand itched on the Big Fifty. "But that is what we have come for." He voiced a sentiment he had heard from other hunters. "If we don't, others will."

Jeff studied the nearest buffalo, some now coming within as little as twenty or thirty yards. "They see us but don't pay us any mind. The Indians ain't been runnin' them, at least not yet." He pointed his chin toward a knoll. "Looks like a good place to set up a stand. There's no time like now to get started."

Smithwick gritted his teeth and felt his hand go sweaty on Cephus Browder's old Fifty. It was going to be a long day.

Twenty-four

CROW FEATHER stared across the valley at the swelling carcasses of the buffalo, stripped naked for their hides, their stink so offensive that he and the rest of the horseback scouting party circled them on the upwind side. Gray wolves slunk away, but not so far as to desert their feast. Anger rose in his throat like bad meat fighting its way up from a disturbed stomach. Not all of it was directed at the heathen whites who had committed this atrocity. Some went to his complacent Comanche brothers who so long had scoffed at his fears that the white hunters would kill all the buffalo and leave the People in hunger.

No one scoffed now. Since they had broken up the winter encampment to follow the migrating herds northward, they had witnessed enough such scenes that all knew the message Crow Feather had brought last fall from the Cheyennes was serious indeed. Some like Man Who Stole the Mules remained content to pick off a hunter here and a skinner there for the pure exhilaration of the kill, but most were beginning to think in terms of a larger goal. One did not attack an ant bed by stepping on one ant here and another yonder. This fight would require a concerted effort, a bold plan to drive out the greedy invaders.

There had been times in the distant past when many villages of the Comanches had gathered in massive numbers to overwhelm a foe. In the youth of Crow Feather's father, the Penateka band to the south had once driven all the way down to the Gulf of Mexico, a thousand strong. They destroyed a Texas seacoast town called Linnville, wading out into the salty waters to kill terrified survivors in their boats as they attempted to escape. They burned the town as they left, driving a great herd of horses and mules. It was a crushing victory. Overconfidence, however, betrayed the Comanches into a disastrous confrontation with vengeful Tejanos at a place the white men called Plum Creek, far inland from the big waters. The People had learned a painful lesson about the Texans' willingness to fight. True, there were cowards among them, but there were more who fought with the ferocity of a cornered bear. Those of the warrior society called Rangers were like the snapping turtle that bit down hard and refused to let go so long as the heart held life.

Crow Feather knew that the *teibos* who now slaughtered the buffalo came from the north, whereas Tejanos lived to the south. He was not sure they were of one tribe, though they looked the same. Their clothing was similar, their faces often covered by a growth of ugly hair, like a bear. So far as he knew they spoke in a single tongue, and it was forked. He reasoned that they might be of different bands but of one people. It did not matter; they were invaders, destroyers, despoilers of that which belonged to Crow Feather's people. They must be turned back, whatever the cost in Comanche and *teibo* blood.

It was not that the People had yet begun to go hungry. The buffalo migration had been late, for rain had been scarce and the grass slow to green, but the numbers had been large. His concern was for the future. It was clear that the hide hunters were already taking far more buffalo than the People would normally kill for their own needs, and spring was just now giving way to hot summer. In autumn, when the north wind blew cool again, time would come for the great hunt to store up meat for winter and process the hides for protection against the bitter cold. By then, if the white men were not stopped, the buffalo might well be reduced to scattered remnants. He had seen it in the land of the Cheyenne.

Before winter his lodge would be home to two more young ones, joining the son he had from White Deer and the daughter given him by Rabbit. It was unthinkable that the milk in their mothers' breasts should dry up for lack of meat.

The alternative he saw to war was painful to contemplate: to accept the reservation the white man offered, to live a virtual prisoner, to become like the dog in camp that tucks its tail and accepts whatever whipping a cruel master might give, then licks the master's hand for every feeding. Some bands of the People had already gone the white man's way. He knew from reports that they were restless and dissatisfied, wishing they had not so easily traded away their freedom. It was a hard thing to live where one must beg permission of inferiors to travel so much as a day's journey and where one was forced to eat the white man's scrawny cattle instead of the nourishing flesh of the buffalo.

Mules remained shortsighted. He wanted to seek out a hunter camp and take whatever scalps came handy. He seemed not to have learned from his experience back in the fall, when he had killed his own horse with a dead hunter's rifle that carried bad medicine. Crow Feather thought it more important to spy out the big new encampment where he heard that white men had built large houses of mud and sod, where the dried skins of many buffalo were stacked without reverence and many wagons came and went daily, bringing more hunters, more rifles, more death for the herds.

This encampment, he thought, was the wasp nest. It did but little good to kill a single wasp, out foraging. One should strike down the nest and quickly drown it or throw it into the flames. Those wasps which survived would seek a new home elsewhere. It seemed reasonable that if the Comanches and allied Kiowas and Cheyennes could destroy this place, which appeared to be a point of supply and dispersement for all the hunters, any who survived would move far away from the People.

If Mules and such foolish friends as Swift Runner could not see beyond the distractions of the moment, Crow Feather had gained other allies to his cause. Goes His Own Way was a brave man in a fight but also wise in council for one who had not known many summers since gaining his status as a warrior and the medicine of a protecting spirit. Goes rode around the perimeter of the buffalo-killing ground, his young face twisted in revulsion. His voice quivered with anger. "Everywhere we see the same. Why do they take so little of the meat? Are there not hungry wives and children in their lodges?"

"I have seen no women and no children with the wagons," Crow Feather said. "They must leave those in some faraway village. But they could dry the meat and carry it to them if they wanted."

"Have they so many tepees that they need all these skins to cover the poles?"

"The Tejano lodges are of wood and stone and mud, not of skins. The Cheyennes say those in the north are much the same."

"Then can it be that their spirits are enemies of the buffalo spirits, that they kill all they find?"

Crow Feather had to think about that a while. The idea had a certain plausibility. Everyone knew that the world was full of opposing spirits, the good and the evil, those who roamed by night and those who lived in the sun. They were ever at war with one another. "The white man's heart is bad, but our spirits are good. If we are careful not to offend them, surely they will help us overpower the white man."

By Comanche reckoning the party was twice times four in number, all of fighting age, veterans of the war trails down into the Texas settlements or much farther, into Mexico. With the exception of Mules and a pair including Swift Runner who followed his lead in the way of eager pups, they were men Crow Feather would gladly choose to have at his side in any conflict.

He heard distant rifle fire. The shots came at a steady pace, indicating a hunter at work. Mules argued loudly for finding the hair-face and dispatching him to join his grandfathers. Acquiring a fresh scalp or two might help scrub away the stain of ridicule Mules had suffered since the unhappy incident with the buffalo rifle and his horse.

The majority followed Crow Feather in overruling him. Crow Feather said impatiently, "Go, if it pleases you, but the rest of us have a more important thing to do."

Mules rode at the rear, grumbling with his two confederates about the missed opportunity. Crow Feather was torn between a wish that the three would break away to attempt the attack on their own and a concern that they might bring a vengeance-seeking party of hunters down upon the entire group, spoiling the larger mission. It soon became evident that Mules had no intention of going with only two warriors beside him. He could not even guess how strong the hunter's camp might be.

Crow Feather knew by description where to find the wagon village. He had hunted over those grounds. Nearby, he had been told, white traders once had built an adobe-brick post to barter with the Indians but had abandoned it because enmity between the several tribes was too strong. Too many had rather spill one another's blood than trade for white-man goods. At the same site, when Crow Feather had not yet been of age, the People had fought a great battle with the pony soldiers and would have overwhelmed them but for the big thunder guns on wheels. These caused the ground to explode with much noise and smoke, killing the warriors' horses or panicking them into an uncontrollable runaway.

The sandy Canadian River lay just south of the wagon lodges. Crow Feather and the others approached from the east, halting amid a heavy stand of sheltering cottonwoods and willows on the banks of a small creek that fed into the river. They could not go farther without being seen, for a broad, open meadow lay between the creek and the cluster of buildings. Crow Feather thought they could see enough, however, from where they were. Several strings of wagons stood in random fashion in front of the buildings. Some were laden with buffalo hides, others canvas-covered. He reasoned that these might have brought supplies from the north, or perhaps they were used for sleeping, though he did not understand why one would want to sleep cramped in a wagon. There was so much more room on the ground, where a man could feel the beating heart of his mother the earth.

A strong corral of upright logs held many horses and mules. He could see men walking about, busy loading or unloading the wagons. At this moment he could sympathize with Mules, for his heart quickened with anger at sight of them, and he wanted to strike at them now.

He remembered this meadow. He remembered once, as a youth, besting Mules in a horserace across its green expanse. He remembered a later time he and a hunting party had chased and killed buffalo here when their camp was badly in need of meat. His memories touched on moments of high exhilaration. The white-man structures, the many wagons, the *teibos* themselves, were a sacrilege, a violation against those happy memories. These interlopers had no business here, these soulless ones who showed no care for sacred places or sacred things. This land belonged to the People. The grandfathers of their grandfathers had come here from the north to slay the Apaches and any others who dared stand against them. Generations of vigilance and warfare had given the People a blood right to this land. Soon the mother earth would drink the blood of these hairy men from the north and sweeten the grass for the buffalo.

He saw a puff of smoke and a moment later heard the report of a rifle. For a startled few seconds he thought someone was shooting at him and his companions. It seemed unreasonable they would attempt such a thing at a range this long. Several more shots were fired without causing any evident excitement among the white men working around the post. It came to him that someone was firing for practice, or perhaps trying out a new rifle. It stood to reason that such a place would trade rifles and bullets to hunters.

That was a happy thought. He and his friends could make good use of such trophies, once all the *teibos* were dead.

He observed, "There are not so many lodges as I had imagined. There cannot be many white men in a place so small. It should not be much of a fight."

Goes His Own Way agreed, to a point. "But it is open ground from here to the walls. They would see us as soon as we leave these trees. You have seen how far their rifles send bullets to bring down the buffalo. They could kill many of us before we could reach them."

Crow Feather grunted. "What if they could not see us?"

"We would attack them at night?" That was not a thing the Comanche liked to do.

"No, at the first coming of the morning sun. It will rise there," he said, pointing back over his shoulder toward the east. "That is the plan. Any white men who might be awake will be blind to us because we will come at them out of the rising sun."

He saw a sun reflection in a distant window. He knew what glass was; he had seen it in Tejano houses. He had seen it in trade mirrors. He knew how easily it was demolished. Even if the doors were barred and could not be broken down, it would be simple to smash in the windows and shoot through them, killing everyone inside.

It should be over quickly. Surprise the white man, still dulled by sleep, and set the wasp nest aflame.

Goes said, "It is a thing for a greater war party than this one."

"So it will be, more warriors than you can count. Not like Mules, who thinks he can drive out the white man by killing a few of the easy ones, but men who will follow the plan."

"The plan of the medicine man Isatai?"

Crow Feather sniffed. "Isatai is a fool, or a trickster like the coyote."

"He says he can make magic that will stop the white man's bullets and cause them to roll off like the rain."

"One can say anything. That does not make it true."

"There are many who believe. Some say they have seen him bring the dead to life and cough up the white man's bullets."

"Surely, Goes, you do not believe in such foolishness."

"I do not believe what I have not seen, but a great many want to believe. Whether his magic is good or not, he can gather many warriors for the fight. Not just of the People but of the Kiowas and the Cheyennes. They have been listening to him."

"The Kiowas can be fooled into believing many things, and the Cheyennes even more. That does not make them true."

"We do not have to believe in Isatai. We can believe in our own spirits, and what they can help us do. Even a fool has his uses."

That was true. Mules had been useful at times. "Isatai is calling for us to have a Sun Dance. That is all right for the Cheyennes. They have done it since before our grandfathers. But it has never been our way."

"These are times like we have never known before. If a Sun Dance might call up spirits that would help us, what is the harm in it?"

"I see no harm except that many may stand back and wait for the spirits to do the work. The spirits will not remove the white man from our land by themselves. That is a thing we must do, with their help."

Rides a Black Horse was a believer, not only in Crow Feather but in Isatai. He suggested, "Isatai talks to spirits that have not spoken to the rest of us. I have heard amazing things."

Crow Feather was not surprised at Black Horse's acceptance of the claims to strong medicine. He perceived that Goes also wanted to believe despite his doubt. "If Isatai can gather enough warriors, it will not matter whether his spirits speak to him or not. Ours will speak to us, and our weapons will speak to the white man." He touched his hand to the Mexican trade knife at his hip.

The Comanche had never been comfortable with the complex religions of other plains folk. His faith was simple and straightforward. He believed in his own personal spirit guides, the powers and the rules of conduct they laid out for him. He respected the medicine of others but put his trust only in his own. From the first, Crow Feather had harbored doubts about the rising young medicine man, though many of the People in their alarm over the white man's incursions had begun to embrace Isatai and invest faith in his promises.

Crow Feather suspected Isatai was using the People to build his own prestige, so he saw no evil in using Isatai. But he would stay clear of the medicine man. If Isatai was even half the shaman he claimed to be, he would easily see the doubt in Crow Feather's heart and perhaps call upon some dark spirit to visit punishment upon his lodge. Crow Feather had never been one to keep his feelings from showing in his eyes. He had never been able to hold a secret from White Deer, though he could sometimes fool Rabbit.

Mules did not want to wait for Isatai to gather a force. He was in favor of staying the night here, then hitting the post at daybreak with the eight warriors present. There would be coups enough for everybody, he declared.

"Eight against so many?" Crow Feather had seen foolhardiness in Mules before, but nothing of this dimension.

"We could kill half of them before they are awake."

"We do not want to kill half. We want to kill them all. We will wait." He turned away from Mules, indicating that the discussion was done before it had fairly started. Mules grumbled and drew his two supporters to his side to continue a one-sided argument. Crow Feather frowned. He wished he knew what to do about Mules. The man's recklessness could kill them all.

He watched the buildings and the wagons for a while more, trying to burn into his mind the location of everything the force would need to strike. If there were enough warriors, he thought, it would be wise to attack in a broad line, hitting every part of the post at the same moment and giving none of the white men time to mount a defense. With even as little as a nod from the spirits, annihilation should be accomplished within a few beats of a drum.

He was about to signal a quiet retreat eastward, keeping the line of trees between the scouting party and the post, when Rides a Black Horse touched his arm and pointed in the direction they were to travel. Three sets of hide wagons appeared, bound for the trading post. For a worrisome while it seemed they might cross the creek where the reconnaissance party waited in hiding. That would bring a fight and almost surely draw white men rushing from the buildings to help their own kind. His heartbeat quickening, Crow Feather crouched and held the nostrils of his horse. The others did likewise to prevent nickering that would give them away.

The man on the front wagon evidently did not care for the crossing where the Comanches waited. He moved beyond it, putting his team into the water some distance downstream. Relieved, Crow Feather expelled a long breath. The white man would never know how lucky he was.

He saw the thought in Mules's eyes, as plain as if it had been painted huge on a deerskin: hit the wagon drivers while they concentrated on getting across the creek without sticking their wheels. Crisply Crow Feather warned, "Do not even consider it, or we will leave you here afoot."

Mules gave him a look of silent but deep resentment that promised a future reckoning.

A lone wagon came along, following the tracks of the earlier three. Crow Feather decided it best to wait until dark before leaving the hiding place. He did not want to disturb the wagon village and cause it to become too alert for the surprise that was planned. So the party sat, watching the post, memorizing its features. Crow Feather knew it well enough to draw a sketch in the sand, correct in its principal details. He would be able to recreate the sketch for guidance of those who had not been here.

With darkness they stole away, making camp at a familiar spring to the east. They built only a very small fire. Another flickered in the distance, much too large to have been built by Indians. The white hunters were everywhere, like the grasshoppers that descended as a plague when summers turned dry and hot, like this one.

Crow Feather stared into the small fire, thinking of White Deer and Rabbit, of the two children he had now and those to come. He wondered what kind of life lay in store for them if the white man could not be turned back. He had been born at a time when the Tejanos were too far away to be considered any threat to his own band, though they had begun serious encroachment against those bands like the Penateka who lived farther to the south. In his youth the Texans, like the Mexicans, had been little more than an object of sport, to be raided, to be challenged, to prove the valor of young warriors in combat. But with these hair-faces greedy for buffalo skins, this was not a question of sport. Survival of the People was at stake.

He poked at the fire, feeling little of its heat. The night was warm, but he shivered, the cold coming from within him.

They moved before daybreak, traversing an open plain where last year's dried grass sheltered a reluctant fresh green growth stunted by a drier-than-usual season. Crow Feather thought darkly that if Isatai were so powerful he should be able to prevail upon some benevolent spirit to make it rain. It would be far better for the horses, and for the buffalo.

The sun had made a good climb when the party moved across a rise in the prairie and came suddenly upon a valley where cottonwoods and other timber lined a meandering creek. Between them and the creek rode a lone horseman. He reined up abruptly, seeing the Comanches at the moment they saw him. Crow Feather knew at a glance that this was a white man.

So did Mules. With a blood shout he drummed his heels against his pony's ribs and set out in headlong pursuit, his two confederates close behind him. Crow Feather yelled at Swift Runner to come back, but it was useless. Mules was no longer to be denied, and Swift Runner was a pup eagerly following an older but no wiser dog.

Goes His Own Way pulled his horse in close beside Crow Feather. "Should we not go and help them?"

"Help three barking dogs? They leave the trail of a bear to chase a rabbit."

The hunter was no rabbit. He dismounted, stepped behind his horse, leveled a long-barreled rifle and fired. One of the three horses went down. Mules hesitated only a moment to be sure the rider himself was not hit. As he plunged ahead, the rifle spoke again. Mules's remaining companion lurched forward, then tumbled.

Crow Feather cried out in dismay. The fallen rider was Swift Runner, his brother-in-law. He motioned for the others to stay behind while he pushed his horse forward.

Mules turned back. The loose horse kept going. There was no chance of recovering it in the face of the hunter's marksmanship. Mules dismounted and knelt beside Swift Runner. Crow Feather knew by his actions that the warrior was dead. As Crow Feather reached the scene, Mules cried out in anger, "Why did you not come and help us?"

"Three fools was enough."

"You have let your sister's husband die."

"No, I tried to stop him. You led him to his death." Crow Feather felt his voice break with sorrow. "Let us get him away from this place."

Scowling, Mules lifted the body for Crow Feather to receive and carry in front of him across his horse. Mules picked up the fallen shield lest it pass into enemy hands and be used to make bad medicine against the departed. He remounted and leaned low, trying to be a poor target. The warrior who had been set afoot trotted along beside him as they returned to those who waited.

A bullet kicked up dust near the feet of Crow Feather's horse. The range was formidable, yet the hunter had missed by only a little. Crow Feather thought the white man must have spirits of his own that guided his bullets so far. These were indeed rifles that could shoot today and kill tomorrow.

Further rebuke would serve no purpose. Mules was crestfallen, spattered with blood from the wound that had killed his friend. The bullet had gone into the chest and made a large hole in the warrior's back as it had exited. Crow Feather dreaded the lamentations that would accompany the party's return to camp. In her mourning, his sister Calling Bird would cut off her hair and slash her arms and body until she bled half to death. The unborn baby that swelled her stomach would never see the face of its true father.

Crow Feather looked gravely at Goes His Own Way. "This is a bad beginning," he said.

Twenty-five

S WEAT, SALTY AND BURNING, rolled into Nigel Smithwick's eye just as his finger tightened on the trigger. The moment the rifle roared, he knew he had fired a bad shot. The buffalo cow he had intended to hit in the lungs made a frightened leap and broke into headlong, bawling flight. The rest of the buffalo had stood by in confusion while cows fell about them one by one, but now thirty or so set off in a clattering run. The cow which had sparked the alarm went about fifty yards and fell. The others rushed past her in full stampede.

Arletta sat twenty feet from Smithwick, her rifle barrel balanced upon two long crossed sticks. She had drawn a bead but lowered the rifle stock and eased the hammer down. A good marksman in her own right, she wanted to harvest as many buffalo as possible before they were thinned out by the wholesale hunting that had spread across the upper Texas plains. Because Cap Doolittle took care of the cooking, she had been going out with Smithwick some days, Jeff or Ike on others. The uncertainty of the Indian situation made it risky for her to go alone, but she refused to remain in camp.

She would have good reason for anger over the loss of this stand, for she and Smithwick had stood a good chance of bringing down every animal in the bunch. But she wiped a sleeve across her face and smiled tentatively. "We've had a fair-enough day. I probably would've spilled them if you hadn't."

"It's difficult to see the sights when perspiration keeps stinging your eyes. I wonder if June is always so hot here." Summer had come early, its temperatures high. The grass was dry and brittle, badly in need of a rejuvenating rain. As he moved from his prone position to sit upright, a jumping grasshopper threatened to go down his open collar. He brushed it away, addressing it sharply beneath his breath. "Away from me, you beggar." He blinked at the glare from the bleaching old grass. "It was never this hot in England."

She studied him with concern. "It's been a while since I heard you say anything about goin' back."

"I was merely commenting about the weather."

"This is different from Ohio too," she conceded, standing up, brushing dust from the long, shapeless gray dress she always wore, in camp or out hunting. "But all in all it seems like a healthy country. Jeff seems to glory in it."

"Because this is Texas, and he is a Texan. A pity he cannot go farther south to his old home."

"Has he ever told you why?"

"He avoids the subject. It seems there was a killing." He ran a cloth patch through his rifle barrel. "Sorry about the stand."

"We don't have to bring them all down in one day." She frowned. "Somehow I get a feelin' that your heart ain't in this anymore."

"Can you honestly say that yours is?"

"I take no pleasure in the killin'. But any time my trigger finger hesitates, I remember Papa."

He gathered up his unused cartridges as well as the spent shells to be reloaded in camp. Brass cost too much to waste. "I shall tell Barney and Herman they can begin their work."

She cocked her head toward the sound of a wagon. "They're already comin'. They heard the buffalo run."

The hide wagon climbed the slope from a plum grove behind which the skinners had waited out of sight. Smithwick looked up at the afternoon sun, gauging the time. He saw little purpose in seeking out more buffalo to kill today even though the number they had dropped was short of expectations. "If you would like to return to camp, I'll stand watch over Barney and Herman."

"They don't really need us to guard them. Me and you, we don't spend much time together."

"It is probably better that way."

"No it isn't. It's hell."

Barney Gibson pulled the team to a halt and surveyed the thin scattering of fallen buffalo awaiting the skinning knives. "I'm glad I'm bein' paid by the day and not by the hide."

Arletta said, "You'll get to eat supper early. Me and Nigel, we're goin' out to locate a bunch for tomorrow."

Barney nodded a little too knowingly, Smithwick thought. Herman jumped down from the wagon and cautiously checked the nearest cow to be certain no life remained. He would not make the mistake that once had almost killed Gantry Folsom. "Barney," he shouted, "is it to sit you are paid, or is it to work?"

Barney scratched beneath his armpit. "If I was paid for every buffalo louse I pick up, I'd be richer than Colonel Cregar." He climbed down from the wagon, whetting his skinning knife as he walked. Tonight he would bathe in the creek near camp and throw these clothes on an ant bed to let the ants seek out the lice.

Arletta gave Smithwick that faint smile again. "The buffalo are waitin'."

They rode southward a couple of miles, the wind at their backs, and paused to water their horses in the pleasant shade of cottonwoods and willows that lined a clear, cool creek. It had no name that Smithwick knew of. A bit farther on they ascended a rising ground and came upon a scene that never failed to stir him. He rough-counted as many as five hundred buffalo scattered in small bunches over a mile or more of open prairie framed by a distant line of blue hills. The nearest animals were no more than two hundred yards away. A cow raised her head, sniffing the wind and finding something in it that disturbed her. She snorted and began to move nervously away. Others responded to her alarm and stopped their grazing.

"She has caught our scent," Smithwick said. "We had best draw away."

"Even though I know I have to kill them, the sight of them does somethin' good for my soul."

"A sight you had best enjoy while you can. It will soon be gone, and ours will be the hands that destroy it."

"You're makin' me feel guilty."

"Of late, dropping these poor dumb beasts, I have begun to feel guilty enough for both of us." The thrill he had taken from his first shooting last fall had dulled. He had seen blood enough. Jeff Layne's reservations about killing as sport had begun to sink in.

They retreated, Arletta looking back over her shoulder as long as the buffalo remained in view. "Would it make any difference in the long run if me and you quit shootin' them?"

"Not a whit. The slaughter has gone too far to stop. Hunters will hound them until the last herd has gone to the ground."

They halted at the creek again, dismounting to give the horses another chance to drink, though the animals barely more than nuzzled the water. The dun pawed in it, stirring up mud for no good reason that Smithwick could see.

Arletta's laugh was soft and musical. "I never could figure out why they do that."

"Horses probably wonder sometimes why we humans do the things we do."

Arletta turned into Smithwick's arms. "I wonder too, Nigel. I wonder why we open ourselves up to so much hurt when stoppin' it would be so easy."

His blood warmed, and he held her, wanting to sink to the ground with her, knowing she wanted it too. "We can't. You know we can't."

"I know. But hold me for a while, please."

"We should not go off together anymore. Sooner or later you know what it will lead to."

"I wouldn't mind if it did."

"You would. Later you would."

"How long must we keep paying for my mistake, Nigel?"

"*Our* mistake. I wanted you but listened to my doubts. And the day I brought you the money, I should have turned around and gone right back."

"But you couldn't. And I couldn't've let you."

Of late he had considered often her suggestion that they go away together somewhere, to a place where no one knew them, where no one would care. But he knew they wouldn't. She was stronger than that, and he hoped he was. When time came for the leaving, they wouldn't do it.

He held her and asked himself the question that had tormented him for weeks: *What is ever to become of us?*

THEY FOUND Barney and Herman had finished the skinning and were on the move, the fresh hides folded and stacked in the wagon bed. Flies in noisome number sought the blood and the thin tallow that still clung to the skins. Flies and buffalo lice and the eternal smell . . . he thought it little wonder that the luster had faded, that for him the sport had degenerated into a grim business. Were it not for Arletta, he would turn his back on it in a moment.

On the way to camp they joined Jeff and his skinners, whose wagon carried a larger load. Jeff made no comment, but it was obvious he noticed.

Smithwick said, "My fault. I spoiled the stand. I wonder sometimes why you put up with me."

"Because you work cheap." Jeff turned in his saddle and looked behind him. A mild alarm came into his eyes. "Do you hear that?"

At first Smithwick heard only the rattle of the wagons and the plodding of horses' hooves. Gradually he became conscious of a low rumble. It could have been distant thunder; gray clouds were building to the north, holding forth a possibility of rain. But the sound came from the south. "Buffalo running?"

Jeff's face creased with concern. "A lot of them, and they're comin' towards us." He motioned to Barney, on the lead wagon. "Be ready to put that team into a run. Arletta, you better stay close to the wagons. English, me and you are goin' back and take a look-see."

Smithwick saw nothing yet, at least not for certain. He thought he detected a rising of dust, but it had been a dry season. The wind often whipped up hoof-churned dust where large congregations of buffalo had grazed grass off to the surface. The plains had a deceptive appearance of flatness, but in reality they rose and fell in an irregular rolling pattern that fooled the eye. Often Smithwick had ridden unexpectedly upon buffalo he had not seen because they grazed or rested in low ground hidden from him. Natural playa lake beds, some fully a half mile across, caught and held runoff from the higher ground that surrounded them. Most were dry or nearly dry now because rainfall had been scarce.

The wind at their backs, he and Jeff climbed an almost imperceptible rise. The breath caught in Smithwick's throat. A mass of buffalo rushed toward them, stirring dust that rose in a brown cloud so dense he could not determine the depth of the herd. The ground trembled. It was thunder, rightly enough, the thunder of thousands of pounding hooves. He had wondered sometimes what might put genuine fear in Jeff's eyes. He saw fear there now. "What'll we do?"

Jeff declared, "Run like hell!" and whipped his black horse around. He had no need to use quirt or spurs. The horse sensed the peril and was more than ready to run. Smithwick trailed after, leaning over Dunny's neck and slapping the animal's rump with his hat. Dunny caught the contagion of fright.

Jeff fired his pistol to alert the wagon drivers. Seeing for themselves the buffalo spilling over the rise, they set the teams into a run. The wagons bounced across the rough ground. Several hides fell off, but it would be foolhardy to stop and retrieve them. Arletta galloped her horse alongside the lead wagon, watching over her shoulder.

Jeff gained on the wagons and waved his hat. "Pull to the left! To the left!"

Smithwick saw that in that direction they had a chance to draw clear of the stampede, for the main mass of buffalo was to their right. He remembered someone telling him that buffalo usually stampeded into the wind. The wind was out of the north, and north was the direction of camp.

He maneuvered to get behind Arletta. It was in his mind that if her horse fell he would be in position to grab her up and carry her to safety. But it was Dunny which stumbled. Smithwick hit the ground rolling and lost most of his breath. For a moment he was too stunned to move. The horse gained its feet and ran on without him, the stirrups flopping.

Jeff slid his horse to a stop and came back. Smithwick had been holding Archie Grosvenor's Big Fifty across his lap. He looked frantically for it.

Jeff shouted urgently, "Come on! Get up here with me!"

"I lost the rifle."

"To hell with the rifle! Get up here!" Jeff freed his left stirrup so Smithwick could swing up behind him. It was a precarious seat, and he felt in danger of sliding off over the horse's rump. He held his arms tightly around Jeff as the Texan put the mount back into a run.

Shortly they were clear. The main body of the herd swept by, missing them. A few animals along the fringe of the bunch passed to their left. He felt that he might choke on the heavy and oppressive dust, though much of his problem was the dirt he had swallowed when he fell. He looked for the dun horse. It was still running toward camp, its stride awkward. It appeared to have lamed itself.

The wagons slowed to a stop. Arletta hurried toward Jeff's black horse. "Are you all right, Nigel?"

Smithwick slid to the ground, coughing up dirt. Arletta dismounted and slapped his back. It did not help.

Barney Gibson said, "I'm afraid we lost some hides."

Jeff grunted. "As long as we didn't lose our own, I'd say we came out pretty good."

The last of the buffalo passed on. Jeff looked anxiously northward. "I hope the boys in camp don't get caught unawares."

Volleys of gunfire began in that direction. Jeff said, "They're tryin' to turn the herd or make it split around. We'd better lope up and see."

The ground was pulverized where the buffalo had run. The wind whipped fresh dust in their wake, adding to the dust the hooves had raised. When Smithwick's throat was clear he asked, "How many do you suppose there were?"

Jeff said, "I didn't take time to count. Couple thousand, maybe more."

Arletta wiped dirt from Smithwick's face with a cloth she had brought along for cleaning her rifle. "What do you suppose touched them off, Jeff?"

"It doesn't take much if they're already nervous. One spooks at somethin' and they all go. Could have been anything . . . a wolf, even a jackrabbit." But his face betrayed his doubt.

Arletta asked, "Could it have been Indians?"

"We ain't seen any."

"But could it have been?"

"Buffalo ain't overly smart; it doesn't take much to make them run."

Something in Jeff's eyes made Smithwick suspect he was trying to shelter Arletta.

Left afoot, his dun horse gone out of sight, he climbed upon the wagon with Barney and Herman. The distant shooting subsided, then stopped. Smithwick felt a tingling of apprehension until he began to see movement. A dozen or more buffalo lay dead or dying. The beaten ground showed that the herd had skirted the edge of camp.

Elijah Layne and Cap Doolittle walked out to meet the wagons. Both were visibly shaken. Elijah said, "Son, we thought they was comin' right over the top of us. Had to kill a bunch of them, but they shied off at the last minute."

Jeff asked, "Any damage?"

Cap said ruefully, "They made kindlin' out of the supply wagon. Played hell with most of what was in it. I hope you can get along without coffee, because they tromped it into the dirt. Sugar too, and most of our flour."

Jeff looked darkly at the destroyed wagon and spoiled supplies. "We can probably borrow a little from Colonel's camp, but looks like we'll have to send a wagon to Adobe Walls with a load of hides to trade." He turned to Smithwick. "How would you like a couple of days rest from killin' buffalo?"

Smithwick was not sure how to answer. He welcomed the prospect of not watching the big animals die. He was not pleased at the idea of leaving Arletta. He searched her face, seeking her reaction.

"I guess it has to be done," she said reluctantly.

The stock tender came up leading the dun horse. The saddle had turned under its belly. "He came runnin' into the bunch," he told Smithwick. "Looks like he might've lamed himself a mite."

The horse was still nervous. Smithwick patted him on the neck and talked softly to him before he dropped the saddle to the ground. He ran his hand down the shoulder to Dunny's left foreleg. "There doesn't seem to be anything broken. He probably bruised himself or pulled a muscle when he fell. I'd best not ride him for a few days."

"You'll be ridin' a wagon anyway," Jeff said.

Smithwick saddled another horse to go back and look for the lost rifle. Jeff said, "You're not goin' alone. I'll ride with you." When they had left camp behind, Jeff confirmed Smithwick's suspicion. "I didn't want to upset Arletta, but I think there's a good chance it was Indians set them buffalo to runnin'. Maybe just huntin', or maybe they hoped to stampede them over us."

Despite the narrow escape, Smithwick found a certain rough justice in the idea. "It seems appropriate when you consider it, sending the buffalo to rid themselves of buffalo hunters."

Jeff held out little hope that they would find the rifle, but they did, after an hour's search. It had been stomped into the dirt, the wooden stock broken. Jeff said, "You can wrap wet rawhide around the stock. When it dries it'll shrink and hold like a vise. It won't be much for pretty, but it'll do till we get back to Dodge. Otherwise, the gun looks like it's all right."

"Looks like." Smithwick found himself slipping into the Texan's vernacular. He had noticed it happening more and more.

Colonel Cregar arrived in camp at the same time they did. He had seen the buffalo stampede from afar and had run his horse until it was lathered with sweat. He rushed past everyone else to reach Arletta. "You're not hurt?" The shrillness of his normally deep voice betrayed his apprehension.

"I'm all right. It was nip and tuck for a minute or two, but we all came out in good shape."

"God!" he declared. "I was all but certain they swept right over your camp."

"They might near did, but I wasn't here. I was out shootin'."

"Shooting?" His eyes widened. "Haven't I told you how dangerous that is?" He turned accusingly to Jeff and Smithwick. "How can you allow her to do such a thing?"

Jeff shrugged. "She doesn't listen to me and English. Arletta does whatever Arletta wants to do."

She pushed the subject aside. "Colonel, you can see what they did to our supply wagon. Reckon you could give us the borry of a few supplies while we can send a wagon to the post?"

"Of course. But I want you to promise me that you won't be out shooting again. A passing hunter told me today that he saw Indians skulking around."

Jeff said, "She won't be out for a few days. Won't be anybody shootin' except Ike till me and English get back from Adobe Walls with supplies."

That caught Smithwick off guard. He had assumed he would travel alone, or take one of the skinners with him.

Arletta leaned against him. "I wish you didn't have to go, Nigel. We could send somebody else." She placed her hand against his chest.

Cregar's eyes narrowed, covering up whatever emotion he might feel at seeing his son's wife in another man's arms.

Smithwick said, "We shall be back as quickly as we can."

THE ADOBE WALLS trading post had grown considerably since he had witnessed its rough beginnings. He sat on the wagon seat, the reins in his hands, Jeff riding alongside on his black horse. The wagon was piled high with dried hides. Smithwick's first impression was of a small stick-and-mud village. One building fronted the northeast corner of a large horse-and-mule corral of upright cottonwood logs. Construction had begun on the corral before he had gone south in search of buffalo. The building, as he recalled, would be the Myers and Leonard store. Drawing closer, he saw that it was of pickets, daubed with red clay to turn wind and rain.

To the south stood a sod-block building of roughly the same dimensions, fronting a hide yard four times its size. Between the two were a blacksmith shop and the saloon the hunters had been promised. The buildings spanned a space he estimated at perhaps three hundred yards long and a hundred or so wide.

Though crude, the little village had a certain straight-line symmetry. It was not a place that would impress a man who had spent most of his life in and around the mannered villages of England, but he made allowances for its isolation and limited resources. Give it a hundred years and it might come up to civilized standards. Most English villages had required far longer.

Passing hunters had told Jeff and Smithwick that Charles Rath had built a store at Adobe Walls after Myers and Leonard had completed theirs. He assumed it to be the southernmost of the structures. Rath and his partners had gotten a late start. Their corral was still under construction, only two or three courses of sod squares run so far.

Because Jeff had done business with Rath in Dodge City, he pointed Smithwick in the direction of that store. The manager was a young Irishman named James Langton. Smithwick stood back to let Jeff take care of whatever bargaining was to be done. He had never liked haggling; it compromised dignity, he thought. The Texan was not a haggler either. He simply told Langton how many hides were on the wagon, and Langton told him the current market price, two dollars.

"Fair enough," Jeff said. The market might be higher in Dodge, but Dodge was a long way off. He presented a list of necessities he and Cap and Arletta had worked out. "On that gunpowder, I don't want any low-grade American stuff. I want that English grained kind. It fires cleaner and has a right smart more power."

Smithwick indulged himself in a bit of pride over the fact that the Texan chose an English commodity.

Jeff said, "We'd like to get the hides unloaded and the goods put on the wagon tonight so we can start back at daylight in the mornin'."

Langton saw no problem. "Wouldn't you like to stay around and enjoy the luxuries of Adobe Walls a few days?" His smile indicated that he was enjoying his little irony.

Jeff said, "One night'll have to do us. A hunter we passed along the way said we could get a woman-cooked meal here."

Langton pointed his thumb toward a partition. "That's our restaurant. Hannah Olds presides over the stove, and her husband clerks for us. You'll not eat from tin plates, either, but real ironstone dishes like the best places in Dodge City."

Jeff grinned at Smithwick. "They got anything better in London?"

"Not everywhere." The rude sod and picket buildings did not lead him to high hopes, but he reserved final judgment. He had been in places back home that boasted crystal, china and the best English silverware but offered food that would turn away a mongrel dog.

"Long as I'm here," Jeff said, "I want to take Tar Baby to the blacksmith shop and get him reshod. Tom O'Keefe is a lot better at it than I am."

Smithwick remembered several of the men they encountered in the saloon, for they had been in the wagon train that had come down from Dodge in March to establish this place. Jeff had known them much longer, having crossed their trails north of the Arkansas. There was, for example, a young long-haired hunter named Billy Dixon, reputed to have one of the best shooting eyes anywhere on the buffalo range. There was James Hanrahan, the saloon-keeper, a strong-minded Pennsylvanian who had been on the frontier long enough to adapt and thrive on its ways. And there was a hunter, younger than Dixon, who went by the nickname Bat. Smithwick thought the last name was Masterson; he had not heard it clearly enough to be certain. They were, all in all, a most varied lot, far more colorful than one was likely to find in the typical English pub.

He and Jeff had a couple of drinks in the saloon, then walked outside, intending to eat supper in the Rath restaurant on ironstone dishes, as Langton had promised. "With all due respect to Cap Doolittle," Jeff said, "there's no substitute for a woman's hand on the stirrin' spoon, and no campfire quite the equal of an iron stove."

Smithwick could only agree.

He stopped in midstride, recognizing a familiar figure. His heart sinking, he grabbed Jeff's arm and pointed.

Jeff swore. "I thought the son of a bitch had gone east."

Farrell Cregar strode toward them from a hide yard. His clothes were ragged, one sleeve of his brown checkered shirt ripped halfway down the arm, and they were dirtier than Smithwick had ever seen them. But there was no mistaking the man. Farrell did not attempt to shake hands. He probably knew neither man would welcome the gesture.

"I just heard that somebody was in from your camp."

Jeff demanded, "What're you doin' here, Farrell?"

"Looking for my wife."

Smithwick said, "A few months late, aren't you?"

"I tried to trail you soon after you left Dodge, but the best I could do was to find Adobe Walls. Tracks led off from here in every direction, and nobody could tell me which way you'd gone. So I've been working at this place ever since, waiting for some of you to come in. Where's Arletta?"

Smithwick's stomach had gone cold. "She's no longer any business of yours. You burned that bridge when you robbed her."

"I was angry and jealous, and more than a little drunk. I'm cold sober now and have been for a long time. I married her to spite my father as much as anything. But I came to realize that I really love her."

Smithwick said, "Perhaps. Or perhaps you figure she has a new supply of buffalo hides, and you want to rob her again. If I were a braver man I'd shoot you here and now."

Jeff offered, "I'd furnish the pistol."

Farrell said, "If you won't tell me where she is, I'll find her for myself. I'll backtrack your wagon."

Smithwick knotted his fists. "Stay away from her, Farrell. She doesn't want you anymore."

"Let's see if she tells me that." He turned and walked toward a stable.

Smithwick declared, "We've got to stop him, Jeff."

"I don't see a way, unless you aim to shoot him."

In a few minutes Farrell left the stable on horseback. He stopped briefly at the Myers and Leonard store, coming out with a sack, which he tied behind his saddle. He rode past Smithwick and Jeff without a word and moved on, following the tracks left by their wagon.

Desperately Smithwick said, "We've got to leave here, Jeff. We've got to get back to camp before he does."

Jeff shook his head. "We're in bad need of supplies. That's what we came for."

"But Farrell . . ."

"He's a greenhorn. He'll find so many tracks out yonder that he won't have any idea which ones to follow. He'll wind up lost like last summer's wages. Leavin' here at daylight, we'll beat him there . . . if he ever finds the place at all."

□ □ □ □

AFTER SEEING that Tar Baby and the wagon team were fed and securely staked for the night, the two repaired to the saloon to while away the evening and help Hanrahan reduce his liquor stock. It was of equal to better quality than most Smithwick had tasted in Dodge.

He heard some disquieting talk about an Englishman and a German having been killed by Indians in a hide camp on the Salt Fork, and earlier, two other men on Chicken Creek. Jeff made no comment, but his dour expression gave Smithwick pause. He asked, "Do you still think that buffalo stampede . . ." He broke off, for Jeff surely knew the rest of what he was trying to say.

Jeff only stared into his drink. "We'd better be gettin' back tomorrow the fastest we can. And not just because of Farrell."

The saloon became fairly crowded with hunters, skinners and teamsters after dark. They played cards and swapped stories of their adventures, some of them possibly true. They helped diminish the supply of liquor while Hanrahan and bartender Oscar Shepherd smiled a lot and counted the change. Jeff listened but did not join in. Smithwick knew he was worried about the camp. As for himself, he only half listened, his mind on Arletta, on Farrell . . . on opportunities missed and regretted.

His attention was caught by a crow, which evidently had become something of a pet. The black bird flew in at the door and landed on the back of a chair. One of the men rubbed the top of its head with the tip of his finger and asked if it would like a drink. The crow answered by flying out an open window.

When Jeff had sampled enough of the Hanrahan whiskey, he said, "It's cooler outside. I'm goin' to spread my roll out there and catch me some sleep."

Smithwick had been ready for an hour or more but had not wanted to spoil Jeff's rare chance to indulge himself. He had not been in his blankets but a few minutes when he heard Jeff starting to snore. He thought Jeff could sleep through a buffalo stampede. Off toward the creek, he heard owls hooting. Closer in, horses and mules moved restlessly in the corrals or on picketlines to which they were tied.

Smithwick slept but little, staring up at the stars, the full moon, wondering. What if Farrell *did* find the camp before they got back?

What if he somehow talked Arletta into giving him another chance?

It was a short night. Smithwick had finally dozed off in the wee hours of the morning when he was awakened by a sharp sound, like a shot. He heard a buzz of excitement in the saloon nearby. Someone shouted that the ridgepole had cracked. The saloon roof was in danger of falling in. The weight of its sod covering could kill somebody.

Jeff growled as he crawled out of his bedroll. "Well, hell. A man has more need of a lantern than a blanket in this place." He and Smithwick went to help. In a little while it seemed that half the men at the post were in or around the saloon, cutting a prop and wedging it under the ridgepole, or on top of the dirt-covered roof building, shoveling off some of the weight.

By the time the job was done, daybreak's first rosy glow began lighting the eastern horizon, haloing the line of cottonwoods, willows and other timber along Walls Creek. Dixon said he had just as well stay up and get an early start to the buffalo range. Billy Ogg started off afoot to bring up horses turned loose to graze between the buildings and the creek. Above the Myers and Leonard store, two German brothers named Scheidler slept in one of the wagons with which they were to start for Dodge City. With them was a big Newfoundland dog which had formed an uneasy relationship with several other dogs that had taken up residence around the post.

Jeff said, "We'd just as well eat a little breakfast and get us an early start too. I wonder if Mrs. Olds is up yet?"

Smithwick was about to reply that he was ready to start, breakfast or not. He heard a shot, then distant shouting. He wheeled around, facing east, and his breath left him.

Charging toward him from out of the blinding sunrise came what looked like all the Indians in the world.

Twenty-six

AT FIRST he assumed the Indians were after the horses turned out to graze between the post and the creek. He saw Billy Ogg desperately racing afoot toward the buildings, trying to outrun the horseback warriors who were gaining on him. Smithwick felt a stab of fear for Ogg. Even if their primary aim was the horses, they would gladly take the scalp of any white man who fell into their hands. He reached beneath his blankets for the rifle he had placed there to keep it from the morning dew. Bringing the rawhide-wrapped stock to his shoulder, he fired a shot in the general direction of the Indians, hoping to discourage them enough that Ogg could reach safety.

Dixon's horse plunged in terror against the picket rope that held him. Anxious eyes fixed on the Indians, Dixon hurriedly retied him close against his wagon to prevent the animal from jerking free and being carried away with the rest of the horses.

Very quickly it became evident that the warriors' primary interest was not the horses and mules. Whooping, screaming, they swept through the frightened and confused animals and bore down on the post like a terrible summer storm.

Smithwick went numb, mesmerized by the barbaric splendor. In morning's first light he saw what he thought must be two to three hundred Indians charging toward him, raising a din that bristled the hair on the back of his neck. Their faces were streaked with garish color, their horses war-painted, all manner of bright feathers and plumes streaming from their bullhide shields, their horses' manes and tails. If this magnificent but terrible panoply was calculated to freeze their enemies, it worked in Smithwick's case. He tried to bring the rifle to his shoulder but could not. He seemed unable to move.

Jeff grabbed his arm and violently shook him out of his trance. "Good God, English, you goin' to stand here and let them take you? They're comin' to kill us!"

Smithwick shivered as if struck by a sudden cold wind. He realized the Indians meant to overrun the post, to overwhelm its small force in one grand rush. Again he reached between his blankets, retrieving his pistol and its belt, and a canvas belt of ammunition for the rifle. The pounding of hooves and the Indians' shouting sounded as if they were almost on top of him. Holding his breath, he sprinted after Jeff. They hurried through the open door of the nearest building, Hanrahan's saloon. Someone slammed the door shut and braced his body against it, shouting, "Where's the bar?"

He heard pounding and an excited yell. Dixon hollered to be let in. He entered in a rush, rifle in his hand. Billy Ogg, arms flailing in panic, breezed through the door and collapsed on the hard-packed dirt floor, so exhausted he could barely draw breath. The door was shut again and quickly barred. Bullets and arrows thumped against it. Slugs ripped through the wood, showering splinters, snarling across the room and impacting against the furniture, the opposite wall.

Bullets shattered the glass windows so recently freighted down from Dodge City. Smithwick ducked away from the shower of sharp fragments, then peered through the nearest opening. He saw Indians swarming against the building in numbers too large to count. The door shuddered as a warrior threw his body against it, trying to smash it open. Warriors hammered on it with lances and rifle butts. The green cottonwood bar rattled but held the door against the assault.

For a moment a primitive fear bound Smithwick's arms and held him helpless, unable even to breathe. He saw his death in those furious painted faces, heard it in the fierce blood cries so loud that they seemed to come from within the room.

As before, Jeff broke him free of his paralysis. He grabbed him by the shoulders and shook him. "If you're not goin' to use that window, step aside and give me room."

Smithwick's voice trembled, as did his hands. "There is room here for both of us."

At such a close range he thought the pistol more practical than the Big Fifty. A warrior backed his horse against the door, trying to break it in with the animal's weight. Smithwick fired, aiming not at any one warrior but at the swirling mass of war-painted men. He heard a cry of agony. Other defenders crouched at other windows, firing whatever they had at hand, pistols or rifles. The deafening roar echoed within the confines of the small building and seemed to shake its sod walls.

The Indians made a hair-raising racket with their war cries, confident they would overpower the post in minutes through sheer force of numbers. They came like storm waves breaking upon a beach, one surge and then another and another. But the thick earthen walls did not yield. They gave protection to the men inside, while the attackers outside had none.

The first desperate volleys from the saloon exacted a harsh toll in blood. Warriors fell. Wounded horses screamed, some falling, some kicking and pitching, throwing riders to be trampled by other horses or exposed to deadly fire from the windows. The Indians began to waver, their initial confidence broken by confusion over the ferocity of the defense. Some pulled back in bewilderment while others kept hurling themselves against the walls.

Bullets droned through the broken windows. An arrow whispered between Smithwick and Jeff, driving itself against a row of whiskey bottles and knocking them to the dirt floor. Indians in pairs raced to pick up fallen comrades and carry them off between their horses. Even as Smithwick fired into the milling congregation of warriors, fighting for his life, he felt an incongruous admiration for their wild courage.

The first minutes were so hectic that he had little idea of time between the initial charge and the Indians' partial retreat. Firing continued, but most of the warriors reluctantly pulled back from the building, perplexed and disappointed.

In a momentary lull, Smithwick reloaded the pistol while he tried to regain his breath. The weapon was hot enough to burn his hands. Dust from outside swirled through the broken window. His heart was pounding, his chest tight from excitement.

Having survived the first wild flush of panic, the fearful expectation of being overrun at any moment, the other men had settled to a grim, quiet determination. They no longer fired indiscriminately into the frenzied melee but chose their targets and took deliberate aim.

Smithwick wondered if the people in the other buildings had held out or if they had been overwhelmed. "What do you suppose has happened to everybody else?"

Jeff switched pistol for rifle. His eyes were grave. "For all we know they may be dead."

They were not. As firing eased from within the smoke-filled saloon, Smithwick heard shots from both north and south. A defense was being put up in the two stores on either side. He felt a measure of relief. "We are not alone."

Jeff's face was smudged from the black powder smoke. "We're cut off from one another. If they decide to join up and take us one buildin' at a time, we're dead."

"I wonder why they did not do that the first time."

"Indians don't fight like an army. Every man does what he wants to, and they seldom all want to do the same thing. Like this one comin' now." A lone Indian was charging the door on his own. Jeff rested his rifle on what was left of the splintered windowsill and fired. Hard hit, the Indian tumbled as his horse cut back sharply, frightened by the gunshot. Two warriors came up in a gallop, bent down and grabbed the wounded man by his upraised arms.

Jeff aimed the rifle, then let the stock sag. It pleased Smithwick that the Texan chose not to shoot at men on a perilous mission of mercy.

Someone across the room held no such reservations. A rifle boomed, and one of the rescuers slumped forward, letting go the arm he held. The second rider managed to keep hold of the other arm and continue dragging the wounded man away from the battlefield. The rider who had been struck clung to his horse for fifty yards, then fell. The horse galloped away, head high in fright, leaving him motionless in the grass.

Smithwick felt regret. Such valor deserved better than a bullet in the back. Yet he realized that every Indian brought down was one less to continue the fight.

This was no time, he thought, to consider the viewpoint of the other side. He had to concentrate on one thing: survival.

The attacks resumed, coming in waves, but none was as fierce and determined as the first. Each met a stubborn wall of flame belching from the windows and was repulsed with losses. Smithwick used his rifle for the long shots, his pistol for close targets, pausing frequently to rub eyes irritated by the burned powder and the dust that fogged in from outside. He coughed spasmodically against the smoke and the powder and the dust that invaded his lungs.

After a time, the bold frontal assaults ceased. The Indians withdrew to what they must have thought was a safe distance and began a harassing long-range fire at the buildings. A number earlier had dismounted to throw themselves at the doors, front and back, and the windows. Now these men afoot became ready targets, vulnerable to the white men's guns. Some flattened themselves against the sod walls, where it was difficult for the defenders to reach them without being exposed to Indian fire.

One, armed with a pistol, shoved his hand through a broken window and blindly emptied the cylinder. He hit no one, but he left a pall of black smoke slow to dissipate. Several of the men in the room fired back, adding to the choking powder.

Wiping sweat from his face onto his sleeve, Smithwick was keyed to a high pitch, like a drumhead stretched to the breaking point. He turned to take stock of the defenders' situation. He did not know how much ammunition the other men might have, but he had used up a considerable part of his own.

He wished the first charge had given him time for contemplation, for he would prefer to have taken refuge in one of the stores, which stocked rifles and ammunition. To try to reach one of them now would be suicide. Indians had taken up positions behind hide stacks, behind the picket horse corral and Rath's partially finished sod enclosure.

He ached to know what was going on in the other buildings, who and how many might still be alive. The violence of the first charge made him marvel that anyone had survived. It occurred to him that had the saloon ridgepole not cracked, so that a number of men were awake and stirring when the attack began, they might all have been overrun and slaughtered with the sleep still in their eyes. That clearly had been the Indians' intention.

A lucky coincidence, most would say. But Sully would have had another explanation for it.

Firing was desultory now, but black powder smoke hovered in the poorly ventilated room. Smithwick's eyes and nose burned unmercifully. He broke into fits of coughing that threatened not to stop. In the rising morning heat, sweat rolled down the defenders' sober faces, cutting through the grime. Some men were only half dressed, for the first alarm had caught them in their blankets. Their clothing was soaked with perspiration, streaked with dirt and grease and black powder.

By noon, Smithwick thought, this closed room would be hot enough to bake bread. Only the shattered windows admitted any air from outside. It would be reckless to open the doors.

Through his window he saw horses down, dead or dying, others standing droop-headed, mute in their torment and slowly bleeding to death. Some had belonged to the post and the hunters, some to the Indians. His throat tightened as he shared their helpless pain, knowing he could do nothing except put them out of their misery. He tried that but gave it up. Shooting buffalo had become distasteful. To shoot horses was too much to bear.

Jeff muttered, "My God! Tar Baby!"

His black horse had staggered up near the building, half a dozen arrows protruding from its side. Blood flowed down its legs and dripped from its belly. Agony was in its glazed eyes.

Jeff aimed, then grimaced and lowered the rifle, working up his courage. He raised it quickly and fired, putting a bullet through the horse's brain. The animal dropped like a stone.

Smithwick said, "Jeff, I'm sorry." He saw tears in Jeff's eyes, but they might have come from the smoke and the dust.

He heard a fluttering sound. The pet crow flew in a window, cawing loudly, disturbed by the frantic action and the shooting. It settled on the bar, making its raucous noise until one of the men, nerves on thin edge, ran shouting at it and waved a hat. The startled crow flew out another window, still cawing.

"Damned crow," the man said. "It's a sign of death."

Whose death? Smithwick wondered. *Ours, or theirs?*

He looked dismally out the window, sick at his stomach over the sight of Indians in grotesque attitudes of death, so close to the buildings that their fellow warriors had been unable to pick them up, and over the many horses fallen innocent victim to man's violence. "There would appear to be enough death to go around."

So far, despite hundreds of rounds of ammunition and countless arrows sent at them, not a man in the saloon had been wounded. He could not imagine that everyone on the post had been so lucky.

As the hours wore on his mouth became desperately dry. Though tension showed in Jeff's face, he never betrayed despair. Smithwick had not heard Jeff say much about the war, but he knew he had been through more than one battle. He was aware of an old bullet wound that still plagued the Texan when he rode too long or walked too far.

Smithwick said, "I suppose you became hardened to this sort of thing, fighting in the war."

The smoke and grime made Jeff's face seem to bear more lines than Smithwick had seen there before. "You never get hardened enough. It's hell every time."

The Indians settled now mostly for sniper fire from a distance or from reasonably safe cover. At a back window the long-haired Billy Dixon discovered an Indian hiding behind a stack of hides, peering out now and again to fire a quick shot. Dixon held his aim on the corner of the stack until he saw a hint of movement, then squeezed the trigger. The heavy bullet ripped through the hides. The Indian jumped, yelping. He ran a zigzag pattern for a short way, then went down.

Warriors at intervals rode back and forth, taunting the defenders from a distance, inviting them in sign to come outside and fight in the open. Two waved fresh scalps and whooped in derision, trying to provoke a reckless response. The men in the saloon cursed and fired at the Indians and speculated gloomily on whose hair it might be. Every so often a buffalo gun would pick off a rider at several hundred yards. Many Indians had rifles or pistols, but their range was no match for Sharps and Remington weapons in the hands of veteran hunters accustomed to killing buffalo at long distances.

Borrowing from Jeff's courage, Smithwick gradually began to entertain serious hope of survival. The Indians must have been dismayed at the stiff defense and the heavy losses they had endured, instead of the quick and easy victory they probably had expected. It seemed unlikely they would attempt any more suicidal charges like those of the first half hour or so.

Jeff said, "They're whipped, English. All we've got to do now is hold on. And we will unless we run out of ammunition."

A worried Hanrahan said they were dangerously near to doing just that. Some of the men had used up all that fitted their rifles. After a short discussion, weighing the odds, he and Dixon decided to make a rush for the Rath store, the nearest to the saloon. After the others wished them luck and went to the windows to give them covering fire, the pair set off in a dead run. Indians shot at them from afar, bullets kicking up dust but missing them. A door swung open at Rath's to receive the men, and they made it safely inside. After a time the door opened again and Hanrahan came sprinting back, carrying a large sack over his shoulder. Bullets buzzed around him while men at the windows fired at the distant Indians in an effort to make them keep their heads down. Hanrahan reached the saloon untouched and dropped the bag of ammunition on the earthen floor while he gasped for breath.

When he was able to talk, he said, "Everybody is all right over at Rath's. There is not a real hunter among them, though. They begged Billy to stay because he is one of the best shots around. They have Mrs. Olds to protect."

Somebody said he should have come back; it was every man for himself in this battle. Jeff said curtly, "He did right. That good woman needs him more than we do."

Sporadic firing continued far into the afternoon. It came mostly from a distance, too far for accuracy. Even that quieted eventually.

Once the Indians gave up on frontal attack and withdrew or lost those who had dismounted as snipers behind the horse corral fence and the hide stacks, small numbers continued to show themselves at what they probably judged to be a safe distance. Their error was demonstrated more than once as a buffalo rifle brought down a horse or a man at a range that must have seemed incredible to them. But marksmanship was these buffalo runners' stock in trade.

Smithwick felt little apprehension now for himself. His concern shifted again to Arletta. What if Jeff was wrong about Farrell being unable to find the camp? What if he was already there?

Well past midafternoon a man known as Bermuda Carlyle ventured outside to pick up a tempting Indian trinket he had been watching through the window. Smithwick thought him rash; no souvenir was worth a man's life. He waited for the shots that might cripple or kill Carlyle, but none came. Shortly more men went out, leaving the sweatbox that the saloon had become, letting the warm wind work its cooling effect against the perspiration that had stuck their clothing to their bodies. The defenders at last were able to compare experiences with those who dared leave the other buildings.

The first report left Smithwick heartsick. Three men had been killed. The first rush had trapped the two German brothers in their wagon, where they had slept near the Leonard and Myers store. Their Newfoundland dog must have put up a fight, for the Indians had killed him and had taken a strip of hide in lieu of scalping him as they did the two brothers. Young Billy Tyler had been shot at the back door of the same store and had died within half an hour.

Smithwick tried to rationalize that the news, bad as it was, could have been far worse. He was amazed that the death toll had not been much higher in view of the suddenness and massive nature of the assault.

Sully crossed his mind again. Sully would have had an explanation.

The defenders were emboldened by failure of the Indians to fire upon them as they moved around outside, though they could see warriors far away, in the line of trees beyond the flat and open meadow and at times mounting a distant small butte for better observation. It was a foregone conclusion that they were keeping the place surrounded.

Smithwick's stomach stirred queasily as he walked among dead Indians scattered near the buildings. It had been one thing to watch from a distance as the warriors fell. It was another to see them close-up, flies buzzing restlessly about them, crawling over glazed eyes, exploring mouths locked open in death. In life they had seemed something alien and barbaric, not unlike the wild animals with which they shared these plains. In death he saw their humanity, and he shuddered, cold despite the heat of the June sun. He felt no desire to count the bodies, but others said they found more than a dozen. They could only guess how many dead and wounded had been carried away.

"Poor brave, bloody bastards," he said shakily. "My God, Jeff, was this all necessary?"

Jeff appeared uneasy too. "This is war, and war is an ugly business. Like it or not, we did what we had to. We saved our lives."

"But at such a bloody awful cost."

"It can be a bloody awful world sometimes. I never told you it'd always be pretty out here. It can be mean as hell, and today it was. You do the best you can and hope someday it'll be better."

"Not for these poor beggars it won't. Their day is done."

"So now maybe it's our day for a little while. Colonel would say we're just livin' out another chapter of history, the way it's always been. Somebody gets strong and runs over the weak, like these Comanches did to whoever was here before. Now we're runnin' over the Comanches. Someday, when we're not watchin', somebody may come along and run over *us*. Colonel says that's the way the world has always been, the way it'll always be."

"We could change it if we wanted badly enough to do it."

"But we won't. When we're the strong ones we don't *want* to change it. When we're the weak ones, we won't be able to."

Smithwick had noticed a small leather bag hanging around each Indian's neck. He knelt to examine one.

"Medicine pouch," Jeff explained. "Each man has got some special medicine that belongs just to him."

"I wonder what it contains," Smithwick said, looking for a way to undo its tight lacing.

Jeff touched his arm to stop him. "I wouldn't. There's no tellin' what might come of it."

"Superstitious?"

"No. Well, maybe a little. There's things in this world we don't understand. I don't feel like takin' chances."

The defenders tallied some fifty horses brought down either by the Indians or by the whites barricaded in the buildings. All the Scheidlers' oxen had been killed. Not one live horse or mule was

left. Jeff grieved over his black horse Tar Baby, which lay stiff
where he had dropped it. Those animals not killed had been driven
away, including the wagon team that had brought Smithwick here.
The implication was ominous.

Jeff sounded grave. "We can't send for help. Any man out there
afoot wouldn't make it a mile. Even mounted, they'd run him a hell
of a horserace, and likely win."

Smithwick's worries went in another direction. "Then we can't
get out to warn the camps, either . . . Arletta and the rest. If
these Indians can't take us, they'll go looking for targets they *can*
get."

Smithwick saw real fear in Jeff's eyes, not for himself but for
others. "If they attack our camp it'll take every gun to turn them
back. Dad can't see good enough to hit a horse at ten paces, much
less a man."

Dixon came up with an Indian bridle to which was attached a
scalp, its hair long and brown. Smithwick felt more distressed than
ever as he conjured up a mental image of the woman to whom it
had belonged, a young woman probably, for he saw no sign of
gray. He thought of Arletta and what Mrs. Thomason had said in
Dodge about Arletta's long red hair hanging in an Indian lodge.

Against that threat, Farrell Cregar faded into insignificance.

"Jeff, I can slip away after dark. If I can make it as far as the
river . . ."

Jeff grimly shook his head. "You wouldn't. They'll be lookin' for
somebody to try. Not even a dog could slip through tonight."

"I can't just sit here."

"You have to. We both have to. You're no good to Arletta dead,
any more than I could help Dad by gettin' myself killed. All we can
do is wait and hope that somebody has seen the Indians and spread
the alarm."

The excitement of the pitched battle had stretched Smithwick's
nerves almost to the breaking point. Now, in the dead silence of
the bloodstained battlefield, his knees felt as if they might not
continue to hold his weight. He was overwhelmed by a sense of
helplessness worse than he had experienced when he was thrown
from the train. But now his fear was not for himself.

Jeff said, "There's one consolation."

"I fail to see it."

"Colonel Cregar's camp is not far from Arletta's. Sure, he's a damnyankee, tough as a boot and mean as hell, but his battle scars are all in front. No enemy ever saw his back."

Late that day, the three white victims of the battle—Billy Tyler and the Scheidler brothers—were solemnly but without ceremony lowered into a single grave. Nobody read from the Bible or preached a sermon, but many a hardened frontiersman said his own prayer in the silence of his heart.

SMITHWICK lay sleepless, staring into the darkness, reliving the violence of the early morning, wondering, worrying about Arletta. He had seen far fewer Indians in the afternoon than in the early part of the attack. They might be hidden in the timber along the creek, contemplating another try, or their frustration and anger might have driven them on to seek out more vulnerable targets. He burned with anxiety. Should they strike Arletta's hunting camp with even a little of the strength they had thrown against Adobe Walls, it could not possibly stand.

He thought seriously about trying his luck despite what Jeff had said, slipping out in the darkness and attempting to escape afoot. But he heard bird calls at a distance around the post. He suspected not all of them were made by birds.

Jeff had said little in a direct way, but his voice betrayed the same anxiety that Smithwick felt. "You awake, English?"

"I have been all night."

"Somethin' told me I oughtn't to've brought Dad on this trip. He's gettin' too old and stove up. Bob Wright offered him a nice easy job so he could stay in Dodge, but I hated to go off and leave him."

"Be thankful you still have him with you. We buried mine four years ago."

"I hope you were on good terms with him."

"We quarreled, frightfully at times. Sometimes he was wrong, but I realize now that he was right more often than I knew. I wish I could have told him so."

"I know it hurts to lose one, but it also hurts to watch one grow old, to see the strength and the will go out of him. I look at Dad sometimes and feel like I've already lost him." Jeff lighted a half-smoked cigar left from Hanrahan's saloon. "We had our arguments, but we made peace a long time ago. There was one thing I never could do for him, though. I never could take him back to Texas."

"I suppose he did not want to go alone."

"He couldn't. People have always figured it was me the law wants down there, and I've let them keep thinkin' that way. But he's the one they've got paper on."

Surprised, Smithwick sat upright on his blankets. "Your father? That gentle old soul? What could he possibly have done?"

"You wouldn't think so to look at him now, but there was a time when he didn't back up for anybody. After the war the carpetbaggers and scalawags came down on us like a plague of locusts. They took our place for the taxes. I guess most people wouldn't count it as much of a place, but it was ours. Dad had worked himself into an old man on it, and we had family buried there. My mother, a brother and a baby sister.

"I'd started up the trail to Kansas with a throwed-together herd when the state police came to put Dad off of the place. He tried to make a fight of it, and they took the double of a rope to him. Ever see him with his clothes off? He's still got a rope scar across one shoulder.

"He took to drinkin' and broodin' till the weight of it was more than his old shoulders could carry. He went out there with the notion of takin' our place back and shot those carpetbaggers, three of them. Killed them deader than hell. Wasn't nothin' left but to run. Losin' his home, the killin', that all took the heart out of him. I get the feelin' sometimes that he's just lookin' for a good place to die."

The thought of frail old Elijah Layne killing anyone was almost beyond Smithwick's comprehension. "Kansas is not that far from Texas. Didn't they ever come after him?"

"They did, and I'd manage to hide him someplace. Finally they quit comin' to look. But the paper is still out on him. If he ever tried to go home . . ."

Smithwick frowned in sympathy. "At least he has never had reason to feel ashamed of a wayward son, as mine did."

"I worried about you at first, English, but there's more to you than shows on top. You'll do to ride with. Your daddy would be proud of you, if he could know. And who can say that he *doesn't?*"

Smithwick half expected another charge at dawn, but it did not come. As the day wore on, he saw only an occasional Indian or two, always at a distance that would challenge the buffalo rifles. This only intensified his anxiety that most of them had gone, that they were looking for easier prey. He watched the pet crow flying around on the battlefield, moving from one dead horse to another, making its gravel-throated cry.

A rising stench from the dead animals and Indian warriors forced the men of the post to tie ropes to dried buffalo hides and roll the bodies onto them. As many as three or four men were required to drag the heavy horses away.

The first non-Indian to come into the post was a German freighter named George Bellfield. Approaching from the direction of the Canadian River, he became aware of the many dead horses and whipped his team into a run. Unaccountably, he had not seen an Indian.

He lent his only spare horse for a courier to be sent to Dodge City for help.

Encouraged by the fact that Bellfield had gotten through, Nigel Smithwick and Jeff Layne set out on foot after dark, determined to reach their hunting camp.

Twenty-seven

CROW FEATHER recoiled in bitter disappointment from the disaster at the white-man houses. It should have been finished before the morning sun lifted above the cottonwoods along the creek. Instead, the white men appeared strongly entrenched, while the Indian dead had to be counted with the fingers of both hands, three or four times over. The only *teibos* known killed were two caught by surprise in their wagon, the way all the white men were supposed to have been taken. Another had been seen to fall but had been dragged into a building, so no one knew whether he had lived or died.

Something had gone dreadfully wrong. Crow Feather gazed with burning suspicion at the medicine man Isatai. Now, on the second day, the shaman sat on his horse, naked except for his head-dress, paint smeared over his body. He had made powerful medicine with the spirits, or so he claimed, that would assure quick success without harm to any Indians.

Either Isatai or his spirits were false, that was clear. Crow Feather had never put much confidence in the shaman's preachings. He had seen none of the professed miracles himself, and he had always distrusted reports from those excitable ones who bent in whatever direction the wind blew. He thought it likely that only the wind had spoken to Isatai, not the spirits. The wind was ever changeable.

Man Who Stole the Mules was in his usual quarrelsome mood,

quick to fix blame on others, regarding his own actions as without blemish. "There were too many who gave in to their fears at the first gun. Look, the white men are walking around in the open. If we rush at them now we might kill a few of them before they can go back into their houses."

The bitter-ash taste of defeat had Crow Feather ready to lash out in any direction. "We came here to cut off the head of the snake, not just to take its rattles."

"Something must have spoiled Isatai's medicine."

"Perhaps it never was good. Perhaps it was only in his mind." It was a rare thing for one Comanche to kill another, but Crow Feather thought the spirits might not be too angry if someone sent Isatai to join his grandfathers. The shaman had promised that the white man's bullets would roll away as harmlessly as raindrops. But many of the People's bravest lay broken and bleeding or dead from the heavy bullets of the big-medicine guns. Also among the killed were Kiowa and Cheyenne, whose loss was lamentable but less personal to him. He considered them more dispensable than the Comanche.

He saw that the white men were using dried buffalo skins like sleds to drag horses away from the buildings. By this time the animals were beginning to stink. He wondered if the whites were dragging Indian bodies away with the same indifference, leaving them to the buzzards and the wolves. The thought intensified his indignation, his simmering desire for retaliation.

Isatai remained the nominal spiritual leader of the expedition despite his failure, though the authority rested uneasily upon his shoulders. Plains Indians were under no compulsion to honor a leader whose performance no longer satisfied them, and Comanches in particular were proud of their independence as warriors. Isatai sat with some of his more faithful followers atop a small butte which gave them a good view of the white-man houses. Despite much disaffection among the warriors, he had argued that nothing was wrong with his medicine; a Cheyenne had compromised it by killing a skunk and thereby breaking a taboo. Isatai had promised to make new medicine and set things aright. But Crow Feather had never heard of medicine strong enough to bring the dead back to life.

One of Isatai's followers snapped back as if he had been struck by a war club. He tumbled over his horse's hip and fell lifeless to the ground. The distant sound of a rifle echoed from one of the buildings.

Whatever might be said for Isatai's medicine, that which attached itself to the white men's rifles was stronger, Crow Feather decided. It seemed incredible that a bullet fired so far could find its target without help from a guiding spirit. It must be a spirit that hated buffalo, for so many had been killed by these rifles. Now it appeared to hate the People and their allies as well.

To make himself less of a target, he dismounted and stood beside his notch-eared horse, which rolled on the ground and rubbed away much of the warpaint Crow Feather had applied to it before the battle. The loss of the color seemed symbolic of this spoiled campaign against the white-man post. The paint was supposed to ward off bullets, but he had given little credence to that idea even before he saw the first grand charge disintegrate into a slaughter. He knew now that he never should have come. He had fasted long and asked for guidance by the bear, his guardian spirit, but the bear had never answered.

Isatai's followers, realizing their vulnerability, moved down from the butte, carrying their fallen comrade. Isatai remained at first, stubbornly refusing to concede. But after a bullet kicked up dust near his horse's feet, he reluctantly gave up the high ground.

Crow Feather considered it the worst of luck to find oneself caught up in a battle between spirits, in this case the white man's and Isatai's. It was like being trapped between two fighting buffalo bulls.

It was clear that a majority of the war party had lost faith in Isatai's leadership. Though Crow Feather was strongly inclined to leave this battle, he did not want to be the first to declare it lost. He seethed with suppressed recriminations. Mules was nearby, so he sought release by aiming a good share of his anger at him. "Had you not been so interested in taking horses and had stayed with me in the first charge, we might have been strong enough to break into the house and finish the fight."

"I was afraid the Cheyennes would get them all."

Mules had always been easily distracted from the task at hand.

His thoughts were small and confined, like a sweat lodge, not large and free like the open prairie. And always, they were centered upon himself.

Goes His Own Way thought on a larger scale. He gave Crow Feather the opening he needed. "I think we should depart this place," Goes said. "The medicine has turned against us."

"It will not be a good thing, returning in failure. What do we tell the widows?"

"We need not go back in failure. We will find another battle first, a battle we can win."

The same idea had been brewing in Crow Feather's mind. He had waited to present it when the time seemed proper and enough men appeared to be in a mood to accept it. He had been ready to leave yesterday when it became apparent that the raid was a shambles, but the weight of failure was too great a burden to carry back to his family and others of the band who waited in camp far to the southeast.

White Deer should be delivering her child soon now, if she had not already. It was unthinkable that the first time a new son saw its father's face, that face should be painted black as a symbol of defeat and death.

White-man hunting camps were scattered in all directions, some farther than a hard day's horseback ride. The main purpose of this expedition had been to demonstrate Indian power by destroying their trading post. It had been anticipated that the raid would so demoralize the remaining hunters that they would abandon the buffalo range and return to the far-north villages from which they had come. Now Crow Feather was ready to accept a second choice. Perhaps the same effect could be achieved if some of the camps were overrun and their hunters sent to whatever spirit land dead white men went to.

He said bitterly, "These *teibos* have the walls to protect them. But many there are who have only their wagon camps. There will be no walls to stop us."

Mules argued, "This is what I have said from the beginning."

"But you have been interested only in scalps and horses. My purpose is larger."

Goes said, "Some still want to keep trying here. They think the medicine will change. But I am ready to follow you, Crow Feather, if you will lead us from this place."

Mules protested, "Why Crow Feather? Why not me?"

Goes made a nasty reply that brought anger to Mules's eyes. "Crow Feather has had horses shot from under him in battle, but never has he shot his own."

Crow Feather did not give voice to his thought: *Nor has he ever led foolish young men to a needless death.* His sister Calling Bird had almost died from self-mutilation in grief for her husband, and she had aborted her child. He said to Goes, "See how many want to go. Bring them to me."

Thus it was that he crossed the Canadian River with a party that numbered three times four, seeking hunter camps vulnerable to the wrath of a people whose land had been violated, whose *cattle* were wantonly slaughtered by rapacious hair-faced men who had no respect for the ancient traditions of a proud race.

Before he was done, Crow Feather promised himself, the white men would learn that respect . . . those the spirits allowed to survive. He would kill as many as his own spirits would permit him. They would fear the Comanche; his very name would make them tremble.

A sense of foreboding settled over him when Mules chose to ride with his party. He had expected that Mules would gather some of his own kind, the careless ones who acted on impulse rather than reason, and strike out in a different direction. To have Mules beside him was like having a malevolent spirit sitting on his shoulder. But the other men seemed to accept. Cries Like the Hawk, an able warrior, pointed out that Mules had demonstrated his bravery and his boldness many times.

That he had learned much from past grievous mistakes was yet to be shown, Crow Feather thought. But he felt compelled to accept the judgment of the rest.

South of the river they encountered killing grounds that sickened Crow Feather's heart: buffalo rotting, their hides gone, their flesh dried and blackened. Meat that should have warmed the bellies of children was crawling with maggots and flies. With the revulsion came a building wrath, a yearning for vengeance. He stopped to freshen his warpaint, to smoke and to call upon the spirits and ask that they guide his hand. He could see the fire of hatred burning in the eyes of the men who rode beside him. It was good that they feel that fire.

It carried them with the fury of a thunderstorm over the first hunter camp they encountered. Two white men were turning hides that had been staked to dry, and they did not see until too late the warriors who bore down like lightning upon them. Stone war clubs smashed their skulls even as they ran for their rifles. Crow Feather had ruled out gunfire that might alert other hair-faces nearby. Mules took one scalp, Cries Like the Hawk the other. Mules wanted to ransack the supply wagon, but Crow Feather said they had more important business. They might revisit the wagon later, if that was still their wish.

Evenly spaced rifleshots told him that a hunter was nearby, killing buffalo, unaware of what had happened in his camp. He rode toward the sound, halting after a time, signaling the others to remain out of sight while he and Goes His Own Way went forward as wolves to scout the ground. He remembered all too well the incident the preceding autumn when he had ridden with the Kiowas and the Cheyennes far to the north. They had attacked a pair of shooters but had overlooked two wagon men behind a hill. Though wounded, the two shooters with the wagon men's help had been able to escape to their camp. Two Cheyennes had been killed. He would not repeat that error.

This time he saw but one shooter. Two men waited with a wagon to steal the skins from the buffalo once the man with the rifle was done. One of the pair appeared to be asleep. The other was whetting a large knife on a small slab of stone. Crow Feather discussed the problem with Goes. If they struck the two first, the shooter would be alerted and turn that medicine gun on the warriors. If they hit him first, the wagon men would have time to set up a defense. Though they would probably be killed in any case, the chance was great that they might take some of the warriors to the other world with them.

"We must strike them all at one time," he told Goes. "He held up four fingers. "This many of us will get the one who kills the buffalo. The men with the wagon are for you and the rest."

Goes nodded approval, with one reservation. "Which of us must take Mules?"

"He is angrier at you because you reminded him that he killed his own horse. I will take him."

The tactic appeared to be working well. The party split as planned and quietly approached the white men without their knowledge. But Mules could not restrain himself. He rushed ahead of the others the final distance, shouting his war cry. The shooter had been sitting cross-legged, balancing his rifle barrel over a pair of crossed sticks while he brought down the buffalo one by one. He whirled around on his knees, swinging the heavy rifle. Before he could fire, Mules drove an arrow deep into his chest. The rifle roared, the bullet tearing through the dry grass and burying itself in the ground.

Mules's action had been premature, giving the skinners time to grab rifles—smaller ones than the shooter used—and take shelter behind the wagon. Goes's party circled them and brought both of them down, but not before a cousin of Goes had been shot through the lungs. The heart seemed to die in Goes as he saw the fallen warrior's lifeblood pulsing out into the dust, soaking into the dry ground. Dull-eyed, Goes watched others slice away the scalps. One of the wagon men groaned until a warrior slit his throat.

"I must go now and tell my cousin's wife she is a widow," Goes said plaintively.

Mules and a couple of his followers rode up, Mules waving the gray-peppered scalp of the shooter, laughing until he saw Goes's cousin. Crow Feather thought he might have to rescue Mules from a lashing by Goes's quirt, a thing he would be reluctant to do. But Goes was too distraught to think of retaliation.

A suitable place was found for the warrior's burial. His shield, his bow, arrows and quiver were placed with him beneath a pile of stones on the east side of a rock outcrop where the morning's first sun would always touch his resting place. When feasible it was customary to sacrifice a dead warrior's best horse and leave it for him to ride to the spirit world, but under the circumstances an extra horse might be needed should one of the party lose his own in a fight. They cut off most of the horse's tail and left it as a symbolic gesture.

The war party was thus reduced by three, one dead, Goes and another cousin leaving to carry the sad news home. That left two times four to ride with Crow Feather. Dark was approaching as they finished the burial, but they rode on for a time; the Comanche was always uncomfortable in the presence of the dead. They made a dry camp and ate pemmican in lieu of fresh meat.

That night Crow Feather had a dream that brought him awake in a cold sweat. He saw a buffalo-hunting camp on the bank of a small stream. It was littered with the bodies of Comanche slain. He could see the faces. They were men of his own band. He saw the white hunters riding in triumph, running their horses among the fallen, carelessly stepping upon the dead.

He had not always been able to discern the difference between a vision and a dream. A dream could be a trickster, like the coyote, but a vision was not to be dismissed, for it came directly from the spirits. Trembling, he slept no more. He waited in the darkness for the bear to send him some sign that this had been only a dream, not a true glimpse into a future terrible to contemplate.

Two young warriors rode out in advance of the party, acting as wolves while Crow Feather remained with the others. He kept a resentful watch over Mules, whose appetite for blood seemed only to have been intensified by their annihilation of the first hunting camp. Mules showed no sign that he recognized the tragedy his impetuous action had caused.

The shadows were almost directly beneath the horses' bellies when the wolves brought word. They had located another hunter camp, much larger than the first. It had many wagons, but they had counted only five men. It appeared likely that others were out killing and skinning buffalo. Divided, the hunters should not be difficult to overrun, they said.

"Five men?" Crow Feather asked. "You are sure?"

"We watched them a long time," said one of the wolves.

"Five men, and also a woman," said the other.

Mules brought his horse in close. "A woman, you say?" He appeared dubious.

It was not common for these hunters to bring their women. Crow Feather had never seen one in a wagon camp. He had pondered often over this. Among the People, custom clearly delineated what was proper as a man's work and what was a woman's. It was obvious that white men in a hunter camp were doing work that a woman should have done. He had wondered if white women were too weak or too lazy to do their part like Comanche wives and daughters. This had reinforced his conviction that white people were of an inferior race.

He asked the wolves about the opportunity for concealment so the party could approach undetected and strike before the white men could fortify themselves. The wolves conceded that the hunters had chosen their campsite wisely. The ground was open for some distance on both sides. Brush along the creek might provide limited cover for an approach that way, but the risk was high at best.

Given his choice, Crow Feather had never liked to attack across a stretch of open ground. That had proven the undoing of the allied force at the big wagon post. Ambush was far more effective, but it worked only against moving parties.

He said, "We will follow the creek, then, and hope the spirits blind the *teibos'* eyes. Let there be no shouting or shooting until we are among them." He looked sternly at Mules.

Mules paid little attention. He was questioning the wolves about the woman. Was she young, or was she old?

The wolves had been too far away to give him much information about her beyond the fact that her hair was dark and long.

Mules said, "That is good. It will make a fine decoration for my lance."

Cries Like the Hawk taunted him. "How do you know you will be the one who takes her? I may reach her first."

Brusquely Crow Feather declared, "It is not of importance who gets the woman. It is important that we destroy the camp without more loss to ourselves." He motioned for the wolves to lead the way.

They entered the creek downstream so that the current would carry no mud stirred by the horses and give warning of their approach. In a while they reached a place where there was a break in the timber. From this point on they could be seen by any white man who happened to be alert. The warriors laid their blankets and other equipage on the ground so they would be no hindrance. They would carry only their weapons into the battle.

Crow Feather studied the camp. It appeared at first like others he had seen. Three men were turning hides to dry the side that had been against the grass. Two more were in camp, one moving with the slowness of many years. The other, a fat man, was near a fire. It appeared that he was cooking, though that seemed a strange thing for a man to do if a woman was present. He did not see the woman and began to wonder if the wolves had imagined her. Then she appeared, coming out of a canvas tepee. She stopped to talk with the old man.

A chill rolled over Crow Feather. He had seen this camp before. It was the camp that had appeared in his dream, or had it truly been a vision?

"Wait," he said. "Our medicine is bad. We must go back."

Mules gave him an incredulous look. "Go back, when there are two of us to their one? It is not the medicine that has gone bad. It is your courage. Who will go with Man Who Stole the Mules?"

Without waiting for an answer, he pressed his horse up out of the creek and set off in a run toward the camp. He could not resist a war whoop. Whatever Mules did, he always did with a flourish. Four of the warriors gave Crow Feather a quick glance, then followed Mules.

Crow Feather tried to shout for them to come back, but the words lodged in his throat.

The white men at the hide ground ran for the cover of their wagons. The fat man who had been cooking seemed almost instantly to have a rifle in his hand. The old man rushed to the woman and pushed her behind a wagon.

Mules, his knees tucked under a hair rope, leaned low on the right side, letting the horse's body shield him. He was the first to breach the hunter camp, leaping his mount over a wagon tongue. He seemed impervious to the white men's bullets as he raced toward the woman. The old man threw himself in front of her. Mules struck him across the head with his stone club. The old man's rifle fired as the blow crushed his skull, the bullet driving into a wagon box. The woman had fired her rifle and was attempting to ram another cartridge into the breech when Mules grabbed her about the waist and pulled her up against his horse. He gave a whoop and leaped the mount back over the wagon tongue.

The fat man brought a rifle to his shoulder. Flame spat from its muzzle. Mules pitched forward, dropping the woman and almost falling from his horse. The woman scrambled hurriedly back to the protection of the nearest wagon.

Two of the warriors who had followed Mules fell to the white men's fire. Mules's frightened horse carried him partway back to where Crow Feather and a remnant of the party waited in the creek bed. Mules slid from the animal's back and rolled on the ground as the mount stampeded on. He did not move again. The recklessness that had cost the lives of so many others had finally taken his own.

The two warriors who had survived the charge retreated. They managed to rescue one of the fallen and carry him back to the creek between them. His shoulder was smashed. The way blood coursed from the gaping wound, Crow Feather doubted that his spirit could remain long within his shattered body.

Mules and one other lay where they had fallen.

Crow Feather knew now with a terrible despair: it had been a vision, not simply a dream.

What Mules had done had been foolish, but he could not be left there to the mercy of his enemies. That part of the vision, at least, Crow Feather could not allow to come to pass. "We must go and bring back those who have fallen."

Cries Like the Hawk shouted angrily, "That is not enough. We must avenge them or return in shame."

"The medicine is bad."

"Your medicine perhaps, but not mine." Cries Like the Hawk turned, looking to the others. "Who goes with me?"

The remaining warriors raised a shout. Cries Like the Hawk led them up over the creek bank and raced toward the wagons. Belatedly, Crow Feather followed them, though he knew in his heart that it was a bad thing.

The camp's rifles blazed. A bullet struck a glancing blow against his bullhide shield and almost wrested it from his arm. It lost some of its feathers that had long ago been blessed by the spirits.

He felt the wind hot in his face. It was a dark wind.

From across the creek he became aware of movement. Horse-men were coming, white men, as many as the fingers on both hands. Bullets buzzed like hornets. He saw the other warriors fall-ing before they reached the wagons. He glimpsed the woman, looking at him over a rifle barrel. Flame leaped. The impact slammed the shield hard against his ribs. Breath left him, and fire blazed where breath had been. The bullet had driven through the flint-hard leather. Blood flowed hot down his side.

The sky seemed to turn above him, and the ground danced be-neath his horse's feet. He saw that every warrior had fallen. Only he remained. The white riders still came, spurring, firing as they rode. In a moment, as in the vision, their horses would be tram-pling the slain.

Without his bidding, his horse turned back, plunging down the creekbank and galloping away in panic. The fire in Crow Feather's belly grew stronger, then seemed to go cold. He felt strangely detached from the world around him. He seemed to be floating on air. He saw the face of the bear, as through a fog, and appealed to that benevolent spirit to guide his way.

The bear gave him no answer.

Crow Feather felt despair come over him, cold as a winter night. Always his people had depended upon the cloudy, unseen world of their spirits to guide them. Somehow that guiding hand was gone. Could the spirits have turned their backs on their chosen people? Or, worse, could it be that they had never existed except in the minds of those who wanted to believe? That thought was too terri-ble. He would not allow himself to consider it.

"Where are you?" he cried in anguish to the bear. "Why do you not know me anymore?"

Still the bear did not answer.

Crow Feather's knees slipped from beneath the horsehair rope, and he was falling. Cold water splashed over his body. He strug-gled for breath that would not come. He turned over onto his back and saw the sun high overhead, moving in circles like a golden hawk.

Then he saw no more.

Twenty-eight

CAUTION would have suggested that Smithwick and Jeff walk by night and hide by day, but anxiety over what might be happening at the camp allowed them to rest only a little while before they resumed traveling. They had cut the faint days-old trail made by their wagon, so they backtracked it. They noticed intermittent blown-out tracks of a horse that had followed the same trace south.

"Farrell?" Smithwick asked worriedly.

Jeff shrugged. "I figured he was still a greenhorn, but maybe he's been out here long enough to learn some things."

"Surely she would not take him back, not after what he has done."

"A man never can know for sure what's in a woman's heart."

Smithwick hastened his gait until he realized it was fatiguing him. He slowed, trying to pace himself.

They saw, after a time, where the horse tracks suddenly veered from the wagon trail and headed due west. Jeff knelt, fingering one that remained plainer than the rest. "Farrell or whoever he was, he put the horse into a run. A hard run."

A few yards farther they found the tracks of many horses. "They were runnin' too. The other horse was shod. These weren't."

Smithwick shivered. "Indians."

"I reckon." Jeff squinted, looking off to the west. "Buzzards. See them?"

Smithwick did. He shivered again.

Jeff said, "You know what we're apt to find if we go down there. Do you really want to?"

"I think we ought to know. We owe it to Arletta. And to Colonel Cregar."

Fully three days old, the body was in bad condition, ants and other insects crawling over it, feeding on it. It lay facedown at the edge of a dry creek bed. The scalp had been taken. Buzzards had torn at the arms and back. Smithwick shuddered at the nauseous sick-sweet smell of death.

Jeff said, "Does that look to you like the shirt Farrell was wearin'?"

Enough was left that Smithwick could see the brown checkered pattern. And the sleeve was ripped where he remembered it. "It does."

"Poor devil, he gave them a run for it," Jeff observed. "I reckon they got off with his horse."

Smithwick grimaced. "There were times when I wished him dead. But not this way. Hadn't we better bury him?"

"We've got no shovel to dig with, and I don't see any rocks close by to cover him up. Best we can do is pile enough dead timber over him that the buzzards can't get at him anymore till we can come back and do it right."

HE HAD NEVER IMAGINED Colonel Cregar could look so good as he did, riding out from Arletta's camp with Illinois Ike to meet the two men who trudged in afoot from Adobe Walls. Cregar's face was solemn. "We saw that you were white men, but we could not tell who you were. By the fact that you are walking, I assume you encountered Indians?"

"A few," Jeff replied dryly. "How's everybody here?"

It struck Smithwick odd that Cregar and Ike were riding together. They belonged in separate outfits. Anxiously he asked, "What about Arletta?"

Ike said, "She's all right." He glanced expectantly at Cregar, then rested regretful eyes on Jeff.

Cregar cleared his throat and stepped down from his horse. He placed a big hand on Jeff's shoulder. "I have sad news. We buried your father last evening."

Jeff stood in wooden silence, his eyes gone bleak. His voice, when he spoke, was strained. "How did he die?"

"Indians attacked Arletta's camp. Your father fell like a good soldier, protecting her. We got there a few minutes too late to save him."

Smithwick felt sorrow for Jeff but had to know. "You say Arletta is all right?"

Cregar gave him a dark and unreadable look. "I told her from the first, it is much too dangerous out here for a woman. An Indian tried to make off with her. Elijah delayed him just long enough that Doolittle was able to bring him down. She was shaken a bit, that is all."

Smithwick was relieved but could not rejoice, knowing the jolt Jeff had received, the jolt Cregar was about to receive.

Jeff stared at the ground. "Dad lived in dread that sooner or later they'd find him. He was afraid he'd die a sick old man in some dirty Texas jailhouse. At least he's been spared that."

Ike said, "He met his Lord a fighting man, Jeff. I read over him. We sent him away the best we could."

Jeff squared his shoulders. "Thank you, Ike. He'd've appreciated that." He started to wipe a sleeve across his eyes but blinked rapidly instead. "He'd've liked knowin' he was buried in Texas."

Smithwick placed a comforting hand on Jeff's shoulder, then soberly gave his attention to Cregar. "I'm afraid we have sad news for you too, Colonel." He told about Farrell.

Cregar swayed. Turning his back, he leaned to his horse, his head against his saddle. "Can you tell me what he said?"

"He told us he was sorry for what he had done to Arletta. He wanted to make it up to her."

Cregar kept his back toward the others. "Then he did come around after all. I just wish he hadn't waited so long." He raised his chin. "Did he say anything about me?"

Smithwick considered what Farrell *should* have said. "He told us he wanted to make everything up to you too. He said he was sorry for all the hurt he had brought you."

Colonel's big hand clutched the bay horse's mane. "Thank you.

Thank you for telling me." He mounted without turning to face Smithwick. He started toward camp alone, his shoulders bent.

Jeff said softly, "You're a liar, English."

"I doubt that I shall go to hell for it."

"Adobe Walls was hell enough. I think this lie might help you get to heaven. No time soon, of course."

Ike said, "I'm surprised that you two made it through afoot. Indians have been roaming over this country like packs of wolves. They have hit several camps very hard."

Smithwick said, "They hit Adobe Walls too." He described briefly the fight at the trading post.

This was the first Ike had heard of it. "Then Colonel and Arletta made the right decision. We combined the two outfits. The men are loading the wagons now to leave for Dodge City. Parson Parkhill pulled in with us last night. I doubt that any raiding party will want to go against that kind of strength."

Smithwick could hardly believe. "You are abandoning the buffalo range?"

"For the time being. But Colonel says he will be back."

Jeff said, "He may. I won't. I've had enough. What about you, English?"

Smithwick frowned. "I will see what Arletta wants to do."

Nearing camp, he saw her standing beside a wagon, watching, waiting. As she came running, he met her and swept her into his arms. There was no need to speak. They embraced one another with all the strength they had.

At last she said, "I was afraid they'd killed you."

"And I feared they had killed *you*."

She said, "They might've if Colonel and his men hadn't come chargin' in when they did." She dropped her head to his shoulder. "Colonel just told me about Farrell. He's takin' it hard."

"How are you taking it?"

She considered before she answered. "I wish it could've been different. But I don't know if I can weep for him."

"Weep for him if you feel like it. It's a way of closing a door. When the weeping is done we'll open another door, the two of us."

On their way north the combined outfits stopped at the creek bank where Farrell had died. He was given a proper burial, and

Parson Parkhill preached a glowing sermon over the grave, touching on the story of the prodigal son who returned repentant to the fold. Smithwick had never seen Colonel Cregar so haggard. He had lost the two people who meant the most to him, Sully on the last trip, Farrell on this one.

The parties withdrew to allow Cregar time alone at the graveside. Smithwick and Arletta walked together, though for Colonel's sake they did not touch one another.

Parson Parkhill studied them intently. "I am hardly a blind man, nor am I deaf to rumors whispered around camp. I believe you two young people are also in need of my services."

Smithwick and Arletta gazed at one another. Smithwick said, "I think it might be seemly if we wait a bit, for Colonel Cregar's sake."

Arletta took his arm. "We've waited this long. I reckon we can wait till we reach Dodge City."

By the time the wagons arrived at Adobe Walls, the population there had expanded greatly. Hunters had gathered from all around for mutual protection. Hanrahan's bullet-marked saloon was doing a thriving business, but Smithwick sensed that the prosperity would be of a short-term nature. It was evident, despite some boastful whiskey talk, that the attack on the post and on scattered camps had cast a pall over the hunters. Most would not admit to fear, but it appeared that a majority were ready to return to Dodge City.

Fighting Indians was the army's job, several said. Until the army saw fit to clear this region of hostiles, the hide trade would have to go on hiatus.

Still so new that some of the planned construction was not yet complete, Adobe Walls was doomed to be abandoned. For the moment, though the Indians had lost the battle, they had won their goal. For a time the buffalo would graze in peace. The plains would not echo to the roar of the killing guns. For a time . . .

MOVING NORTH toward Dodge City, the wagon train met a relief column riding south to bolster the fighting strength at Adobe Walls. The courier had gotten through.

At times Smithwick rode rear guard, but more often he rode

alongside Arletta's wagon. He had lost her once, to Farrell Cregar, and he had almost lost her to a bold Comanche. He had no intention of letting her far out of his sight, ever again.

Beside the campfire at night, Smithwick found Jeff squatting on his heels, absently poking a stick at the glowing coals. He said, "You told the colonel you are not returning to the buffalo range. What will you do?"

Jeff lighted a cigar with the burning end of the stick. "With Dad gone, there's nothin' to keep me from goin' back home. Me and Cap, we've been talkin' about buyin' steers in South Texas and drivin' them up the trail to the railroad. It's cleaner than killin' buffalo. What about you, English? You and Arletta goin' to buy that Ohio farm?"

"She has not spoken of it lately. She may have changed her mind."

"Somehow I don't see you as an Ohio farmer. Your hands don't look like they'd fit a plow handle. You could partner up with me and Cap and give the cattle business a try."

The prospect aroused his interest. "I shall give it some thought."

Jeff looked toward Arletta's tent. "Good woman, Arletta. You're lucky to have her. You need a good woman."

"A wife might be a blessing for you too."

Jeff stared off beyond the wagons. "That night we laid awake at Adobe Walls, I thought a lot about Charity. She's a decent woman at heart. She had some bad breaks that pushed her into the wrong kind of life, is all. I've been no angel myself. You see any reason a woman like her ought not to be dealt a new hand?"

Smithwick remembered what Charity had told him, that the past had foreclosed any future for her with Jeff. But he said, "If what she has been makes no difference to you, I see no reason anyone else should have a say in the matter."

"She's never been to Texas. It'd be a fresh start. I'm goin' to ask her, English."

"I'll buy the flowers."

"A bottle of good sippin'-whiskey would be more like it."

A CONSIDERABLE PERCENTAGE of Dodge City's population stood along the street, watching the approach of the hide train from Adobe Walls. Within a few days the battle would begin moving toward legendary status. The facts were already being overwhelmed by exaggeration and fancy. A few hundred Indians would soon become a thousand or more. Grand tales of heroism would be told about men who basically had done neither more nor less than to fight desperately for their lives.

And though the number who had been there at the moment of the charge had totaled but twenty-eight men and a woman, a tally of those who would claim to have been would easily come to double that many.

As had always been his custom, Colonel Cregar had ridden ahead to gather bids. The burden of grief still heavy in his face, he met the wagons as Jeff, Smithwick and Arletta pulled into the camping grounds. To Arletta he said, "I have made a deal with Charles Rath for all my hides. He will offer the same price for yours."

Arletta said, "Me and Jeff have talked it over. Papa always sold to Mr. Thomason. We'll give him first refusal."

"I hope you have not changed your mind about getting out of this dangerous business."

"We're cashin' in our wagons and teams. We won't be goin' back where the buffalo are."

"Good. But *I* plan to return as soon as the hunting grounds are reasonably safe. I would be glad to buy you out."

"How much?"

"Inquire about town. I will match the highest bid and add five hundred dollars."

Arletta's face lighted as she looked first at Smithwick, then at Jeff. "You're a fair man, Colonel. It's a pleasure doin' business with you. Come to the hotel tonight and we'll settle up."

Cregar gave Jeff a cordial nod. He started to ride away, then turned his horse and came back. He gave Smithwick a moment's keen study. "I've been aware for a long time of a strong feeling between you and Arletta. I admit that I resented it. But I bow to reality. If you have plans together, do not delay them on my account."

Arletta blinked away tears and took Smithwick's arm. "Thank you, Colonel. I'm glad you understand."

Smithwick extended his hand to Cregar. "And I shall admit that I have not always liked you, sir. But you are a gentleman, and you have my respect."

Colonel turned abruptly away, toward Rath's and his outfit.

Parson Parkhill performed the wedding ceremony an hour later at the wagons, in the presence of the crew. Once the hides were sold and unloaded, Arletta paid off the men one by one. Her eyes glistened while she thanked each for his help and bade him good-bye. She gave extra time to Barney Gibson and Herman Scholtz, who had been special friends of her father's, and to the solemn Illinois Ike. She and Jeff split what was left, for they had been equal partners. She said, "Nigel and me, we're takin' a room over at the hotel. We'd be tickled to have you come eat supper with us, Jeff."

"Thanks, but I expect a supper for two would be a lot more fitten tonight. Anyway, I'm goin' to see a lady."

Smithwick had told her. She placed her hand on Jeff's. "I wish you the best."

Jeff said, "English has already got the best."

She smiled.

DARKNESS FELL while they dawdled over coffee and a slice of cake apiece, their gaze fastened to one another. She said, "It's about time for Colonel to come and find out what the outfit is goin' to cost him. Let's go wait for him in the lobby."

They had waited only a few minutes when Smithwick saw a familiar figure pass the door. "Jeff," he called, "wait a minute." He arose from the deep horsehair divan and hurried to the door. Arletta followed.

Jeff appeared reluctant to stop, but he did. Smithwick smelled whiskey on the Texan's breath.

Jeff's shoulders were slumped. "She's gone."

"Gone?" Smithwick's jaw fell. "You mean dead?"

"Just gone. Left two months ago. Nobody has any idea whichaway she went."

"Perhaps you can find her. We'll help you, Arletta and I."

"Where would we start lookin'? She could've gone anywhere." He leaned against a gallery post and looked at the ground. "I should've asked her a long time ago. It's too late now."

Smithwick wanted to say something that might bring comfort, but nothing came.

Arletta said, "Jeff, we're waitin' for Colonel Cregar. You've got a big stake in this. How about stayin' here with us?"

Jeff shook his head. "You take care of my part for me. I'm goin' to see if I can locate Cap and find out how drunk two old Texas boys can get in one night." He walked on.

Arletta watched him worriedly. "Maybe you'd better go and keep an eye on him, Nigel."

"No, this is something he will have to work out for himself. And he will. He's been to hell and back before."

They waited in the lobby, sitting tightly together in the center of the divan. Arm around Arletta's waist, he was warmed by her glowing smile, the weight of her head against his shoulder. He wished Colonel would hurry and get here so they could finish their business transaction and go upstairs.

Cregar came, finally. "I am sorry to be late. I had other business." His dark eyes were still hollow. "Parson Parkhill told me you two had your ceremony. I hope you will not think ill of me for not coming. It would have been awkward for all of us."

Arletta said, "We understand. We hope you do."

"I must admit to some pain, but I understand. Now, to business . . ."

A voice spoke sharply from the sidewalk outside. "Cregar! Turn around!" Colonel's eyes widened in recognition of the voice. He complied slowly, defiantly.

Gantry Folsom stepped into the doorway. In his hands was the rifle he had carried the last time Smithwick had seen him. Its muzzle was pointed at Cregar's broad chest.

Folsom had been drinking; Smithwick could smell the whiskey halfway across the room. He saw hatred in Folsom's eyes, hatred and murder. "You left me for the Indians, Cregar. I tried to kill you the last time you were in town. This time I ain't going to miss."

Arletta pleaded, "Please, Folsom, don't."

Smithwick pushed her to one side, well out of the line of fire. He took a long step toward Folsom but stopped when Folsom swung the muzzle toward him. "Listen to her. She saved your life. She gave you a horse and saddle when you were set afoot."

"It didn't cost her nothin'. She got them back."

Cregar neither moved nor spoke. He seemed to call upon whatever steel nerve had carried him through a war and through all the rigors of the buffalo range.

Smithwick saw then why Cregar could be so calm. Someone moved behind Folsom. Jeff Layne's voice was stern. "Drop that rifle, Gant, or I'll blow you out like a lamp."

Folsom's mouth dropped open. He started to whirl around but never made it halfway. Jeff's pistol came down across his head. Folsom sprawled, his hat rolling across the floor. He squeezed the trigger in reflex. The bullet smashed harmlessly into the wall. Cregar quickly jerked the smoking weapon from Folsom's hand.

Jeff saw how Smithwick and Arletta stared at him in surprise. "I couldn't find Cap," he explained.

Folsom tried without much success to push himself up. Some of the old fire seemed to return to Cregar's eyes. "I would have hit him a lot harder."

Jeff shrugged. "I might've, but I've had a drink or two."

Colonel said, "I'll buy you another, after we drag this man down to the sheriff." He turned. "Arletta . . . Smith . . . I've lost my taste for business tonight. If it is all right with you, I had rather wait until morning. I may not be very early."

Arletta put her arm around Smithwick's waist. Smiling at him, she said, "Be as late as you want to."

She leaned her head against Smithwick's shoulder until Jeff and Colonel and Folsom were gone. Then, arms around one another, they walked up the stairs.

Twenty-nine

FOR WEEKS the village in the shadow of the Double Mountains had awaited word from those of its young men who had set out with Crow Feather to raid hunting camps after the collapse of the siege against Adobe Walls. The last heard from them had been the arrival of Goes His Own Way, carrying woeful news about the death of his cousin. There had already been wailing in the village over men lost at the walls. Goes had brought a black cloud that would not lift.

White Deer had delivered her baby, a second son for Crow Feather. The older boy, Little Squirrel, spent much of his time riding his gentle pony around the edge of camp, practicing with a small bow his father had made for him and watching the west for sign of Crow Feather's return. White Deer had tried to mask her own anxieties so she would not add to the distress of her younger sister. Rabbit was having problems with her second pregnancy. White Deer suspected it was a sickness of the spirit as much as anything physical. Rabbit spent much of her time weeping, convinced she would never again know the comfort of her husband's strong arms.

Some other women of the band had already resigned themselves to widowhood, for it was not reasonable that their men would have been gone so long without somehow sending word. There had been much keening, cutting of hair and bloody self-mutilation to demonstrate their grief.

White Deer still forcibly resisted the notion that Crow Feather was dead. Though the spirits ordinarily did not speak as liberally to women as to men, she had always assumed that should something happen to her husband, she would know it in her heart. He would come to her or send his bear spirit to tell her. So she nursed her new son and cared for her grieving sister and struggled within herself to keep the faith.

There were compensations. Warriors returning from other raids said most of the white hunters had left the buffalo-killing grounds. Though the massive attack on the new trading post had failed to breach its walls, the *teibos* had abandoned it, carrying away most of the goods they had stored there. Many of the hides they had hoped to sell had spoiled in the rain, a triumph of the buffalo spirits over *teibo* greed. They had left foodstuffs behind, but the warriors had resisted the temptation to eat. White men were of bad heart. It would be in their cruel nature to have poisoned the food to kill Indians as they poisoned buffalo hides to kill insects. It was clear that they regarded the People in much the same way as they regarded the bugs.

The feeling was mutual. The warriors had torched that part of the post which pleased the flames and had pulled down much that would not burn. Brave men had died at the walls of the white-man houses. The pull-out of the hunters meant at least that those deaths had not been in vain.

But deep concerns persisted. Goes His Own Way had come home dark in spirit, and that darkness had remained over him like a bitter winter cloud. He voiced an opinion that the victory was not to last forever. Adobe Walls had shown that the People's medicine was no longer strong enough to counter that of the whites. Somehow the spirits were failing the People, or the People had failed the spirits. Whatever the case, prayers were no longer answered. He said the hunters would call upon the blue-clad soldiers to administer punishment, to drive as many as possible to the reservation and to kill those who would not go. Then the big guns would return, and the buffalo would fall until the last one had rotted back to the earth from which it came.

It was a sad premonition, and many argued that Goes was wrong. But White Deer's deepest instinct told her he was not. She wept inside, for her husband and for all her people. Her children would not live the life she had known, the life Crow Feather had led. Theirs would be a different world, a white man's world. With or without their father, the journey would be long and hard. She wondered despondently if they would find their way or if they would wander in a spiritual darkness, forever searching, forever lost.

She received little help from her sister, for Rabbit was too ill to carry her share of the work. White Deer had brought the shaman Terrapin Shell to sprinkle his magic powders and to sing his healing chants, but the dark spirits which had invaded her body and mind fought back and retained their hold. The failure of Isatai's medicine might have compromised the medicine of all the others and added to the strength of the black powers, the shaman speculated bleakly. He feared these powers would take Rabbit and her unborn child.

White Deer worried too about the fall buffalo hunt. It was the People's way to care for widows and orphans, but it would not be the same as if she had a husband to provide for her and Rabbit and their children. Should the hunt be poor, the men would see to the needs of their own families first. Those who depended upon charity would have to content themselves with whatever was left over, and it might not be much.

An alternative was remarriage. Because of the hazards of the hunt and of warfare, females were usually in surplus. A man proficient in raiding and in the chase might take more than one widow to wife, spreading the burden of labor as well as assuring himself of children to see to his welfare in his later years. Finds the Good Water had begun to watch White Deer when she was about her outside duties. It was not the tribe's way for the man to be overly bold and forthright at first, but by fleeting looks he revealed his interest, smoothing the way for the day when he would ask her. She did, after all, still retain some of the charm that had drawn Crow Feather to her. She had strong arms and back for the work, and she was younger than the two wives he already had, young enough to make his nights interesting again.

But Finds the Good Water was a man of some arrogance, and without any tenderness that she had seen. Worse, she knew his wives. The oldest, who sat by him in the lodge, would always be the number-one woman. White Deer knew her to be evil of tongue, a cruel taskmaster to the number-two woman, who was not her sister. White Deer's nature had never allowed her to suffer abuse in silence. Were she to become the third wife, they would sooner or later resort to hand-to-hand battle and probable injury to both.

Finds the Good Water at last broached the question while White Deer knelt to the tanning of a deerhide. She told him flatly, "I have a husband. His name is Crow Feather." By saying his name she perpetuated the faith that he still lived. One did not speak the name of the dead.

"I do not see him."

"He will come."

"Only if the dead rise up and walk." Finds the Good Water seemed affronted by her refusal. "I am rich in horses. I have two other wives, so there would be three of you to share the labor. Your life would be easy."

"A woman's life is never easy."

"You have three children. Four, if your sickly sister lives long enough to deliver hers. How many men can you find who would accept such a burden?"

Stubbornly she said, "I have a man. He has never complained of his burden."

Finds the Good Water frowned with impatience. "You are a foolish woman. I shall speak to your father. He has no son-in-law now to keep him in meat. If I offer him horses he will listen to me, and you will listen to him."

Watching him walk stiffly away, White Deer felt suddenly chilled. Though she was a mature woman, under the circumstances it would be difficult to defy her father. He was likely to be impressed by an offer of horses, and the suggestion that not having a son-in-law left him vulnerable to hunger.

And what if Finds the Good Water was right? What if Crow Feather was indeed dead? What if some evil force had prevented him from coming to her or sending the bear spirit to tell her? Life could indeed be hard for a widow no man took to wife. Crow Feather owned many horses, wrested from the Tejanos and the

Mexicans, but once she accepted him as dead she would be expected by tribal custom to give the horses away. And though her children would not be allowed to starve, they might well grow up poor, pitied objects of charity.

She pushed to her feet, standing away from her work. She looked for her first son but did not see him. He was probably down by the river, where half-grown boys watched over the grazing of the horse herd. He had taken more and more of late to following the novices, learning from them what they had learned from fathers and uncles and grandfathers.

She heard her sister cry inside the tepee. Rabbit had seemed very weak this morning, unable to rise to her feet without help. White Deer had begun to despair of her living to deliver the child that kicked so restlessly in her belly.

To her surprise she found Rabbit sitting up on her blankets, her black eyes wide with wonder. "Sister," Rabbit declared, "I have seen him."

"Him? Who?"

"Our husband. He appeared to me just now."

"You had a dream."

"It was more than a dream. He was there, where you stand. He has been hurt, and he is terribly thin, but he is not dead. He said for me to wait, that he is coming."

"A dream. That is all it was." But White Deer trembled as if a cold wind had entered the tepee. Crow Feather had promised that if anything ever happened to him he would come to her, or send the bear spirit. Could it be that he had come to Rabbit instead?

Seldom had she allowed herself to succumb to jealousy, even when Crow Feather gave more of himself to Rabbit than to her. Jealousy came over her now for a fleeting moment. She realized she was older than Rabbit, that lines were beginning to crease her face, that her desire for lovemaking had cooled while her sister's had remained high. She could understand that her husband was drawn to Rabbit, but was she not still the number-one wife?

Rabbit cried, "Help me to my feet. He must not find me like this when he comes."

"No, you are ill." But she saw color in Rabbit's cheeks, color she had not seen in a long time. She saw in Rabbit's eyes a will to live that had all but faded away.

Perhaps it was time for the baby. That would explain the hallucination, the light in Rabbit's eyes. She must hurry and fetch the life-giver woman. "You lie still. I will not be long."

She hurried through the flap and took the direction of the midwife's tepee. She stopped suddenly, for she felt that someone had called her name. She had not actually heard a voice, but the feeling was too strong to put down. Turning quickly, she saw no one except three women, cooking in front of their lodges. She started again for the midwife, and again the feeling came. She heard the call through her mind, not through her ear.

She froze. He had not come only to her sister. He had come to White Deer as well.

She found herself drawn toward the edge of camp, toward the horse herd. Her heart pounded with excitement.

She saw him then. He was walking along beside the boy's pony, his arm around the boy's waist. She could not yet see his face, but she knew him by the set of his shoulders, by the way he moved. He was too far for her to have heard him call in a normal way, but the People knew not to question the power of the spirits; they had ways of their own.

She shouted his name and went running to meet him.

ABOUT THE AUTHOR

ELMER KELTON was raised on a West Texas ranch and spent his for-
mative years among cowboys and old-timers. He is the author of more
than thirty novels, the winner of three Western Heritage Awards from the
National Cowboy Hall of Fame, four Spur Awards from the Western
Writers of America, and the Levi Strauss Golden Saddleman Award for
lifetime achievement in Western literature, as well as honors from the
Texas Institute of Letters and the Western Literature Association. Mr.
Kelton lives in San Angelo, Texas.